SCIENCE FICTION
DOUBLE FEATURE

Liverpool Science Fiction Texts and Studies, 52

Liverpool Science Fiction Texts and Studies

Recent titles in the series

SCIENCE FICTION
DOUBLE FEATURE

The Science Fiction Film as Cult Text

EDITED BY

J. P. TELOTTE AND GERALD DUCHOVNAY

LIVERPOOL UNIVERSITY PRESS

First published 2015 by
Liverpool University Press
4 Cambridge Street
Liverpool
L69 7ZU

British Library Cataloguing-in-Publication data
A British Library CIP record is available

ISBN 978-1-78138-183-0 cased

Typeset by Carnegie Book Production, Lancaster
Printed and bound by CPI Group (UK) Ltd, Croydon CR0 4YY

Contents

List of Illustrations

Notes on Contributors

Stacey Abbott is a Reader in Film and Television Studies at the University of Roehampton. She is the author of *Celluloid Vampires* (U of Texas P, 2007), co-author, with Lorna Jowett, of *TV Horror* (I. B. Tauris, 2013), and the editor of *The Cult TV Book* (I. B. Tauris, 2010). She has contributed to *The Routledge Companion to Science Fiction* (2009) and *Fifty Key Figures in Science Fiction* (Routledge, 2009), and written on the relationship between computer-generated effects and sf for the journal *Science Fiction Studies*. She is currently writing a book on twenty-first-century dystopian vampire and zombie films and TV.

M. Keith Booker is the James E. and Ellen Wadley Roper Professor of English at the University of Arkansas. He has authored or edited more than 30 books on literature, film, and television, including *Monsters, Mushroom Clouds, and the Cold War: American Science Fiction and the Roots of Postmodernism, 1946–1964* (Greenwood, 2001), *Strange TV: Innovative Television Series from* The Twilight Zone *to* The X-Files (Greenwood, 2002), *Science Fiction Television* (Praeger, 2004), *Alternate Americas: Science Fiction Film and American Culture* (Praeger, 2006), *Postmodern Hollywood: What's New in Film and Why It Makes Us Feel So Strange* (Praeger, 2007), and, with Anne-Marie Thomas, *The Science Fiction Handbook* (Wiley-Blackwell, 2009).

Mark Bould is Reader in Film and Literature at the University of the West of England and co-editor of the journal *Science Fiction Film and Television*. He is the author of *Film Noir: From Berlin to Sin City* (Wallflower Press, 2005) and *The Cinema of John Sayles: Lone Star* (Wallflower, 2009), co-author of *The Routledge Concise History of Science Fiction* (2011), and co-editor of *Parietal Games: Critical Writings by and on M. John Harrison* (Science Fiction Foundation, 2005), *The Routledge Companion to Science Fiction* (2009), *Fifty Key Figures in Science Fiction* (Routledge, 2009), *Red*

Planets: Marxism and Science Fiction (Pluto/Wesleyan, 2009), and *Neo-Noir* (Wallflower, 2009). His most recent publication is *Science Fiction: The Routledge Film Guidebook* (2012). He is an advisory editor for the journals *Extrapolation, Historical Materialism, Paradoxa,* and *Science Fiction Studies.*

Gerald Duchovnay, Professor of English and Film at Texas A&M University-Commerce, is the founding and general editor of *Post Script: Essays in Film and the Humanities.* He has published numerous articles on film, literature, and media. His books include *Humphrey Bogart: A Bio-Bibliography* (Greenwood, 1999) and *Film Voices* (SUNY, 2004); he has also co-edited (with J. P. Telotte) *Science Fiction Film, Television, and Adaptation: Across the Screens* (Routledge, 2012).

Rodney F. Hill teaches film in the Lawrence Herbert School of Communication at Hofstra University. He is co-author of *The Francis Ford Coppola Encyclopedia* (Scarecrow, 2010) and *The Encyclopedia of Stanley Kubrick* (Checkmark, 2002), co-editor of *Francis Ford Coppola: Interviews* (UP of Mississippi, 2004), and is a contributor to several other books, including *The Essential Science Fiction Television Reader* (UP of Kentucky, 2008), *The Stanley Kubrick Archives* (Taschen, 2005), and *Science Fiction Film, Television, and Adaptation: Across the Screens* (Routledge, 2012). His essays have appeared in *Film Quarterly, Cinema Journal, Literature/Film Quarterly, Post Script,* and elsewhere.

Matt Hills is Professor in Film and TV Studies at Aberystwyth University. The author or editor of six books, including *Fan Cultures* (Routledge, 2002) and *Triumph of a Time Lord: Regenerating Doctor Who in the Twenty-first Century* (I. B. Tauris, 2010), Matt is an associate editor of *Cinema Journal,* and has published widely on cult media and fandom.

Nicolle Lamerichs is an independent Dutch researcher previously at Utrecht University. Her dissertation "Productive Fandom: Intermediality and Affective Reception in Fan Cultures" (Maastricht University, 2013) discusses fandom as a cultural phenomenon that is lived, shared, and felt, as it examines fan fiction, cosplay, and role playing through traditional as well as virtual ethnography. Nicolle has published peer-reviewed articles in *Transformative Works and Cultures, Participations: Journal of Audience & Reception Studies,* and she has contributed to several edited collections, including *Sherlock and Transmedia Fandom* (McFarland, 2012).

Rob Latham is Professor of English at the University of California-Riverside, where he is developing a program in Science Fiction and

Technoculture Studies. A senior editor of *Science Fiction Studies* since 1997, he is the author of *Consuming Youth: Vampires, Cyborgs, and the Culture of Consumption* (Chicago, 2002) and co-editor of the *Wesleyan Anthology of Science Fiction* (2010). He is currently editing *The Oxford Handbook of Science Fiction* and completing a book on new wave sf of the 1960s and 1970s.

Sharalyn Orbaugh is a professor in the Department of Asian Studies at the University of British Columbia. Her research addresses issues of race, gender, sexuality, and visuality in Japanese fiction, film, and popular media, such as manga and anime. She is co-editor of *The Columbia Companion to Modern East Asian Literature*, a member of the editorial board for *Science Fiction Film and Television*, and author of *Japanese Fiction of the Allied Occupation* (Brill, 2007).

Takayuki Tatsumi is professor of American Literature at Keio University, Tokyo. President of the American Literary Society of Japan, he is on the editorial board of *Journal of Transnational American Studies*. His major books are: *Cyberpunk America* (Keiso, 1988), winner of the American Studies Book Prize; *New Americanist Poetics* (Seidosha, 1995), winner of the Yukichi Fukuzawa Award; and *Full Metal Apache: Transactions between Cyberpunk Japan and Avant-Pop America* (Duke UP, 2006), winner of the 2010 IAFA Distinguished Scholarship Award. Co-editor of the New Japanese Fiction issue of *Review of Contemporary Fiction* (Summer 2002), he has also published numerous essays, including "Literary History on the Road: Transatlantic Crossings and Transpacific Crossovers" (*PMLA*) and "Planet of the Frogs: Thoreau, Anderson and Murakami" (*Narrative*).

J. P. Telotte is a professor of film and media and former Chair of the School of Literature, Media, and Communication at Georgia Tech, where he teaches courses in film history, film genres, and film and television. Author of more than 100 articles on film, television, and literature and co-editor of the journal *Post Script*, he has published numerous books; among the more recent are: *The Mouse Machine: Disney and Technology* (U of Illinois P, 2008), *The Essential Science Fiction Television Reader* (Kentucky, 2008), *Animating Space: From Mickey to WALL-E* (U of Kentucky P, 2010), and *Science Fiction TV* (Routledge, 2014).

Chuck Tryon is an associate professor in the Department of English at Fayetteville State University. His research focuses on the transformations of movie and television consumption in the era of digital distribution. He is the author of *Reinventing Cinema: Movies in the Age of Media Convergence* (2009) and *On-Demand Culture: Digital Delivery and the Future of Movies*

(2013), both from Rutgers University Press. He has also published essays in *The Journal of Film and Video, Jump Cut, Popular Communication,* and *Screen,* as well as the anthologies *Moving Data: The iPhone and My Media* (Columbia UP, 2013) and *Science Fiction Film, Television, and Adaptation: Across the Screens* (Routledge, 2012).

Sherryl Vint is a professor in the Department of English at University of California-Riverside, the author of *Bodies of Tomorrow: Technology, Subjectivity, Science Fiction* (U of Toronto P, 2007) and *Animal Alterity* (Liverpool UP, 2010), and co-author of *The Routledge Concise History of Science Fiction* (2011). She has co-edited the collections *Fifty Key Figures in Science Fiction* (Routledge, 2009), *The Routledge Companion to Science Fiction* (2009), and *Beyond Cyberpunk* (Taylor & Francis, 2010), and she is a founding co-editor of the journal *Science Fiction Film and Television.* She is also First Vice-President of the International Association for the Fantastic in the Arts.

Jeffrey Weinstock is Professor of English and the graduate program coordinator at Central Michigan University. A specialist in fantasy and the gothic, he has published widely on American literature, culture, and media. Among his books are *Spectral America: Phantoms and the American Imagination* (Wisconsin, 2004), *Reading Rocky: The Rocky Horror Picture Show and Popular Culture* (Palgrave, 2008), and *Vampires: Undead Cinema* (Wallflower, 2012).

Rhonda V. Wilcox, Ph.D., is Professor of English at Gordon State College and past president of the Whedon Studies Association. She is editor of *Studies in Popular Culture* and coeditor of *Slayage: The Journal of the Whedon Studies Association.* She is the author of *Why* Buffy *Matters: The Art of* Buffy the Vampire Slayer (I. B. Tauris, 2005); coeditor, with David Lavery, of *Fighting the Forces: What's at Stake in* Buffy the Vampire Slayer (Rowman & Littlefield, 2002); with Tanya R. Cochran, of *Investigating* Firefly *and* Serenity: *Science Fiction on the Frontier* (I. B. Tauris, 2008); and, with Sue Turnbull, of *Investigating Veronica Mars* (McFarland, 2011). Rhonda is currently editing *Reading Joss Whedon,* forthcoming from Syracuse University Press.

Introduction:
Science Fiction Double Feature

J. P. Telotte

I

The most well-known, and certainly the most frequently discussed cult film, *The Rocky Horror Picture Show* (1975), opens with an arresting image, a close-up of bright red lips mouthing the film's theme song, "Science Fiction Double Feature." Both image and song have become practically iconic—emblems of the cult film, signs of its generally transgressive, sometimes campy nature, celebrations of the way such films, in contrast to most traditional Hollywood cinema, seem to directly address their audience, even, as Timothy Corrigan allusively puts it, placing them "oddly inscribed" within the film text (34). While *Rocky Horror*—the film—no longer seems to evoke the shocks (of recognition or of recoil) that it once did, both song and lips retain something of this evocative and subversive power. In fact, I would suggest that, because of what we might term their *separation* from the text itself—a separation that was always implicit, thanks to their placement as a prologue, prior to the actual start of the narrative—we might see in them some additional resonance, use them as our own prologue to thinking about the cult film and its place in our experience of film genres.

This volume aims to draw on that resonance, specifically by tracking the relationship between the cult film and the genre of science fiction (sf), exploring a connection that has always seemed closer, somehow even more *natural*—although some might find that term an ill fit for the cult experience which always seems intent on questioning what is "natural"—than in the case of most other film genres. In fact, sf has typically enjoyed a special version of that relationship between audience and text that critics often cite as one of the defining features of the cult film experience. We might recall that, even in its formative period (for both literature and film) in the 1920s and 1930s—a period that saw the emergence of the great pulp magazines that helped shape the modern literary sf narrative—the sf genre was already marked by what John Cheng describes as a curiously "participatory rhetoric" (10). That rhetoric can be traced through a wide variety of genre-associated activities: participation in letter and discussion columns, the development of specialized clubs, the publication of fanzines printing fan-originated fiction, and the organization of the first cons (or fan conventions), all of which helped to establish "a subculture of amateur fan activity related to but independent of" the world of professional sf text production (Cheng 10). That description of the fan and fan activity as "related to but independent of" sf itself strikes another note of *separation*, yet at the same time it attests to the audience's deep involvement with the texts of sf. In effect, it suggests a kind of *double* relationship that gives some reason to the frequent assertion that the audience for sf, whether in its literary, cinematic, or televisual forms, has always been rather different from that for other genres: more enthusiastic, more open to speculation, more interested in connecting with other, similar fans.

This notion of a double relationship or double character—a doubleness that takes many forms—provides the focal point for this study, and it is one I would like to begin describing by returning briefly to *Rocky Horror* and considering that theme song mouthed by those large, disembodied red lips. The tune is a deeply reflexive one, or as Robert Wood describes it, a kind of "celebration of filmgoing" (159). As such, it not only obliquely forecasts the film's admittedly pastiche plot, but also lovingly—if a bit perversely—wraps that plot within something else that it celebrates, the familiar conventions of a host of sf films, many from the 1950s, and expressly named for the audience: *Doctor X* (1932), *The Invisible Man* (1933), *The Day the Earth Stood Still* (1951), *When Worlds Collide* (1951), *It Came from Outer Space* (1953), *Forbidden Planet* (1956), and others. This initial move is significant not only because it clearly situates this very unconventional film within a long tradition of (conventional) sf films, but also because it asserts a level of cinematic knowledge, particularly about sf, that the film's audience apparently should have—or at least might *pretend* to have—in order to properly appreciate the work: their stars (such as Claude Rains and Anne Francis), their plots, their look, even their costuming (as when the song notes Flash Gordon's "silver underwear"). More than just a "celebration" of the movies, that song claims a generic relationship and an audience intimacy that are being *confidently* tapped in *The Rocky Horror Picture Show*, as if the film and its makers were sure of a group of knowing sf viewers—like those sf literature fans Cheng describes—who would recognize, draw some pleasure from, and enjoy celebrating that kinship.

And yet, we have to recognize another hint of separation, of distance, of detached commentary—thus the frequent suggestion of this film's camp rather than straightforward sf appeal. For in the period when *Rocky Horror* first appeared, a pre-*Star Wars* (1977), pre-*Close Encounters of the Third Kind* (1977), pre-*Alien* (1979) era, and one before the sf film had become practically a mainstream sign of the summer blockbuster exhibition period, the genre was actually in a period of decline. As the song "Science Fiction Double Feature" readily reminds us, the sf film had become associated with cheaply made B-films, works of a long-gone Hollywood establishment and a long-lost innocence that might be satirically—if also nostalgically—evoked for *Rocky Horror*'s recent and disillusioned post-Vietnam audience. The song was, in effect, already playing upon a double attitude towards sf: as something a bit cheap and tawdry, perhaps rather time-worn, but also quite worth a certain fondness as well as an added attention, given its often strange look and exaggerated actions, that is, elements conducive to the sort of "cognitive estrangement" described by genre theorist Darko Suvin (7).

Yet those exaggerated, overly red lips—resonant of the full-scale lips of Allison Hayes, star of the 1950s *Attack of the 50 Foot Woman* (1958), as well as another appropriately titled film of the era, *The Disembodied* (1957)—add a further dimension to that introduction. Not so much an icon of "love," although an element of cinephilia is invariably part of the nostalgia bound up in recollections of those earlier sf double features, the lips speak of a repressed message inherent in most of those films to which homage is being paid, and perhaps in the larger sf film experience. For even as those 1950s-era works recounted their tales of flying saucers and alien invasion, of atomic apocalypse and atomic mutation, of machines running amok and mad doctors, or of shrinking men and colossal women (with colossal lips and other parts), they also persistently pulled back from these science and technology-connected anxieties to remind audiences of something else—a humanity that remained anchored not in all of our technological devices, science, or the minds of geniuses (mad or otherwise), but in our bodies (small *or* large), our feelings, our emotions—and, of course, our lips as well.

In fact, we might briefly note another version of that recoil and a more articulate version of that threat in another film of the period with some cult standing, and one that turns on contact with a pair of exaggerated lips. When Miles Bennell of *Invasion of the Body Snatchers* (1956) moves in to kiss his girlfriend Becky Driscoll, to reassure her of his love, even as all others in their community of Santa Mira have apparently been taken over by lifeless, emotionless pod invaders, he suddenly starts back from that intimate contact and confesses, in a quavering voice-over that accompanies an extreme close-up of her face: "I never knew the real meaning of fear until ... until I kissed Becky." For that kiss—and her lips looming so large and distorted due to the Superscope anamorphic process the film used—signified not only his very real love for her, but also his shock of recognition that she had been taken over by those plant-like invaders whose signature effect is to deprive humans of any feeling, any capacity for love—including, we might assume, a love of the movies. That kiss thus carries its own "double" message, one crucial to the sf genre, but also one that, again, could bear some significance for our thinking about the cult film.

For the cult cinema, as this volume will repeatedly argue, is fundamentally linked to the sf film—and perhaps more broadly to fantasy—in large part because of this doubleness that we keep noting in various forms that seems implicit in and driving both. So beyond those giant mutant lips of Allison Hayes that, even in their monstrous form, still clearly evoked sexuality and an impossible desire for love, we also need to acknowledge the long tradition of similar paradoxical elements and narrative events—often straining credulity—that run throughout the sf film tradition and that repeatedly turn not so much on *ideas*, as many commentators on the genre would prefer to argue, but on our problematic *emotional* responses, including the sort usually associated with the cult experience. As examples of this sort of doubleness, we might quickly note the robotic Maria of Fritz Lang's epic *Metropolis* (1927), a *mechanical* figure whose real power is both tested and frighteningly demonstrated in a striptease before the young men of the city that effectively demonstrates her ability to stir their *emotions*, even prompting them to kill each other; or *Forbidden Planet*'s revelation that the "culmination" of the advanced scientific knowledge of the alien Krell race was the destructive unleashing of "monsters from the Id," the mobilized repressed emotions and deadly impulses of that entire people; or *Serenity*'s (2005) story of how the government's efforts at a scientific eradication of all extreme emotions on the colony of Miranda leads, on the one hand, to a populace that in its complete passivity no longer even cares to live, and on the other, to a percentage—the Reavers, as they are termed—who become so violent and destructive that they turn into *self*-destructive, emotion-run-amok cannibals. In this cinema, it seems, the most extreme reaches of reason, science, and technology almost invariably have a recoil, breeding emotional or sensory extremes, even destructively so. And such paradoxical circumstances, a common and rather literal *double* feature of the genre, seem equally at work—or play—in our cult films, as they both embrace and send up the forms, plots, and characters of popular cinema, as they embrace the pleasures but also the problematic possibilities of the body and of our feelings, and especially as they situate themselves, just as *Rocky Horror* paradigmatically did, both within and without our common generic expectations.

This "within and without" character has led many to see the cult film's real attraction as residing simply in its pastiche-like, boundary-crossing blending of various text types—of pieces taken from one set of generic conventions and mixed with those from outside, from another generic supertext, by way of confounding—while at the same time reinvigorating—our usual experience. In reference, we might here recall Ingeborg Hoesterey's discussion of the pastiche as a form that implies, on the one hand, "a pâté of various ingredients," and on the other, a mixture that relies on a "selection aesthetic" (1–2), enabling the text (and textual author) to produce striking linkages of disparate elements. Thus, Hoesterey offers, "the falsities that make up a pastiche create a kind of truth" and deliberately so (6). In noting this connection, though, we might also recognize how the cult work ultimately seems just to escape Hoesterey's influential definition of the pastiche. For the cult film is typically something more than a disparate blending, if also something that we would with difficulty describe as *ruled* by a "selection aesthetic" of any sort. Its various parts, as *Rocky Horror* emphatically announces, remain distinct and *identifiable* (even *self*-identified, as the song "Science Fiction Double Feature" suggests) for those who will look, even as the pleasures of the cult almost invariably seem too *accidental* and inconsistent a mash-up for the latter notion. And yet Hoesterey's observation that pastiche texts often result in a "double visuality" (60), that is, an audience experience of strange "juxtapositions" (65), a "conflation," or even "paradox" (67), clearly strikes a chord and helps explain some of that sf kinship we began by noting.

That sense of the paradoxical, as we have already suggested, has always been an important marker in sf cinema—as a form that seems to draw so much of its very identity from the work of science, technology, and reason, while also consistently cautioning against or qualifying our attitudes towards that work as it depicts the sort of destructive consequences we have described or recoils into the seemingly more comfortable realm of the emotions. And while I do not mean to suggest an easy equation here, that the sf text is invariably a cult work or that the cult film should primarily be seen through the lens of sf, I do, much as *Rocky Horror* does, want to emphasize that connection, want to suggest that we should—as the following essays in this volume undertake to do—pursue those often strange "juxtapositions" and instances of "paradox," whether thought deliberate or not, to better understand both cinematic categories. Doubleness—whether we describe it as a *double* feature potential or a "double visuality"—seems fundamental in both cases, allowing for the sort of textual richness that helps to explain the resonance such texts have, their appeal to what are often seen as specialized audiences, and ultimately a kind of generic connectedness, even if only by way of reminding us of how quickly both sorts of texts try to slide away from or deny any easy generic categorization.

So while we might be hard pressed today to see *Rocky Horror* as a paradigm for examining either cult film or sf cinema—there are simply so many other such works that have now followed its lead—we should note that it has helped instigate much study of the cult phenomenon, that it has probably brought more critical attention to cult cinema than any other single work, and that its emphasis on sf is itself noteworthy. In fact, it serves as a reminder that the link between the cult and sf has largely gone unexplored—despite the presence of so many sf works on any list of key cult films, works like *Robot Monster* (1953), *The Giant Claw* (1957), *Plan 9 from Outer Space* (1958), *The Man Who Fell to Earth* (1976), *Zardoz* (1974), *Blade Runner* (1982), *The Fifth Element* (1997), and many others cited and discussed in this volume. A wide-ranging study like Mathijs and Mendik's *The Cult Film Reader* (2008) with its collection of

a. Rick Deckard (Harrison Ford) explores a world of doubles in *Blade Runner* (1982).

b. *Star Wars* cultists: The 501st Legion Marches at Walt Disney World.

43 essays curiously, even somewhat improbably, steers clear of almost all sf—with the predictable exception of *Rocky Horror*—as it tries to draw a complete portrait of cinematic cult activity while leaving out what this volume argues is perhaps the key, if unacknowledged, generic player. So while no single essay here examines *Rocky Horror*, that film, with its sf theme song, distinctive imagery, and self-reflexive anchorage in the larger world of sf cinema, points us in an important direction, inviting us with those giant lips to focus more deliberately on the sf film as cult phenomenon, and to speak, as if through them, about the cultish aspects of the whole sf genre.

Working from this cinematic and cultural signpost, the following, specially targeted case studies trace out various dimensions of that linkage between the peculiar cinephilia bound up in the cult film experience and the sf genre's own frequent embrace of human emotion and feeling—which always seems a bit "peculiar" in light of the form's visual and thematic emphases on reason, science, and technology. But then our cult film activity is more than just a sign of our love for certain films or types of films.[1] It also involves a quite pleasurable cultural working out of limits, contradictions, paradoxes, or peculiarities that might seem proscribed or addressed only with some difficulty in what is often labeled mainstream film; thus its simple but accurate description by Mark Jancovich et al. as an "oppositional form of cinema" (1) and the dominant focus much of the criticism has taken on that form's generally subversive nature. It is the same sort of work that has long found a ready home in the sf film, which, thanks to its embrace of another, and even more fundamental sort of doubleness—that is, as simultaneously *science* and *fiction*—is already and always engaged in creating a distinct narrative space of difference: a space of double vision, a space for exploring cultural paradox, and a space that has simply become especially important for addressing the science- and technology-haunted cultural environment we inhabit today.

II

But *why* is it especially useful or important for us to focus our attention specifically on sf texts for this investigation? After all, as other research has shown, cult activity—in film, television, and more generally in popular culture—really knows no clear generic boundaries.[2] In fact, critical discussion has generally suggested that one of the more common characteristics of the cinematic cult text has been its very slipperiness, especially its tendency, as we have noted, to straddle boundaries, to reach for or pull into range unexpected generic material, and in the process to juxtapose different sets of conventions, narrative formulae, or character types for the almost surreal pleasures that might arise from such surprising comparisons or collisions—or the sort of "anachronistic juxtapositions" Hoesterey notes. Admittedly, that is one of the cult experience's fundamental pleasures, the *bricoleur*-like encounters in which the film can implicate its audience, encounters assuredly imaged in a work like *Robot Monster* with its alien invader, who is represented by an actor in a gorilla suit wearing a fishbowl-like space helmet, and photographed in a 3D process that often made him/it seem to be walking into the theater, amongst the audience, meeting us half-way, quite literally invading *our space* (a cultural and psychological space) if not the Earth itself.

But just like the cult work, the sf genre has always offered such strange encounters while operating at the margins of the normal film experience, offering audiences images of and narratives about what our conventional films could not: other worlds, other ways of living, even other life forms that might, in their own ways, "invade" our world—in effect, fantasies that challenge, estrange, and in the process help to broaden—or burst—our sense of boundaries. And it seems noteworthy that our sf cinema has done most of this work at approximately the same time—from the 1950s to the present—when the cult film was also emerging as a distinct cultural phenomenon (as if awakened by the same cultural and technological forces that would awake the sf film, as well as such sf stars as Godzilla, Rodan, etc.). Because of that coincidence, sf has helped to define the cinematic cult: by drawing into the same orbit such strange convention bedfellows as the robots, cowboys, and musical numbers of *The Phantom Empire* (1935); by giving license to its own unconventional narrative explorations (after all, what Vernian "Journey to the Center of the Earth" does not forecast the similar inward journeys of the typical cult text, such as John Waters's *Pink Flamingos* [1972]); or by introducing us to strangely intriguing hybrid figures, such as *Robot Monster*'s alien "Ro-Man," who is also, as Rodney Hill's essay in this volume will suggest, near kin to the eponymous central figure of the Ed Wood, Jr. work about another very strange double, *Glen or Glenda?* (1953).

And while the cult film cuts across all generic types, it is a form that, in another kinship to the sf world, has tended to privilege the audience and the peculiar nature of the audience experience, in effect, to be marked by a level of self-awareness that, while unusual for most mainstream cinema, has typically been one of the hallmarks of sf. The cult film usually accomplishes this privileging in two key ways: either it allows viewers a kind of access to the text that they do not normally enjoy, as in the case of the *immersive* invitations found throughout—and indeed celebrated as part of the screening activity of—a work like *The Rocky Horror Picture Show*, or it places them in a new position to the text, effectively *distanced* from it, at a point where they can, knowingly, appreciate it in ways that non-cultists simply cannot. We can especially see this repositioning in the case of a film like *Blade Runner* (1982), thanks to its multiple versions—including its strange situation of having several different "director's cuts"—and the extensive critical annotation that has grown up about the text, providing a comforting "critical" context for its own cult following. If the former type of cult film is about a level of immersion that is relatively rare in Hollywood cinema, the latter is about the sort of detachment that instinctively troubles film producers precisely because of the way it calls attention to the fan experience and thereby threatens to undermine the conventional pleasurable immersion most audiences—and exhibitors—usually anticipate. And yet both types (of films and of responses) rely for their very status on a kind of two-way (one more *double* feature) relationship that is long familiar to sf fans: on an audience embrace or appreciation of its special scientific/technological vision of our world and on the text's peculiarly self-conscious, distant, and indeed *different* nature from that world.

In fact, while that special fan embrace, which has also produced a wide variety of overt and extra-cinematic cult behaviors, has long been an acknowledged dimension of the sf film experience, it is the other, reflexive component that makes the genre such an especially fertile ground for this sort of study. For the sf film is, as has often been remarked, one of the most self-conscious of popular film types,[3] typically marked by an imagery that recalls—and in some cases, such as John Carpenter's early comic sf film *Dark Star* (1974), even mocks—its own process of production and exhibition. Through its insistent concern with technology and its ubiquitous images of monitors, video screens, scanners, and various machinery of reproduction, not to mention its thematic explorations of the implications of technological replication, including the replication of the self, the sf film text always generates a level of transparency that seemingly invites us, as do so many cult films, to see right through the text, to become aware of its mechanisms and consider their implications. Thus, it builds into its generic experience a kind of destabilizing potential that echoes those most common descriptions of the cult as a subversive form.

And in another dimension of that transparent effect, we might recognize the extent to which the sf text also tends to become an involving drama of "screens." For it constantly asserts the place of its technological vision somewhere beyond the cinema, beyond the cinematic (or television, computer, or iPad) screen on which it unfolds, but ultimately in our own lives. For what the sf film always seems to argue for and wants us to embrace are those utopian realms, futuristic technologies, and even new ways of thinking that it visualizes for us, as it encourages us not just to dream them, but to find a practical place for them in our lives, to bring fantasy off the screen and to (or at least *towards*) life, as those cultists who still attend *Rocky Horror* and other midnight screenings ritually do, and as those sf fans of the various cons—ComicCon, DragonCon, WorldCon, etc.—so dedicatedly do in their cosplay, mock combats, balls, and role-playing games. Both the sf and cult film experiences, in effect, suggest that we might indeed "live it"—that other world or set of possibilities that is on the screen but from which, in our more conventional film (and everyday) experiences, we typically seem so screened off.

In his discussion of what he describes as the "post-cinematic affect" found in much recent media, Steven Shaviro offers a more nuanced lead in this direction, as he notes an "underlying *flexibility*" that marks certain film and video texts today (1). It is an apparent "ability to take on any shape as needed, a capacity to adapt quickly and smoothly to the demands of any form, or any procedure" (14), a characteristic coincident with—and responding to—an increasing experience of the breakdown of conventional generic boundaries and even textual types. Exploring how this "flexibility"—or a limited flexibility, a *doubleness*—works in a specific cult sf film, Richard Kelly's *Southland Tales* (2007), Shaviro observes how that text seems to rely on both the persistence of the past and the insistence of the future, how it requires that its audience adopt a kind of double vision (67) by the way it evokes our expectations of conventional Hollywood narrative, while it also pushes us to read it outside of that context, as a product of our culture's "sensory-overload barrage of lo-fi video footage, Internet and cable-TV news feeds, commercials, and simulated CGI environments" (68). In the context of this description, *Southland Tales* comes to seem like a film trying to become something other than film, something that is indeed "post-cinematic." And in that process, I would suggest, it hints at what may be the real and parallel trajectory/destiny for all of our sf/cult films, the true source of their "double" character, even the basis of their appeal. For in what I term their drama of screens, in their pointing to what might lie beyond those screens, in trying to take us across them, these films consistently signal something of what Shaviro terms the "post-cinematic." They suggest the possibility of escaping the current state of cinema (and cinematic texts), of moving beyond—or striking through—its screens, of *becoming* (although becoming *what* is not really the issue), as they/we celebrate that possibility.

III

The chapters that follow this introduction lay out the broad parameters of a shared cult/sf identity through a mix of broader contextualizing pieces and discussions of specific sf cult texts, all of them drawing on the informing conceit of the pairing's double character—or "double feature" experience. These case studies are organized around three dimensions of the sf/cult film experience. The first portfolio of studies is devoted to another sort of contextualizing, one that emphasizes how each sf cult work gains an element of its character by asking us to see doubly, through a melding of diverse forms: different genres, different cinematic impulses or trends, different characters and actors, even different national traditions. That melding, as these essays demonstrate, allows audiences to experience not only the pleasures of such new or unexpected combinations, but also a kind of shock of difference, as they recognize the possible implications of these conjoined characteristics. For example, a work like the British *Attack the Block* (2011), with its postmodern mixture of urban gang, coming-of-age, alien invasion, and self-reflexive components, easily suggests the range of such cult work, as it not only demonstrates new and compelling narrative possibilities, but also forces audiences—much like the various characters at the end of the film—to cheer for a figure like the protagonist Moses who, because of his race, involvement in subculture activities, and criminal background, initially seems a most unlikely embodiment of humanity's best hope in the face of a hostile and invasive universe.

And that sort of "shock," as many will readily recognize, has typically provided one of the great appeals of the sf genre. The lead essay in this section, Matt Hills's study of the "multiverses" involved in the production of J. J. Abrams's rebootings of *Star Trek*, immediately reminds us of the expectations audiences bring to any text, but especially ones that operate within an already established cult context. The studies that follow explore different dimensions of the larger sf cult multiverse, drawing on such varied works as *Zardoz* (1974), the sf/horror films of Larry Cohen and David Cronenberg, the Coen brothers' *The Man Who Wasn't There* (2001), and the Japanese anime tradition, all of them suggesting how the sf film has often and effectively drawn together varied narrative impulses, producing a mash-up that invites audiences to perceive in it something "other," something that often generates what we typically label as a cult response. In some instances, as Mark Bould's examination of *The Man Who Wasn't There* illustrates, it is the clash of various genre components that prompts a kind of double vision. In others, as co-editor Gerald Duchovnay explores, it is the echoes that result from casting actors well known for one sort of role in a different—and quite unlikely—sort of narrative vehicle. And in still others, it is the rather "ghostly" effect of bringing different animation styles to bear, as we see in a film like *Ghost in the Shell* (1995) and its sequel *Innocence* (2004). In most cases, these entries describe a kind of sampling activity that is at work in many of our sf cult films, although it is a sampling of a special sort, something that, because it is seldom neat and systematic, might better be described as *splattering*—a term from which Stacey Abbott's discussion draws other sorts of double potentials. In a way that results in a more (for want of a better term) *surprising* experience, the various works she examines often seem, with almost a violent impulse, to *splatter* bits and pieces of various forms, various conventions, etc. throughout their narratives, with the result that the irregular and certainly unconventional appearance of those splatters, matched up with the horrific visceral splattering on which her chosen texts focus, confronts viewers with a type of film experience that they have and have not seen before—literally an sf double feature.

Following this section, a second portfolio of case studies focuses more precisely on fan reaction and involvement in the cult sf work, as this section explores the special nature of audience activity, or what might even be described as *interactivity*, that these films commonly inspire. Extrapolating from an observation made by Mark Jancovich et al. in *Defining Cult Movies*, these essays underscore the notion that the cult audience's relation to a film "is not coherent" (2); that is, when considered as a phenomenon, it seems to proceed from no single concern, appreciation, or even venue, but rather emerges from what Jancovich and his colleagues rather elusively term a "subcultural ideology" that might be located in a specific audience, a film-maker's approach, or even some dynamic component of the film itself (1). To frame that difficult sense of "incoherence" (a term that bears some obvious kinship to the "splattering" previously suggested), this portfolio's essays view sf cult activity from a variety of vantages—gender, media, culture—while also incorporating several extra-cinematic dimensions. Thus Rhonda Wilcox details how the "Browncoat" movement arising from Joss Whedon's failed *Firefly* television series (2002–03) and its cinematic continuation *Serenity* (2005) sought to continue the spirit of those texts, extending them beyond the film and television experience and effecting a cultural impact as a result of various sorts of fan activities, such as charity fund raising and media protests. Through such behaviors, the Browncoats effectively pose a question, one neatly articulated in *Serenity*, of who actually owns "the signal," that is, both the text that speaks meaningfully to people as it finds a cult life, and the very media through which it manages to gain that life. Nicolle Lamerichs's essay complements this broad consideration of fan activity by documenting the more immediate, personal events typically encountered in European sf conventions (or cons), while also offering a revealing portrait of the typical con attendee. As her highly personal piece suggests, in spite of many preconceptions about both sf and cult film audiences (both often seen as predominantly male), these ritualistic sites are heavily populated by women, who increasingly find themselves attracted to the alternate worlds, realities, and the *possibilities* that sf has always envisioned—and from which culture has frequently blocked them.[4]

Another version of this cult audience-text activity is that which occurs *across* normal borders, both economic and cultural. While recalling the Browncoats' efforts on behalf of *Firefly* and *Serenity*, Chuck Tryon's entry explores some new economic territory for fan and text interactivity, as he details the practices of "crowdsourcing" and "crowdfunding." That practice of attracting wide-based audience support for a project, demonstrated most successfully in the cult sf film *Iron Sky*, opens the door for questions about whether a text might indeed be tailored for a cult audience, and thus whether cult activity is in various ways predictable after all. Takayuki Tatsumi's entry takes that border crossing potential of the cult text as both the literal and cultural context for his examination of the South African sf work *District 9* (2009). This film about an apparently accidental alien "invasion" capitalizes on our sense of cultural geography by examining the transnational image transactions to be found in Japanese and South African sf films. What this sort of transaction points up, as we shall see, is another kind of doubleness, one that reminds us of the cult text's ultimate resistance to a restrictive *cult*-ural harnessing: that for all of a work's apparent grounding in a very specific cultural embrace, it ultimately belongs to no single culture, and often confounds efforts to identify it with a particular culture.

The volume's third portfolio examines a selection of films that have often proved to be the stalking horses in discussions of the cult phenomenon, even as they have also troubled some of the theoretical discussions that go on around cult activity: those often described as "transgressive" films,[5] sometimes as components of a "cinema of excess,"[6] or even more simply as "bad" movies. These are works that some claim to like precisely because of their "badness," and they include such varied titles as *Plan 9 from Outer Space* (described by some as the worst film ever made), the previously cited *Attack of the 50 Foot Woman*, *Robot Monster*, a wave of low-budget sf/horror films that appeared in the 1970s, challenging conventions of taste and representation, and more recent efforts like the comic sf works *Space Truckers* (1996) and *Bubba Ho-tep* (2002). Because of their typically problematic nature as "serious" works, their hyperbolic representations, or the difficulties they pose to a segment of the audience who believe sf should ultimately engage in plausible depictions of science and technology—as Gary Westfahl's recent book *The Spacesuit Film* argues at great length—these works have often been segregated under the heading of "camp" and, as a consequence, then simply dismissed from "serious" critical or classroom discussion as works whose very weaknesses or "over-the-top" effects are their chief, and implicitly only, real attractions.

However, these sorts of films also foreground a key dynamic that seems to be involved in most cult formation. For they have often resulted in what my discussion of *Robot Monster* terms an *occulting* of the cult. Put more simply, these films provide a rationale for cult appreciation and cult behavior by virtue of their very trajectory of dismissal, by the fact that, for a majority of moviegoers, they seem to *mystify* the category's qualities, much as they also mystify conventional aesthetics. Jeffrey Sconce locates one positive dimension in this sort of cult film when he suggests that studying "bad" texts can be a highly useful exercise, teaching us much "about film itself—as a practice, as an art, as an object" (33). Yet there is also the haunting sense—and indeed respected critical opinions—that ultimately we cannot really know what constitutes a "bad" film, or how such a text might be differentiated from another that is intentionally working to subvert our conventional film experience—as in the case of *Southland Tales*. Thus, those who can appreciate these sorts of films, it may well seem, comprise a group of special cognoscenti; in their hip knowingness, they seem to "get" what most viewers do not, and in their ability to do so they demonstrate yet another sort of doubleness at work in the cult text: that of the seemingly bad film that is also able to speak quite meaningfully—to those capable of "hearing"—in the language of cinema.

This "occulting" approach sustains and partly explains the popular response to the work of the legendarily bad film-maker Ed Wood, Jr.— responsible not only for *Plan 9 from Outer Space*, but also such works as *Bride of the Monster* (1955) and *Glen or Glenda?* (1953). His works have come in for cultic appreciation not only for their legendarily slapdash creation, but also for Wood's minimalist "aesthetic" and the cultural implications of the films, that is, as works that invert and in the process render transparent some of the worst impulses of Hollywood filmmaking, even in a period like the '50s marked by a horde of quickly and cheaply produced sf films. However, with a work like *Attack of the 50 Foot Woman*, and a host of similar films, as Sherryl Vint demonstrates, we can see a different dimension of that occulting activity, in this instance the appreciation of the work precisely for the ways in which the sexual or gender dynamics of its era are quite literally writ large in its text, a process that also allows contemporary audiences to situate themselves at a great distance culturally from the world depicted there. In this "occulting" approach, then, we can find instances of both those immersive and those distancing practices previously described in this Introduction.

Another group of films in this "occult" branch of cult sf demonstrates precisely the sort of serious notes that might be struck, even by works that choose to play at the margins of conventional sf cinema. Rob Latham situates a series of low-budget sf films of the 1970s in the context of the literary genre's new wave that had begun to emerge in the previous decade, noting in these works some of the signature new wave-like characteristics that would prove foundational for a later mainstream sf cinema. In his study of the sf satire *Space Truckers*, M. Keith Booker explores a paradox that he argues is at work in most capitalist texts, but which surfaces most obviously—and usefully—in the sf cult film.

In considering how this film deploys the principles of "camp," typically associated with cult development, he offers a new perspective on how effective a cult work can be as social and political commentary. And in a similar vein, Jeffrey Weinstock uses the sf/horror mash-up *Bubba Ho-tep* to consider the strategic possibilities inherent in the level of silliness— actually a superficial non-seriousness—that often seems to mark cult works. While acknowledging the over-the-top potential of much that we find in the sf cult vein, Weinstock mines *Bubba Ho-tep* to reveal what he terms a "seriously silly" lode, the sort of unexpected gold that, as most of the contributors to this volume would attest, is frequently to be found in the most unexpected—or cultic—of places.

IV

More than twenty years ago, the academic study of the cult film was effectively inaugurated with a volume published by the University of Texas Press, *The Cult Film Experience: Against All Reason*. Containing essays by more than a dozen prominent film critics and historians, that book set out to define the emerging but still vaguely conceived form of the cult film, particularly in light of what were, at that time, two dominant trends in the typical cult experience, and around which most critical commentary of the time had clustered: first, the classical film narrative, exemplified by a work like *Casablanca* (1942), with its devoted, often nostalgic audience that supported the then popular repertory cinema exhibition of older, well-loved movies, and that reveled in the ability to *look back* at an earlier age of film; and second, the midnight movie, the sort of transgressive film that at one time found its key outlet and chief site of its cult worship in late-night showings at small urban theaters—a practice that continues, if somewhat more muted, to the present day. These very different types—of films and exhibition practices—were both obviously keyed to a special kind of fan experience (or re-experience), as well as to a manner of film distribution that has since, thanks to the internet, cable, satellite transmission, Netflix, iTunes, Flickr, Hulu, and various other new or still emerging venues for image hosting and dissemination, become almost irrelevant to the creation or support of a cult following.

In fact, the very variety of media sources we note—and that Chuck Tryon's contribution here helps to frame—begins to argue for a new way of thinking about what we previously termed "the cult film *experience*." For rather than disappearing along with its specialized venues, that experience now seems almost fundamentally linked to the fractures,

segmentation, and narrow casting that have increasingly come to characterize the popular film and, more broadly, much of our media experience
today (a characteristic we might also see paralleled in that "splattering"
aesthetic which often marks our cult texts). It is an experience that
does not evict the cult, but rather offers new ways of advancing and
reinforcing it: by what would at one time have seemed very much like
science fictional activities—the tweet, blog, YouTube self-distribution
and dissemination, crowdsourcing, etc.

While the original *Cult Film Experience* took as its central guiding
principle a kind of Dionysian spirit that attached to those two types
of experience—a spirit broadly alluded to by Andrew Sarris's originary
comment that the term "cultist" was "justified for those of us who loved
movies beyond all reason" (13), and one visibly demonstrated in the sort
of revels that attended midnight screenings of films like *The Rocky Horror
Picture Show* and that linger in the parades and other activities of the *Star
Wars* 501st Legion members; the extended spirit, even (as Rhonda Wilcox
argues) the *ethic* of the *Firefly/Serenity* Browncoats; and the great variety
of cosplay and mock activities found at various national and international
cons (as well as in reality shows like *Heroes of Cosplay* that celebrate
this spirit)—that principle too seems an insufficient guide for assessing
the contemporary cult film experience, especially as the cult so often
intersects with the world of sf and its particular fandom. There is, simply,
a certain amount of *reason* that appears fundamental to the activity of
cult today, a calculus that rather quickly projects a film like *Saw* (and
its multiple sequels) or a television series such as *Lost* into another level
of experience and audience connection. The aim of this study, then, is
to let in a bit of that *reason*—or more precisely, the multiple sorts of
reason, reasons that often end in the kinds of paradoxes described above,
and reasons that especially tend to be foregrounded in the sf text—at
work in the contemporary cult media experience. Particularly, we
want to emphasize the curious yet inevitably technologically informed
nature of that contemporary "experience." And we want to establish a
new guiding principle for reconsidering and redefining today's "cultist"
behavior: the notion that the cult text is essentially the site at which
those ruptures and fractures noted above call attention to themselves,
show the very fissures in the larger film or media experience (and by
extension in the culture that produces such experiences), while also—
as again we see that doubling principle at work—celebrating them as
important, even vital. The key spot for doing so, we would once more
offer, is that preeminent cultural site of such technological reflection,
the sf film with its own inherent fascination with (and critiques of) the
very workings of reason and its own keenly sensed appreciation of how

those ruptures/fractures/fissures inevitably surface in or seem attracted to a world of reason, science, and technology.

As an aid to further research and better appreciation of the evolving cult form, the volume concludes with several tools that we hope will prove useful in extending this discussion of cult work. It includes an extensive bibliography of works that explore the intersections of sf and the cult, including some of those intersections that occur on other screens, such as television and computational media. And it provides an extensive filmography of the primary works which, our contributors have determined, operate at that point of intersection: sf films that have, for a variety of reasons, attracted a large cult following and, regardless of their other appeals, have staked out an important yet largely unexplored place in both our cinematic and cultural history. However, that filmography also reflects the fact that the very category of the cult is constantly changing, that it is, as Jancovich et al. nicely put it, "essentially eclectic" (1), and is always open to discovering *new audiences* with other reasons for "celebration." This listing should prove a useful tool for those who want to do more extensive examinations or offer more nuanced historical accounts of both sf and cinematic cult activity.

Finally, we believe that the discussions that follow will fill an important gap in the scholarship on both sf and cult activity. While sf is very much on the critical agenda of late, as evidenced by a great many recent books, including Mark Bould's *Science Fiction* (2012), Telotte and Duchovnay's *Science Fiction Film, Television, and Adaptation: Across the Screens* (2012), Lincoln Geraghty's *American Science Fiction Film and Television* (2009), and Christine Cornea's *Science Fiction Cinema: Between Fantasy and Reality* (2007), cult studies, as we earlier noted, have generally paid little specific attention to the form. While Mathijs and Sexton's *Cult Cinema* observes that sf "is a genre that has often been closely connected to cult cinema" (205), and briefly treats several examples, its textbook-style effort at surveying the entire cult phenomenon militates against a detailed examination of sf. Jancovich et al.'s *Defining Cult Movies* gives a great deal of attention to another sort of fantasy, the horror film—with individual essays on Spanish horror, Italian horror, "sex-horror," and David Cronenberg horror—but limits its concern with sf to a routine discussion of fandom. A theoretically informed but also focused text, one that situates sf properly, near the very core of cinematic cult activity today, can help to fill this gap, while also proving informative to students, scholars, and a general readership. We hope that *Science Fiction Double Feature: The Science Fiction Cult Text* begins to address this need.

Notes

[1] In my earlier *The Cult Film Experience*, I suggested that an analysis of the cult film as phenomenon might well begin by acknowledging a dynamic that such works involve, that they point to a love *beyond all reason*, in effect, that they situate our response in contrast to a *reasonable*—perhaps even a scientific—explanation (5). At that point, I preferred to examine that response largely in terms of "difference," as a way of thinking about the various ways in which cult audiences pointedly sought to differentiate themselves from other filmgoers, even to claim, if only temporarily and within the precincts of the movie theater, another identity for themselves, sometimes quite literally by dressing up as a film character and acting out parts of the film.

[2] As a gauge of the variety of cult film activity, we might consider Ernest Mathijs and Xavier Mendik's collection *The Cult Film Reader*, as well as David Lavery's anthology *The Essential Cult TV Reader*. Both identify a wide variety of cult film and television texts, in fact, such a variety that it almost seems that anything one wants to claim a cult following for might be fair game for inclusion. That inclusive approach has the advantage of avoiding what is commonly referred to as the "empiricist dilemma," that is the problem of placing something in a critical category that can itself only be established by accepting things for and grouping them in that category. See Andrew Tudor's discussion of this issue in "Genre" (4–5). Of course, that approach also runs the risk of suggesting that the cult *is* the mainstream and that the only defining component of the cult is the specific, yet fragmented audience for each text.

[3] For a summary of and commentary on that recurrent self-reflexive activity that marks the sf media text, see Telotte and Duchovnay's *Science Fiction Film, Television, and Adaptation: Across the Screens* (especially xvii–xix), or Annette Kuhn's "Introduction" to *Alien Zone* (1–12).

[4] Jancovich et al., following the lead of many others, simply assert that "cult fans ... are largely middle-class and male" (2).

[5] For a discussion of the "transgressive" cult film, see Joan Hawkins's "Midnight Sex-Horror Movies and the Downtown Avant-Garde" (especially 227–28).

[6] See Mike King's discussion of such films in *The American Cinema of Excess*, particularly as he describes another sort of cinematic "double feature": how certain films "of excess" can "reveal the unique madnesses of the American mind," as well as "its unique strengths" (3).

Works Cited

Bould, Mark. *Science Fiction*. London: Routledge, 2012.

Cheng, John. *Astounding Wonder: Imagining Science and Science Fiction in Interwar America*. Philadelphia: U of Pennsylvania P, 2012.

Cornea, Christine. *Science Fiction Cinema: Between Fantasy and Reality*. Edinburgh: Edinburgh UP, 2007.

Corrigan, Timothy. "Film and the Culture of the Cult." *The Cult Film Experience: Beyond All Reason.* Ed. J. P. Telotte. Austin: U of Texas P, 1991. 26–37.

Geraghty, Lincoln. *American Science Fiction Film and Television.* Oxford: Berg, 2009.

Hawkins, Joan. "Midnight Sex-Horror Movies and the Downtown Avant-Garde." *Defining Cult Movies: The Cultural Politics of Oppositional Tastes.* Ed. Mark Jancovich, Antonio Lazaro Reboll, Julian Stringer, and Andy Willis. Manchester: Manchester UP, 2003. 223–34.

Hoesterey, Ingeborg. *Pastiche: Cultural Memory in Art, Film, and Literature.* Bloomington: Indiana UP, 2001.

Jancovich, Mark, Antonio Lazaro Reboll, Julian Stringer, and Andy Willis. "Introduction." *Defining Cult Movies: The Cultural Politics of Oppositional Tastes.* Ed. Mark Jancovich, Antonio Lazaro Reboll, Julian Stringer, and Andy Willis, Manchester: Manchester UP, 2003. 1–13.

King, Mike. *The American Cinema of Excess.* Jefferson: McFarland, 2008.

Kuhn, Annette. "Introduction: Cultural Theory and Science Fiction Cinema." *Alien Zone: Cultural Theory and Contemporary Science Fiction Cinema.* Ed. Annette Kuhn. London: Verso, 1990. 1–12.

Mathijs, Ernest, and Jamie Sexton. *Cult Cinema.* Oxford: Wiley-Blackwell, 2011.

Mathijs, Ernest, and Xavier Mendik, eds. *The Cult Film Reader.* New York: McGraw-Hill, 2008.

Sarris, Andrew. *Confessions of a Cultist: On the Cinema, 1955–1969.* New York: Simon and Schuster, 1970.

Sconce, Jeffrey. "Esper, the Renunciator: Teaching 'Bad' Movies to Good Students." *Defining Cult Movies: The Cultural Politics of Oppositional Tastes.* Ed. Mark Jancovich, Antonio Lazaro Reboll, Julian Stringer, and Andy Willis. Manchester: Manchester UP, 2003. 14–34.

Shaviro, Steven. *Post-Cinematic Affect.* Winchester: Zero Books, 2010.

Suvin, Darko. *Metamorphoses of Science Fiction.* New Haven: Yale UP, 1979.

Telotte, J. P., ed. *The Cult Film Experience: Beyond All Reason.* Austin: U of Texas P, 1991.

Telotte, J. P., and Gerald Duchovnay, eds. *Science Fiction Film, Television, and Adaptation: Across the Screens.* London: Routledge, 2012.

Tudor, Andrew. "Genre." *Film Genre Reader III.* Ed. Barry Keith Grant. Austin: U of Texas P, 2003. 3–11.

Westfahl, Gary. *The Spacesuit Film: A History, 1918–1969.* Jefferson: McFarland, 2012.

Wood, Robert E. "Don't Dream It: Performance and *The Rocky Horror Picture Show.*" *The Cult Film Experience: Beyond All Reason.* Ed. J. P. Telotte. Austin: U of Texas P, 1991. 156–66.

1. From "Multiverse" to "Abramsverse": *Blade Runner, Star Trek,* Multiplicity, and the Authorizing of Cult/SF Worlds

Matt Hills

When theorizing how a cinematic cult status develops, we should bear in mind that there may be more than one kind of media cult, and also more than one way for audiences to meaningfully approach films and franchises as cults. Prior research has emphasized different *types* of cult texts, whether by distinguishing "the midnight movie from the classical cult film" (Telotte, "Beyond" 10), "residual" from "emergent" audience valorizations (see my own "Realising the Cult Blockbuster"), or transgressive cult movies from "cult blockbusters" (Mathijs and Sexton 214). Some writers have explicitly identified branches of cult movies: "One ... branch of cult adores, worships and scrutinizes our leading actors, performers and celebrities," while "the alternate branch ... focuses on the very nature of strange worlds and unusual tales" (Havis 1–2). Of course, these may not be wholly separate branches: cult stars, for example, can appear in films depicting fantastical worlds (see the essay in this volume by Gerald Duchovnay). So cult value suggests a series of parallel universes—forked paths and expanding possibilities—rather than a single coherent logic. However, moving beyond these binaries, I will argue that cult films inhabit four categories that are not mutually exclusive and may come into tension with one another. These categories depend on differing processes of cult development: world-based, auteur-based, star-based, and production-based.

This chapter focuses primarily on the first two, examining how world-based and auteur-based cults operate in relation to two exemplary sf texts, *Blade Runner* (1982) and the rebooted *Star Trek* (2009) franchise. Despite the emergence of significant work on cult stardom (see that by Egan and Thomas, Nicanor Loreti, Jason Scott, and my own "Cult Movies"), I will not focus on cult stars here, but will emphasize questions of multiplicity and authority via cult world-building—or "world-sharing"—and authorship.

Cult worlds typically offer an expansive narrative space, which fan audiences can learn about, fill in via the creation of their own fan fiction, and imaginatively inhabit through such practices as cosplay or replica prop making. The intersection of cult and fantasy/sf is supported by this mode of cult development. Thus Ernest Mathijs and Jamie Sexton note that one of the special appeals of sf films

> is the creation of detailed environments that are strikingly different from those that we experience in our daily lives ... The creation of imaginary spaces can lead to cultic followings through inducing a sense of wonder ... leading to subsequent investigations of such spaces through re-readings. (209)

Fantasy/sf therefore lends itself especially to world-based cult creation by audiences, since it typically proffers what Umberto Eco terms "completely furnished worlds" (68) which fans can map. However, no sf *mise-en-scène* can ever sustain a "fully" furnished world. The camera moves across design details, giving a fleeting glimpse of some and prioritizing a few details of the narrative world while denying access to others. At best, as Sara Jones offers, a "completely furnished world" can only be implied rather than directly shown, as there "is always a deficit between what is (or can be) shown and what the avid audience wants to see ... and know" (13). As such, it might be said that Eco's "completely furnished worlds" and Jones's "incompletely furnished worlds" (12) capture aspects of the same cult/sf phenomenon: that *implied, extensible, transtextual worlds* characterize many conjunctions between sf and cult movies.

Of course, sf cinema's narrative spaces are typically otherworldly (or represent an intrusion of something alien into our mundane world). Compared to more naturalistic genres, spectacle and special effects play a greater role in sf movies. As J. P. Telotte observes: "Simply put, these films, more than any others, reflect the technology that makes them possible" (*Science Fiction* 25). Piers Britton in "Design for Screen SF" suggests that although the genre's design work needs to draw on "extended *common sense*" in order to look plausible to viewers (341), sf cinema, particularly since the 1970s, has emphasized "highly textured, visually complex" design, privileging materiality rather than sleek minimalism (344). The fact that sf cinema is called upon to construct fantastic profilmic spaces enhanced by extensive post-production and CGI work, means that it displays "a very particular kind of 'to-be-looked-at-ness'" (342).

On occasion, this effect can tip over into visual excess, with costume or production design drowning out characters and dominating an entire narrative world, as happens in *Flash Gordon* (1980), which Mark Bould cites as an example of "camp" sf (*Science Fiction* 107). The tension between "common sense" (cultural plausibility) and its "extended" extrapolation in sf design, identified by Britton, means that sf not only calls attention to its visuals, but also to its very constructedness. *Production-based* cult processes can thus unite cult and sf in alternative ways. By highlighting moments where sf's visions are "failed" or excessive, fans can align films with "bad film" or "trash" versions of camp cult, dubbed "paracinema" by Jeffrey Sconce (101). Furthermore, research into sf fandom and sf as a genre has drawn on Pierre Bourdieu's sociology to theorize cult/sf in relation to (sub)cultural capital and cultural distinctions (see work by Nathan Hunt and Andrew Milner).

But cult and sf are not only articulated in the category of "trash" movies. Blockbuster sf can also attain cult followings, with expensive, state-of-the-art special effects (SFX) being celebrated by audiences for their display of technical craft. Far from what Derek Johnson terms "the critical dismissal of effects as 'empty'" (41), or the unhelpful binary of spectacle versus narrative, SFX can instead interact with film narratives—and production histories—as part of the sf text's cult formation, sustaining types of fan knowledge and helping to position movies as what Roz Kaveney terms "thick texts":

> understanding how the look of a particular film derives in part from the technical accomplishment and creative innovation of its designers, make-up crew, CGI technicians ... is what makes all films, but most especially SF films, thick texts ... The precondition of ... recognizing a thick text is that we accept that ... texts ... contain all the stages of that process within them like ... vestigial organs. (5)

Kaveney's concept emphasizes the extent to which sf films' constructed worlds not only draw fans into diegetic elaborations such as fan fiction, but also incite them to explore production histories and contingencies. However, Kaveney does not push the notion of a "thick text" far enough: intersections of the cult and sf result in more than various sorts of paratextual proliferations, such as DVD/blu-ray extras, making-of books, or assorted merchandise allowing some texts, as Jonathan Gray comments, to "claim more paratexts than others, with, for instance, blockbusters and cult texts often sporting sizeable posses" (114). In some cases, films can be re-released with augmented SFX sequences as "Special Editions." So a cult audience's interest can go beyond just recognizing the "vestigial" traces of production in a "thick text" to (re-)consuming (and sometimes not approving of) textually amended and thus multiple versions of cult sf films. Thus, cult/sf texts may be thickened not just by "making-of" features, but also by *textual iterations,* meaning that production-based cultification can occur both around "camp," trashy sf and around commercial, re-released, and re-edited sf texts.

This multiplication of cult/sf textual versions can occur gradually over a period of decades, as with the various incarnations of *Blade Runner* and *Star Wars,* along with 1979's *Star Trek: The Motion Picture,* modified as *The Director's Edition* in 2001. And cult cinema's multi-generational fan popularity means that such films are readily amenable to *periodic* re-commoditization. But textual multiples can also occur within rapid cycles of cult commercialization, as was the case for *Donnie Darko,* which followed its initial 2001 release with a 2004 *Director's Cut* that included "explanatory material that had existed at the margins," and that shifted "from website ... to DVD extras—moved into the text itself" (King, *Donnie* 28), rendering the latter version less cryptic and more straightforwardly science-fictional than its predecessor.

So while cult/sf films do often correlate with large numbers of paratexts, my particular interest here is in the ways in which intersections of cult status and sf cinema have generated such *textual* multiplications, as we can see when contrasting *Blade Runner*'s situation with that of the *Star Trek* franchise. Ridley Scott's *Blade Runner* currently exists as a series of five commercially available versions (included in the *Ultimate Collector's Edition* [*UCE*]), although commentators have identified others, including the letterboxed Criterion laserdisc. The recently released *30ᵗʰ Anniversary Collector's Edition* supplements the previous *UCE* with a production photo archive. By contrast, J. J. Abrams's *Star Trek* (2009) and *Star Trek Into Darkness* (2013) might appear to be wholly singular texts. However, while *Star Trek Into Darkness* has been exhibited in IMAX and "standard" prints, as well as in 2D and 3D, both it and Abrams's first *Trek* film adopt a specific relationship to previous *Star Trek* franchise entries, simultaneously recognizing alternative, prior texts and seeking to *overwrite* them.

While *Blade Runner* permits a cultish textual multiplicity, amounting to what Will Brooker has described as "a network of possible alternate routes" through its hyperdiegesis ("All" 79), Abrams's *Star Trek* allows yet also marginalizes an "unruly multiverse" ("All" 90), imagining a binary of "cult" versus "mainstream" audience readings. One of the issues that cult/sf film generates, then, is how such resulting textual multiplicity— either specific re-versioning or franchise rebooting—can be discursively authorized. I will suggest that, in the case of *Blade Runner,* world-based and auteur-based cult developments come into conflict, only being uneasily and paradoxically held together, whereas these two specific cult-generating processes are reflexively unified in *Star Trek* (2009). In part, these differences are related to the fact that *Blade Runner* was not initially designed for cult audiences, and has what we might think of as a "retrofitted" cult quality, whereas Abrams's *Trek* of necessity had to anticipate the cult fandom of Trekkers (see Anders).

Blade Runner's Multiverse: Multiple Texts and Cult Authorizations?

Blade Runner may well be the ultimate "thick text," its production errors and inconsistencies having been emphasized by what Mark Bould describes as "text-clusters" of multiple variants ("Preserving" 165), and illuminated through ongoing fan/academic discussion. As Nick Lacey points out, if *"Blade Runner* had not become such a cult movie," its various "discontinuities would never have become so widely known" (80–81), such as when the character Bryant refers to "six" escaped replicants with "one" shot, suggesting that five should be loose on the streets, rather than the four we encounter. *The Final Cut* fixes many such "vestigial" traces of the original production. As Sean Redmond observes, "Batty's death scene, where a dove is released into a bright, blue world, is now shot against a bleak, tumultuous-looking night sky" (91). And the riddle posed by replicant numbers—a mistake, as the numbers referred to an additional replicant character, Mary, whose role was cut during rewrites—is also corrected in the 2007 version. Previously, the miscount enabled fans to speculate that Deckard himself was the missing member of the replicant team, but, as Will Brooker notes, the "minor adjustment to Bryant's dialogue sends ... significant ripples throughout the text ... This hole has been closed" ("All" 81), and the number of replicants adds up neatly.

It may seem as if the *Final Cut*'s tendency is simply "to clean up ambiguities and close down multiple choices" (Brooker, "All" 83), therefore providing a "definitive" authorial statement. Indeed, the *UCE* included "A Letter from Ridley Scott," printed on acetate as if to render it part of the science-fictional diegetic world. Concluding with Scott's printed signature, the message assures fan-consumers:

> I have included the four previously seen versions of the film ...
> My goal was to give you the film in whatever form you prefer ...
> And finally, I've assembled a collection of in-depth documentaries,
> multi-faceted commentaries, never-seen-before footage and rare

artwork to give you a deeper appreciation of all the work that went into the making of this film. I can now wholeheartedly say that *Blade Runner: The Final Cut* is my definitive director's cut.

A process overseen by others—Charles de Lauzirika acted as the restoration producer, for instance—is personalized as Scott's labor alone: "I have included," and "I have assembled." While the "multi-faceted commentaries" and "never-seen-before" footage testify to "a continuing movement beyond the original boundaries of the text" (Bukatman 40), there is an incredibly strong auteurist bent to this paratextual framing of the *UCE*, as it implies that *Blade Runner*'s multiple texts have been personally authorized by Ridley Scott's imprimatur. *The Final Cut* is "wholeheartedly" claimed as his true vision—invoking not only auteurist ownership but also a mode of (fan-like) passion for the narrative world depicted. Mark Bould's observation in relation to the 1992 (and somewhat mis-named) *Director's Cut* is even more apposite in relation to *The Final Cut*, as he argues that scholarly "complicity in promoting the re-mix too easily slides back into declaring the director to be the source and guarantee of the movie's meaning" ("Preserving" 166).

Such auteur-based cult generation operates by prioritizing specific entries within the multiple texts of cult/sf cinema, leading to "core texts ... assumed to hold 'answers' to ... inconsistencies, ambiguities" (Brooker, "Internet" 61), and textual multiplicity being resolved into a

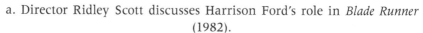

a. Director Ridley Scott discusses Harrison Ford's role in *Blade Runner* (1982).

b. *Star Trek: Into Darkness* (2013): J. J. Abrams revisions the relationship between the series' central characters, Kirk and Spock.

"canon of valid 'evidence'" (62) by fans' reading protocols and auteurist discourses. Yet this process of cult author-ization can involve an element of hesitancy:

> a degree of uncertainty [is] felt by some *Blade Runner* fans as to whom they should turn to for authorial meaning … [They are] torn between … [a] belief that Ridley Scott is the true auteur of the film and … knowledge that Philip K. Dick created many of the characters and ideas translated to the screen. (Gray 154)

Despite this oscillation between Dick and Scott as the "definitive" *Blade Runner* auteur, other authorial voices are firmly excluded in most fan discourse. For example, Christy Gray notes that K. W. Jeter's "continuation" novels are viewed "by many *Blade Runner* fans as trash to be read mainly as a means of satisfying one's need for more material" (155–56). In this instance, a powerfully auteurist reading linked to Scott's filmic realization seems to rule out, or at least subordinate, some of the transmedia extensions that have emerged over time, leaving the cinematic world of *Blade Runner* in place as the (nevertheless fractured and multiple) "origin" of textual meaning and fan debate.

Although such auteur-based activations of cult status have played a significant role in *Blade Runner*'s cult development, these processes can come into conflict with world-based readings. Different pathways to cult value may sometimes overlap, but they can also operate in tension with one another, with author-based cults exceeded by fans' investments in story-worlds and characters that can go well beyond authorial statements and even an author's sense of "ownership." Will Brooker recognizes this tension in discussing the *Ultimate Collector's Edition*, which he interprets as

> Satisfying ... twin desires for an ultimate edition of *Blade Runner*, which to many fans meant an auteurist expression of Ridley Scott's personal vision ... and for the continued ambiguity and aperture created by the multiple versions and their sheer inconsistencies ... this privileging of the director as auteur on Disc 1 is tempered by the surrounding material on other discs ... many other voices, of comparable cultural status, are placed in dialogue with ... [Scott's] own. ("All" 84)

Of course, "ambiguity and aperture" emerge not only through the film's multiple texts, but also through fans' attempts to rationalize its hyper-detailed narrative world. So *Blade Runner* has produced a paradoxical collision of auteur-based and world-based cults, with fans wanting to hold open questions emerging out of the world of 2029 Los Angeles *and* appreciate Scott's seemingly "definitive" answers.

This collision could be read as a philosophical problem requiring its own theoretical resolution. Indeed, I have previously approached the topic in this way, arguing that Umberto Eco's analysis of the "living textuality" of cult worlds is falsified by cult auteurism (*Fan Cultures* 132–33). However, it may be more productive to tolerate contradiction here rather than adjudicating between *Blade Runner*'s world-based and auteur-based cultifications. As Eco argues of the cult film:

> outside the conscious control of its creators, it becomes a sort of textual syllabus, a living example of living textuality. Its addressee must suspect it is not true that works are created by their authors ... texts are created by texts, all together they speak to each other independently of the intentions of their authors. (68)

This process creates multiple points of origin for fan readings. Scott simply represents *one* originary source of meaning, but *Blade Runner*'s expansive, detailed narrative universe represents another, with fans seeking new textual details and rejecting many of Scott's favored interpretations. One might almost suggest that cult worlds become a type of supplementary "author"—or at least an additional mode of author-ization—sustaining what Michel Foucault terms "a 'transdiscursive' position" as "initiators of discursive practices" (24–25). Although Foucault reserves this position for the creators of grand theory such as Marx and Freud, ruling out novelists who generate new genre patterns and identities, such as the "gothic," his separation of genre ("resemblances and analogies") and theory ("differences") seems unconvincing. I do not mean to suggest that narrative worlds work in exactly the same way as Foucault's "author-function," but these worlds nonetheless appear to secure authenticity for fans, working to code material as "canonical" (see my "Academic Textual Poachers" 138–39) and operating as a rival principle of classification and value.

Blade Runner's "transdiscursive" narrative world readily raises questions about self-identity/humanity, allowing its texts to be positioned in terms of their intertextual cultural capital and status as sf film art (see my "The Question" 444). As "initiators of discursive practices," its variants also raise the issue of "Otherness"—a key characteristic of cult movies for Barry Keith Grant—positioning Roy Batty less as a "black hat" villain and more as a sympathetic figure, while also implying that Deckard may himself deconstruct the self/other binary of the blade runner and replicant (135). But these "transdiscursive" generators of meaning also enable *Blade Runner*'s cult world, perhaps unsurprisingly, to be commodified in the form of physical collectibles and fan-targeted merchandise. Thus a plastic "origami" unicorn accompanied the US "Limited Edition Gift Set" of the *UCE*, while a die-cast "concept" Spinner formed part of the 30th Anniversary limited edition re-issue, enabling fan interactions with various diegetic objects reproduced as extradiegetic collectibles. In such engagements with world-based cult, Ridley Scott's role as auteur recedes, and emphasis instead falls, as Will Brooker observes, on fans' playful inhabitation of *Blade Runner* "as a story-world" treated "more like a *game*" ("All" 86). The *UCE*'s acetate "Letter from Ridley Scott" attempts to unify these two reading protocols by merging an auteurist sentiment with hyperdiegetic gaming mimicry, but it is a highly unusual artifact in this respect. More generally, *Blade Runner*'s multiple texts and paratexts hold world-based and auteur-based cultifications in tension, meaning that there are distinct cult author-izations and discourses in play. However, given that *Blade Runner* has essentially had cult status thrust upon it over time, rather than being designed *for this status*, perhaps we should not be too surprised by such contradictory contexts. Despite the (para-)textual work of the *Director's Cut* and *The Final Cut*, *Blade Runner*'s hyperdetailed *mise-en-scène* (coupled with narrative puzzles and Philip K. Dick's source text) has never fully cohered into a "Scottverse." However, a far more strategically unified case of auteur-based and world-based cult discourses surfaces in what we might term the "Abramsverse" of *Star Trek*.

Star Trek's Multiple Texts and "Mainstream Cult" Authorization?

Although *Star Trek*'s initial creator-auteur figure was Gene Roddenberry, the franchise has been handed across a series of "torchbearers," as Mark Wolf notes: "While torchbearers work for ... the franchise's corporate owners, they are more than just employees, since they fill the role vacated by the world's main author, actively setting ... the course of the ... imaginary world" (276). Jeffrey Jacob Abrams is just the latest in this line of heirs to Roddenberry's role. As such, rather than world-building, Abrams is, as Derek Johnson describes it, effectively a "world-sharing" figure (109). He's taken over creative control of a narrative universe that has been expanding for more than four decades, one wherein the devoted audience experiences a hyperdiegetic world that "not only achieves saturation of mind, but virtually exceeds the audience's ability to encounter it all in its entirety" (Wolf 135).

However, unlike *Blade Runner*'s tension between world-based and auteur-based cultifying processes, Abrams and his team from Bad Robot Productions (including Roberto Orci, Alex Kurtman, and Damon Lindelof) adopt a "world-sharing" strategy that amounts to a sort of "world-containing." The encyclopedia of *Trek*'s prior timeline is abruptly set to one side by *Star Trek* (2009) via the use of time-travel as a plot device. The Romulan villain Nero (Eric Bana) goes back in time, and his interventions send the narrative off on a tangent wherein Kirk's father is killed just as Kirk is born, and where Spock's home planet is destroyed along with his mother. As a franchise, *Star Trek* has utilized parallel universe, time-travel storylines before, but Abrams's initial outing as director-producer, Karma Waltonen argues, "is unique in its failure to restore the timeline" to established events (172). In essence, Abrams et al. jettison the notion that *Trek*'s "fully furnished world" needs to be learned or known; they "unfurnish" previous subcultural capital and fan knowledge in one fell swoop.

The preceding TV franchise entry, *Enterprise* (2001–05), had itself become ensnared in producer/fan wrangling over accurate continuity, with "torchbearer" Brannon Braga attacking hardcore fans as "continuity pornographers" who would not allow his production team even minimally to contravene established lore (Ina Rae Hark 148). Fans' cultish, accumulated sense of *Star Trek*'s "imaginary world" diverged from that represented in much of *Enterprise*, and this disagreement was accompanied by falling ratings and vitriolic fan criticism. *Enterprise*, in effect, represented the triumph of a world-based cult over an auteur-based cult, fans turning their backs on the show in favor of the hyperdiegetic universe they were attached to, and which paratexts such as *Star Trek: The Official Magazine* have worked to unify (Lincoln Geraghty 35). Robert Kozinets frames this dilemma:

> Should *Star Trek* be used to critique *Star Trek*? Fans' already well-developed creative proclivity has now been married to abhorrence for manifestations of *Star Trek*. The fans hated ... recent TV series (particularly *Enterprise*). Their animosity creates considerable fan activity aimed at ... dissociating ... it from the official lore of *Star Trek*. (202)

Abrams et al. learned from this fan disgruntlement, simultaneously suspending fans' capacity to nitpick their continuity decisions, and leaving the "fully furnished world" of prior *Star Trek* in place as an alternative timeline. In fact, this "original" *Trek* was even honored via the moniker given to its version of Spock (Leonard Nimoy) in paratextual end credits where the character is dubbed "Spock Prime." But this designation is buried in the credits, since referring to Leonard Nimoy's character as "Spock Prime" in the narrative could create the impression that its world is somehow not the "true" one. While Abrams seems content to leave this implication in play for long-term Trekkers, he does not permit any such sentiment to leak into the film itself, where Chris Pine and Zachary Quinto are now definitively Kirk and Spock rather than sub-prime incarnations.

The *Star Trek* already beloved by long-term cult fans may be the "Prime" universe, but it is reflexively *not* the universe of Abrams's films, which has been described in fan parlance as the "Abramsverse" (see the *Trek* fan wiki, "Memory Alpha" 2013). As writer Roberto Orci puts it, almost *contra* Kozinets: "*Trek* already had the time travel set-up ... We used the rules of *Star Trek* to free *Star Trek* from itself" (qtd. in O'Hara 85). Mark Wolf interprets this move as an effort to reinvent the franchise, "while still trying to position new works as an extension of the original" (216), and it can certainly be said that *Star Trek* and *Star Trek Into Darkness* adopt a multivocal, dialogic relationship to the franchise's established story-world. Reduced to a matter of intertextual referencing or remixing, *Star Trek: The Original Series* is not so much adapted as transformatively and selectively cited. This pattern shows that the Abramsverse can pick and choose how it engages with *Trek*'s continuity, signaling to both "mainstream" and new audiences that they do not need to be familiar with what Sue Short terms "forty-odd years of mythology" (188).

The Abramsverse also ambiguously ranks what has been called "fan service" (Anders), where fan knowledge is intertextually drawn upon, alongside what might be termed "fan disservice," where continuity is pointedly ignored, revised, or discarded. The latter has aggravated scholar-fans, who dismiss *Star Trek* (2009) as "a noisy, effects-driven actioner without a shred of substance ... [featuring] a half-Vulcan who is now more in touch with his human side ... without the conflict that made him so dramatically interesting" (Short 189), while arguing that Chris Pine's "sophomoric, leering Kirk ... doesn't have anything like the authentic daring or sensitivity of the original ... [Zachary] Quinto's Spock replaces Nimoy's dignity and quiet emotional anguish with snideness and coiled rage" (Greven 208–09). The "triumvirate" of Kirk-Spock-McCoy, often represented as central to the appeal of *ST: TOS*, is also seen as diminished by the Abramsverse in favor of emphasizing the Kirk-Spock relationship, with Spock's newfound emotionality making him more akin to his captain (Lynnette Porter 26).

As David Greven astutely remarks, the Abramsverse demonstrates that "*Trek* has joined the postmodern collage of American culture, become the stuff of citation and allusion—which is to say that at last, in cultural terms, it has arrived" (208–09). But whereas the metaphorical, messy "multiverse" of *Blade Runner* and its multiple texts generate a game for fans—who can choose to dissent from Ridley Scott's textual interpretation—the Abramsverse makes *Star Trek*'s multiverse a diegetic assertion, officially edging out rival histories and changing previously canonical events within its storylines. Fans can still dissent, of course, but the alignment of the auteur and post-2009 franchise means that such disagreement comes up against a powerfully authorized timeline that explicitly defines its textual pathway as *neo-canon*, set against older, phased-out continuity. If Ridley Scott's auteur-based cult operates in tension with *Blade Runner*'s world-based "living textuality," the Abramsverse seeks to close down any such tension. It does so by articulating its "unshared" world (i.e., a new timeline) and its torchbearer's vision—addressing cult fans intertextually (often relying on citations of *The Wrath of Khan*, whether through the Kobayashi Maru and Spock's dialogue or through the character of Khan), while at the same time drawing on what Derek Johnson terms *Trek*'s "persistent visual design tradition" (117). But by refusing to engage in full-blown franchise "world-sharing," and thus ruling out prior continuity, the Abramsverse defines itself as accessible to new, casual, and non-Trekker audiences; hence the importance of coding fans' prior investments as subtextual or intertextual at best.

Working to unify world-creation and Abrams's transformative take on *Star Trek*, the franchise centers not on the cult world versus the author, but rather cult versus mainstream readings. Scholar-fans like

Short (189) and Greven (208) who reject Abrams's work as lacking "substance" and as "dumbing-down" the narrative world implicitly replay this binary of cult connoisseurship and intellect "in opposition to an imagined feminized 'mainstream'" (Hollows 41). Likewise, websites that attack *Star Trek Into Darkness* for catering too strongly to *Trek* fandom also replay a cult/mainstream binary, albeit positioning the 2013 film on the other side of the fence:

> Abrams' first *Star Trek* movie took a ... more restrained approach to fan-service—the story was more or less new, and the movie took some huge liberties, but then Abrams and friends threw some bones to the fans. Like, we saw Kirk take the Kobayashi Maru test, we saw a Tribble ... But the fan-service never took over the film, to the point of derailing the actual story. (Anders)

This "cult/mainstream" discourse also frames discussion of the Abramsverse as allegedly being SFX-driven and action-oriented rather than a logical and cerebral sf narrative (the latter implicitly demarcating "authentic" *Trek*). Yet scholarship on previous TV-to-film adaptations of *Star Trek* has emphasized how successful *Trek* films, such as *The Wrath of Khan*, have always more closely followed the "adventure/romance" formula of *ST: TOS*, while relying "more on emotion than cognition to engage" audiences (Booker 111). Indeed, of all the *Trek* movies perhaps only *The Motion Picture* edges into the realm of cognitively estranging sf, rather than embracing "the adventure/romance pole of the genre continuum" (Booker 111), and even *ST: TMP* can hardly be accused of neglecting spectacle.

Attacking the Abramsverse for offering mindless action just recuperates the cult/mainstream binary that the franchise has seemingly tried to bridge via Abrams's authority as what Hark terms a "trendy cult writer-director" (150). It also neglects to consider how *Trek* film producers—even those seeking to deactivate more than 40 years of accumulated continuity—must "balance delicately between spectacle and narrative in a manner [not] required ... of producers of one-off sci-fi films" (Pearson and Messenger-Davies 104), since they need to combine cinematic visuals, special effects, and production values with at least a degree of "consistency with ... characters' previously established traits and backstory" (Waltonen 172). Roberta Pearson and Maire Messenger-Davies have thus convincingly argued that blockbuster cinema's "conditions of production and reception" led to *Star Trek*'s TV characters becoming action heroes rather than cerebral heroes, noting: "if ... cinema *Trek* has to add spectacle but retain a focus on familiar characters, then your hero must figure prominently in the spectacular sequences" (113–14).

Thus, critiquing post-2009 *Trek* for its "mainstream" dumbing-down rather than its ability to offer a "pure" cult/sf aesthetic plays into the very concept of an "Abramsverse" by overestimating Abrams's authority and agency. In a sense, options for revitalizing the *Trek* franchise are precisely hemmed in by the "conditions of production and reception," framing how a blockbuster has to operate, and how something recognizable as *Star Trek* has to function. Rather than selling out *Star Trek*'s cult status, the Abramsverse has attempted to authorize one diegetic possibility, one timeline among others, to shape a "mainstream cult" coalition text, thereby allowing *Trek*'s old-school, world-based cultification to be intertextually carried, while Abrams's auteur-based cultification harnesses his "cult cachet" for new generations of fans and new audiences (Short 169).

I have here sought to compare two very different sf/cult multiverses that have both arisen out of multiple texts and their auteurist authorizations. *Blade Runner*'s "unruly multiverse" emerges out of variant cuts of the film. Its (para-)textual proliferation pits Umberto Eco's notion of a "living textuality" against Ridley Scott's efforts at an authorial closure of meaning, with these two impulses struggling over *Blade Runner*'s authenticities. In contrast, *Star Trek*'s hyperdiegetic multiverse represents a production strategy for managing the franchise's unwieldy, accumulated "imaginary world." In this instance, its multiple texts have generated such a vast mass of continuity constraints—outrunning any one author-function—that this "living textuality" has to be "stunned," if you will, without being entirely killed off, so as to craft a new "mainstream cult" authorization. However, key tensions continue to underscore cult versus mainstream imagined readings. For all that Abrams's agency may be overstated in cult fans' resistance, the Abramsverse actually works to unify cult's world-based and auteur-based discourses.

What these two different cases indicate is that the development of cult status is not singular or wedded to one coherent logic. Instead, a text's cult value can be energized in multiple ways: as world-based, auteur-based, star-based, and production-based framings. Although I have only focused significantly on the former two categories here, each of these can facilitate the collision of sf and cult status. What is so fascinating about auteur-based and world-based cults is that these potentials can be activated around the same series of texts—whether *Star Trek* or *Blade Runner*—and yet exist in tension with one another, as some fan audiences stress authorial vision and others emphasize the narrative universe that they love exploring, documenting, and speculating about. Cult/sf isn't just a doubling of categories; cult sf really can mean different things to different (fan) readers.

Works Cited

Anders, Charlie Jane. "*Star Trek* into Dumbness." *io9*, May 16, 2013. Web. Accessed 18 May 2013.

Booker, M. Keith. "*Star Trek* and the Birth of a Film Franchise." *Science Fiction Film, Television, and Adaptation: Across the Screens*. Ed. J. P. Telotte and Gerald Duchovnay. London: Routledge, 2012. 101–14.

Bould, Mark. "Preserving machines: Recentering the decentred subject in *Blade Runner* and *Johnny Mnemonic*." *Writing and Cinema*. Ed. Jonathan Bignell. Harlow: Pearson Education, 1999. 164–78.

—. *Science Fiction*. London: Routledge, 2012.

Britton, Piers D. "Design for Screen SF." *The Routledge Companion to Science Fiction*. Ed. Mark Bould, Andrew M. Butler, Adam Roberts, and Sherryl Vint. London: Routledge, 2009. 341–49.

Brooker, Will. "Internet Fandom and the Continuing Narratives of *Star Wars*, *Blade Runner* and *Alien*." *Alien Zone II: The Spaces of Science Fiction Cinema*. Ed. Annette Kuhn. London: Verso, 1999. 50–72.

—. "All Our Variant Futures: The Many Narratives of *Blade Runner: The Final Cut*." *Popular Communication* 7.2 (2009): 79–91.

Bukatman, Scott. *Blade Runner*. London: BFI, 1997.

Eco, Umberto. "*Casablanca*: Cult Movies and Intertextual Collage." *The Cult Film Reader*. Ed. Ernest Mathijs and Xavier Mendik. New York: McGraw-Hill, 2008. 67–75.

Egan, Kate, and Sarah Thomas. "Introduction: Star-Making, Cult-Making and Forms of Authenticity." *Cult Film Stardom*. Ed. Kate Egan and Sarah Thomas. New York: Palgrave-Macmillan, 2013. 1–17.

Foucault, Michel. "What is an Author?" *Screen* 20.1 (1979): 13–33.

Geraghty, Lincoln. *Living with* Star Trek*: American Culture and the Star Trek Universe*. London: I. B. Tauris, 2007.

Grant, Barry Keith. "Science Fiction Double Feature: Ideology in the Cult Film." *The Cult Film Experience*. Ed. J. P. Telotte. Austin: U of Texas P, 1991. 122–37.

Gray, Christy. "Originals and Copies: The Fans of Philip K. Dick, *Blade Runner* and K. W. Jeter." *The Blade Runner Experience*. Ed. Will Brooker. London: Wallflower, 2005. 142–56.

Gray, Jonathan. *Show Sold Separately: Promos, Spoilers, and Other Media Paratexts*. New York: New York UP, 2010.

Greven, David. *Gender and Sexuality in* Star Trek*: Allegories of Desire in the Television Series and Films*. Jefferson: McFarland, 2009.

Hark, Ina Rae. *Star Trek*. London: BFI, 2008.

Havis, Allan. *Cult Films: Taboo and Transgression*. Lanham: UP of America, 2008.

Hills, Matt. "Academic Textual Poachers: *Blade Runner* as Cult Canonical

Movie." *The Blade Runner Experience*. Ed. Will Brooker. London: Wallflower, 2005. 124–41.

—. "Cult Movies With and Without Cult Stars: Differentiating Discourses of Stardom." *Cult Film Stardom*. Ed. Kate Egan and Sarah Thomas. New York: Palgrave-Macmillan, 2013. 21–36.

—. *Cultographies: Blade Runner*. New York: Columbia UP, 2011.

—. *Fan Cultures*. London: Routledge, 2002.

—. "The Question of Genre in Cult Film and Fandom: Between Contract and Discourse." *The Sage Handbook of Film Studies*. Ed. James Donald and Michael Renov. London: Sage, 2008. 436–53.

—. "Realising the Cult Blockbuster: *The Lord of the Rings* Fandom and Residual/Emergent Cult Status in 'the Mainstream.'" *The Lord of the Rings: Popular Culture in Global Context*. Ed. Ernest Mathijs. London: Wallflower, 2006. 160–71.

Hollows, Joanne. "The Masculinity of Cult." *Defining Cult Movies*. Ed. Mark Jancovich, Antonio Lázaro Reboll, Julian Stringer, and Andy Willis. Manchester: Manchester UP, 2003. 35–53.

Hunt, Nathan. "The Importance of Trivia: Ownership, Exclusion and Authority in Science Fiction Fandom." *Defining Cult Movies*. Ed. Mark Jancovich, Antonio Lázaro Reboll, Julian Stringer, and Andy Willis. Manchester: Manchester UP, 2003. 185–201.

Johnson, Derek. *Media Franchising: Creative License and Collaboration in the Culture Industries*. New York: New York UP, 2013.

Johnston, Keith M. *Science Fiction Film: A Critical Introduction*. Oxford: Berg, 2011.

Jones, Sara Gwenllian. "Starring Lucy Lawless?" *Continuum* 14.1 (2000): 9–22.

Kaveney, Roz. *From Alien to the Matrix: Reading Science Fiction Film*. London: I. B. Tauris, 2005.

King, Geoff. *Donnie Darko*. London: Wallflower, 2007.

Kozinets, Robert V. "Inno-tribes: *Star Trek* as Wikimedia." *Consumer Tribes*. Ed. Bernard Cova, Robert V. Kozinets, and Avi Shankar. Oxford: Butterworth-Heinemann, 2007. 194–211.

Lacey, Nick. *York Film Notes: Blade Runner*. Harlow: Pearson Education, 2000.

Loreti, Nicanor. *Cult People: Tales from Hollywood's Exploitation A-list*. London: Headpress, 2010.

Mathijs, Ernest, and Jamie Sexton. *Cult Cinema*. Oxford: Wiley-Blackwell, 2011.

Memory Alpha. "AlternateReality." Web. Accessed 21 May 2013.

Milner, Andrew. *Locating Science Fiction*. Liverpool: Liverpool UP, 2012.

O'Hara, Helen. "Out of Orbit: *Star Trek Into Darkness*." *Empire* May 2013: 82–93.

Pearson, Roberta E., and Maire Messenger-Davies. "'You're not going to see that on TV': *Star Trek: The Next Generation* in Film and Television." *Quality Popular Television*. Ed. Mark Jancovich and James Lyons. London: BFI, 2003. 103–17.

Porter, Lynnette. *Tarnished Heroes, Charming Villains and Modern Monsters:*

Science Fiction in Shades of Gray on 21st Century Television. Jefferson: McFarland, 2010.

Redmond, Sean. *Studying Blade Runner*. Leighton Buzzard: Auteur, 2008.

Sconce, Jeffrey. "'Trashing' the Academy: Taste, Excess, and an Emerging Politics of Cinematic Style." *The Cult Film Reader*. Ed. Ernest Mathijs and Xavier Mendik. New York: McGraw-Hill, 2008. 100–18.

Scott, Jason. "From Behind the Masks to Inside: Acting, Authenticity and the *Star Wars* Co-Stars." *Cult Film Stardom*. Ed. Kate Egan and Sarah Thomas. New York: Palgrave-Macmillan, 2013. 90–106.

Short, Sue. *Cult Telefantasy Series: A Critical Analysis of* The Prisoner, Twin Peaks, The X-Files, Buffy the Vampire Slayer, Lost, Heroes, Doctor Who *and* Star Trek. Jefferson: McFarland, 2011.

Telotte, J. P. "Beyond All Reason: The Nature of the Cult." *The Cult Film Experience*. Ed. J. P. Telotte. Austin: U of Texas P, 1991. 5–17.

—. *Science Fiction Film*. Cambridge: Cambridge UP, 2001.

Waltonen, Karma. "To Boldly Go When No One Has Gone Before (or After): *Star Trek*'s Timelines." Star Trek *and History*. Ed. Nancy R. Reagin. Oxford: Wiley-Blackwell, 2013. 158–75.

Wolf, Mark J. P. *Building Imaginary Worlds: The Theory and History of Subcreation*. New York: Routledge, 2012.

2. The Coy Cult Text:
The Man Who Wasn't There as Noir SF

Mark Bould

They got this guy in Germany. Fritz, something-or-other. Or is it? Maybe it's Werner. Anyway, he's got this theory, you want to test something, you know, scientifically—how the planets go around the sun, what sunspots are made of, why the water comes out of the tap—well, you gotta look at it. But sometimes, you look at it, your looking changes it. You can't know the reality of what happened, or what would've happened if you hadn't've stuck in your own goddamn schnozz. So there is no "what happened." Looking at something changes it. They call it "the uncertainty principle." Sure, it sounds screwy, but even Einstein says the guy's onto something ... Sometimes, the more you look, the less you really know.

> —Freddy Riedenschneider (Tony Shalhoub),
> *The Man Who Wasn't There*

Many attempts to define cult movies and to describe their appeal are characterized by notions of doubleness, contradiction, and introjection. For example, J. P. Telotte finds in the "etymological underpinnings of 'cult'" (14) a complex of potential meanings pointing to a dialectical impulse to possess and to be possessed, to express selfhood through surrendering to an external other. Thus, he suggests, the cult movie transgresses norms, enabling the cultist "to fashion a statement of difference" (14), even as it establishes "a stable ground from which to make that assertion, a ground *within* the very boundaries" that are being transgressed (15). Sam Kitt suggests that cult audiences "need to identify with something" external to themselves that is nonetheless "emblematic of their feelings" (qtd in Telotte 15), while Timothy Corrigan depicts the movie cultist as embracing certain public images and making them part of his or her private space (26). The cultists, as he says, "wrench representations from their naturalized and centralized positions" and relocate them within a personal and "glorious[ly] incoheren[t]" cultural repertoire (28). Although Corrigan considers this effect specifically as a variety of audience activity, it resonates strongly with our post-structuralist understandings of textuality (albeit retaining a greater sense of agency than normally survives the putative death of the author). Furthermore, it suggests the extent to which an authoring agency such as the Coen brothers, the partnership responsible for a cult text like *The Man Who Wasn't There* (2001), might be understood not merely as objects of cultist fascination but as cultists themselves.

Most of the Coens' films can be characterized in the sort of doubled terms noted above, in part through Joel and Ethan's chiasmically intertwined film-maker identity. They alternate top billing on co-authored screenplays and co-edit their films under the pseudonym Roderick Jaynes. That most of their films credit Joel as sole director and Ethan as sole producer is largely a consequence of Directors Guild of America rules rather than an accurate representation of the division—or non-division— of their actual labor. They are typically described as "function[ing] interchangeably on the set and work[ing] together throughout every step of the filmmaking process," and as "finish[ing] each other's sentences, laugh[ing] soundlessly at each other's deadpan humor, and reportedly communicat[ing] regularly on a near-telepathic basis" (Russell 2). Indeed, Ronald Bergan's "bi-graphy" (2) of the brothers is so troubled by this sense of the Coens as neither a single person nor quite two people that it starts with a bizarre violent fantasy: he describes Joel shooting Ethan and then himself, leaving behind a suicide note with a quote from Edgar Allan Poe's doppelganger-murder-suicide story "William Wilson" (1839); the note turns out to have been written by (the non-existent) Roderick Jaynes (1–2). That such a hagiography should start so aggressively refracts, like its remorseless punning, what Bergan somehow neglects to describe as the "coentradictions" that distinguish his subjects, as well as their films, which have attracted such a staunch cult following.

Two of these contradictory impulses—both of which resonate with the activity of cult fans as Corrigan describes them—will be the focus here. First, I will discuss the Coens' genre proficiency and playfulness. Second, I will consider the ways in which the Coens situate specific objects in their *mise-en-scène* so as to imbue them with meaningfulness, while simultaneously rendering their meanings ambiguous. As we shall see, these objects function like metaphors (and, indeed, puns), pulling together otherwise distinct conceptual domains so as to create brief, sometimes awkward, moments of playful, energetic semiosis (see Kövecses). For example, in *The Man Who Wasn't There*, the objects to which I shall draw attention combine, in a science-fictional mode, two key cult effects: what Stephen J. Greenblatt describes as *resonance*—"the power of the object displayed to reach out beyond its formal boundaries to a larger world, to evoke … the complex dynamic cultural forces from which it has emerged and for which … it may be taken … to stand"—and *wonder*—that is, the power "to stop the viewer in his tracks, to convey an arresting sense of uniqueness, to evoke an exalted attention" (170; see also Milner 18–21).

Most of the Coens' films are more or less idiosyncratic pastiches of pulp fiction or Hollywood sources: *Blood Simple* (1984) sets a James M. Cain story in a Jim Thompson milieu; *Miller's Crossing* (1990) reworks Dashiel Hammett's *Red Harvest* (1929) as an ethnic gangster movie of the sort made in Hollywood before the Production Code was enforced; *The Hudsucker Proxy* (1994) plays like a Frank Capra movie, with a little bit of Preston Sturges in it; *O Brother, Where Art Thou?* (2000) takes its title from the unmade film-within-the-film of Sturges's *Sullivan's Travels* (1941), but it also adapts, or so it claims, Homer's *Odyssey*. *No Country for Old Men* (2007) and *True Grit* (2010) are both adapted from rather literary westerns, the former in the style of a modern-dress thriller, the latter also—like their *The Ladykillers* (2004) and their screenplay for *Gambit* (Hoffman 2012)—reworking an identically titled earlier film. In every case, the identity of the Coens' films is partially formed by the presence within it of another text, and by that other text's absence—just as, for example, in *Barton Fink* (1991), Barton (John Turturro) both is and is not playwright Clifford Odets and/or Herman Melville's Bartleby the Scrivener; Jack Lipnick (Michael Lerner) and Bill Mayhew (John Mahoney) both are and are not, respectively, studio boss Louis B. Mayer and novelist William Faulkner; and Charlie Meadows (John Goodman) is also, and not, an hallucination, the serial killer Madman Mundt, and/or an irreal manifestation of the Hotel Earle itself.

Furthermore, as *Barton Fink—Künstlerroman*, horror, noir, buddy comedy, pulp-Adorno Hollywood exposé—also demonstrates, the Coens seem drawn to what is problematically known as generic hybrids,[1] especially the crime comedy, as we see in *Raising Arizona* (1987), *Fargo* (1996), *The Ladykillers*, and the Raymond Chandler-inspired *The Big Lebowksi* (1998), a film that has been variously described as "the only psychowesternoircheechandchonginvietnambuddy genre pic in existence" (Comentale and Jaffe 3), and as a "stitching together" of "the 'bowling noir' film" with "the Busby Berkeley musical, the Vietnam movie, the pornographic movie, the screwball comedy, the buddy film, and the 1960s romantic quest à la *Easy Rider*" (Ashe 55). While *The Man Who Wasn't There* does not aspire to such a level of "genre-mulching" (Raczkowski 101), it nonetheless introduces a variety of sf elements into its insistently film noir world. Set in Santa Rosa, the California town where Alfred Hitchcock shot *Shadow of a Doubt* (1943), it plays a variation on James M. Cain's murderous love triangle narrative, borrowing heavily from his novels *The Postman Always Rings Twice* (1934), *Double Indemnity* (1936), and *Mildred Pierce* (1941), and from their mid-1940s film adaptations directed by, Tay Garnett, Billy Wilder, and Michael Curtiz, respectively, while also importing flying saucers and aliens from the space invasion films that would follow in the 1950s.

The central figure in *The Man Who Wasn't There* is Ed Crane (Billy Bob Thornton) who works the second chair in the family-owned barbershop run by his brother-in-law Frank (Michael Badalucco). Ed's wife Doris (Frances McDormand) is the bookkeeper at Nirdlinger's department store, managed by Big Dave Brewster (James Gandolfini) but owned by his wife's family. The laconic, withdrawn Ed is not particularly bothered by the affair he suspects between Doris and Dave, who has, with her assistance, been embezzling from Nirdlinger's so as to open up his own store, which she will manage. When Creighton Tolliver (Jon Polito), an entrepreneur passing through Santa Rosa in search of $10,000 with which to start up a dry-cleaning chain, tells Ed that he has been let down by a local investor (i.e., Dave) whose capital is now committed to his own business expansion plans, the affectless barber raises the funds himself by anonymously blackmailing Dave. After paying the embezzled money to, he believes, Tolliver, Dave finds out the truth and assaults Ed, but Ed kills him and seems to get away with it. The police, however, uncover evidence of the embezzlement and arrest Doris for Dave's murder. Frank mortgages the family business so that Ed can hire fast-talking lawyer Freddy Riedenschneider to defend Doris. Ed even confesses his own guilt, but Riedenschneider does not believe him. But then Riedenschneider does not remotely care about the truth, just about being able to construct a narrative that will persuade the jury of Doris's innocence—even if it means invoking a little-understood scientific concept, Heisenberg's uncertainty principle, to do so. Tolliver, the only person able to corroborate Ed's confession, cannot be found, and Doris, pregnant by Dave, commits suicide on the eve of her trial. However, these noirish narrative convolutions do not end here.

During Doris's pre-trial incarceration, Ed becomes attached to the teenaged Rachel "Birdy" Abundas (Scarlett Johansson), whose piano playing soothes him. He arranges for her to be auditioned by Jacques Carcanogue (Adam Alexi-Malle), but the maestro dismisses her as merely technically competent and refuses to take her on as a student. On the drive back to Santa Rosa, unconcerned by the blunted possibility of a musical career, Birdy attempts to fellate the unsuspecting Ed to thank him for his thoughtfulness. Horrified by this unsought attention, he crashes the car. When he regains consciousness, he is arrested for murder. It transpires that Dave had not merely beaten the truth out of Tolliver but killed him, and when Tolliver's body was discovered, so was the partnership contract Ed signed. The voice-over narrative is then revealed as Ed's account of what happened as, on death row, he writes his story for a true crime magazine. The film ends with Ed in the electric chair. The switch is thrown. Fade to white.

If this was all that happened in *The Man Who Wasn't There*, it would be nothing more than a particularly well-done Cain pastiche, its most remarkable features being its cinematography (shot in color, but digitally converted to black and white in post-production) and the effectiveness of Thornton's minimalist performance as the taciturn barber. However, two specific sequences, and a host of related moments, cast a strangely sf shadow. First, when Doris is awaiting trial, Dave's skittish widow, Ann Nirdlinger-Brewster (Katherine Borowitz), turns up late one night on Ed's doorstep, her eyes wide and unblinking, and tells him about a camping trip she and Dave took the previous summer near Eugene, Oregon. There were lights in the sky, she says, and aliens took Dave aboard their spacecraft, but he never told anyone about what happened. Ann implies that the government and other powerful institutions are involved in a cover-up and are perhaps responsible for Dave's death. Second, on the night before his execution, Ed wakes to find his cell

a. Doubled imagery in *The Man Who Wasn't There* (2001), as a low-key noir scene recalls Ann's tale about circular lights and a mysterious UFO.

b. The UFO visits Ed in the prison yard at the end of *The Man Who Wasn't There* (2001).

door open and wanders out into the prison yard, above which a flying saucer hovers. He nods at it and returns to his cell.

Anyone concerned with the rigid policing of genre boundaries could easily dismiss Ann's account of alien abduction as one character's hysterical delusion, and various commentators, including sources as "authoritative" as Wikipedia, describe Ed's UFO sighting as a dream. But what if these scenes are more than just amusing little B-movie, pulp culture riffs? What if, despite their limited duration, they constitute the film's generic dominant? What if they are to be understood as moments akin to the one in *Dark City* (Proyas 1998) when Murdoch (Rufus Sewell) and Bumstead (William Hurt) break through the wall to discover that the noir city in which they live is actually an alien construct floating in outer space? What if such moments leave you generically suspended? And what if you choose, as many cultists might, to accept a generic indeterminacy?

Carl Freedman has mapped the relationship between film noir and sf onto the "dialectical tension at the heart of Marxism, which is inflationary and deflationary at once" ("Marxism" 72). The deflationary impulse, exemplified by Marx's demystifying critique of capital and by the tradition of ideology-critique, is matched by noir's "neo-Hobbesian" universe, in which "the most widely and reliably operative human motives turn out to be the most obvious, familiar and selfish ones, mainly greed and lust" (79). Marxism's inflationary impulse—"the positive project of human liberation and self-realisation" (72) found in the post-capitalist future briefly, ambiguously, and only occasionally hinted at in Marx's "mainly deflationary scientific analysis" (74) of capitalism—resembles sf's "impulse to transcend the mundane and to imply a depth and richness of reality ... beyond any empirical norm" (70). Freedman also links sf's "inflationary bent" (69) to Ernst Bloch's discussions of the traces of utopian hope found in everyday life. Marxist reality, Bloch argues, consists of "reality plus the future within it" (162). However, one does not need to be a Marxist to develop such a complex sense of current reality. For example, Paul Ricoeur describes the threefold nature of the present moment, which is also composed of the past (memory) and the future (expectation): "not a future time, a past time, and a present time, but ... a present of future things, a present of past things, and a present of present things" (*Time* 60).

Just as the role of the Stranger (Sam Elliott) in *The Big Lebowski*, the narrator who also appears as a character, "is to underscore" that film's "combinatorial critical agenda about the shared American genome of the western and detective genres" (Commentale and Jaffe 32), so *The Man Who Wasn't There*'s flying saucers and alien abductions point to the concern film noir shares with sf about a present moment, heavy with the past yet infiltrated by, and opening out onto, potential futures and future potentials. While sf has a panoply of familiar semantic and syntactic devices—aliens, robots, future cities, time travel, other worlds—with which it articulates this concern, film noir more typically displaces it into its *mise-en-scène*. For example, *Double Indemnity*, a story told by a dying man to a dumb machine that enables his voice to survive his death, sets Los Angeles architecture and shifting social relations against a pristine, actuarial imaginary: on the one hand, Phyllis Dietrichson (Barbara Stanwyck), doubly excluded from material wealth by her gender and her working-class origins, murdering her way into a loveless marriage and a dust-filled house, its décor reeking of an already receding past; on the other, the statistical analysis of masses of people in order to determine probabilities, police human behavior, and rationally predict, in limited ways, the future. Set in 1938, at the end of the Depression, it prefigures the "postwar world in which the manipulation of FIRE (finance, insurance, and real estate) increasingly trumps the production of tangible things" (Freedman, "End" 70). *White Heat* (Curtiz 1949) commences with Cody Jarrett (James Cagney) and his gang holding up a train as if they are Wild West outlaws, but it quickly gives way to urban settings and the cutting-edge instruments of the state's panoptical apparatus. Vast bureaucracies are brought into play to place an undercover cop in Cody's gang, and he himself learns the value of simulation, feigning symptoms of the derangement from which he suffers, becoming a simulacrum of himself so as to bust out of jail. Police use maps and three radio cars to tail Cody's Ma covertly; and as the film approaches its climax a more complex technological and institutional apparatus is brought to bear on the gangster, with multiple vehicles, centrally co-ordinated, triangulating Cody's position and trajectory across the city as he heads towards a chemical plant that looks like an intrusion from some dystopian future or machinic alien world, and to his apocalyptic immolation. *Kiss Me Deadly* (Aldrich 1955), a tale of stolen nuclear materials, ends on a similarly apocalyptic note, culminating in a radioactive explosion and blaze, accompanied by what sounds suspiciously like the electronic throbbing of a flying saucer. A key intertext for such sf films as *Repo Man* (Cox 1984), which substitutes Roswell aliens for nuclear materials, and *Southland Tales* (Kelly 2006), *Kiss Me Deadly* contains further material which is particularly instructive in grasping the sf character of *The Man Who Wasn't There*.

First, we might consider the sequence in which the hospitalized Mike Hammer (Ralph Meeker) slowly regains consciousness. It begins with a black screen, accompanied by music that sounds halfway between eerie instrumentation and low-key electronica, and thus cannot help but connote science-fictional strangeness. Cut to a low-angle, medium shot, the focus swimming, of two women looking down as if seen from underwater. The woman on the right, the one who is not a nurse, repeats Mike's name, over and again, but her voice sounds far away, unfixed and drifting. Cut to a high-angle shot of Mike, slowly stirring in his hospital bed. The swirling soundtrack—not exactly music, not exactly a sound effect, suggesting a radio dial being turned, searching for but not quite finding a specific frequency—threatens to drown the woman's voice. Mike opens his eyes slightly. A reverse shot reveals a flying saucer, hovering just out of focus, and the curious noise gains a diegetic source: it is the sound of the alien craft's engines. But the camera immediately racks focus, and the flying saucer becomes just a circular light shade, and the sound extra-diegetic music, as Mike blinks and turns his head. Another reverse shot shows the two women again, in focus this time, although their presence is far from reassuring. The music rises to a crescendo as they loom over Mike, weird and threatening. Mike recognizes Velda (Maxine Cooper), his secretary and lover, and smiles as he says her name. But again the uncanniness persists. As Velda leans down to kiss Mike, the film cuts to a long shot, sideways on to the full length of the bed, at a Dutch angle, disturbing what should, now that Mike is conscious, be a stable space.

This scene provides a key for unlocking the film's mapping out of the complex temporality of the present moment through architecture and interior design. Mike's swish Wilshire Boulevard apartment—the epitome of the 1950s *Playboy* bachelor pad (see Cohan 267–75)— contains a reel-to-reel telephone answering machine, a television that looks like a cross between a jukebox and Robbie the Robot, and light fittings that resemble UFOs. Its airiness, clean edges, and moderne furnishings contrast sharply with the battered tables and chairs seen elsewhere, as in Harvey Wallace's (Strother Martin) crowded kitchen and Carmen Trivago's (Fortunio Bonanova) cluttered, laundry-strewn room in a Bunker Hill residential hotel—and especially with their dusty, old-fashioned lampshades that look not at all like flying saucers.

The Coens' *mise-en-scène* similarly pays particular attention to the specificity of objects—objects that either belong precisely where they are but which are never otherwise attended to, or—resonating with Corrigan's account of cult fan activity—objects torn from their familiar contexts and inserted into new ones. Edward P. Comentale and Aaron Jaffe argue that, when presented in such a way, such objects heighten "the tension between everyday life and its irrational subtexts" (9). They note, for example, how *The Big Lebowski* took shape around "a set of unrelated objects ... and the fraternal challenge of putting them all in the same film" (11), resulting in "a dream of objects, not just a dream that contains objects, but a dream that objects may have, once freed from their practical, everyday use" (12), a "new poetry of common objects" which opens our eyes to "a world in which each mundane thing is both drained [of] and saturated with meaning—a world stupid, stubborn, mute, and a world vibrant, charged, and ecstatic" (13). Christopher Raczkowski explains such objects in terms of metaphor and metonymy. The hat blown through the woods in *Miller's Crossing*'s title sequence is "an oddly extrinsic figure" (100), mutely metonymic. Like protagonist Tom Regan (Gabriel Byrne), to whom it is connected and whose loquacity is somehow taciturn, it gives nothing away. In contrast, the tumbleweed that blows in from the desert to Santa Monica Boulevard at the start of *The Big Lebowski* is (excessively) metaphoric, taking on more and more potential meanings as it moves through shifting contexts. In both instances, the object signals its significance but not its meaning, deflecting or endlessly deferring interpretation, suggesting a fantastic surplus of significance. In contrast, Dennis and Susan Grove Hall associate *The Big Lebowski*— and indeed "all cult films"—with metonymy because, they contend, "metaphor [and its] extensions into symbol and allegory ... tend to fix meaning" (323). Regardless of this diametrically opposed reading, what remains at stake is a tension between meaningfulness and meaning, between materiality and semiosis—between all that the world could be and what little it presently seems to be. In the Coens' attention to the specificity of objects, Allan Smithee finds an "underlying nostalgia for wholeness and lost origins, a nostalgia for a past that is not so much accessed through memory as mediated through objects of the material world" and which expresses "desire for that elusive object that might precede the precession of simulacra and subtend the surface level of the mere play of differences" (257–58).

The Man Who Wasn't There, however, is not concerned with the recuperation of the past but with the utopian futurity implied by the commodity form, and with the barrenness of this promise. The flying saucer that Ed sees at the end of the film is merely the culmination of a series of images of moderne commodities. In Ed's copy of *Life*, an article called "Dry Cleaning: The Wave of the Future" is followed by one about the Roswell flying saucer incident. As with *Kiss Me Deadly*, certain light fittings insistently recall UFOs: in Nirdlinger's department store, a fleet of flying saucers hovers behind Ed when Dave confesses his affair, and one of them apparently follows Ed to observe his first meeting with Birdy; others hover above the route from his cell to the prison yard and to the death chamber. Echoing the scene in which Mike regains consciousness, when Ed crashes, a mundane circular object transforms into the potential futurity contained within its metallic sheen. The image spins wildly, creating a circular blur; when it comes to a stop, the car sails gracefully through the air, from left to right, past tall trees. A hubcap bounces through the air and rolls through the grass and trees, recalling the escaped hula hoop in *The Hudsucker Proxy*, the Coens' comedy about the difference between use-value and exchange-value. The hubcap is superimposed over a slowly rotating aerial shot of the unconscious Ed, which then fades out, replaced by blackness, into which the still-spinning hubcap retreats, suggesting to all intents and purposes a flying saucer climbing into the night sky. Cut to a scene—a memory, perhaps—in which Doris returns home, sees off the salesman trying to persuade Ed to upgrade their driveway by resurfacing it with tarmac, pours herself a drink, and settles onto the sofa. Ed joins her, but she cuts off his attempt at conversation. The screen again turns to black, and the flying saucer descends. However, when it comes into focus, the image is no longer a hubcap but the dazzlingly lit mirror on a doctor's headband, as his distorted voice, like Velda's, calls the patient back to consciousness.

Consequently, Ed's ambivalent response to the flying saucer that visits his prison (and the placidity with which he approaches and sits in the electric chair, his final gaze taking in not the faces of those who have come to witness his execution but their haircuts) constitutes a rejection of certain varieties of futurity: of those corporate dreams of thoroughly commodified futures familiar from the 1939 New York World's Fair, of Frank R. Paul's *Amazing Stories* cityscape covers, of advertising copy of the period, and of the alien salvation that *The Day the Earth Stood Still* (Wise 1951) and such early accounts of extraterrestrial visitations as George Adamski and Desmond Leslie's *Flying Saucers Have Landed* (1953) promised.[2] In their place, Ed chooses noir: death and the quasi-religious transcendence—along with a posthumous reunion with Doris—of the sort signaled at the conclusion of such films noir as *You Only Live Once* (Lang US 1937) and *The Postman Always Rings Twice*.

While flying saucers and their avatars offer one route into comprehending *The Man Who Wasn't There*'s and *Kiss Me Deadly*'s cultic ambivalence about a commodity culture which seems simultaneously to be introjected from and to unfurl into all possible futures, both films also draw upon the sf tradition of depicting aliens passing for humans. In *Kiss Me Deadly*, this effect derives from casting decisions. We might consider the awkward acting of Gaby Rodgers, who plays Gabrielle, who pretends to be Lily Carver; of Albert Dekker, whose portentous dialogue as Dr. Soberin, international atomic spy, sounds like it has been looped, badly, in post-production, even when it has not; and of Wesley Addy, whose Lt. Pat Murphy somehow manages a stilted drawl and can barely conceal his queer attraction to Meeker's hard-boiled dick. Each of these performances suggests a subject who is so alienated by his or her passage through the world—and by having to pass as someone he or she is not—that they have no real sense of how to be in the world. They come across like alien facsimiles of human beings, as if they really belong not in a Mickey Spillane adaptation but in *Invaders from Mars* (Menzies 1953), *It Came from Outer Space* (Arnold 1953), or *Invasion of the Body Snatchers* (Siegel 1956).[3] Each of these films uses the alien facsimile as a metaphor to express the stultifying conformity of Eisenhower's placid and alienating decade of corporate culture, consumerism, and suburbia.

Two sequences in *The Man Who Wasn't There* frame Ed's viewpoint in this same context, as if he were just such an alien. In the first, shot in slow motion, Ed drives down Main Street, observing the decelerated bustle of the affluent townsfolk. It is as if he occupies some other temporal plane, or can alter the speed of his sensory inputs so as to observe humans more clearly. While the distended duration of their passage lends them the appearance of the dehumanized modern subject that the 1950s aliens-passing-as-humans cycle so dreaded, Ed's voice-over simultaneously implies that he has achieved transcendence *through* his alienation:

There they were, all going about their business. It seemed like I knew a secret, a bigger one even than what had really happened to Big Dave. Something none of them knew. Like I had made it to the outside somehow and they were all still struggling way down below.

This sequence is immediately followed by Ann's nocturnal revelation about Dave's alien abduction, which *could* be seen as hinting at something of Ed's own true nature.

In the second sequence, also done in slow motion, Ed walks down Main Street, moving from left to right, with the camera tracking in the same direction, while the vast majority of other pedestrians move from right to left. This disharmony creates the illusion that he moves through the world differently and at a different pace to other humans. His voice-over emphasizes his spectrality, his increasingly tenuous connection to the community in which he lives:

When I walked home it seemed like everyone avoided looking at me. As if I'd caught some disease. This thing with Doris, nobody wanted to talk about it. It was like I was a ghost walking down the street. And when I got home now, the place felt empty. I sat in the house, but there was nobody there. I was a ghost. I didn't see anyone, no-one saw me. I was the barber.

As he enters his house, the film returns to normal speed, but Ed's pace remains glacial. He makes his way to the sofa and sits down, leaving us with the sense that he may well stay perched there all night until it is time to return to work next morning, that the house is just a prop, a cover, for someone who lives among humans but does not comprehend the purpose of a home. In his awkward occupation of this space, Ed resembles the alien who passes as the newlywed Bill Farrell (Tom Tryon) in *I Married a Monster from Outer Space* (Fowler, Jr. 1958), a film that plays like the creature-feature version of a melodrama about repressed homosexuality by Douglas Sirk, Vincente Minnelli, or Nicholas Ray.[4] Indeed, Ed himself—sexually indifferent to women, his life devoted to male grooming—could be read as queer. Tolliver certainly thinks so, making an awkward pass at him. The film's reconstruction of a past that was more overtly repressive of queer sexualities and its display of material that could not have been shown on US screens in the year in which the film is set—the contrast between Tolliver's clumsy hesitancy and the clarity with which it is represented—opens onto a moment of queer futurity, onto the possibility that things might be different. Ed, however, is uninterested in the polymorphous plenitude, the increase in "intensive and extensive pleasure," and "the production of a libidinous, that is, happy environment" that Herbert Marcuse (19) associates with the utopian drive. Indeed, if Tolliver holds any kind of appeal for Ed, it would be associated not with the man himself, but with his toupee.

Ed is, after all, a half-hearted barber. The haircuts he performs—the Butch, the Heinie, the Flat-Top, the Ivy, the Crew, the Vanguard, the Junior Contour, even the Executive Contour—are, for him, not so much distinct styles as a repertoire of moves to keep the uncanny materiality of the world at bay. Hair very simply disturbs him:

> Do you ever wonder about it? ... how it keeps on coming? It just keeps growing ... it keeps growing. It's part of us, and we cut it off and throw it away ... I'm going to take this hair and throw it out in the dirt ... I'm going to mingle it with common house-dirt.

Beyond its distressingly ambiguous nature (Is it part of us or not? When does it cease to be human and start to be dirt?), hair also brings Ed into troubling proximity to others. Anyone can come in off the street and require his presence, his touch, his attention. So it is little wonder that Ed is drawn to the aseptic chemical business of—and futurity suggested by—a dry-cleaning enterprise; as Tolliver explains, "*Dry* cleaning. Wash, without water. No suds, no tumble, no stress on the clothes. It's all done with chemicals." Such a process dangles before the reluctant barber the prospect of a scientific future—inorganic, pristine—in which commodities persist but human contact is minimized, and in which such utter alienation seems like a promise of transcendence.

In the barbershop, when Ed starts to comb Tolliver's hair, the florid entrepreneur interrupts him, peeling off his improbable coiffure, revealing it as a hairpiece that "fools even the experts—one hundred percent human hair, handcrafted by Jacques of San Francisco." Later, when hitting on Ed, Tolliver begins by straightening his toupee, drawing attention to its artifice, its detachability: it is human hair that has finally ceased to grow, and it is not (yet) common house-dirt. It is as close to the future promised by the commodity form that something so human, so organic, so material can get. But it is still not enough. Its sterility—the utopian separation and perfection it promises—is too burdened by its history and by the inevitability of its decay. It remains liminal. Like so many of the Coens' particular objects, wherever they fall on the metaphoric/metonymic axis, it is a marker of irresolvable in-between-ness, of uncertainty. Hair or hairpiece? Hubcap or UFO? Flying saucer or light fitting? Film noir or science fiction? The presence or the absence of the man who wasn't there?

Freddy Riedenschneider says, "sometimes, you look at it, your looking changes it," but the Coens' adventures in ambiguous, proliferating semiosis go even further than this explanation allows. Meaning is made, they instruct us, not fixed; meaning is overdetermined, immanent, evanescent; meaning is, indeed, coentradictory. And it is the ludic practice and privilege of the cultist—whether film-maker, fan, or both—not merely to have it both ways, but to have it all ways and every which way.

Notes

1   On the problems with "genre hybridity," see Staiger and Bould.
2   Although the imagery on the cover of the issue of the (fake) magazine *The Unheard-Of* seen in Ed's cell seems more or less authentic to the period— it might not look out of place on the cover of Raymond Palmer's *Other Worlds/Flying Saucers, the Magazine of Space Conquest* or EC Comics' *Weird Science*—its cover story, entitled "I was abducted by aliens!" is anachronistic. Alien abduction narratives did not really become widely reported or part of ufological lore until after the October 20, 1975 broadcast of the television movie *The UFO Incident*, adapted from Betty and Barney Hill's account of their September 1961 encounter with a UFO.
3   This is not, of course, to suggest that Spillane's characters in any way resemble human beings. Of these films, *Invasion of the Body Snatchers*—with its paranoid entrapment narrative, expressionist lighting and camerawork, and its anxieties about consumer culture, suburban/corporate emasculation, and female sexuality—is especially open to recuperation as a film noir. Like *The Man Who Wasn't There*, it opposes (nostalgia for some sense of) authenticity with the alienation of (debased) commodity forms. Compare, for example, the scene in which Miles (Kevin MacCarthy) and Becky (Dana Wynter) discover that a jukebox has replaced the nightclub band with the scene in which Ed first finds Birdy, playing a Beethoven sonata on a baby grand piano—music they both prefer to the swing band at the raucous department store party below.
4   For a queer reading of *I Married a Monster*, see Ostherr 111–18.

Works cited

Ashe, Fred. "The Really Big Sleep: Jeffrey Lebowski as the Second Coming of Rip Van Winkle." *The Year's Work in Lebowski Studies.* Ed. Edward P. Comentale and Aaron Jaffe. Bloomington: Indiana UP, 2009. 41–57.
Bergan, Ronald. *The Coen Brothers.* London: Orion, 2000.
Bloch, Ernst. "Marxism and Poetry." *The Utopian Function of Art and Literature: Selected Essays.* Ed. and trans. Jack Zipes and Frank Mecklenburg. Cambridge: MIT Press, 1988. 156–62.
Bould, Mark. "Genre, Hybridity, Heterogeneity; or, the Noir-sf-vampire-zombie-splatter-romance-comedy-action-thriller Problem." *A Companion*

to Film Noir. Ed. Andrew Spicer and Helen Hanson. Oxford: Blackwell, 2013. 33–49.

Cohan, Steven. *Masked Men: Masculinity and the Movies in the Fifties*. Bloomington: Indiana UP, 1997.

Comentale, Edward P., and Aaron Jaffe. "Introduction." *The Year's Work in Lebowski Studies*. Ed. Edward P. Comentale and Aaron Jaffe. Bloomington: Indiana UP, 2009. 1–37.

Corrigan, Timothy. "Film and the Culture of Cult." *The Cult Film Experience: Beyond All Reason*. Ed. J. P. Telotte. Austin: U of Texas P, 1991. 26–37.

Freedman, Carl. "The End of Work: From *Double Indemnity* to *Body Heat*." *Neo-noir*. Ed. Mark Bould, Kathrina Glitre, and Greg Tuck. London: Wallflower, 2009. 61–74.

—. "Marxism, Cinema and Some Dialectics of Science Fiction and Film Noir." *Red Planet: Marxism and Science Fiction*. Ed. Mark Bould and China Miéville. London: Pluto, 2009. 66–82.

Greenblatt, Stephen J. "Resonance and Wonder." *Learning to Curse: Essays in Early Modern Culture*. London: Routledge, 1990. 161–83.

Kövecses, Zoltan. *Metaphor: A Practical Introduction*. Oxford: Oxford UP, 2002.

The Man Who Wasn't There. Wikipedia. Web. Accessed 4 March 2013.

Marcuse, Herbert. *Five Lectures: Psychoanalysis, Politics, and Utopia*. Trans. Jeremy J. Shapiro and Shierry M. Weber. Boston: Beacon, 1970.

Milner, Andrew. *Locating Science Fiction*. Liverpool: Liverpool UP, 2012.

Ostherr, Kirsten. *Cinematic Prophylaxis: Globalization and Contagion in the Discourse of World Health*. Durham: Duke UP, 2005.

Raczkowski, Christopher. "Metonymic Hats and Metaphoric Tumbleweeds: Noir Literary Aesthetics in *Miller's Crossing* and *The Big Lebowski*." *The Year's Work in Lebowski Studies*. Ed. Edward P. Comentale and Aaron Jaffe. Bloomington: Indiana UP, 2009. 98–123.

Ricoeur, Paul. *Time and Narrative*. Vol. 1. Trans. Kathleen McLaughlin and David Pellauer. Chicago: U of Chicago P, 1984.

Russell, Carolyn. *The Films of Joel and Ethan Coen*. Jefferson: McFarland, 2001.

Smithee, Allan. "What Condition the Postmodern Condition Is In: Collecting Culture in *The Big Lebowski*." *The Year's Work in Lebowski Studies*. Ed. Edward P. Comentale and Aaron Jaffe. Bloomington: Indiana UP, 2009. 255–75.

Staiger, Janet. "Hybrid or Inbred: The Purity Hypothesis and Hollywood Genre History." *Perverse Spectators: The Practices of Film Reception*. New York: New York UP, 2003. 61–76.

Telotte, J. P. "Beyond All Reason: The Nature of Cult." *The Cult Film Experience: Beyond All Reason*. Ed. J. P. Telotte. Austin: U of Texas P, 1991. 5–17.

3. "It's Alive!":
The Splattering of SF Films

Stacey Abbott

You wanted to blow other people's minds and you wanted to blow your own.

—David Cronenberg (*The American Nightmare*)

The 1970s represent one of the great transitional periods for Hollywood, producing an increasingly independent and confrontational approach to cinema in terms of both narrative content and aesthetic display. Film-makers sought to break violently with film-making conventions by reimaging genre tropes through a more visceral and realistic style, challenging audiences with graphic, nihilistic, and often brutal imagery. Thus, John Carpenter, director of *The Thing* (1982), confesses that he "wanted something savage to happen. I don't believe I could do that now. I don't believe they'd let me do that," while David Cronenberg explains that he "wanted to blow other people's minds" (both qtd in *The American Nightmare*). This attitude was particularly apparent within film genres as they were being reimagined in this period. For instance, the western *The Wild Bunch* (1969), the outlaw film *Bonnie and Clyde* (1967), and the gangster film *The Godfather* (1972) all featured dramatic shootouts in which the bodies of protagonists were riddled with bullets in an orgy of bloodletting and violence. Similarly, big budget Hollywood horror films were reworking their scare tactics through visual display and special effects, both *The Exorcist* (1973) and *The Omen* (1976) featuring regular and escalating set pieces in which the body comes under brutal attack by the devil and his minions. Nowhere was this emphasis on graphic imagery—defined by John McCarty as "splatter"—felt more keenly than in the arena of independent exploitation or underground cinema. McCarty argues that splatter cinema is a type of film whose aim was "not to scare their audiences, necessarily, nor to drive them to the edges of their seats in suspense, but to mortify them with scenes of explicit gore. In splatter movies, mutilation is indeed the message" (1).

While we most commonly associate splatter with horror, many of the era's exploitation film-makers were increasingly rethinking the nature of genre, blurring the lines not only between art and exploitation, but between sf and horror. Splatter especially served to reimagine sf within the context of increasingly independent modes of film production and a growing cult audience.

This commentary will look precisely at the manner in which the sf genre was cultified not just through a "splatter" imagery, but through the "splattering" of sf tropes themselves, particularly those surrounding the science/military machine and the creation of monsters, within the changing production context of the 1960s/1970s that privileged independent film production typified by cult auteurs George Romero, Larry Cohen, and David Cronenberg. It will consider how the conventions of exploitation merged with sf to create a series of subversive texts, targeted at the growing cult cinema audience of the 1970s, whose "interests and concerns—drugs, rock music, sexual experience, alienation from their parents and established society—clearly surfaced in such films" (Telotte 10). This new confrontational aesthetic made sf an ideal genre with which to express the cultural rupture at the heart of the decade.

Independent Cinema and the Case of *Night of the Living Dead*

The 1970s is a period often heralded as a golden age of Hollywood independent cinema, although the transition to increasingly independent modes of film production began much earlier. Janet Staiger explains that

> *economic* incentives enhanced the changeover to independent production. These incentives included the elimination by a 1940 consent decree of blind selling and block booking, certain effects of World War II, and an apparent tax advantage. After the war, the movement intensified because of income losses, the divorcement decree, and new distribution strategies. (331)

Furthermore, by the 1950s, declining audiences—a natural result of the gradual population migration away from city centers (where cinemas were largely located) to the suburbs and the expansion of domestic recreation—meant that the film industry came to "recognise its audience as increasingly segmented" and its methods of distribution and exhibition changed accordingly (Maltby 168).

Production companies and distributors increasingly sought to target niche urban audiences, leading to the growing importation of European art house and exploitation cinema in the 1950s and 1960s to cater to reinvented urban, art house cinemas (Neale 406). Similarly, American exploitation cinema, produced by independent companies like American International Pictures (AIP) and Allied Artists, served the 8,000 cinemas in the US still screening double bills following the decline in the production of B-movies by the studios (Maltby 169). As a result of these varied developments, there were increasing opportunities for small production companies to produce independent films on micro-budgets, often privately funded (or, in the case of David Cronenberg, through tax incentives and Canadian federal funding), and aimed at niche audiences. Additionally, this diversification of film production, with increasing emphasis upon exploitation and art house products, led to a relaxation of censorship and film exhibition regulations (Neale 406–07). In 1968, the Motion Picture Association of American launched its modern rating system to replace the Production Code, which had been in effect since the 1930s. This transition aimed to remove limitations upon artistic expression within cinema and to acknowledge the growing liberalization of American culture.

A film that stands as evidence of these various industrial changes is George Romero's independently produced *Night of the Living Dead* (1968), shot in Pittsburgh for a budget of $114,000 (Hervey 13). Romero signed a distribution deal with Continental Film Distributors, a company specializing in distributing a combination of European art films, horror/exploitation cinema, and commercial releases to niche markets in urban cinemas via their Walter Reade cinema chain (Heffernan 203–08).[1] The film received scathing reviews for both its embrace of splatter techniques that emphasized graphic depictions of violence and gore, and its low-budget, independent aesthetic. For instance, Lee Beaupre of *Daily Variety* described it as "repellent," "distasteful," "amateurish," and an attack "on the integrity and social responsibility of its Pittsburgh-based makers." As a result, Continental opted to treat the film as a "programmer," promoting it on its extreme terror factor, even advertising a $50,000 insurance payout for anyone scared to death by the film (Rubine qtd in Lebowitz, Hackett, and Cutrone 39). Negative reviews, along with a splashy marketing campaign promising something schlocky, terrifying, and transgressive, gradually built the film's cult reputation, while rave reviews in Andy Warhol's *INTERVIEW Magazine*, *The Village Voice*, *Sight and Sound*, and *Positif* provided the film crossover art house appeal. This reception culminated in a 1970 screening of the film at the Museum of Modern Art in New York as part of a program on new auteurs (Hervey 17). In 1971, it received its first midnight showing in Washington, before finding a home at the Waverley Cinema in New York where, according to Ben Hervey, the cult of *Night of the Living Dead* took root (7). Weekend midnight screenings of the film spread across the country, and the film "ran continuously at midnight in New York for over two years, from May 1971 through mid-July 1973" (Hoberman and Rosenbaum 126). While Romero's film did not start the practice of midnight screenings, it helped popularize them, becoming a landmark cult movie that demonstrated the cult/art house crossover potential for splatter sf.

These diverse industrial factors, along with *Night of the Living Dead*'s success, meant that by the 1970s a space had opened up on the periphery of the film industry where independent film-makers such as Cronenberg and Cohen, among others, were able to produce unusual and transgressive film material, attracting a new cult audience. These fans were drawn to films that seemingly challenged the status quo not only in terms of their content, but also in terms of form and genre. As *The Village Voice* reviewer pointed out about *Night of the Living Dead*, the film undermines the campy expectations of "most horror movies" by providing the audience undiluted terror through "a combination of incredibly graphic grisliness, the grim realism of the locale, and the ultimate plausibility of the characters." This reviewer's experience of watching the film at a midnight screening at the Waverley, in which "obligatory guffaws and verbal macho-tactics" gave way to "uneasy silence" and eventually "shrieking and groaning" with "people hiding their heads in their hands," reinforces Telotte's argument that this new experience created a type of cinemagoing as a "rite of passage," while embracing "a form that, in its very difference, transgresses, violates our sense of the reasonable" (6). The merging of splatter techniques with the conventions of sf in the films of Romero, Cronenberg, and Cohen, among others, offered this rite of passage experience where, as McCarty claims, mutilation did indeed become the message, displacing the conventional preoccupations of sf cinema—associated with a sense of wonder at the world, technology, and the cosmos—with a brutal and transgressive reimagining of the genre.

Science/Military Machine

A common motif within many sf films, particularly in the 1950s and 1960s, is the often fractious relationship between science and the military, particularly following the use of the atom bomb to end the Second World War, as well as the subsequent Hydrogen bomb experiments. As Christopher Frayling explains, many sf films in the 1950s "include a sequence where in effect the politician or soldier turns to the scientist and says 'It's all your fault—you built the bomb', and the scientist turns to the soldier and says, 'Yeah, but you dropped it'" (204). However, Peter Biskind notes that the participant held responsible for the misuse of power can vary from film to film. In *Them!* (1954), science is given moral authority, resisting the military option of dropping the bomb on the giant ants and choosing to gas them instead, while in *The Thing from Another World* (1951), it is the pragmatic military men who ignore the lead scientist's pleas to "reason" with the alien, choosing instead to destroy it and save the whole of humanity (319–20). But despite their differences, science and the military are repeatedly presented as having to work together, albeit with one party in charge.

The splatter sf films of the late 1960s and early 1970s—particularly films such as *Night of the Living Dead, The Crazies* (1973), and *Rabid* (1977)—often revisit this relationship between science and the military. In fact, these films have much in common with 1950s sf. Both periods are marked by a blurring of sf and horror tropes, and these later indie films seem deliberately to hark back to the earlier alien invasion films. While not necessarily about an alien invasion, they chronicle an outbreak—virus, zombies—that must somehow be contained and that often requires the collaboration of the military and science. However, in contrast to the earlier works, these films do not privilege one group over the other, but instead present the science/military machine as dysfunctional and broken. Unable to contain the outbreak, both groups are presented as ineffectual and, often, equally culpable.

For instance, in Romero's *Night of the Living Dead*, America is again under attack, not by giant ants or alien invaders, but rather the dead, returned to a form of zombie life in which they hunt down and feed on the living. The focus of the story is on an isolated group of survivors— Ben, Barbara, Tom, Judy, Mr. and Mrs. Cooper, and their daughter Karen—hiding in an abandoned farmhouse. There are no represent- atives from the military or the scientific community to explain the situation or to provide a coherent plan to defeat the zombies. The only glimpses of these authority figures come in the form of news bulletins, featuring interviews with experts attempting to provide guidance and explanations. Yet these figures clearly do not understand what they are facing any more than our lone survivors. The attempt by the press to link the rise of the dead to radiation emanating from a satellite sent to Venus but destroyed before it re-entered earth's atmosphere seems to be an allusion to 1950s sf, associating the zombies with the threat of radiation, but unlike these earlier films, this suggestion is never confirmed. Journalists report that the FBI, CIA, Joint Chiefs of Staff, and "space experts" have been meeting to determine the cause of this unusual outbreak, but their conclusions are not made public. When questioned by a journalist (played by Romero), the scientists and military representative openly disagree about the connection between the radiation and the zombie outbreak. The scientists claim that there is in all likelihood a connection, while the military representative equivocates. He cautions his scientific colleagues to be more circumspect in their assertions and refuses to speak on behalf of the military. This sequence presents the military and science as at odds with one another, while the military's response suggests a cover-up.[2]

Furthermore, the comparatively measured, if somewhat stressed, tones of the journalists, scientists, and military figures presented in these news reports stand in contrast to the trauma experienced by the first-hand survivors, like Barbara, who oscillates from silent shock to near hysterics. The journalists, delivering reports based upon second-hand accounts, struggle to find the right words to describe what is happening, using phrases such as "epidemic of mass murder," "a virtual army of unidentified assassins," and "wholesale murder ... engulfing the

a. One of the slug-like parasites emerges from a drain in Cronenberg's *Shivers* (1975).

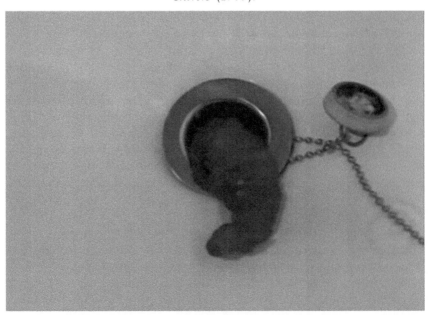

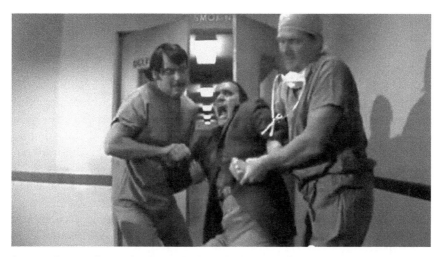

b. Frank recoils at the horrific hospital birth, the centerpiece of Larry
Cohen's *It's Alive* (1974).

nation." As the facts become more fantastic, with stories of "killers ...
eating the flesh" of their victims, and the recently deceased "returning
to life," the journalists express their own doubts, stating, "it is difficult
to imagine such a thing actually happening but these are the reports
we have been receiving," and "it is hard for us here to believe what
we are reporting to you but it does seem to be a fact." The disjunction
between the media's skeptical reporting of second-hand accounts and
our characters' first-hand experience of the zombie outbreak is enhanced
by the adoption of splatter techniques. The journalists may struggle to
believe the substance of their reports, but the audience is confronted
by visceral and all-too believable images of the zombies eating the
flesh, bones, and intestines of the young couple Tom and Judy, shot in
close-up and in graphic detail, or the Coopers' daughter Karen eating
her father's flesh and then stabbing her mother with a trowel as blood
splatters on the wall. The use of graphic effects drives home the reality
of these events, and the ever-expanding gulf between the survivors and
the authorities ostensibly responsible for their protection.

This gulf seems even wider when we consider the fact that in *Night
of the Living Dead* and Romero's 1973 film *The Crazies*, these figures of
military and scientific authority do not offer any useful solutions for
those who are directly affected. In *Night of the Living Dead*, the association
between radiation and the zombie outbreak fundamentally serves no
narrative purpose. It does mark the key transition of the zombie from

the realm of horror to sf—or in Tzvetan Todorov's terms, from the marvelous to the fantastic—since the cause of the outbreak is not linked to the overt supernatural realm of curses and voodoo (marvelous) as in *White Zombie* (1932), *Revolt of the Zombies* (1936), and *I Walked with a Zombie* (1943) (25, 42). Instead, the film attempts to provide a rational scientific explanation, suggesting the possibility of a solution, but with an emphasis upon the uncertainty of these explanations and the lack of practical guidance on how to stay alive and destroy the zombies (fantastic)—something the survivors have by this point figured out through trial and error.[3] These news reports and interviews with scientists purport to offer assistance but end up undermining the value of information by offering no practical solution.

In *The Crazies*—a film about the spread of a bio-weapon accidentally released in the water supply—the only apparent solution available to the military and science is to round up and contain all of those who are infected until they die. In the similarly themed David Cronenberg film *Rabid*, about the spread of a rabies-like virus through Montreal, the Director of the World Health Organization explains that "shooting down the victims is as good a way of handling them as we've got"—the same tactic employed in *The Crazies*. As a result, the military and scientists are not absent but all too present within these films. *The Crazies* begins after the military have already descended upon the town, setting up a perimeter and rounding up its inhabitants in an attempt to contain the spread of the bacteriological contaminant. In the case of *Rabid*, the military arrive about halfway through the film to impose martial law in a similar attempt to contain the spread of an infection, this time caused by one woman who is a virus carrier. Soldiers and military vehicles are displayed throughout both films, while scientists are presented as struggling to understand the nature of the outbreak. The emphasis on the visibility of these institutions highlights their inability to solve or even contain the outbreak.

Like *Night of the Living Dead*, *The Crazies* again alludes to the alien invasion films of the 1950s, but this time the military is itself presented as the invading force: setting up patrols on Main Street, bursting into private homes, rounding up civilians, and quelling any resistance with force. Their own *alien* presence is made all the more frightening by the fact that all members of the military and scientific communities are outfitted in identical white hazmat suits and black gasmasks, visualizing them as an alien presence divorced from the civilian forces they are supposedly protecting but actually treating like an enemy. Rather than allude to the films of the 1950s, Cronenberg's *Rabid* seems to evoke Romero's film by presenting the soldiers in the same protective clothing to create a similar effect. The masks cause everyone to speak with the same muffled voices, while the suits remove any markers of individual identity, including signifiers of field (science or military) or rank. This loss of identity recalls the aliens in *Invasion of the Body Snatchers* (1956), but while the aliens in that film are a highly organized and efficient communal body, in *The Crazies* these military/scientific invaders are presented as struggling against the tide, incapable of finding a solution or stemming the infection, except by killing everyone in the town. The film's climax reinforces this attitude, as the general who oversaw the quarantine of Evans City is sent to another town showing signs of infection. In *Rabid*, the military and science are not merely presented as out of their depth, but as completely incapable of stemming the outbreak. Instead, they serve as a clean-up crew, driving through the city in big garbage trucks, collecting and disposing of bodies like common household waste.

Splatter in both films is used to emphasize the violent repercussions of the military and scientific communities losing control. The brutal confrontations between the military, the police, the infected, and the uninfected are presented through bloody detail as bodies are torn apart, riddled with bullets, or set on fire. In his first color film, Romero playfully highlights this violence by repeatedly featuring the bright red blood splatter on the white hazmat suits. In *Rabid*, a pre-Christmas mall location, featuring casual shoppers and children visiting Santa, is disrupted when an infected man attacks another, biting into his throat and leaving blood dripping down his victim's neck. A security guard armed with a machine gun pursues the infected man and, in a panicked desire to stop him, opens fire, killing both the man and Santa. As the shoppers run from the mall, the guard looks on in horror at Santa's bloodstained body.

This visible emphasis on the violence of the military presence speaks openly to contemporary anxieties about the military. *The Crazies* alludes to Vietnam in its depiction of violent skirmishes between the soldiers and the local residents of Evans City, both those who are infected and those defending themselves against this unexplained incursion. This link is perhaps best exemplified by the priest who protests the arrival of the soldiers by dousing himself in gasoline and setting himself on fire, calling to mind Buddhist monks who performed similar acts of self-immolation in Vietnam. The emphasis upon the violence committed by soldiers against other Americans is also alluded to when the Vietnam veteran David claims that the military presence in the town will inevitably lead to violence, pointing out how "they can turn a campus protest into a war," thereby recalling the Kent State Massacre in May 1970. Similarly, the images of soldiers and military vehicles on the streets of Montreal, checking IDs, segregating suspect individuals from the crowds, directly recalls the imposition of the War Measures Act and the deployment of Canadian Forces in Montreal as a result of a local terrorist crisis in October 1970.[4] The splattering of the alien invasion narrative in these films, therefore, serves to reposition sf as a genre that speaks to contemporary anxieties about authority, in the form of both the military and science, as these institutions push forward developments in science and technology.

Splattering *Frankenstein*

These cult films not only echo the sf films of the 1950s as part of their reimagining of the genre through the language of splatter, but they also hark back to a much earlier ancestor—one that has had a pervasive influence on the genre—namely Mary Shelley's *Frankenstein*. They do this by revisiting and reimagining Shelley's man-made monster. While *Frankenstein* is now regarded as an originary classic of sf and the gothic, its relationship with splatter movies is not a distant one. In fact, its preoccupation with the macabre, finding root in Victor Frankenstein's construction of a man from the body parts of the dead, makes the novel, according to John McCarty, "the *Hamlet* of splatter"(84). The novel wallows in the morbid and macabre, as Frankenstein prepares to bring life from death, collecting his "materials" from graveyards, charnel houses, dissecting tables, and slaughterhouses.[5] The films of David Cronenberg and Larry Cohen—works like *Shivers* (1975), *Rabid*, *The Brood* (1979), *It's Alive* (1974), and *It Lives Again* (1979) — return to that creation myth and explore the conditions and repercussions of scientific interventions in this process, expressed through the language of splatter. As Cronenberg explains, "A lot of my films—all of them, in fact, up to and including *Videodrome*—have to do with creators, people who create monster children in some sense and who have to deal with their own creation once it comes back to them" (qtd in McCarty 84).

Each of these films is about the scientific creation of monsters, but no longer a monster stitched together from body parts scrounged from the grave—signaling anxieties about life, death, and decay—but rather an abject, organic creation that emerges from the living body itself. Each monster, be it slug-like parasite, vampiric virus carrier, monster feral children, or monster babies, is a mixture of the natural and the scientifically enhanced, gestating in the human body—both male and female—and then bursting forth to wreak havoc. While Shelley's monster was an erudite and articulate creation, raising existential questions about the nature of existence, Cronenberg and Cohen's creations are driven by primal instincts of self-preservation and reproduction. They equally raise questions about the nature of being, but in these films it is a form of being defined by our relationship to the body and not the mind. Here splatter is crucial to the reworking of the Frankenstein story, for the monsters are defined by their abject physicality, confronting the audience with their monstrous appearances: the feces-like parasite in *Shivers*, the phallic appendage that emerges from Rose's armpit when she feeds in *Rabid*, the gender-less children in *The Brood*, and the fanged and clawed monster babies in Cohen's *It's Alive* films.

The creation or birthing scenes in particular feature the eruption of splatter, replacing James Whale's natural thunder claps and lightning strikes with screams and a monstrous viscerality. Rather than highlighting the spark of life, creation in these films comes from a highly physicalized birth. In *Shivers*, the scientifically engineered parasites are shown moving around just beneath the skin of their male host, who speaks to them like children before eventually vomiting them out one by one. In *The Brood*, Dr. Raglan's therapeutic techniques known as "psychoplasmics," in which patients project their inner trauma externally on their body, cause Nola to form an external birthing sac in which the children of her rage gestate. Their birth occurs when Nola bites into the sac, rips it open, pulls the baby out, and licks off the afterbirth. John McCarty claims that "Cronenberg's brand of splatter cinema is a unique blend of the absurd and the physically revolting," a reaction reaffirmed by the look of horror on Nola's husband's face as he watches her clean her child. While these scenes do, as McCarty argues, "revel" in "detailing the utter corruption of the human body," they also celebrate its inherent physicality (77). As Cronenberg explains, the body is "the first fact of human existence" (qtd in *David Cronenberg and Cinema of the Extremes*). Thus his films force audiences "to confront ... some very hard truths about the human condition ... particularly with the human body" (Cronenberg qtd in McCarty 78).

In *It's Alive* and *It Lives Again*, Cohen presents the birth of these monster babies as a clash between the primal body and the clinical world of science, perceived by many contemporary critics as a commentary on the thalidomide scandal (Hinxman; Robinson) and broader scientific and technological interventions within the natural order: "pollution, radiation and the increasing use of drugs" (Thirkell). In the first film, the birth of Frank and Lenore's baby takes place in a standard sanitized and medicalized labor room, as Lenore lies on a delivery table with her legs strapped in the stirrups. The male doctor asserts complete control over the process, ignoring Lenore's expressions of concern that something is wrong, knowledge gained not from formal scientific training but from lived, physical experience. He reasserts that there is nothing wrong but intervenes in the birth by cutting Lenore and applying forceps to force the baby out. The sequence then cuts to outside the room, where Frank sees an orderly emerge only to collapse, his throat covered in blood. When Frank looks for his wife, he finds the labor room no longer anonymous and sanitized but the site of chaos, with furniture overturned, Lenore hanging off the gurney, screaming to see her child, the room covered in pools of blood spatter, and the entire medical team dead. The confrontational nature of these images is enhanced by Cohen's visceral—even schlocky—aesthetic style, which uses wide-angle lenses mixed with hand-held camera movements to signal a loss of control and the world turned upside down.

The second film in the series takes this *mise-en-scène* further by having the parents, Gene and Jody, arrive at a hospital surrounded by police and medical officers, prepared to kill the baby at birth should it prove to be one of the deformed children. The labor room is no longer simply medicalized but militarized, as the doctor conceals a gun among the surgical tools, and police wearing medical masks surround the mother. Even the mobile labor room, where Jody is eventually brought by Frank—the father in the first film—in a daring rescue from the hospital, is a cold and sterile space in which a large *caged* incubator dominates the *mise-en-scène*. In these spaces, the lone woman is surrounded by masculine authority, even within the seeming sanctuary of a mobile room designed to provide a safe place for the birth. Like the first film, both husband and doctors ignore the mother's cries, this time to see her baby. Upon seeing the child, one doctor shockingly claims that it "shouldn't be allowed to live"—in stark contrast to Frankenstein's orgasmic exclamation of "It's Alive!" in the James Whale film that provided this work's title—resulting in the eruption of splatter as the child horribly mauls the doctor. While science may seek to sanitize birth, these babies remind us that it remains a bloody business.

This fusion of splatter techniques with sf tropes has refocused the genre in new directions. Barry Keith Grant argues that the "appeal of science fiction is primarily cognitive," suggesting that its often described "sense of wonder" embodies a "philosophical openness" (17). But the use of splatter in sf as I have described it here merges the cognitive with the visceral in a way that redirects the "philosophical openness" away from "wonder" to a form of social critique, one that deconstructs the traditional hierarchies of power represented within the genre. In this manner the films create a confrontational aesthetic, depicting the destabilization of society and the overarching institutions upon which it is built. Cronenberg and Cohen offer a reimagining of the Frankenstein myth, extolling the abjectness of the body at the center of creation, thereby undercutting the authority of the cold and clinical world of science. Romero utilizes splatter to present a vision of authority—whether media, scientific, or military—as, at best, out of touch with the violent realities of the real world or, at worst, the cause of them. With this reworking through splatter, sf has become part of a reappropriation within cult cinema of traditionally "negative forms of affect such as disgust, revulsion, and aversion" (Mathijs and Sexton 97) to serve the drive toward social and cultural transgression so welcomed by the cult film audience.

Notes

1 *Night of the Living Dead* was turned down for distribution by Columbia and AIP.

2 In his 1973 film *The Crazies*, in which a bacterial weapon has contaminated the water supply in the town of Evans City, Pennsylvania, Romero takes us inside a series of similar meetings between officials to confirm that the main aim of the government, including the President, present on a video hook-up, is cover-up, the group planning to destroy the town and present a story about a radiation "leak" to conceal their culpability in developing bio-weapons.

3 *Night of the Living Dead* operates within Todorov's concept of the fantastic, in which there is uncertainty as to the cause, supernatural or scientific, of the zombie outbreak. Contemporary zombie films and television series from *28 Days Later* (2002) to *The Walking Dead* (2010–), however, increasingly position the zombie within the realm of Todorov's notion of the uncanny in which there is a clear rational explanation, i.e., it is caused by a viral outbreak.

4 Cronenberg acknowledges the relationship of the imagery in his film to the October crisis in the documentary *David Cronenberg and Cinema of the Extreme* and claims that "no one in Canada seeing this movie would not make the connection" (qtd in Mathijs 40).

5 This legacy of splatter has always haunted the adaptations of Shelley's novel. While James Whale's *Frankenstein* (1931) downplays the visceral in favor of a spectacular machine age creation scene, Hammer's *Curse of Frankenstein* (1957) reinfused the narrative with the sights and sounds of the charnel house through the visceral emphasis upon blood smears and body parts photographed in color. By 1973, Paul Morrissey's *Flesh for Frankenstein* took the gothic grotesque of Hammer and exploded it into an orgy of splatter, shot in glorious 3D.

Works Cited

American Nightmare, The. Dir. Adam Simon. Minerva, 2000.

Beaupre, Lee. "*Night of the Living Dead.*" *Daily Variety*, October 15, 1968. Available from the BFI Reuban Library Cuttings Collection.

Biskind, Peter. "The Russians are Coming, Aren't They? *Them!* and *The Thing.*" *Liquid Metal: The Science Fiction Film Reader.* Ed. Sean Redmond. London: Wallflower Press, 2004. 318–24.

Bonnie and Clyde. Dir. Arthur Penn. Warner, 1967.

Brood, The. Dir. David Cronenberg. Canadian Film Development Corporation, 1979.

Crazies, The. Dir. George Romero. Cambist Films, 1973.

Curse of Frankenstein, The. Dir. Terence Fischer. Hammer, 1957.

David Cronenberg and Cinema of the Extreme. Prod. Nick Freand Jones. BBC2 1997.

Exorcist, The. Dir. William Friedkin. Warner, 1973.

Flesh for Frankenstein. Dir. Paul Morrissey. Bryanston Distribution, 1973.

Frankenstein. Dir. James Whale. Universal, 1931.

Frayling, Christopher. *Mad, Bad and Dangerous? The Scientist and the Cinema.* London: Reaktion Books, 2005.

Godfather, The. Dir. Francis Ford Coppola. Paramount, 1972.

Grant, Barry Keith. "Sensuous Elaboration: Reason and the Visible in the Science Fiction Film." *Liquid Metal: The Science Fiction Film Reader.* Ed. Sean Redmond. London: Wallflower Press, 2004. 17–23.

Heffernan, Kevin. *Ghouls, Gimmicks, and Gold: Horror Film and the American Movies, 1953–1968.* Durham and London: Duke UP, 2004.

Hervey, Ben. *Night of the Living Dead.* London: BFI Publishing, 2008.

Hinxman, Margaret. "*It's Alive!*" *Daily Mail*, May 10, 1975. Available from the BFI Library Cuttings Collection.

Hoberman, J., and Jonathan Rosenbaum. *Midnight Movies.* New York: DaCapo Press, 1991.

I Walked with a Zombie. Dir. Jacques Tourneur. RKO Radio Pictures, 1943.

It's Alive. Dir. Larry Cohen. Warner, 1974.

It Lives Again. Dir. Larry Cohen. Warner, 1979.

Lebowitz, Fran, Pat Hackett, and Ronnie Cutrone. "George Romero: From *Night of the Living Dead* to *The Crazies.*" (Originally Published in *INTERVIEW Magazine*, April 1973, 30–31, 45). Reprinted in *George A. Romero Interviews.* Ed. Tony Williams. Jackson: UP of Mississippi, 2011. 36–46.

Maltby, Richard. *Hollywood Cinema.* Oxford: Blackwell Publishing, 2003.

Mathijs, Ernest. *The Cinema of David Cronenberg: From Baron of Blood to Cultural Hero.* London: Wallflower Press, 2008.

Mathijs, Ernest, and Jamie Sexton. *Cult Cinema.* Oxford: Wiley Blackwell, 2011.

McCarty, John. *Splatter Movies: Breaking the Last Taboo of the Screen.* New York: St. Martin's, 1984.

Monthly Film Bulletin. "Review of *Curse of Frankenstein.*" *MFB*, 24.281 (June 1957): 70.

Neale, Steve. "Arties and Imports, Exports and Runaways, Adult Film and Exploitation." *The Classical Hollywood Reader.* Ed. Steve Neale. London: Routledge, 2012. 399–411.

Night of the Living Dead. Dir. George Romero. Walter Reade Organization, 1968.

Omen, The. Dir. Richard Donner. 20th Century Fox, 1976.

Rabid. Dir. David Cronenberg. Canadian Film Development Corporation, 1977.

Revolt of the Zombies. Dir. Victor Helperin. Academy Pictures Distributing Corporation, 1936.

Robinson, David. "*It's Alive!*" *The Times,* May 9, 1975. Available from the BFI Reuban Library Cuttings Collection.

Skal, David J. *The Monster Show: A Cultural History of Horror.* London: Plexus, 1993.

Staiger, Janet. "Individualism vs Collectivism: The Shift to Independent Production in the US Film Industry." *The Classical Hollywood Reader.* Ed. Steve Neale. London: Routledge, 2012. 331–42.

Telotte, J. P. "Beyond All Reason: The Nature of the Cult." *The Cult Film Experience: Beyond All Reason.* Ed. J. P. Telotte. Austin: U of Texas P, 1991. 5–17.

Them! Dir. Gordon Douglas. Warner, 1954.

Thing, The. Dir. John Carpenter. Universal Pictures, 1982.

Thing from Another World, The. Dir. Christian Nyby. RKO Radio Pictures, 1951.

Thirkell, Arthur. "Watch for the Little Horror." *Daily Mirror,* May 9, 1975.

Todorov, Tzvetan. *The Fantastic: A Structural Approach to a Literary Genre.* Trans. Richard Howard. Ithaca: Cornell UP, 1973.

"*Night of the Living Dead.*" *The Village Voice,* July 17, 1971.

White Zombie. Dir. Victor Halperin. United Artists, 1932.

Wild Bunch, The. Dir. Sam Peckinpah. Warner, 1969.

4. Sean Connery Reconfigured: From Bond to Cult Science Fiction Figure[1]

Gerald Duchovnay

While histories of cinema, especially US cinema, typically discuss the development of the star system, only in recent decades has much attention been paid to actors as performers, and still less attention is given to actors as cult performers. As Wade Jennings observes, compared to regular stardom, "Cult stardom is a relatively recent phenomenon," and one that, "over time ... can emerge as a quite different phenomenon" (90). Exploring the discourses related to this "different phenomenon," Matt Hills notes how, "across their lifetime, some cult stars become hemmed in by their most famous roles (where a specific character has taken on a cult following, or been linked to a cult text)" (28). For example, while William Shatner was "recast" from his TV image, he, like other cult figures, continued "to be shadowed by his cult identification with Captain Kirk" (28). Meanwhile, as Hills offers, Harrison Ford's Hollywood career, "as a 'mainstream' star," has undermined his "cult status despite his multiple appearances in cult movies such as *Blade Runner*," because Ford's performance always "connotes conventions of Hollywood acting, being discursively linked to 'mainstream' cinema" (31–33). There are, in fact, few international stars like Ford who have shifted their focus from mainstream, even blockbuster films, to cult or non-mainstream works that have resulted in a problematic persona that successfully challenges audience expectations.

Dennis Bingham, in writing about Clint Eastwood, notes that:

> Not much has been said ... about the star who acts against the grain of his or her own persona, the effect that such a deviation has upon the ideological meanings of the persona, and the reaction of audience groups who have learned to "read" the performance codes in one particular way. (40)

One star who deviated from the expected and challenged those "performance codes" at a relatively early stage in his career—and did so perhaps most spectacularly within the realm of sf—is Sean Connery.

Fifty years and multiple James Bond films later, while much debate continues as to who is the best Bond, for many Sean Connery *is* Bond, the star who helped to create the franchise. To John Cork and Bruce Scivally, the initial Bond/Connery appeal focused on teenage boys who found "007 [to be] everything an adolescent male dreams of becoming: a sexually irresistible, socially astute, witty, dangerous, heroic enigma— the dedicated individualist the rest of the world cannot live without" (7).[2] Yet even beyond the adolescent audience, the Bond films (and Connery) have found a widespread appeal, as a 1965 *Saturday Evening Post* cover story suggests, reporting how photographers and reporters for mainstream newspapers, magazines, and television networks from around the world descended on the Bahamas for the making of the fourth Bond film:

> It wasn't any mere Dominican uprising or Cuban blockade. It was even bigger than that—the new James Bond movie was being filmed in the Bahamas! The men who made *Dr. No* and *From Russia with Love* and *Goldfinger* were back in action, stirring up a new epic, this one more colossal than ever. *Thunderball!* Guns and girls ... and sex! All this and Sean Connery too ... . (Zinsser 77)

To the public, Connery was essential to the successful Bond formula, which made him a matinee idol and thus a marketable and highly desirable commodity. Yet at the height of this popularity, Connery opted to deviate from the Bond persona, as well as from the mainstream performance codes embodied in his portrayal of agent 007. In what, for a variety of reasons, had to seem an unlikely development of his persona, he chose a role in John Boorman's sf effort *Zardoz* (1974), a film in which he played Zed, a rapist, killer, and truth seeker. The resulting film—and Connery along with it—was roundly criticized. *Zardoz* was panned as "a joke," a "cheaply made" film (Avery 185), a "glittering cultural trash pile" (Kael 276), marked by "pretentious intellectualism" (Pfeiffer and Lisa 127) and "impenetrable psycho-babble" (Bray 183). However, some found the film's subversive narrative an effective commentary on the culture of the time and a somewhat visionary, if "weird," sf film that broke away from conventional morality (Smalley)—all signs of a cult appeal in the making.

One of the questions most often asked by those who have seen *Zardoz* and have not followed Connery's career moves is why the actor would opt to go from being the franchise star in the lucrative early Bond films to taking the lead in a dystopian sf effort, a type in which he had seemingly shown little interest. Moreover, the role required him to be seen in one scene donning a woman's wedding dress and for the rest of the film wearing a ponytail and moustache, red boots, and what has variously been described as a red nappy or red jock strap—not only a far remove from Bond's tuxedos and tailored suits, but precisely the sort of unusual dress that would invite commentary because of its radical and quite literal *redressing* of "Bond."

When word first went out that one of Ian Fleming's novels was to be made into a film, a British TV station had run a poll on who should play Bond, and Connery, based largely on his recent television work, came out on top. While the producers discounted the poll, Connery received an offer to screen test for the movie. He refused but did meet with the producers, who were unimpressed by his appearance and clothing and could not see him as a refined or debonair secret agent or in a tuxedo or Savile Row suit, although they did like his rough and tumble demeanor and the way he carried himself (Pfeiffer and Lisa 14). According to some accounts, when one of the producer's wives was asked about Connery, she said he "was a sexy guy." Whatever the cause, producers Albert Broccoli and Harry Saltzman eventually agreed to cast the relatively unknown actor as Bond, offered him £6,000, or a little less than $17,000 (*Playboy* interview) out of a total budget of approximately 1 million dollars. Though hungry for money and a role that would give him greater visibility, Connery was initially hesitant to take the part:

> I didn't want to do it because I could see that, properly made, it would have to be the first in a series, and I wasn't sure if I wanted to get involved with that and the contract that would go with it. Contracts choke you, and I wanted to be free … However, I did see this would be a start—a marvelous opening. (Pfeiffer and Lisa 15)

Stardom is a funny thing. When actors are struggling to make it in television, movies, or the stage, they desperately want recognition. Once they achieve star status they often want to run and hide from the fame and publicity it attracts—as well as from the public self that, ironically, facilitates that recognition. Michael Caine tells the story of how Harry Salzman put him up

> in a very grand suite at the Carlton Hotel [at Cannes] and I reveled in the luxury of it, but as soon as *Ipcress* [*The Ipcress File*, 1965] was shown I saw that my days of freedom were over. I couldn't leave the hotel without being mobbed by the press. Sean Connery was

also in town and he hated it so much—he couldn't even get to the hotel dining room in peace—that he left the same day. (72–73)

By this time, Connery was an international superstar and sex symbol. Yet he wanted to avoid being "a piece of merchandise, a public institution" (*Playboy* interview). What he wanted to be was an actor, recognized for his growing skills on the screen.

Wanting to avoid being typecast, Connery made several films between his Bond efforts, including *Shalako* (1968) with Bridget Bardot, *The Molly Maguires* (1970), and *The Red Tent* (1971), but they were not successful at the box office. After George Lazenby's outing as Bond in *On Her Majesty's Secret Service* (1969), Broccoli and Saltzman, money in hand, lured Connery back for *Diamonds are Forever* (1971). Fans rejoiced and Connery became a "hot property" again, only to leave the Bond franchise once more to make Sidney Lumet's *The Offence* (1973) and then Boorman's *Zardoz* (1974), the latter one of the most interesting if not bewildering dystopian sf films produced in the late 1960s and early 1970s.

Agreeing to play roles that were unlike anything he had done before was part of Connery's professional strategy. In 1972, when his agent was leaving to become a producer and partner of Richard Selinger, Connery had a meeting with Selinger, who was one of the top Hollywood agents and also handled Connery's friend Michael Caine. According to Andrew Yule, Selinger told Connery:

> … you've made an awful lot of money out of Bond and since then you don't seem to be very interested in working. In the last three years you've made two or three pretty bad movies. Because of that you're going to find it very difficult to get the good parts. All you will be offered are Bond lookalikes—which you shouldn't do. (137)

When asked what he should do, Selinger, who was soon to become Connery's agent, told him to follow Michael Caine's path: "make three or four pictures a year. If two bomb out, one of them has got a chance of making it. It's hard work, but once you get back in, then you can pick and choose" (137).

This conversation with Selinger occurred a short time before Connery's meeting with Boorman about *Zardoz*. Boorman was coming off the highly successful *Deliverance* (1972) and knew that he could do almost anything he wanted: "I was hot. I had made a hit, a genuine blockbuster. The picture had not been expensive. The studio had made lots of money. I had earned myself the power to make what I wanted" (Boorman, *Adventures* 204)—but not the one film he wanted to do more than any other—*The Lord of the Rings*. Frustrated because he could not find the necessary financial backing for that project, and lamenting that "Our lives are frittered away on movies we fail to make" (203), he channeled his energies and ideas into writing, producing, casting, and directing a far less conventional sort of story, *Zardoz*.

Originally Burt Reynolds was to be the male lead in *Zardoz*. He had worked with Boorman on *Deliverance*, was one of the ten most profitable stars in 1973 (Kerr 110), and had posed nude for *Cosmopolitan* magazine a year earlier, when Helen Gurley Brown, a few years before Laura Mulvey's seminal essay on visual pleasure in the cinema, championed his photos "as a victory for women whose 'visual appetites' had been ignored by male magazine editors and proprietors" ("Burt Reynolds Nude"). But Reynolds had to withdraw for medical reasons. After Richard Harris, Boorman's second choice, failed to keep a scheduled appointment, he turned to Sean Connery who, from the early Bond films until 1971, had become one of the ten most profitable box office stars (Kerr 109–10) and had physical attributes and sex appeal similar to Reynolds. With his background as a former Mr. Universe contestant, Connery also offered Boorman an actor uninhibited by his body, who could meet the physicality of Zed, the main character, and appeal to the "visual appetites" of a female audience that might not normally be attracted to a sf film.

Connery liked the vision and dramatic action, and signed to do the film within days of receiving the script; as he noted:

> What gripped me especially was the direction the people in it were taking in this future existence, as opposed to space ships and rockets

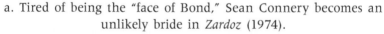

a. Tired of being the "face of Bond," Sean Connery becomes an unlikely bride in *Zardoz* (1974).

b. Sean Connery as a Brutal is examined in *Zardoz* (1974).

and all that. I am not a science fiction buff … What does interest
me is the possible development of society in centuries to come. The
way different levels and types evolve in the script is intriguing and
refreshing, and could well be true. The fact that people would not
die, for example. (Gow 11)

In addition, as unlikely as it seems given the success of his Bond
films, Connery told Boorman he "was finding it difficult to get work"
(Boorman Director Commentary).[3] Known for his parsimonious ways,
Connery did not choose to work with Boorman for the money. He was
tired of being the face of the Bond franchise, and even though he had
returned to make *Diamonds are Forever*, and then a decade later to do
the ironically titled *Never Say Never Again*, he was trained as an actor,
had by this time performed for some years in the theatre, wanted to
avoid total identification as James Bond, and, as Selinger had suggested,
wanted to be cast in as many films a year as he could make.

For many directors, casting is the essential element of a film. As
Martin Scorsese observes at the opening of the documentary *Casting By*
(2012), "99% of directing a picture is the right casting." In addition to
the casting of Connery, Boorman chose Charlotte Rampling as Connery's
co-star. At the time, Rampling, like Connery, had something of her own
cult following for her beauty and big screen sex appeal. She started her
film career in the mid-1960s with Richard Lester's *The Knack, and How
to Get It* (1965) and Silvio Narizzo's *Georgy Girl* (1966). She subsequently
took on controversial roles in Luchino Visconti's *The Damned* (1969) and
Liliana Caviani's *The Night Porter* (1974); as a result of performances
in those films, but especially *The Night Porter*, Rampling would secure

her own cult status as "the muse *extravagante* of Seventies art-house depravity" (Macaulay). Dirk Bogarde, the star of *The Damned* and *The Night Porter*, is credited for assigning Rampling her nickname, "The Look," a term still used today[4] that conveys her sensuality, imperiousness, aloofness, intensity, mystery, and seductiveness, all traits she brought to the role of Consuella in *Zardoz*. Rampling, like Connery, developed her "culticity" in part because of her appearance and demeanor, but also because of the roles she chose to play; of those roles, Rampling has said:

> I generally don't make films to entertain people. I choose the parts that challenge me to break through my own barriers. A need to devour, punish, humiliate, or surrender seems to be a primal part of human nature, and it's certainly a big part of sex. To discover what normal means, you have to surf a tide of weirdness. ("Charlotte Rampling")

For many viewers, *Zardoz* itself seems to "surf" that "tide of weirdness" with its difficult narrative and disarming presentation of ideas and characters. When Boorman first screened the film for critics, he asked them to see it twice before commenting on it (Pfeiffer and Lisa 130), and he subsequently added a prologue to help audiences better understand the film. The story takes place in 2293, when the populace, not unlike the people of Fritz Lang's *Metropolis* (1927), is divided by class and geography. The Eternals are young, emotionless intellectuals who, unable to procreate, live forever in a communal environment inside the Vortex, a land protected by an invisible force field and controlled by the Tabernacle, a computer that holds all knowledge. The outlands are populated by the Brutals (savage slave laborers) and Exterminators (killers) who worship Zardoz, a Floating Head. Zardoz exacts tributes of grain from the Brutals and spits out guns and bullets to the Exterminators so that they might kill some of the Brutals in order to control their population. Zed (Sean Connery), the leader of the Exterminators, pillages and rapes at will amongst the Brutals, until one day he becomes curious and stows away in the Floating Head. He encounters and kills Zardoz's creator, Arthur Frayn (Niall Buggy), and subsequently penetrates the Vortex. Once inside the Vortex, Zed encounters the Eternals, led by two women: Consuella (Charlotte Rampling), who wants him killed before he corrupts their culture and destabilizes their way of life, and May (Sarah Kestleman), who, intrigued by his sexuality, wants to study him. Fascinated and then overcome by his passion and vitality, the Eternals (especially the women) easily fall prey to Zed's energy and sexuality, almost as if he were some primitive Bond.

Once he decodes the secrets of the Eternals and understands how they control the social order, Zed reintroduces emotion and passion to their world. He shows his fellow Exterminators how to enter the Vortex, where they kill off most of the Eternals. In establishing a new social order by allowing May and some of her followers to escape, transforming his lust to love for Consuella, and granting, through his henchmen, what the Eternals have longed for—death—Zed becomes both avenger and savior. During a massacre of the Eternals by the Exterminators, Zed and Consuella go into hiding and form a nuclear family by having a son, who eventually leaves to make his way in the new world. As the film ends, in a time-transition scene, we witness Zed and Consuella quickly age and die, holding hands, leaving behind their skeletal remains and two handprints on a cave wall.

While the film's visual style is often applauded by critics and fans, the interpretations of the characters and events of *Zardoz* are varied, with most commentators sticking on its seemingly paradoxical characteristics. Marsha Kinder, for example, found it "a film of paradox ... liberated and experimental in form, yet fascist and sexist in content" (49). Michael Ciment saw in it "a cautionary tale coloured by Boorman's concern for the evolution of humanity" (135). To Roger Ebert, the film was "genuinely quirky" but also "an exercise in self-indulgence," while Brian Hoyle saw it as a "critical and commercial disaster, but one that nonetheless merits careful attention" (91). Ryan Britt, one of many recent commentators on the film, sums up a rather different take on the film, one characteristic of the cult appeal it has found. He sees it as "accidentally funny, visually preposterous, borderline offensive," while "trying to be a very earnest, very arty science fiction movie"; "It's not that *Zardoz* is simply a bad movie. It's just hard to believe that it even exists" (Britt). Given this range of response, it is hardly surprising that the film has attained a solid cult status, with sf fans repeatedly viewing the film, some enjoying it simply for what they see as its "badness," others finding an appeal in its "offensive" strategy, some finding links to other sf films such as *Metropolis* or *Things to Come*, as well as literary texts such as *Utopia*, *Gulliver's Travels*, *Brave New World*, or *News from Nowhere*, and still others appreciating Connery's physicality and his cult turn in the subversive role of Zed. A significant part of that attraction, though, also rests in the almost unavoidable sense that there is Bond in that Zed.

Audiences often go to a film for the star; they appreciate consistency in an actor's persona, whether it be Adam Sandler, Humphrey Bogart, Katharine Hepburn, or Sandra Bullock. Changing—or challenging—a persona can be off-putting to mainstream audiences. Connery as Bond was carrying on what one critic calls the tradition of "The Great

Appeal" found in male stars during the Studio System and into the '60s. Male actors appealed to both sexes by conveying confidence, glamor, sex appeal, social graces, and "desirable and imitable" traits that catered to "national unity or national virtues," and "national needs and hopes" (Spoto 49). In the '70s, that appeal was often "linked with sociopolitical integrity, or at least with some social issue" (Spoto 83). Some of the non-Bond films were greenlighted because Connery had "the great appeal," but most who came to see Connery in *Zardoz* were puzzled. Connery's persona and actions were obviously far away in time and place from James Bond and the Bond narratives, although those very deviations—in appearance, dress, and action—opened up another dimension for audiences, part of the appeal cult sf fans have embraced.

Connery's first appearances in *Dr. No* and in *Zardoz* are telling as they demonstrate a kind of deliberate "doubleness" that was at work in his image—what David Robinson calls a "dual image" (92) that might serve as a template for how Connery would both use and deviate from the Bond persona. When Connery first appears in *Dr. No*, he is at the *chemin de fer* table, playing opposite the seductive Sylvia Trench (Eunice Grayson). Connery is handsome, debonair, dapper, sophisticated, with a distinct voice, and stylish in his immaculately tailored tuxedo. His back is to the camera until Trench asks him to whom the check for her losses should be made out. Director Terence Young had Connery do several takes to perfect the timing as he flicks his cigarette lighter and pronounces the iconic line, "Bond, James Bond," to convey a bit of humor as well as identifying Ian Fleming's secret agent for the first time on film (Young).

In contrast, the actor's initial appearance as Zed in *Zardoz* is something of a throwback to his blue collar background and images in films he made between 1957 and 1962, when he conveyed a "stylish mayhem" that "exudes a rich, dark animal presence that is almost overpowering," although it was a presence that did not work well (Crichton 408). As in *Dr. No*, as if quoting that film, there is a time delay before we see the protagonist. The camera moves from the back of Zed's head and ponytail to a frontal close up. When Connery/Zed turns full face to the camera, his first action echoes the opening credits of the Bond films, as well as the last shot in Edwin S. Porter's *The Great Train Robbery* (1903): he points his gun at the camera and shoots. Connery as Zed in ponytail, red briefs, red boots, gun belt slung over his shoulder, shooting Brutals in the back, and raping women is a shocking deviation from the Bond persona, but his savagery, appearance, some of the film's dialogue ("The gun is good. The penis is evil"), and the utopian/dystopian environment in *Zardoz* helped to establish Connery's cult sf ethos.[5] What many mainstream viewers missed—but was clearly picked up by cult followers—is how in *Zardoz* there is less of a perceived radical difference and more of a doubleness with Connery as both 007 and Zed.

Of course, what we might forget is that while Connery's Bond is urbane, stylish, suave, and a seducer of women, he is also, like Zed, an amoral killer for hire who works to reinforce the social order.[6] No doubt the jarring physical image that Connery projected as Zed, the rapes, the brutal violence, and the obfuscated narrative with intertextual references to the likes of T. S. Eliot, William Blake, and Frederick Nietzsche, were off-putting to Bond/Connery fans, but the fundamental nature of the character, as well as other key elements of the Bond franchise film formula are also present in *Zardoz*. Until he kills him, for example, Zed is having his strings pulled by Frayn, the puppetmaster, in a fashion similar to M's control of Bond.

While Boorman uses no spaceships and few gadgets like jet packs (*Thunderball*), a fully armed Aston Martin DB5 (*Goldfinger*), or rigged briefcase (*From Russia with Love*), he does have Zed enter the Vortex via the flying stone head, and in his quest for answers ("the truth"), Zed encounters life-nourishing inflatables, holograms, and a crystal ring that offers encyclopedic knowledge about his new environment. After Zed's initial exploration of this new land, always with gun in hand, he encounters May, one of the leaders of the Eternals, who disarms him through telepathy and eye power. She brings Zed to an examination room, where she and Consuella review images from Zed's memory of his life as an Exterminator. Zed's physical presence disturbs Consuella, who asks May "for our love" to "quench," "quell," and "kill" Zed, whom she sees as a threat to their stability and the tranquility of the Vortex. When May rejects her pleas and suspecting May's attraction is more than scientific, Consuella, who considers herself immune to Zed's physical appeal, forces May to bring their prisoner before a council of primarily female Eternals to decide his fate. Zed's animal magnetism, not unlike Bond's physical attractiveness, is conveyed by the intense interest the women display in his body as they intently gaze upon and then touch the captive. When a vote is taken, that physical interest clearly sways them, as Zed is allowed to live for three weeks so that May can complete her study.

During his captivity, Zed is again brought before the Council members and forced to watch various erotic images to see what might cause the Exterminator to have an erection, a biological reaction long since extinguished in the male Eternals. Bond-like Zed does not respond to any of the projected images, but when he looks Consuella in the eye, the Council members chuckle at Zed's physical acumen, while Zed, in a droll moment, looks down and then, without uttering a word, smiles at an infuriated Consuella. The humor in the Bond films is most often verbal, as in *Goldfinger*, when Pussy Galore introduces herself and Bond says, "I must be dreaming," or, in *Thunderball*, when Tanya laments that her mouth is too big, and Bond replies, "No, it's the right size ... for me that is." While there are occasional sexual allusions in Boorman's dialogue, such as when May tells Zed that "no Brutal has ever penetrated a Vortex" or the Tabernacle says to him, "You have penetrated me ... Come into my center," more often the humor in *Zardoz* is conveyed through images of Zed/Connery's physical presence, starting with the shock to Bond fans of his first appearance as an Exterminator, his display before the Eternals, and his appearance as a woman in a wedding dress while fleeing from the Eternals.

Throughout his time in the Vortex, Zed's advances are rejected by Consuella, who wants him destroyed. When she has the opportunity to kill him, though, she is unable to, seduced by Zed's transformation from an Exterminator to a life-giving force. With his survival skills, the assistance of May and Consuella, and the ability to absorb all knowledge (unbeknownst to Zed, he was bred by Frayn to be superior to all other Eternals), Zed is able to realign the ideology of his adversaries to destroy the "indestructible and everlasting" Tabernacle. In so doing, Zed establishes, or re-establishes, a new order by sending one consort, May, and some of her followers off to a new, more human world and establishing a (somewhat conservative) nuclear family social dynamic with Consuella, the woman who wanted him killed.

On the surface, the images and actions of Connery as Zed subvert audience expectations and deviate from the Bond persona, but for all the film's grounding in *au courant* ideas (population explosion, the haves vs the have-nots, technology, communal living), there are consistent echoes of the Bond film formula: a star with mass audience appeal; a truth seeker who investigates an oppressor and infiltrates the oppressor's sanctuary; a seducer who turns hostile women to his purpose in defeating his adversary; a destroyer of oppressive and destructive technology who uses guile, resourcefulness, luck, and violence to achieve his goals; and a man who winds up in the arms of a woman.

While the Bond films appeal to male and female fantasies worldwide, the films had special appeal to British audiences at a time when the class system was in decline. After the Second World War, the United Kingdom was suffering from having lost its power base and leadership in the world. Bond was one of the antidotes for those losses; his persona and actions offered viewers the fulfillment of their dreams, desires, and fantasies, as well as a renewed cultural self-esteem. As Simon Winder notes in his study of Bond's impact on UK audiences,

As the 1960s progressed, Bond's ability to maim and kill foreigners became a great consolation to millions of embittered and confused people whose traditional world picture had changed with alarming speed. Bond in fact became in the 1960s pretty much the only British national capable of damaging anybody at all. (190)

Of course, Boorman's *Zardoz* offers little of that sort of consolation to the nation beyond the clichéd ending that, not unlike the double meaning (Latin and Greek translations) of the title of Sir Thomas More's *Utopia*—"the good place" and "no place." It suggests that what we are left with is our humanity and love, and if we can find a mate, we can create order and love in a very circumscribed world without technology and without hostility. Both Bond/Connery and Zed/Connery are fabrications that satisfy the double life that many wish for or have. One is a world where dreams and desires are made right by our actions and where we are in control of technology and can overcome evil; the other is a world described by Hobbes in *Leviathan* as "nasty, brutish, and short." As J. P. Telotte notes, "our ability to control reality, to fashion and refashion the images of humans and our world, are the essential *raison d'être* of the science fiction film" (*Replications* 17). While Bond kills to save the world and control his reality, Zed initially kills for the pleasure of killing, but at the end destroys the corrupt scientific system that has created him, returning to a more "normal" though violent world, where technology no longer controls destinies and where individuals have emotions, can bear children, and even die.

While many mainstream filmgoers continue to cherish Connery for his role as Bond, sf enthusiasts have in part relished *Zardoz* precisely for the ways it brings together elements of those earlier roles, for its double ability: to play with—and against—his culturally embraced Bond persona. *Zardoz* was simply something of a shock to mainstream Bond/Connery fans, thanks to its thematically complex ("bad" and innovative in its complex, if not confusing ideas), violent, and transgressive nature. But those effects depended at least partly on the "double" feature built into this sf text through its casting. For Boorman and Connery capitalized on the Bond persona, with the character of Zed both upsetting audience expectations in transgressive and amoral ways, while also drawing on many of the Bond figure's fundamental attractions.

David Thomson has noted how Sean Connery seems to have made "strange choices" in the roles he opts to play (173), *Zardoz* among them. However, those choices were probably ones Connery felt worth making to free himself of Bondage. In bringing together elements of sf and fantasy, as well as some of the impulses established in the Bond films, *Zardoz* forced audiences to experience a kind of shock of difference, especially if they recognized the multiple conjoined characteristics, or paradoxes, built into the Connery persona and revealed by John Boorman's sf text. Connery's performance as Zed contextualizes one dimension of the cult film's "double feature" character. Looking back on this complex creation, Connery rather slyly allows, "I have a splendid memory of [*Zardoz*]" (Sesti 142). And if we can believe biographer Christopher Bray, *Zardoz* "may just have been the movie that [began] to turn round Connery's career in the depths of his post-Bond doldrums" (183), allowing him to be Bond, but also to send up that figure to which he had become so stiflingly bond-ed.

Notes

I want to thank Michele Lellouche for her help in the early stages of research for this project. She shares no responsibility for any misstatements or errors of fact or interpretation.

¹ Leo Braudy suggests as much in *World in a Frame* when he notes the need for scholars to examine acting more closely (194). There soon followed a number of academic studies, including Charles Affron's *Star Acting* (1977) and *Cinema and Sentiment* (1982), Richard Dyer's *Stars* (1979), James Naremore's *Acting in the Cinema* (1988), Christine Gledhill's *Stardom* (1991), Jackie Stacey's *Star Gazing* (1994), and Carole Zucker's *Figures of Light* (1995). More recently, Matt Hills has focused attention on the phenomenon of cult stardom, while Kate Egan and Sarah Thomas have edited a collection of essays on the topic.

² The fantasy of desiring to be James Bond is conveyed in the song "I Wish I was James Bond" (2007), on the debut album of Scouting for Girls, in an album of the same name. The cult appeal of Rampling is captured in the performances in the early '90s of Kinky Machine's "Charlottte Rampling Lyrics"; the most notable lines are: "I always wanted to be your trampoline/Charlotte Rampling/Charlotte Rampling."

³ Except for Hitchcock's *Marnie* (1964), which itself was not well received when it opened, Connery's box office flops between *Dr. No* and *Zardoz*, include *Woman of Straw, The Hill, A Fine Madness, Shalako, The Molly Maguires, The Red Tent*, and *The Offence*. While Pfeiffer and Lisa (and others) consider *The Hill* and *The Offence* Connery's best yet least seen screen performances (122–23), of his non-Bond films, only *The Anderson Tapes* (1971) showed him to be a box office draw.

⁴ In 2011 Angelina Maccarone released the documentary *The Look: A Self-Portrait through Others*, a series of conversations with Rampling and friends and colleagues about her views on life. Dirk Bogarde's nickname for Rampling had been used years earlier for another model turned actress, Lauren Bacall.

⁵ To Fredric Jameson, Connery's performance here is more substantive than

in what he considers the vacuous Bond films: "Sean Connery's heavy features have indeed rarely been so expressive in their basic inexpressiveness. Scowls, blank looks, a raised eyebrow or a sudden sharp light in the eye, the most economical gestures are here charged with density of meaning, with the accumulated reactions of a whole character structure." Aside from what many consider to be its confusing dystopian narrative, four aspects of the film appear in most discussions of *Zardoz*'s cult appeal: the appearance of the floating head, the dispersals of guns to the Brutals followed by the slogan about the penis, Sean Connery's appearance in briefs and ponytail, and his wearing a dress. Connery often appeared bare-chested in Bond films, and wearing briefs and a ponytail was not a stretch for someone who, only a decade before, was competing for Mr. Universe. Wearing the wedding dress, though, was a major deviation for Connery's persona, and while he argued against it, Boorman prevailed (Director Commentary).

6 In an interview with Sheldon Lane, Connery says, "I saw him [Bond] as a complete sensualist—senses highly tuned, awake to everything, quite amoral. I particularly like him because he thrives on conflict" (Cork and Scivally 37). In *Dr. No*, Bond "goes to the dark side" when he kills Professor Dent after Dent's attempted assassination of Bond. Director Terence Young "fought hard for the scene to remain intact, insisting that Bond 'is an executioner—we must not forget that'" (Benson 167).

Works Cited

Affron, Charles. *Star Acting: Gish, Garbo, Davis*. New York: Dutton, 1977.

—. *Cinema and Sentiment*. Chicago: U of Chicago P, 1982.

Avery, William. "Zardoz." Rev. *Films in Review*, March 1975: 185.

Benson, Raymond. *The James Bond Bedside Companion*. New York: Dodd and Mead, 1984.

Bingham, Dennis. "Masculinity, Star Reception, and the Desire to Perform: Clint Eastwood in *White Hunter, Black Heart*." *Post Script* 12.2 (1993): 40–53.

Boorman, John. *Adventures of a Suburban Boy*. London: Faber and Faber, 2003.

—. "Director's Commentary." *Zardoz*. DVD. 20th Century Fox, 1974.

Braudy, Leo. *The World in a Frame*. New York: Anchor/Doubleday, 1976.

Bray, Christopher. *Sean Connery: The Measure of a Man*. London: Faber and Faber, 2010.

Britt, Ryan. "Stay Inside My Aura: Why *Zardoz* is the Arty Dystopian Film You Can't Believe Exists." Web. Accessed 15 April 2013.

"Burt Reynolds Nude: 10 facts about the Cosmo centerfold." Web. Accessed 2 September 2013.

Caine, Michael. *The Elephant to Hollywood*. New York: Henry Holt, 2010.

Casting By. Dir. Tom Donahue. HBO Documentary Films, 2012.

Ciment, Michael. *John Boorman*. Trans. Gilbert Adair. London: Faber and Faber, 1986.

Cork, John, and Bruce Scivally. *James Bond: The Legacy*. New York: Abrams, 2002.

Crichton, Michael. "Sean Connery: A Propensity for Stylish Mayhem." *Close-ups: The Movie Star Book*. Ed. Danny Peary. New York: Galahad, 1978. 408–11.

Dyer, Richard. *Stars*. London: BFI, 1979.

Ebert, Roger. "Zardoz." Review. *Sun Times*, January 1, 1974. Web. Accessed 8 February 2013.

Egan, Kate, and Sarah Thomas, eds. *Cult Film Stardom*. London: Palgrave Macmillan, 2012.

Gledhill, Christine, ed. *Stardom: Industry of Desire*. London: Routledge, 1991.

Gow, Gordon. "A Secretive Person: Sean Connery Interview." *Films and Filming* 20.6 (1974): 10–17.

Hills, Matt. "Cult Movies with and without Cult Stars: Differentiating Discourses of Stardom." *Cult Film Stardom*. Ed. Kate Egan and Sarah Thomas. London: Palgrave Macmillan, 2012. 21–36.

Hoyle, Brian. *The Cinema of John Boorman*. Lanham: Scarecrow, 2012.

Jameson, Frederick. "History and the Death Wish: *Zardoz* as Open Form." *Jump Cut* 3 (1974): 5–8. Web. Accessed 8 February 2013.

Jennings, Wade. "The Star as Cult Icon: Judy Garland." *The Cult Film Experience: Beyond All Reason*. Ed. J. P. Telotte. Austin: U of Texas P, 1991. 90–101.

Kael, Pauline. "O Consuella." Rev. of *Zardoz*. *The New Yorker*, February 18, 1974. Rpt. *Reeling*. Boston: Little Brown, 1976. 276–82.

Kerr, Paul. "Stars and Stardom." *Anatomy of the Movies*. Ed. David Pirie. New York: Macmillan, 1981. 104–15.

Kinder, Marsha. "Zardoz." Rev. *Film Quarterly* 27.4 (1974): 49–57.

Macaulay, Sean. "My Life was Dark: Charlotte Rampling Interview." *Telegraph*, May 3, 2013. Web. Accessed 20 October 2013.

Mulvey, Laura. "Visual Pleasure and Narrative Cinema." *Screen* 16.3 (1975): 6–18.

Naremore, James. *Acting in the Cinema*. Berkeley: U California P, 1988.

Peary, Danny, ed. *Close-ups: The Movie Star Book*. New York: Galahad, 1978.

Pfeiffer, Lee, and Philip Lisa. *The Films of Sean Connery*. Secaucus: Citadel, 1997.

"*Playboy* Interview: Sean Connery." *Playboy*, November 1965. Web. Accessed 23 April 2013.

"Rampling, Charlotte." Imdb. Web. Accessed 10 October 2013.

Robinson, David. "The Star Who Stayed Human." *Sean Connery*. Ed. Mario Sesti. Milan: Electa, 2006. 92–93.

Sesti, Mario, Ed. *Sean Connery*. Milan: Electa, 2006.

Smalley, G. "78. Zardoz (1974)." 366weirdmovies.com. February 9, 2011. Web. Accessed 4 May 2015.

Spoto, Donald. *Camerado: Hollywood and the American Man*. New York: Signet, 1978.

Stacey, Jackie. *Star Gazing: Hollywood Cinema and Female Spectatorship*. London: Routledge, 1994.

Telotte, J. P., "Beyond All Reason: The Nature of the Cult." *The Cult Film Experience: Beyond All Reason.* Ed. J. P. Telotte. Austin: U of Texas P, 1991. 5–17.

—. *Replications: A Robotic History of the Science Fiction Film.* Urbana and Chicago: U of Illinois P, 1995.

Thomson, David. *The New Biographical Dictionary of Film.* 4th ed. New York: Knopf, 2002.

Winder, Simon. *The Man Who Saved Britain.* New York: Farrar, Straus, 2006.

Young, Terence. "MI6 Commentary." *Dr. No.* DVD. 20th Century Fox, 1974.

Yule, Andrew. *Sean Connery from 007 to Hollywood Icon.* New York: Donald Fine, 1992.

"Zardoz." Sean Connery. Ed. Mario Sesti, Milan: Electa, 2006. 142.

Zinsser, William K. "The James Bond Cult: Girls, Guns and Gadgets," *Saturday Evening Post,* July 17, 1965: 76–81.

Zucker, Carole. *Figures of Light: Actors and Directors Illuminate the Art of Film Acting.* New York and London: Plenum, 1995.

5. The Cult Film as Affective Technology: Anime and Oshii Mamoru's *Innocence*

Sharalyn Orbaugh

Oshii Mamoru's animated *Ghost in the Shell 2: Innocence* (2004, hereafter *Innocence*) is indisputably an sf film, but does it constitute a cult film as well? Is it a cult film for all audiences, or only those outside Japan, fascinated by the world of anime? Perhaps we might better ask: can an animated film for adults, created within Japan for a Japanese audience, be considered anything *but* cult when it circulates in a non-Japanese context?[1] This essay will explore these questions en route to a consideration of the connections between the "cult" elements of the film and the science fiction-esque issues that Oshii explores throughout his oeuvre. By using *Innocence* as a case study, I want to argue that, for Oshii, film is a kind of performed philosophical speculation, and many of the same elements that allow us to define his work as "cult" also function to highlight and enact his theories regarding technobiopolitics—theories typically linked to sf. To define *Innocence* as "cult" here is not a secondary designation; rather, "cult" is a fundamental element in producing the meanings of this sf film.

Oshii Mamoru is not a director of animated film, but rather a director of anime, with all of the technical and stylistic differences that designation implies. In an interview with Ueno Toshiya significantly titled *"Anime* begins from *zure* (disjuncture): on the border between 2D and 3D," Oshii links the concept of *zure*—disjuncture, divergence—with his beliefs about what anime is, and especially what it can do that other cinematic forms cannot. The distinctive mixing of 2D and 3D animation styles in one film is only the most obvious of the various *zure*s Oshii exploits to thematize his post-anthropocentric, anti-humanist philosophy.

This examination will begin with some arguments for designating *Innocence* as a cult film, at least as it circulates outside Japan, from both a phenomenological point of view, concentrating on its reception, and an ontological one, identifying the cult elements of its production—visual, narrative, and technical.[2] Then we shall turn to a discussion of the ways that cult functions in this film beyond a simple genre designation. Like sf, cult here is what I call an "affective technology" that helps evoke particular intellectual and emotional engagements. Through the concept of *zure*, which he identifies as a central characteristic of his anime, Oshii mobilizes the affective potentials of sf and cult—the ways both encourage multivalent, intellectually engaged responses—to enact experiments in posthumanity through visual narrative.

Is *Innocence* a Cult Film?

This essay is not the place for an extended analysis of the reception of *Innocence* or Japanese anime in general.[3] But a quick examination of the ways the film was consumed as it traveled to and within North American and European cinema networks, as well as the responses to it outside Japan, supports the argument that *Innocence* fits a phenomenological definition of the cult.

When considering the reception of *Innocence* outside Japan, we should note several structural phenomena—unrelated to the specific contents of the film—that contributed to its cult reception. For one, any foreign-language film may be more likely to attract a cult following because of the difficulty of obtaining it and the attention that is required to read subtitles and decode unfamiliar cultural clues. Moreover, the use of animation in films *for adults* (which is rare in the English-speaking world and Western Europe) together with the particular visual codes of anime (which must be learned to be understood) make for a viewing experience that may be more likely to inspire extreme responses, whether negative or positive. The non-referentiality of animation as opposed to live-action film strikes some neophyte viewers negatively, as inappropriate to serious topics, and strikes others positively as a useful media characteristic for exploring not-yet realized ontological possibilities, such as cyborgs with full-body prostheses or self-aware androids.[4] In interviews, North American fans of anime have noted exactly those qualities as attractions, implicitly referencing the (sub)cultural capital accompanying membership in such an exotic and intellectually demanding fandom.[5] When these characteristics come together in one work—that is, an animated, hard sf film for adults, in Japanese, created by an auteur director such as Oshii—a film such as *Innocence* is primed to be received as a cult film when seen outside Japan.

The circulation channels of Japanese anime in the English-speaking world and Western Europe are also non-mainstream: rarely are anime films widely released in mainstream theaters; instead, fans often download Japanese materials and provide their own subtitles or dubs before the film is available in English or other language formats.[6] Japanese anime films are screened by anime clubs on college campuses (where favorite, often-screened films generate concerted audience participation and cosplay, à la *Rocky Horror Picture Show*) and occasionally in art house theaters. It is more often word of mouth, via websites and fan networks, not the advertising budget, that leads to the success of anime outside Japan. The editors of *Cineaste* have posed the question of whether "the search for the unknown, obscure object of filmgoing desire that marked the cult adventure [of long ago]" is still conceivable in the context of a voracious and standardizing marketplace, but I would suggest that, for many North Americans, especially young people, that obscure object of cult desire is readily found in anime.[7]

Ernest Mathijs has remarked that "A film is not born a cult film … [i]t becomes one by accident" ("Cult Film"), but in the case of a *sequel* to a film that became cult by accident, the birthing process may include some intentional mobilization of elements that scholars have identified as cult-related: the creation of complex, internally coherent alternative worlds; the use of pastiche and intertextuality, requiring high cultural competence; the inclusion of hard-to-decipher puzzles or narrative twists; self-referentiality, drawing attention to the work's constructedness; challenges to the linear progression of time or narrative; and genre mixing.[8] *Innocence*, as the long-awaited sequel to the undeniably (but accidentally) cult sf film *Kôkaku kidôtai* (*Ghost in the Shell*, 1995), would mobilize a number of such elements in its production, thereby intentionally enhancing the likelihood of its reception as a cult work.

In order to understand how these cult elements work in *Innocence*, it is necessary to know a few things about *Ghost in the Shell*. Oshii Mamoru directed numerous episodes of animated TV series, three live-action, and nine anime films before achieving international recognition for his sf thriller, *Ghost in the Shell* (hereafter *GiTS*).[9] *GiTS* played in Japanese theaters for only four weeks after its release, but was a surprise hit in art house theaters in the United States. The buzz surrounding the film led to large US video sales as well, with *GiTS* reaching the #1 position on *Billboard* magazine's video sales chart in 1996 (Schilling 237). But it is not simply the film's sleeper quality that supports its designation as a cult work. Critics and fans remarked on the film's remarkably detailed and distinctive animation style, and its dense, penetrating, and unsentimental portrayal of the ontology of the cyborg—characteristics that resonate with Matt Hills's comment that cult films use "SFX to create narrative worlds or moments of awe in a particular manner," or create moments of "ontological shock."[10]

The unusual combination of philosophical density and sophisticated animation that characterized *GiTS* inspired a small avalanche of scholarly analysis and critical responses on the part of Japanese studies scholars outside Japan.[11] *GiTS* was also a hot topic among what Hills calls fan-academics or fan-scholars (2)—fans without academic positions who use academic theorizing in their writing about favored texts—leading to the publication of at least two books in English from mainstream US publishers on Oshii Mamoru that were fan-authored.[12] And it was not just Japanese studies geeks and college-aged anime fans who were inspired by Oshii's film: when the Wachowski brothers made *The Matrix* they acknowledged the influence of *GiTS*.[13] In other words, it was a film that inspired an intense and engaged response on the part of a numerically small but significant group of viewers—thus a cult film.

The surprising success of *GiTS outside* Japan had a salutary influence on Oshii's reputation as an auteur director *within* Japan, leading to more projects and bigger budgets. When he wrote and directed *Innocence*, released nine years after *GiTS*, he had near *carte blanche* for his animation budget and a high level of creative control (Ueno and Oshii 64). As a sequel, *Innocence* flaunts its cult appeal through elements both extrinsic to the film (metatextual), such as an exhibition of its ravishing animated cityscapes by the Mori Urban Institute for the Future in Tokyo, and intrinsic (textual). Here I shall concentrate on the latter.

Among the elements within the film that contributed to its reception as a cult work is its tight collage of verbal and visual quotations from a staggering range of sources: text quotations come from Descartes, Buddhist sutras, Confucius, proto-sf novels *L'Ève future* (1886) and *Locus Solus* (1914), the Bible, Milton, Richard Dawkins, Gogol, classical Japanese texts such as *Heike monogatari*, and many others (and the use of dense quotation is itself a quotation of Jean-Luc Godard); visually, the film references the art of Hans Bellmer, *Blade Runner*, *The Matrix*, and Oshii's own previous sf films.[14] Even more so than *GiTS*, *Innocence* is an "intellectual" cult film, aimed at the most engaged and responsive fans of his previous work. But Oshii does not pander to any particular group of fans; his film challenges viewers of any nationality, cultural background, or level of education because of the obscurity and philosophical difficulty of the texts quoted. No single viewer would probably have enough cultural competence to identify all of the elements of the pastiche that constitute the script, although viewers with internet savvy could be capable of tracking down the many visual and verbal quotations. The cultural capital for fans—working alone or together on discussion sites—who manage to read the semiotics of the film and use its complex intertextual references to untangle the plot, therefore, is correspondingly high.

Cult and SF as Affective Technologies

The following section analyzes cult elements intrinsic to the film, and argues that the characteristics that make the film cult are also fundamental to Oshii's sf-inflected theorizing about the nature of human and posthuman evolution. To frame this discussion, we might consider both cult and sf as affective technologies, and as fundamentally tied to what and how the film means. A relatively uncommon term, "affective technology" most commonly refers to a form of technology that can mimic or enhance human affect, such as mobile phones or computers, used to enhance the competence of people with autism. But I want to suggest that we see the "technology" part of the term as designating a *techne*—a craft, an art, a skill, a way of doing or making something—that induces a particular *affective* response or constellation of responses. Film and TV are both clearly affective technologies, but so are less obviously "technological" forms/devices/genres such as the novel or oil painting. As each of these new forms of expression, new *technes*, came into existence, they created the potential for expressing new kinds of affect, or new ways of expressing and understanding already-familiar affects. At the same time, new technologies of expression are experienced—physically and sensorily—in ways that are affective. New affective technologies arise from the specific epistemological and ontological milieu of a time and place, while also helping to create and constitute the affective elements of that milieu.[15]

a. Searching for the truth of "human" relationships in *Innocence* (2004).

b. *Innocence* (2004): Togusa encounters the ball-jointed gynoids.

An example may help clarify this idea. The rise of mechanical printing technology resulted in the wide availability of relatively inexpensive books, followed closely by the rise of the novel as a literary form— this constellation of new *techne*s: printing, book, novel—allowed for increasing numbers of people to consume imaginative fiction in the privacy of their own homes. The subject matter of the novel encouraged subjective identification with the characters (evoking affects such as intimacy or sympathy), and the technology of the book allowed private consumption (as opposed to earlier narrative forms that were more often consumed in groups), which also produced affects such as intimacy or empathetic identification, as well as singularity and uniqueness. Therefore the modern conception of selfhood—of the autonomous, unique, individual subject in a society made up of similar individual subjects—both helped lead to the development of the affective technology of the novel by inspiring writers to create a new narrative form, and was underscored and enhanced by the novel's particular material and genre characteristics. The case of film as an affective technology is perhaps even more striking, given film's ability to capture and transmit embodied experience in previously unknown ways—*showing* not only light but also movement—and further in the fully embodied affective responses it generated, reportedly causing early audiences to recoil when waves or locomotives seemed to come toward them.[16]

Each affective technology highlights or enables the production of specific kinds of affect. The cult film, as a particular kind of film, is itself a type of affective technology and evokes particular affects: weirdness, fascination, engagement, intellectual stimulation, and the uncanny, among others. These affects bear a familial resemblance to those evoked by sf narratives, especially in film: wonder, the sense of seeing behind a façade of illusion to the truth, and disconnection from mundane reality. Setting out to make an sf film is a straightforward proposition, but the same cannot be said for making a cult film, since many films *become* cult by accident. But as we have noted, some scholars argue that cult film can also in some ways be intentionally "made."[17] So we will now turn to the ways in which Oshii used *zure* in *Innocence*, among other operational modes, to marshal not only the affective technologies of sf but also the potential of cult.

The Plot and its Affects

The film opens with an epigraph, taken from the 1886 proto-sf novel *L'Ève future*: "If it is true that our gods and our hopes are no longer anything but scientific, is there any reason why our love should not also be so?"[18] Oshii chose this epigraph for *Innocence* because both the nineteenth-century French novel and the twenty-first-century Japanese film take as their central problematic the connections and disjunctions between emotion and science. More specifically, both pose the question: is love possible only for human beings, or are emotions and affect also possible in artificial beings?[19]

Set in the near future, the plot of *Innocence* takes the form of a detective story, involving the murder of a number of prominent Japanese men by their sex-toy gynoids. The protagonist is Division Nine security officer Batou, a cyborg whose body is almost entirely artificial. Batou and his human (non-cyborg) partner Togusa pursue the mystery of how a particular model of sex-toy gynoid, called Hadaly, has somehow acquired the ability to override the ethical programming common to all robots and become capable of both murder and suicide. The crucial relationship of the film, however, is between Batou and his mostly absent former partner Kusanagi, now reduced (elevated?) to existence as a sentient data stream on the Net (as in *GiTS*). As Batou works to solve the crimes, he constantly thinks of Kusanagi, and Oshii's film asks us to consider the nature of a posthuman emotion: when a masculine-shaped cyborg with an artificial body he does not even own, whose memories and sense of self may have been implanted by the corporation that manufactured him, loves a being that was once a feminine-shaped cyborg like himself but is now a disembodied cybernetic being, who/what can we say is in love with who/what? The subject and object are obscure; only the predicate—the affect, the love—remains.

As I have argued elsewhere, one of the main points of *Innocence* is to explore the ramifications of humanity's march into the state of posthumanity, addressing some of the fundamental questions arising from the ontological changes we shall face (Orbaugh 2008). From the wide range of animate/d beings featured in the film—from the completely organic to the completely mechanical—and the explicit intertextual references—*L'Ève future*, *Locus Solus*, and Oshii's own *Ghost in the Shell*—to the implicit intertextual references—*Blade Runner*, E. T. A. Hoffmann's "The Sandman," the *Matrix* films—*Innocence* makes clear its concern with ontology, evolution, the significance (or lack thereof) of sex/gender/sexuality, and so on—all concerns familiar to any sf fan interested in the technobiopolitics of the posthuman. Here, though, cult, sf, and animation all work together as related affective technologies to highlight key issues of posthuman ontology.

One of the most prominent cult elements of *Innocence* is its mixing of cinematic genres: it draws heavily on cyberpunk, the police procedural, early twentieth-century detective stories, the buddy film, horror, the love story, Asia Extreme, and 1940s noir.[20] This sort of mixing is common to many cult films, prompting both singular (based on genre stereotypes) and multiple interpretative responses. Another cult characteristic that inspires both singular and multiple interpretations is the film's pastiche of quotations. To the extent that the quotations are well known and/or deeply embedded in particular philosophical or religious traditions, they evoke specific, already-set resonances and meanings (in those familiar with the traditions). Yet, at the same time, the overwhelming number of the quotations, from many different languages, countries, cultures, and time periods, leads toward an intellectual and affective response that is multiple, manifold—with viewers required to actively (though possibly unconsciously) create a patchwork-like whole from the disjointed pastiche. And these quotations and references are embedded in gorgeously detailed visuals, which further invites a serious response to the film. In one scene, for example, Batou and Togusa visit a crime lab where a pathologist named Haraway is investigating Hadaly gynoids that have murdered their owners and then committed suicide.[21] The depiction of the lab is striking in its complexity and visual surprises. While drinking in the visuals, the viewer listens to a complex logical deconstruction by Haraway of the uniqueness of human parenthood. She argues that children are ontologically the same as dolls, and that child-rearing is therefore identical to the "fabricated" affective relationship a child develops with a doll. Batou agrees, adding an anecdote about

Descartes's love for his inanimate "daughter" Francine. Their contention that there is no significant difference between animate and inanimate beings shocks Togusa.

In this scene, we see the commonplace—modern, humanist—point of view expressed by (the mostly human) Togusa, while Haraway and (the almost entirely cyborg) Batou express more radical, anti-humanist, non-anthropocentric ideas about continuities between life and non-life, between organic humans and inorganic human-shaped creatures. After listening to Haraway express great sympathy for the frustrated and violent reactions of robots who have been discarded in favor of a newer model, it comes as little surprise to the viewer when, as Batou and Togusa are leaving at the end of this scene, Haraway detaches the top half of her face in order to plug a view-screen into the complex machinery that inhabits her otherwise human-looking skull.

There are several such scenes in *Innocence*, wherein a philosophical discussion, or a series of references and quotations is matched with striking visuals. In fact, the use of quotations forms such a tight but eclectic web that it draws attention to itself, leading us to another aspect of the cult's particular affective technology: self-referentiality. The insistent self-referentiality of *Innocence* constitutes a refusal to let the viewer sink entirely into the experience of the film; instead, it repeatedly marks its own constructedness and artificiality. This unrelenting questioning of the authentic or the genuine is both a common characteristic of the cult's affective work and one of the main themes of this film, as it is of sf itself.

All of the elements of the film enumerated here, which on one level help to encourage its reception as a cult film, involve what in Japanese is called a *zure* (slippage, gap, divergence, disjuncture). Instead of an emphasis on integration, wholeness, and autonomy—which accord with modernist views of human subjectivity and the human place in the cosmos—on many levels, the film places its emphasis on duplication or multiplicity, a breaking down of the conceptual boundaries with which we are comfortable, thereby producing a very postmodern, posthuman point of view.

Animation/Anime as Affective Technology

But *zure* also occurs at a more fundamental, technological level. In the 2004 interview cited above, Oshii explains why he decided to use the particular animation style that makes *Innocence* so visually striking. Even though he was familiar with ultra-3D CGI animation (as in *Shrek* or *Final Fantasy*, both from 2001), and had a budget sufficient for any animation technology, he chose to combine a flat, 2D, manga-esque (or Japanimation-esque) depiction of the characters with richly detailed 3D animation of the backgrounds. Oshii mobilizes the potential of this particular style of animation as another affective technology, as a way of thematizing the film's posthuman point of view. For this combinatorial style draws attention to the materiality of the form—a self-referential impulse. Instead of allowing the viewer to sink comfortably and unthinkingly into a plausibly "realistic" visual world, the viewing mind remains perpetually irritated and thus engaged. This approach also endows the inanimate world with depth (connoting psychological depth, authenticity), even as the film's animate beings are portrayed as flat and "unreal." The fact that the animated creatures differ visually from the world they inhabit is a conceptual *zure* that viewers must resolve for themselves (or fail to resolve).

Digital animation (or the combination of CGI and live action) goes beyond live-action cinema in terms of its "reality effect"; it is almost hyper-real. This effect is in contrast to cel animation, and in even greater contrast to the low-budget stylistic elements characteristic of much "Japanimation," as early TV anime was known.[22] The "reality effect" characteristic of digital animation is about depth (including, again, psychological depth), integration, authenticity (even if only apparent), and wholeness. Anime, in contrast, is about flatness, lack of weight, lack of wholeness, and lack of integration: a denial of the "reality effect." When Oshii juxtaposes the two different affective technologies—2D animation (which looks like old-fashioned anime) and 3D digital animation—the affective disjunctures between them are highlighted. The "human" protagonists are shown as fragmented, depthless, inauthentic, nothing more than nodes of a vast multidimensional web, whereas the spaces they move through are architecturally sound, deep, detailed, rounded, integrated. What the film thereby underscores is the loss of modernist ideas of human authenticity, autonomy, and individuality. But Oshii does not present this loss as a tragic future that must be forestalled, or even something necessarily new; he avoids sentimentalism or nostalgia. In his cinematic vision of the posthuman future, emotion and affect remain, but not in the modern forms we are familiar with. Even the warm final scene, which features the nearly-entirely-human Togusa holding his daughter against the background of his cozy-looking suburban house, is undercut by the presence of the doll in his daughter's arms, whose significance as interchangeable with a "human" child has been made clear throughout the film. The same scene shows the cyborg Batou, with his excessively unnatural looking eye-prosthetics, holding what seems like a natural, warm-bodied creature: his beloved dog. The contrast between the "natural" dog and the "unnatural" cyborg is undercut by our knowledge that the dog has been artificially produced through cloning, and by the linking of Batou and the dog to the Net-like cityscape behind them. Its twinkling nodes of light—inconsistent, insubstantial, but still interconnected—signify Oshii's view of the nature of posthuman subjectivity.[23]

Conclusion

As that final scene underscores, this film poses and deconstructs a crucial question: what is it that loves what? In exploring whether love is possible only for humans and other organic beings, or also possible with and among artificial entities, the film poses and deconstructs further questions: what counts as life, and where do we draw the line between animate and inanimate? In many ways, this film is at its most basic level about animation itself—the act of making the lifeless come alive. Throughout the film we see various kinds of inert matter in various shapes "come alive": a mechanical automaton (*karakuri ningyô*) from Japan's past that mimics human movement and behavior (serving tea); gigantic mechanical animals in a parade, moving their heads and bodies as the parade snakes through the city; and, most obviously, the gynoid dolls that appear throughout the film. In every case, the animated figures are visually and emotionally captivating; but in no case is their movement or animation meant to replicate that of humans. In fact, the exaggerated ball-joint construction of the gynoids accentuates this difference. These figures look not alive, but *animated*.

The script further underscores this effect by repeatedly emphasizing through quotation and dialogue among the characters that the boundary between the live, organic human and the many non-living, artificial entities we encounter is not nearly as fixed and impermeable as we commonly believe. Oshii's script does not underplay the *distinctions* among various entities—at one point a little girl explicitly states that she does not want to become a doll and the gynoid dolls state, through Kusanagi, that they do not want to become human—but neither does it support the conceptual boundaries that humans use to divide themselves from animals and machines.

Ernest Mathijs has suggested that "the most important social function of cult cinema is that it creates an understanding for ambiguity, multitudes, and incompleteness" ("Cult Film"). Creating an understanding for ontological ambiguity, through contrasting visual dimensions and multiple simultaneous interpretive possibilities, leaving the viewer with no single conclusive message—this is precisely the point of Oshii's futuristic cinematic vision, as it is of so many other sf films. By harnessing the potential of cult, sf, and animation as affective technologies, his film makes this point insistently and at every level.

Notes

1 This question was posed by Nathen Clerici in an unpublished research paper. I gratefully acknowledge Dr. Clerici's help in locating many of the sources used in this project.

2 I draw the distinction between phenomenological and ontological approaches to cult film from Mathijs and Mendik, 15–24.

3 The term anime refers to Japanese animated narratives regardless of medium: film, video, or TV. Here I use it to designate animated feature-length films unless otherwise specified.

4 See Napier (2007), 172–73.

5 See Napier (2001), 242; Napier (2007), 134–38; Chin, 218.

6 For more on fan subs and dubs, see Gonzalez, 260–77; Napier (2007), 134–38; Eng, 159–61.

7 From the introductory remarks of "Cult Film, a Critical Symposium" on the *Cinéaste* website (hereafter "Cult Film"). For more on anime as cult in the US, see Eng, *passim*.

8 This list of cult characteristics is drawn from Wilcox, 36–39 and Espenson, 45–52; and from the contributions of Hills, Mathijs, Sexton, and Weinstock to "Cult Film."

9 *GiTS* and *Innocence*, like most of Oshii's previous films, were based on existing manga or TV anime series, which means that each instantly referenced an existing and well-developed fantasy universe.

10 See Hills's "Cult Film." Typical reviews for *GiTS* can be found on the Rotten Tomatoes or imdb websites.

11 See, for example, Bolton, Orbaugh (2002/2007), Silvio, Wong, or Napier (2001), 104–16.

12 These are Ruh (2004) and Cavallero (2006).

13 Ruh, 2, cites the "Chat with the Wachowski Brothers," *Official Matrix Website*, November 6, 1999.

14 For a list of many of the textual and visual quotations and their sources, see Brown, 26–29.

15 My thanks to Yukio Lippit for explaining how oil painting functioned as a new *techne* in modernizing Japan.

16 Kata Kôji describes this kind of reaction on the part of early Japanese film audiences, 30. The necessity to go to a special location and view a film with a group of strangers in a darkened room is another important aspect of film as an affective technology, evoking particular kinds of emotional/cognitive responses.

17 Ernest Mathijs and Jamie Sexton both list qualities that are intrinsic

to cult films, implying that they could be intentionally marshaled by a filmmaker to encourage a cult response ("Cult Film"), and Rhonda Wilcox and Jane Espenson explicitly list such formulas for creating a cult TV series.

[18] My translation of the Japanese epigraph. *L'Ève future* by Jean Marie Mathias Philippe Auguste, comte de Villiers de L'Isle-Adam (1838–89) is available in two English translations: as *Eve of the Future Eden*, by Marilyn Gaddis Rose (Lawrence: Coronado Press, 1981) and as *Tomorrow's Eve*, by Robert Martin Adams (Urbana: U of Illinois P, 1982). (It has also been translated twice into Japanese.)

[19] For detailed analyses of the film's answer to this question, see Orbaugh (2008) and Brown (2010).

[20] Asia Extreme is a cult subgenre categorizing films from East Asia characterized by over-the-top violence and/or sex, typified by the work of directors such as Takashi Miike.

[21] This is an explicit reference to cyborg theorist Donna Haraway.

[22] For more on this see Lamarre (2002), 184–85.

[23] Oshii has written and spoken in interviews at length about his vision of the nature of posthumanity. See Oshii (2004) and Orbaugh (2008).

Works Cited

Bolton, Christopher. "From Wooden Cyborgs to Celluloid Souls: Mechanical Bodies in Anime and Japanese Puppet Theater." *positions* 10.3 (2002): 729–71.

Brown, Steven. *Tokyo Cyberpunk*. New York: Palgrave Macmillan, 2010.

Cavallero, Dani. *Cinema of Oshii Mamoru: Fantasy, Technology, and Politics*. Jefferson: McFarland, 2006.

Chin, Bertha. "Beyond Kung-Fu and Violence: Locating East Asian Cinema Fandom." *Fandom: Identities and Communities in a Mediated World*. Ed. Jonathan Gray, Cornel Sandvoss, and C. Lee Harrington. New York: NYU Press, 2007. 210–19.

Church, David, Matt Hills, Ernest Mathijs, et al. "Cult Film, a Critical Symposium." *Cineaste*. Web. Accessed 20 February 2013.

Clerici, Nathen. "Japanese Film Crossing Borders: Marginality, Genre Appeal, Cult." Unpublished paper. University of British Columbia, 2011.

Eng, Lawrence. "Anime and Manga Fandom as Networked Culture." *Fandom Unbound: Otaku Culture in a Connected World*. Ed. Mizuko Ito, Daisuke Okabe, and Izumi Tsuji. New Haven: Yale UP, 2012. 158–78.

Espenson, Jane. "Playing Hard to 'Get'—How to Write Cult TV." *The Cult TV Book: From* Star Trek *to* Dexter, *New Approaches to TV Outside the Box*. Ed. Stacey Abbott. New York: Soft Skull Press, 2010. 45–54.

Gonzalez, Luis Perez. "Fansubbing Anime: Insights into the 'Butterfly Effect' of Globalisation on Audiovisual Translation." *Perspectives: Studies in Translatology* 14.4 (2006): 260–77.

Hills, Matt. *Fan Cultures*. London: Routledge, 2002.

Kata Kôji. "Shikaku no bunkaron: etoki kara gekiga made" ("A cultural study of vision: From etoki to gekiga"). *Etoku*. Ed. Nagai Hiroo and Ozawa Shôichi. Tokyo: Hakusuisha, 1982. 5–32.

Lamarre, Thomas. "Introduction: Between Cinema and Anime." *Japan Forum* 14.2 (2002): 183–89.

Mathijs, Ernest, and Xavier Mendik. "The Concepts of Cult." *The Cult Film Reader*. New York: McGraw-Hill, 2008. 15–24.

Napier, Susan. *Anime from Akira to The Princess Mononoke: Experiencing Contemporary Japanese Animation*. New York: Palgrave Macmillan, 2001.

—. *From Impressionism to Anime: Japan as Fantasy and Fan Cult in the Mind of the West*. New York: Palgrave Macmillan, 2007.

Orbaugh, Sharalyn. "Emotional Infectivity: The Japanese Cyborg and the Limits of the Human." *Mechademia* 3. Minneapolis: U of Minnesota P, 2008. 150–72.

—. "Sex and the Single Cyborg: Japanese Pop Culture Experiments in Subjectivity." *Robot Ghosts and Wired Dreams: Japanese Science Fiction from Origins to Anime*. Ed. Christopher Bolton, Istvan Csicsery-Ronay, and Takayuki Tatsumi. Minneapolis: U of Minnesota P, 2007. 172–92.

Oshii Mamoru. "Shintai to kioku no higan ni" ("On the equinox between body and memory"). *Oshii Mamoru ron: Memento Mori* (*Essays on Oshii Mamoru: Memento Mori*). Ed. Nihon Terebi. Tokyo: Nihon terebi hôsô kabushikigaisha, 2004. 20–45.

Ruh, Brian. *Stray Dog of Anime: The Films of Oshii Mamoru*. New York: Palgrave Macmillan, 2004.

Schilling, Mark. *Contemporary Japanese Film*. New York: Weatherhill, 1999.

Silvio, Carl. "Refiguring the Radical Cyborg in Mamoru Oshii's *Ghost in the Shell*." *Science Fiction Studies* 26.1 (1999): 54–72.

Ueno, Toshiya, and Ôshii Mamoru. "Anime w azure kara hajimaru: 2D to 3D no hazama de" ("Anime begins from disjuncture: at the border between 2D and 3D"). *Yûriika* (*Eureka*) 36.4 (2004): 58–74.

Wilcox, Rhonda V. "The Aesthetics of Cult Television." *The Cult TV Book: From* Star Trek *to* Dexter, *New Approaches to TV Outside the Box*. Ed. Stacey Abbott. New York: Soft Skull Press, 2010. 31–40.

Wong, Kin Yuen. "On the Edge of Spaces: *Blade Runner, Ghost in the Shell*, and Hong Kong's Cityscape." *Science Fiction Studies* 27.1 (2000): 1–21.

6. Whedon, Browncoats, and the Big Damn Narrative: The Unified Meta-Myth of *Firefly* and *Serenity*

Rhonda V. Wilcox

> Most of what now passes with us for religion and philosophy will be replaced by poetry.
> —Matthew Arnold, "The Study of Poetry" (1248)

> It's not just about what you want to say, it's about inviting them into a world, and the way in which you guys have inhabited this world, this universe ... made you guys part of it, part of the story. You are living *in Firefly*. When I see you guys, I don't think the show's off the air—I don't think there's a show—I think that's what the world is like.
> —Joss Whedon, *Firefly: Browncoats Unite*

The story of *Firefly*'s death and rebirth is fairly well known; indeed, for some, the story has gained the status of myth, a myth that they are "living in." The television series was created by Joss Whedon, famous for the success of *Buffy the Vampire Slayer* (1997–2003), which ran for seven years, and the spin-off *Angel* (1999–2004), which ran for five. The Fox network ran *Firefly* for just three months: September 20, 2002 to December 20, 2002. Yet the fans and the series' makers refused to let it die. Organized expressions of fan interest, such as postcard campaigns and paid advertisements, encouraged the production of a DVD, which the fans carried to first place in sales. (As of this writing, the DVD is still a top seller, number eight in science fiction and number 31 in action-adventure on Amazon.) This success, and the ongoing determination of the makers and the fans (who call themselves "Browncoats," after the resistance fighters in the series), helped propel the production of the 2005 film *Serenity*, which continues the story of the *Firefly* universe. While the film did not make enough money to prompt a sequel, the cult of *Firefly/Serenity* still thrives, as the Whedon epigraph above attests, and the Matthew Arnold comment, if we replace the word "poetry" with "art," may help explain some of the reasons for its continuing life. For years, those who have discussed cult films and television have noted both the connection of the term "cult" to religion and the problems in making such a connection. But Arnold's words tell us how important art can be in our lives—and the discourse of Browncoats suggests they agree. The narrative of this relationship starts with the myth of the series and moves to the meta-myth created around it by and about the fans.

"Cult" and "science fiction" are both charged and complex terms, "religion" even more so. While some might consider the terms sf and religion to be opposed,[1] both in some way deal with the Other; both make us confront something beyond that moves into our reality. Either may make us struggle with apocalyptic possibilities. Some film- or television-based cults rejoice in the playfulness of unreality; others are not so ludic. I would suggest that many Browncoats, like believing members of a religion, attempt to bring beliefs related to *Firefly/Serenity* into the mundane world. After all, while sf narratives commonly present a world that is not, it may yet be.

To enable their actions, Browncoats invest in narrative—the narrative of their own actions as well as the narrative of the fictional TV series and film. From Diana Taylor's *The Archive and the Repertoire* to Lakoff and Johnson's studies of metaphor, scholars have argued that we construct our world (or worlds) through narrative, that the stories we tell ourselves direct our reality. Presumably, each cult creates its own narrative, builds its own origin story. I would argue that the *Firefly* narrative comes in part from some of the same impulses that find release in religion. More specifically, it partakes of the views of what might be termed *prophetic* religion—or, more precisely, the idea of the prophet, the person who rails against social injustice or systemic moral wrong and thinks the world needs to be changed. In the Browncoats' meta-myth, the avowedly atheist Whedon is the prophet (and his various avatars—actors/fans and other Browncoats—share that prophetic message). Such a person emphatically resists the status quo. And this identification of systemic wrong and an implicit call for resistance to it is, of course, part of one sf tradition.

In the case of *Firefly/Serenity*, Browncoats do not simply admire the representation of such resistance within the original fiction of the television series or subsequent film, but break through the fictional walls to a world beyond: they invest belief in their own practice of resistance, as well belief in resistance by the various creators of the original fiction. Furthermore, as is often the case with religions, the myth changes. In the beginning, when Browncoats and their prophet helped resurrect *Firefly*, the goal was to change the world by changing the corporate media model. This sort of systemic change would indeed have been almost science fictional in its gravitational shift. When systemic change did not happen, the goal transmuted to private charity: a way of changing the world, yes; a form of resistance to darkness, indeed; but a much more modest one, incorporated within the current world. The Browncoats' recent social and charitable actions, discussed below, extend the idea of chosen family (an important theme throughout Whedon's work) or, as some religions call it, "the beloved community." It is a kind of resistance that is easier to maintain in a world that is systemically unchanged. Still, Browncoats bring this narrative into reality. As Whedon says, in their communities, "that's what the world is like" (*Firefly: Browncoats Unite*).

It is important, therefore, that we (I consider myself a Browncoat[2]) can tell ourselves the tale of a unified reality within and surrounding *Firefly/Serenity*. The resistance is not just fictional, for as Whedon says, Browncoats "inhabit this world." The idea of resistance just begins with the fictional narrative and series characters. It continues with the real-life narrative of the series' cancellation and fans' resistance, while the film's fictional narrative expands it to the metatextual. These narratives are supported by the persona (or should we say the character?) of the creator Joss Whedon; the persona (or character) of lead actor Nathan Fillion; and the communal personae (or character) of the fans—including other cast and crew members, as well as the broader fan community. The narratives (sf and real-world) and the people within and without the narratives all reiterate ideas of independence, difference, and resistance—the sense of being "Other" that is so typically applied to cult audiences in general and sf fans in particular. But we also see reiterated the idea of resistance constructed as the creation of family or community—the "ethic of care," as Tanya R. Cochran terms it ("Browncoats" 244). Beyond the series' life and the movie's run, these defining qualities of the cult persist.

The fictional narrative of *Firefly* begins with war—a fight against crushing, wealthy power. "Earth-That-Was" has used up all its resources, so in the succeeding centuries humanity has moved to an area of space with planets fit for terraforming. The farther-out of these planets have farms, ranches, cattle, and horses; the inner or "core" planets have futuristic architecture, science, and medicine; and characters move from one planet to another by spaceship. Whedon says that when he conceived the series he was reading *The Killer Angels*, based on the Civil War and focused on the losers—although he emphasizes that his losers never fought for slavery (Whedon 8). Malcolm "Mal" Reynolds (Nathan Fillion) and Zoe Alleyne (Gina Torres) are among the Independents or

Browncoats fighting against the Alliance, the wealthier inner planets attempting to exert governmental control over more recently settled, more frontier-like planets on the rim—a fight the Alliance terms "Unification." In the opening scenes, we see Mal and Zoe in battle. Despite the long odds in the Battle of Serenity Valley, Mal kisses his cross and assures the others that they will succeed—their "angels" will rescue them. But we see the shock in his face when Zoe reports that their air support is withdrawing, leaving them to the Alliance, and Mal watches his angels fly away. Six years later he is the captain of a small, scruffy transport vessel named *Serenity* with Zoe as his second-in-command. In a world controlled by those he fought, Mal sometimes breaks the law, smuggling or stealing to get by, but there are some lines he will not cross. In "The Train Job" (the first episode aired), we see Mal and Zoe return stolen cargo once they discover that it is desperately needed medicine—even though the choice means making a dangerous enemy of the gangster who gave them the job. Fox had required Whedon and co-producer Tim Minear to write this episode over the course of one weekend to replace their original pilot with more action-adventure; but even in such circumstances, they made sure to pair physical action with moral action.

Nine morally and psychologically varied people live on *Serenity*. The ship's kindly pilot, Hoban "Wash" Washburne (Alan Tudyk), is married to Zoe; their mechanic, the sweet-natured Kaylee Frye (Jewel Staite) is clever enough to make do with recycled parts and patch-ups. The notably less clever Jayne Cobb (Adam Baldwin) serves as muscle. Inara Serra, whose career as a highly educated Companion might be compared to the role of a geisha (with more independence), rents one of Serenity's two shuttles. The other regulars include passengers who sign on in the two-hour pilot: Shepherd (or preacher) Derrial Book, and the formerly wealthy young physician Dr. Simon Tamm and his teenage sister River, who is both brilliant and mentally unstable—fugitives because Simon has rescued River from a secret Alliance laboratory which was experimenting on her brain. As more than one person (including Whedon) has said, the mixture of characters echoes the classic Western *Stagecoach* (1939; see Erisman). Furthermore, each character has broken away from or resists the norm in some fashion, whether by breaking the law or simply choosing an unusual path. Simon could have been a wealthy doctor but chose to save his sister, even though it meant becoming a criminal; Inara could have become head of her order (as we learn in the episode "Heart of Gold"), but has departed from the ease of the inner planets; Zoe and Mal have literally fought a war. The story, as Michael Marek argues, is mythic (see also, among others, Wilcox and

Cochran, "'Good Myth'"). Each of the characters has a hidden past, but we learn that each is willing to stand up for his or her values (even the mercenary Jayne)—each is willing to resist the status quo. As Mal makes clear, time and again, those on his crew deserve each other's loyalty. In fourteen episodes, we see them becoming a family. By the time of the last episode in the series chronology, "Objects in Space," even River has earned a place. In this episode, the captain and crew work together with River's guidance to expel an Alliance bounty hunter who has managed to sneak on board the *Serenity*. The last scenes of the regulars show them relaxing together in a ship that has clearly become a home—the home that Browncoats choose metaphorically to occupy.

Since 2002, this narrative has proven to have lasting appeal. The series' post-cancellation success and the often-expressed appreciation of critics and fans are evidence enough. But the Fox network was unable—or unwilling—to perceive the possibilities. Network executives had refused to air the two-hour pilot in which the characters and the world were carefully introduced; instead, they broadcast it last, in December 2002, after the series was cancelled. Scholars from Umberto Eco on have emphasized the importance to the cult text and experience of the fully realized separate world. While *Firefly* certainly fulfills that requirement, it was difficult for Whedon and Minear to convey that world in the substitute one-hour pilot that Fox asked for. I was among many fans who, in watching the episode, wondered if I had somehow managed to miss the pilot. Matthew Pateman argues that Whedon and Minear succeeded in including all the necessary world-building information, but some of it is so densely packed that it is hard to retrieve. Another problem was that the series was scheduled for Friday nights—not considered prime television real estate. The network executives asserted that they hoped for a following like that of *The X-Files*, which started out on Fox Fridays—and this strategy might have worked, had it not been for the fact that Fox had paid a hefty sum to air Major League Baseball playoffs and therefore repeatedly cancelled episodes and disturbed the narrative of *Firefly* (see Pateman for analysis of the Fox/*Firefly* interaction).

Sara Gwenllian-Jones and Roberta E. Pearson have argued that an "understanding and definition of the cult must be predicated on the full circuit of communication, that is, texts, production/distribution, and audiences" (x). Browncoats frequently point to parallels between the problems in *Firefly*'s production/distribution and the internal narrative of the series: specifically, they compare Fox to the wealthy, powerful Alliance with whom the Independents, the Browncoats, are at war—and to whom they lose but keep resisting. When Fox cancelled the series, actor Alan Tudyk said, "We were all fighting this evil empire Alliance on the TV show that Fox immediately became" (*Done the Impossible*). Or, as one fan put it, "The cancellation was sort of our Battle of Serenity" (*Done the Impossible*). Just as the Alliance put down the Independents, Fox killed *Firefly*. In this cultic origins story, in the meta-myth, the conflict is clear.

However, the fans wrote the next part of this cultic narrative. Like many fans of shows cancelled too soon, they resisted, but with more success than perhaps any others except those of the original *Star Trek*. The meta-myth is a story of triumph. They adopted the name Browncoats and worked, online and by snail mail, through advertisements and face-to-face, for the series' resurrection. They supported Whedon's attempts to find a new forum, including selling the show to another network, doing a mini-series, and doing straight-to-DVD work. Their actions encouraged the creation of a DVD of the existing episodes of the series, for which sales were surprisingly high. In less than 22 months, 500,000 copies were sold (Breznican). That a series which had only aired ten of its episodes could be a best seller in DVD form was unprecedented. Fans not only bought copies for themselves but additional ones with which to proselytize to new viewers (successfully, as continuing sales show). The DVD sales figures supported Whedon's quest to find a new outlet for *Firefly* (Breznican), and two years later he began shooting *Serenity* with the entire original cast and many of the crew on board. The parallel between the fans' actions and the narrative of resistance to crushing power by Mal and the crew of the *Serenity* is implicit in that fan name of Browncoats—a similarity often noted by scholars (see, e.g., Abbott, "'Can't Stop'" 237; Cochran, "Browncoats" 243; Telotte, "*Firefly*" 118). In the fan-made documentary *Done the Impossible*, which depicts the journey from series to feature film, Adam Baldwin speaks as host: "'We've done the impossible, and that makes us mighty.' These words, written by Joss Whedon and spoken by his hero Malcolm Reynolds, are about struggles against overwhelming odds. They've become a rallying cry for millions of *Firefly* fans worldwide." And he notes that the phrase "Big Damn Heroes," as the characters termed themselves on a rescue mission ("Safe"), has now been applied to the "Big Damn Movie." That parallel of the fan story to the story within the series supports Whedon's comment to the fans, that *Serenity* is "in an unprecedented sense your movie" ("Joss Whedon Introduction").

Perhaps it is not surprising, then, that within the film's narrative, Whedon chose to incorporate an element of that fan story. J. P. Telotte calls attention to *Serenity*'s foregrounding of media, an invitation to self-consciousness: screens are everywhere, and are both passive and active. A screen in the Maidenhead Bar, for example, triggers (through a commercial for "Fruity Oaty Bars") River's Alliance-embedded violence, and the 17-year-old dancer knocks down dozens of burly bar patrons. Whedon apparently "realized that he might be able to explore the complex media context in which *Firefly*, *Serenity*, and indeed, all of contemporary culture and its popular texts are enmeshed" (Telotte 71). And one specific element of this media environment has escaped the seemingly panoptic Alliance. Off on his own, the character of Mr. Universe (David Krumholz) manages to be in electronic touch with the entire galaxy; he contrasts the signal of truth ("Can't stop the signal," he says) with the "puppet show" of what passes for news/entertainment. Mr. Universe recalls the internet-active fans; and it is only through his self-sacrificing help that Mal and his crew are able to get the truth out in the film's climax. The controlling Alliance has secretly damaged or killed millions of people, and Mal and company must tell about those actions. Just so, Whedon and company get to tell their truth, tell their story, despite the corporate powers arrayed against them. Fans (such as those who created cantstopthesignal.com and cantstopthesignal.co.uk) were well aware of this parallel. The original series showed the band of nine characters resisting the powers that be, and fans were inspired to resist cancellation. This new big-screen narrative had the characters not just winning occasional small battles, but sending a message to the entire Alliance-dominated world—just as fans sent a message to Fox and, they hoped, the Hollywood system. After *Firefly*, their lives had imitated art; but with *Serenity* the art imitated their lives.

a. The cast—and crew—of *Firefly/Serenity* (2002–03 and 2005).

b. *Firefly* (2002–03) cast members and creator (l to r) Alan Tudyk, Nathan Fillion, Joss Whedon, and Summer Glau speak to fans at ComicCon.

The fans have also folded into their meta-myth the creator, whom they see as one of them. While some scholars have expressed concern about Whedon's hagiographic treatment, that term is itself revealing: he does play a special role, as continued sales of the "Joss Whedon Is My Master Now" t-shirt suggest. Fans do typically use his first name, and the fan music group Bedlam Bards sing of "The Man They Call Joss," a parody of *Firefly*'s "The Ballad of Jayne." As Alex Pappademas argues, "Whereas *Star Trek* fans revered Gene Roddenberry mostly for giving them the gift *of Star Trek*, fandom has been to an unprecedented degree about a personal identification with Whedon, or at least with the mordantly self-deprecating, bookish, fanboy-made-good version of himself he played on the web and in interviews." Fans and creator, their discourse aligns. "Yes, I'm an artist; I have things to say, blahblahblah, but at the same time I'm a fan," says Whedon ("Relighting the Firefly"). Jonathan Gray similarly argues that "Whedon positions himself as working toward the same goal as his readers, not 'competing' with them" (*Show Sold* 112). Furthermore, he takes the stance of the resistant outsider, the Independent, the Other. The introductory remarks on the fan-created film *Done the Impossible* speak of "how Joss broke the rules of TV and then with the help of the fans, went on to break the rules of Hollywood." Here the film's fan writers present Joss as the rebel, the prophet who inveighs against the system.[3] These words were written when fans were hopeful that they had indeed challenged the financial pattern of corporate media control, though it later turned out that their challenge was only partially successful: while *Serenity* is a good film, no sequel has followed. The rules of Hollywood survive, as does *Firefly*'s fandom.

Does Whedon's greater Hollywood success mean that he will be written out of the meta-myth? In the intervening years, he created the three-part internet narrative *Dr. Horrible's Sing-Along Blog* (2008). Starring, among others, Nathan Fillion, it was produced during the 2008 writer's strike as another attempt to circumvent standard Hollywood mechanisms. However, by 2012, as the director and writer of the Hollywood blockbuster *Marvel's The Avengers* (2012), Whedon might seem less an outsider battling against the establishment than part of that establishment. Still, in the light of that success, he famously wrote to Whedonesque.com, thanking fans for their support. And immediately after *The Avengers*, he chose to make, in his own house and with his wife as co-producer and friends as actors, a film of Shakespeare's *Much Ado about Nothing*—hardly a blockbuster career move. Making this quick, inexpensive film helps to maintain his credibility as outsider, someone who has not been completely absorbed by the system—a credibility important to the meta-myth. Alexis Denisof, who stars in *Much Ado*, says Whedon "will fight for the story and the people in it ... He will go to the mat against the studios or the Powers That Be" (212). Denisof, who starred in *Angel* and briefly in *Buffy* (and married *Buffy* star Alyson Hannigan), is part of what we might call Whedon's repertory group, part of the family, part of the resistance.

After *Firefly*'s cancellation, Whedon says, "I wouldn't accept it; clearly I'm surrounded by other people who wouldn't accept it," referring to fans and collaborators (*Done the Impossible*). Fans have often shared the following story: in the episode "Out of Gas," Mal stays with his ship (and almost dies) while the others escape in the shuttles. Wash tells him to press a big red button for them to return when his "miracle" arrives. After cancellation, the cast gave Whedon that button to call them back—and he did. In Jewel Staite's words, "He is the true captain" ("Kaylee Speaks" 217). Or, as fan Patrick Donahue rapped in a video uploaded to YouTube in 2011, "as with any good ship, love kept her afloat, / And Joss Whedon gave us one final ride in the boat." Fan reaction at conventions, too, makes clear that Whedon is still a welcome part of the meta-myth.

The person who played the *Serenity*'s captain has also become a representative of the Browncoats, as well as Whedon's avatar. *Firefly* and *Serenity*'s Captain Malcolm Reynolds is a former resistance fighter who still finds ways to resist. Mal, like Whedon, is angry with the system, and the fans love him for it. His nickname "Mal" reminds us of his anger, and the character has some elements of the angry prophet who scorns accepted standards (though this is a prophet who has come to reject religion—in some ways like Whedon himself). After the battlefield revelation of his own side's untrustworthiness, Mal trusts only a few. He despises even more the pretended virtues of the winners, the Alliance. Mal is willing to hide on board his ship a brother and sister who are fugitives from the Alliance; he undergoes torture for the moral choice of returning medicine he had stolen ("War Stories"); in *Serenity*, he suffers mightily in the fight with the Operative (the nameless face of the Alliance). Fans speak of the character of Mal, like Whedon, as a figure of resistance when they quote his comment, "I aim to misbehave" (*Serenity*).

A change in the meta-myth, however, can be seen in the shift from focusing on the character Mal to focusing more frequently on the much milder and more cheerful persona of Nathan Fillion, the actor. Fillion, in the years since *Firefly* and *Serenity*, has become very successful as the star of the mainstream ABC series *Castle* (2009–present). Nevertheless, he has maintained his links to the Browncoats and his working connection with Whedon. He stars in Whedon's award-winning internet mini-series *Dr. Horrible's Sing-Along Blog* (2008) and in the comic role of Dogberry in Whedon's *Much Ado* (2013). He still makes appearances at conventions and, when unable to attend in person, sometimes calls in, as at the 2012 DragonCon in Atlanta, where he bantered by speakerphone with Adam Baldwin, Jewel Staite, and Sean Maher.

Milder though he may be, Fillion has qualities that help him maintain a position as Whedon avatar in the meta-myth. Fans at conventions and on Twitter respond to Fillion's intelligence, humor, self-deprecation, and willingness to foster community. The *Firefly* production set has been described as a very happy place, and many people made it so; while Whedon set the tone, Fillion clearly contributed. When the show was cancelled, it was to Fillion's house that the cast went to party their sorrows away. Gina Torres, like the others, asserts the connection between the actors and their parts, saying that Whedon chose a cast "that he knew could play together, could work together, could *inhabit* these people" (*Firefly: Browncoats Unite*). Without Torres in the room for the reunion, Whedon made the same point even more emphatically, sounding a bit like someone from *Six Characters in Search of an Author*:

"These were the people before I wrote it—and they didn't know it yet—but they were those people before they met me" (*Firefly: Browncoats Unite*). And of Fillion in particular Whedon says, "There was never a moment from the time we met when I did not think you were the captain." While Fillion does not seem to have experienced the sort of trauma and bitterness that Malcolm Reynolds has, he does seem willing to assume the mantle of captain. Furthermore, he echoes "Captain" Whedon in that he does not hesitate to discuss the work in a highly analytical way. The commentary for the series pilot was done by Whedon and Fillion together, and in it Fillion says, "I always had it in my head that crew members on *Serenity* represented ... bits of Mal that he has lost." Fillion has also written the introduction to the 2006 Dark Horse Comics book *Those Left Behind* (which takes place between the narrative of the series and the film), wherein he reveals that, like Whedon, he has been a comic book fan since childhood. In addition, he contributed an essay titled "I, Malcolm" to Jane Espenson's second collection on *Firefly*; in her remarks introducing it, Espenson says, "Listen here to Nathan's voice ... the humor, the authority. Isn't it a little ... I mean ... isn't it a little Mal? And isn't that fantastic?" (49). Again, the meta-myth (made by fans and creators who also declare themselves fans) emphasizes the continuity between performer and part, between the sf and the narrative of action in reality that the fans have created. Like Whedon, Fillion is seen as a fan. As Lynnette Porter says, "The actor also is one of 'us'—the tech nerd, SF fan, game lover, and general geek" (299).

In 2012, a survey of fans' perceptions of values illustrated in *Firefly* was conducted by *Watcher Junior*, a journal of the Whedon Studies Association. The results (which drew on members from a wide variety of currently active internet sites, such as fireflyfans.net, Can't Stop the Serenity, and Whedonesque) indicate that fans think "the primary values shown in this series ... were being capable, courageous, imaginative, independent, and having family security, freedom, and self-respect" (Kociemba). These are values that can be seen in both the fictional narratives and the narratives fans and creators have presented about their involvement—the myth and the meta-myth. They are also values publically endorsed by the Browncoat community.

That community sometimes frames its values in the sort of religious terms we earlier observed. Tanya Cochran notes that Whedon, at early screenings of *Serenity*, invoked "the metaphors of war, resistance, and insurgency" which many fans employ in describing their fight to keep *Firefly* alive ("Browncoats" 243). These words could also be associated with prophetic resistance, as Browncoats do not hesitate to use the discourse of religion: fans in *Done the Impossible* speak of "converting" and "missionary" work as they try to spread appreciation for *Firefly* and *Serenity*, and Adam Baldwin speaks of fans being "faithful." "Resurrection" too is a term widely used, and an important part of the meta-myth. The discourse influences the narrative; the discourse reflects the narrative. While in the narrative, Mal has repudiated religion, Shepherd Book's dying words enjoin Mal to believe—in whatever Mal chooses. Perhaps, since Mal is a good person, we are to consider that any belief of his will be worthy. Browncoats are similarly pluralistic in many ways, both religious and otherwise. As SuEllen Regonini says, "You see rightwingers, you see leftwingers, you see old, you see young—there is no stereotype in this group; I think it's one of the broadest fan bases I've ever seen" (*Done the Impossible*). While their views vary, they share the meta-myth.

And the values in the narrative (both the Browncoats' story and the fictional stories) seem to guide not only ideas but actions. A number of writers have noted that *Firefly/Serenity* engenders a new level of consciousness about the media experience. Writing of *Serenity*, Telotte says that "there is, [Whedon] might suggest, a kind of moral imperative that should attach to our viewing, a need to act as well as see" ("*Serenity*" 78). Focusing not on the text but on fan activism, Cochran draws a similar lesson: "As long as fandom is a conscious, educated choice, fans are not slaves of the studios" ("Browncoats" 249). While the 2005 film is long past, the Browncoats are still active, even though there seems little likelihood of a sequel. They still gather online, at conventions, and in local meetings. The tenth anniversary reunion of Whedon and his cast was held to a wildly enthusiastic response at the 2012 Comic-Con. Fans stood in line for hours for the 2012 DragonCon sessions featuring cast members. Groups like the San Francisco Browncoats and the Atlanta Browncoats still have monthly meetings.

Years after the initial activism that helped get the movie made, Browncoats continue to express their shared values. The activities they engage in might be categorized as creative or charitable (and they are not mutually exclusive). SuEllen Regonini, both a Browncoat and a student of applied anthropology, has described Browncoats' creative (or "prosumer") activities, which include not only fan fiction, art, costumes, and role-playing games, but also "3D modeling, prop building, jewelry making, production of fandom related merchandise ... production of podcasts ... video and/or audio mashups/original productions"—and the list goes on ("They Aim"). Fans continue to create. They also donate to charity. Among many examples, in March 2012, Nathan Fillion invited his Twitter following to give him birthday presents in the form of donations to charity. For Whedon's birthday, fans hold annual charity film screenings (the events are called Can't Stop the Serenity), thus reuniting elements of the myth and meta-myth: the narrative in the film, the fans in the audience, Whedon himself via his birthday, and their mutual choice to enact their resistance through charity. As Cochran makes clear in her article "Past the Brink of Tacit Support," Whedon has asked his fans to transform their resistance—to move from just supporting the texts to supporting change in the world. Probably his most direct appeal was in a message after the April 7, 2007 "honor killing" by stoning in Kurdistan of a young woman named Du'a Khalil Aswad, whose death was filmed by numerous witnesses with cellphones; video of her death virally spread around the internet. In indignation, Whedon condemned those who only watch (like typical members of a TV/film audience), using this particularly heinous event to preach a broader message: "All I ask is this: Do something. Try something. Speaking out, showing up, writing a letter, a check, a strongly worded e-mail. Pick a cause—there are few unworthy ones. And nudge yourself past the brink of tacit support to action" (qtd. in Cochran, "Past" 2.22). While Whedon's (and *Firefly*'s) fandom is not the only one active in real-world causes, this activity is certainly an extension of the Browncoat narrative of resistance, independence, and chosen family/caring. Stars like Angelina Jolie or Jon Bon Jovi (among many others) work for good causes too, but unlike Whedon, these stars are not joined by groups with the unity and identity-beyond-the-cause of the Browncoats. Cochran points out that J. K. Rowling, however, is—with the Harry Potter Alliance ("Past" 4.1). And Regonini notes the same of George Lucas's *Star Wars* fans called The 501st Legion ("When Charity"). What do the 501st, the HPA, and the Browncoats have in common? Narrative.

Famously, some fans have knitted orange woolen hats to match the one given to the ferocious Jayne by his loving off-screen mother; the fans call themselves "Big Damn Knitters," whimsically echoing Zoe's "Big Damn Heroes" comment ("Safe"), while connecting caring and heroism in one wooly swoop. In doing so, these fans choose to make themselves part of the Big Damn Narrative, the meta-myth of *Firefly/ Serenity*. More writers in various disciplines have of late come to realize the importance of our own narratives in structuring our understanding of and therefore our experience of our realities. J. Douglas Rabb and J. Michael Richardson argue for a "narrative ethics" in Whedon's texts. In the case of *Firefly/Serenity*, and their makers/fans—the Browncoats—I see a narrative and set of values that unify multiple levels of experience, that amount to acting on belief. The independent "loser" fights against a seemingly overwhelming power; like many an sf fan, the outsider fights the status quo. If the Browncoats cannot change the standard operations of the media, they can still resist the powers that be.[4] They can make a space for caring, for chosen family—whether the small crew of a rattletrap ship, a repertory company of actors and writers, or a group of devoted fans.[5] It is, of course, not possible to say exactly how much of the vision is shared, how many differences there are in the various forms of "the story." In each mind, there is a different world. But that the sf cult of *Firefly/Serenity* has made some difference in *this* world, there seems little doubt.

Notes

[1] On the other hand, in terms of sociology of religion and religious cults or new religious movements (NRMs), Thomas Robbins identifies "the large *science fiction subculture* which emerged in the 1950s and 1960s" as one of four "generative milieu[x]" (3). The analyses of media scholars and media-centered cults have relatively little overlap with the analyses of sociologists of religion. Nor (to look from a very different angle) does this consider the religious content of works such as *Battlestar Galactica* or *The X-Files.*

[2] While I am certainly a fan of the television series, the film, and Whedon and his collaborators, some fans might not apply the term "Browncoat" to me, since I was not active in the early attempts to save the show (though I do recall signing a petition).

[3] While media cult fandoms often center on a single text (a TV series or a film), Whedon is himself arguably a cult figure. Attachments to performers are not unusual, but attachments to non-performing creators are. Matt Hills notes Quentin Tarantino as another example (x). Acknowledging questions of the sources of creation and the nature of reception, Gray quotes Roland Barthes's famous statement that "the birth of the reader must be at the cost of the death of the author" (qtd. in Gray, *Show Sold* 108). But because of Whedon's conscious interaction with his "readers," Gray also argues that, "As is only fitting for the author of *Buffy the Vampire Slayer,* Whedon was an undead author" (*Show Sold* 113). Scriptwriter Jane Espenson adds another dimension to this relationship, as she notes that "Joss-driven projects inspire a certain cult-of-the-writer, and [on the red carpet] we are hooted at and flash-bulbed at almost as vigorously as the stars" (2). Certainly, many academics and fans focus on both Whedon and his collaborators; in fact, there is a Whedon Studies Association, which publishes two peer-reviewed journals (the original journal, *Slayage,* and more recently a journal for undergraduate work as well, *Watcher Junior*), and runs biennial academic conferences. Gray contends that Whedon "is by no means alone" in his authorial status, citing "Cuse and Lindelof, Straczynski, Kring, Doris Egan, Aaron Sorkin, Jane Espenson, Jason Katims, Toni Graphia, Erik Kripke, Rob Thomas, Josh Schwartz, and others" (*Show Sold* 113), but so far as I know, none of these has an academic association—at least not yet. There is

hardly a bibliography of works written about them (there are two for Whedon, one on the internet by librarian Alysa Hornick and another in print publication by librarian Don Macnaughtan). Moreover, analysis of Whedon is rife at locations such as Whedonesque.com, which is not limited to a single series, although there are also websites specifically devoted to *Firefly/Serenity*. Consideration of what might be called the cult of Whedon has some overlap with the current discussion, but cannot be examined in full here.

4 Compare Robbins's assessment of the need for new religious movements, as they develop, "to maintain a balance between worldly accommodation versus uncompromising sectarianism" (109).

5 Since the final draft of this chapter went to the editors, Cochran has published on related issues of fandom and religious parallels in "By Beholding We Become Changed: Narrative Transubstantiation and the Whedonverses." Thanks go to her and the Reverend Marti Keller for comments on early drafts of this chapter.

Works Cited

Abbott, Stacey. "'Can't Stop the Signal': The Resurrection/Regeneration of *Serenity*." *Investigating* Firefly *and* Serenity: *Science Fiction on the Frontier*. Ed. Rhonda V. Wilcox and Tanya R. Cochran. London: I. B. Tauris, 2008. 227–38.

Arnold, Matthew. "The Study of Poetry." [1880.] *Essays in Criticism, Second Series. English Prose of the Victorian Era*. Ed. Charles Frederick Harrold and William D. Templeman. New York: Oxford UP, 1938. 1247–64.

Breznican, Anthony. "'Firefly' Alights on Big Screen as 'Serenity.'" USAToday. com, September 21, 2005. Web. Accessed 14 May 2013.

Cochran, Tanya R. "By Beholding, We Become Changed: Narrative Transubstantiation and the Whedonverses." *Joss in June: Selected Essays*. Ed. K. Dale Koontz and Ensley Guffey. Special issue of *Slayage: The Journal of the Whedon Studies Association* 11.2/12.1 (2014). Web. Accessed 20 October 2014.

—. "'Past the Brink of Tacit Support': Fan Activism and the Whedonverses." *Transformative Works and Fan Activism*. Ed. Henry Jenkins and Sangita Shrestova. Special issue of *Transformative Works and Cultures* 10 (2012). Web. Accessed 12 March 2013.

—. "The Browncoats Are Coming! *Firefly, Serenity,* and Fan Activism." *Investigating* Firefly *and* Serenity: *Science Fiction on the Frontier*. Ed. Rhonda V. Wilcox and Tanya R. Cochran. London: I. B. Tauris, 2008. 239–49.

Denisof, Alexis. "Interview by Laura Berger." *Joss Whedon: The Complete Companion: The TV Series, The Movies, the Comic Books and More*. Ed. Mary Alice Money. London: Popmatters/Titan, 2012. 205–12.

Done the Impossible: The Fans' Tale of Firefly *and* Serenity. Dir. and prod. Brian Wiser et al. Rivetal, 2006.

Eco, Umberto. "*Casablanca*: Cult Movies and Intertextual Collage." *Travels in Hyperreality*. Trans. William Weaver. New York: Harcourt, Brace, 1986. 197–211.

Erisman, Fred. "*Stagecoach* in Space: The Legacy of *Firefly*." *Extrapolation* 47.2 (2006): 249–58.

Espenson, Jane. "Introduction." *Finding Serenity: Anti-Heroes, Lost Shepherds, and Space Hookers in Joss Whedon's* Firefly. Ed. Jane Espenson. Dallas: Benbella, 2004. 1–3.

Fillion, Nathan. "I, Malcolm." *Serenity Found: More Unauthorized Essays on Joss Whedon's* Firefly *Universe*. Ed. Jane Espenson. Dallas: Benbella, 2007. 49–53.

—. "Introduction." *Serenity: Those Left Behind*. Milwaukee: Dark Horse Comics, 2006. [v].

Firefly: Browncoats Unite [Tenth Anniversary Reunion]. Science Channel. November 11, 2012.

Firefly: The Complete Series. 2002. Created by Joss Whedon. Mutant Enemy/Twentieth Century Fox Home Entertainment, 2003.

Gray, Jonathan. "Joss Whedon: Undead Author." SCW5: The *Slayage* Conference on the Whedonverses. University of British Columbia, Vancouver. July 12–15, 2012. Keynote presentation.

—. *Show Sold Separately: Promos, Spoilers, and Other Media Paratexts*. New York: New York UP, 2010.

Gwenllian-Jones, Sarah, and Roberta E. Pearson. "Introduction." *Cult Television*. Ed. Sara Gwenllian-Jones and Roberta E. Pearson. Minneapolis: U of Minnesota P, 2004. ix–xx.

Hills, Matt. *Fan Cultures*. London: Routledge, 2002.

Hornick, Alysa. *Whedonology: An Academic Whedon Studies Bibliography*. March 30, 2013. Web. Accessed 1 April 2013.

Kociemba, David. "You Can't Take the Sky from Me: *Firefly*'s Values." *Watcher Junior Editor's Blog. Watcher Junior: The Undergraduate Journal of Whedon Studies*. Whedon Studies Association. June 20, 2012. Web. Accessed 3 March 2013.

Macnaughtan, Don. *The Buffyverse Catalog*. Jefferson: McFarland, 2011.

Marek, Michael. "*Firefly*: So Pretty It Could Not Die." *Siths, Slayers, Stargates & Cyborgs: Modern Mythology in the New Millennium*. Ed. David Whitt and John Perlich. New York: Peter Lang, 2008. 99–120.

Pappademas, Alex. "The Geek Shall Inherit the Earth." GQ.com, May 2012. Web. Accessed 14 May 2013.

Pateman, Matthew. "*Firefly*: Of Formats, Franchises, and Fox." *Reading Joss Whedon*. Ed. Rhonda V. Wilcox, Tanya R. Cochran, Cynthea Masson, and David Lavery. Syracuse: Syracuse UP, 2014. 153–68.

Porter, Lynnette. "Nathan Fillion Misbehaves All Across the Whedonverse." *Joss Whedon: The Complete Companion: The TV Series, The Movies, the Comic Books and More*. Ed. Mary Alice Money. London: Titan Books/Popmatters, 2012. 298–303.

Rabb, J. Douglas, and J. Michael Richardson. "Adventures in the Moral Imagination: Memory and Identity in Whedon's Narrative Ethics." *Reading*

Joss Whedon. Ed. Rhonda V. Wilcox, Tanya R. Cochran, Cynthea Masson, and David Lavery. Syracuse: Syracuse UP, 2014.

Regonini, SuEllen. "'They Aim to Misbehave': A Case Study of Technology, Browncoat Fan Activities, and the Prosumer Economy." Popular Culture/American Culture Association in the South Conference. Savannah. 5–7 October, 2006. Conference presentation.

—. "When Charity Met Fantasy: Fandom Charities and Their Function as Paratexts." Popular Culture/American Culture Association in the South Conference. Savannah. 3–5 October, 2013. Conference presentation.

"Relighting the Firefly." Featurette. *Serenity.* Writ. and dir. Joss Whedon. Perf. Nathan Fillion, Summer Glau, and Chiwetel Ejiofor. Mutant Enemy/Universal, 2005.

Robbins, Thomas. *Cults, Converts, and Charisma: The Sociology of New Religious Movements.* London: Sage, 1988.

Serenity. Writ. and dir. Joss Whedon. Perf. Nathan Fillion, Summer Glau, and Chiwetel Ejiofor. Mutant Enemy/Universal, 2005.

Staite, Jewel. "Kaylee Speaks: Jewel Staite on *Firefly.*" *Finding Serenity: Anti-Heroes, Lost Shepherds, and Space Hookers in Joss Whedon's* Firefly. Ed. Jane Espenson. Dallas: Benbella, 2004. 217–27.

Telotte, J. P. "*Serenity,* Cinematisation and the Perils of Adaptation." *Science Fiction Film and Television* 1.1 (Spring 2008): 67–80.

—. "*Firefly.*" *The Essential Cult TV Reader.* Ed. David Lavery. Lexington: UP of Kentucky, 2010. 111–19.

Whedon, Joss. "Taking Back the Sky." *Serenity: The Official Visual Companion.* London: Titan, 2005. 8–11.

—. "Joss Whedon Introduction." *Serenity.* Writ. and dir. Joss Whedon. Perf. Nathan Fillion, Summer Glau, and Chiwetel Ejiofor. Mutant Enemy/Universal, 2005.

Whedon, Joss, and Nathan Fillion. "Serenity" Commentary. *Firefly: The Complete Series.* 2002. Created by Joss Whedon. Mutant Enemy/Twentieth Century Fox Home Entertainment, 2003.

Wilcox, Rhonda V., and Tanya R. Cochran. "'Good Myth': Joss Whedon's Further Worlds." *Investigating* Firefly *and* Serenity: *Science Fiction on the Frontier.* Ed. Rhonda V. Wilcox and Tanya R. Cochran. London: I. B. Tauris, 2008. 1–11.

7. *Iron Sky*'s War Bonds:
Cult SF Cinema and Crowdsourcing

Chuck Tryon

In February 2012, after six years of planning, fundraising, and production, the sf film *Iron Sky* premiered at the Berlin Film Festival. Although *Iron Sky* featured a provocative plot—one in which Nazis who had been hiding on the dark side of the moon return to earth in the year 2018—along with a couple of familiar international stars, including German actor Udo Kier, and a soundtrack by the Slovenian avant-garde band Laibach, the film was discussed most frequently because of its unusual production history, which involved the contributions of thousands of fans and followers who donated time and money in order to see the project reach completion. *Crowdsourcing*, the process of drawing from the wisdom or talents of the crowd, along with the companion practice of *crowdfunding*, tapping into the wallets of supporters, has increasingly shaped the discourses around independent film production, and indeed of cult film formation, in an era of digital delivery.

As one of the first high-profile films to use practices such as crowdsourcing and crowdfunding, *Iron Sky* presented a challenge to critics and reviewers, who were reluctant to criticize a film that deliberately challenged norms of both provocative content and innovative distribution practices. Brian Clark, writing for *Twitch Film*, an online magazine dedicated to promoting international, independent, and cult film, admitted, "I'm torn about how to review *Iron Sky*. Is it really fair to criticize a movie about Nazis from the dark side of the moon invading the earth for being too goofy? Hell, is it really fair to criticize that movie for anything at all?" Similarly, David Rooney of the *Hollywood Reporter* found himself puzzling over the film's uneven efforts to juggle a B-movie premise with a relatively sophisticated use of CGI special effects. Meanwhile, Senh Duong of the blog *Movies with Butter*, reported that searches for news on *Iron Sky* were driving traffic to his website, as fans clamored to find more information about the film, which many of them may have had a hand in making or financing. Notably, all of these critics were describing *Iron Sky* as a cult sf film, even before fans could see the completed work, raising important questions about how that classification is conferred: is it the product of deliberate narrative construction or the result of intense audience attachment?

These reactions to the *Iron Sky* premiere help to open up a set of questions that face our sense of the cult cinema as it intersects with both new modes of delivery and new, fan-based models of production, financing, and promotion. Are there aesthetic traits that are inherent to cult films? Do those traits undergo revision as cult audiences (and the sites where they might encounter cult films) evolve? Can a cult audience be created prior to a film's release, especially given the demonstrated media ability to build an audience prior to a film's release? This essay uses the example of the sf text *Iron Sky* to consider how practices of crowdsourcing and crowdfunding are not only intersecting with the discourses of cult cinema, but also beginning to redefine it.

Typically, definitions of cult cinema have focused on both aesthetic and audience factors. Aesthetically, cult films are often associated with parody, camp, and other forms of aesthetic transgression because of their ability to challenge the norms of Hollywood cinema, while cult audiences are typically assumed to emerge after a film is released, and movies deliberately designed to cultivate that audience are often dismissed as "prefabricated." In this sense, *Iron Sky* challenges many of these preconceptions, even while building a massive international audience that has enthusiastically embraced it, to the point that the film's production team began work on a (crowdfunded and crowdsourced) sequel just months after the original film's festival premiere, having received over $150,000 from fans and supporters (Roxborough).

As most commentators have noted, much of cult cinema exists on the periphery of mainstream film-making, in terms of content, distribution, and reception. The films that make up the cult canon often challenge traditional aesthetic definitions and categories of genre and style. Although many cult films have relationships with traditional genres, especially in the case of sf, they often defy traditional genre categories or, in some cases, offer a calculated rejection of mainstream commercial cinema. In his discussion of what he terms "paracinema," Jeffrey Sconce argues that cult films define themselves against the "purity" of Hollywood cinema (102–03). And because they define themselves in this way, they also typically face difficulty in gaining mainstream theatrical distribution. As a result, cult films often achieve popularity only after their initial theatrical run, at midnight screenings in repertory theaters or on various home video platforms. However, cult status also requires an enthusiastic fan base that embraces—and even proselytizes for—that cult object. As Matt Hills reminds us, cult objects typically entail both specific textual features and an audience that recognizes that object as distinct and worthy of unusual attention (131). Because films cannot achieve cult status by themselves, they typically depend on what Jonathan Gray refers to as "extratextual" features, elements outside the film itself, to direct an audience's interpretation of and investment in a given film project. As Gray's discussion of movie trailers reminds us, audiences rarely encounter films without any prior knowledge of the content or subject matter. Instead, they are guided by different forms of prior knowledge—trailers, star profiles, reviews—that help them make decisions not only on whether to see a movie but on how to interpret it (47–80). The attainment of cult status can also depend on similar textual features. *Rocky Horror Picture Show* achieved cult status not just through word-of-mouth, but also through its depiction as a cult text in a variety of media, including a film like *The Perks of Being a Wallflower*, which shows fans participating in ritualistic midnight screenings.

Thus, many films, including *The Rocky Horror Picture Show, The Blair Witch Project*, and *The Big Lebowski*, gained their cult status not solely because of their content but because of the passionate—and often ritualistic—activity associated with screenings, although that audience role is now undergoing an evolution, as social media technologies become increasingly vital as modes of communication for movie audiences. In this sense, the web has become an important site for both facilitating and complicating cult activity. As J. P. Telotte argues, the film-makers behind *The Blair Witch Project* calculatingly framed the experience of their movie through the website, which helped to reinforce its mock-documentary narrative and to cultivate the intense fandom that flourished in response to the vast narrative world that came to encompass not only the film and its website, but also a second documentary ostensibly about the making of the original film (264). More recently, fans of *The Big Lebowski*, initially a modest box office success at best, created Lebowski Fest, a semi-annual event in which fans, many dressed in costumes referencing the film, such as bathrobes, gather at bowling alleys and drink White Russians to honor that film's slacker protagonist. The fans refer to themselves as "Achiever Nation," in reference to one of the film's gags, and several of the Lebowski Fests have attracted stars from the film, including Jeff Bridges, Julianne Moore, and John Turturro. In both cases, fans were able to connect with others using online tools, building upon the participatory cultures discussed by Henry Jenkins (see his *Convergence Culture*) to extend the cultural significance (and financial value) of these media franchises.

As a number of critics have observed, cult films have also typically existed outside of traditional distribution networks, even if these networks continued to be shaped by commercial imperatives. Thus Mark Jancovich observes that, historically, cult movie distribution occurs outside of the studio system, often aimed at repertory theaters (157). In the 1970s and 1980s, these distribution models began to change as home video became commonplace. According to Timothy Corrigan, cult films proliferated thanks in part to the vast expansion of exhibition venues, including cable television, VHS, and DVDs, so that, as Corrigan put it, "any movie today can become a cult film" (81). Further, home video enabled the circulation of cult texts by allowing audiences to watch movies with sexually explicit or gory content that could not be shown on broadcast television or basic cable. In fact, Caetlin Benson-Allott directly links the horror genre's revival in the 1970s and 1980s to the popularity of the VCR (2). These technologies also allowed users to rediscover and re-watch movies outside their theatrical run. This widespread availability, as part of what Barbara Klinger has called "replay culture," also removed geographic barriers associated with cult cinema, allowing audiences with little access to repertory houses or independent video stores, the pleasures of participating in cult cinema rituals, while diminishing the sense of exclusivity typically associated with such films (*Lebowski* 3). As Klinger points out, a number of early websites specializing in streaming movies, such as BijouFlix, cultivated niche audiences built around cult sf, horror films, and similar genre categories (*Multiplex* 199). As a result, social media tools and digital delivery technologies began to redefine where and how cult audiences congregate, while a film's unusual distribution history also helped to confer cult status.

Crowdsourcing, Crowdfunding, and the
Discourses of Professionalism

Alongside these new distribution models, cult cinema benefits from a highly energetic fan culture that organizes itself through a wide range of social media tools. Many of these tools repurpose or rework past forms of fan activity, such as fan magazines and fan films. However, these tools function not merely as part of the reception process. In fact, social media have become central to the production process, particularly through those processes of crowdsourcing and crowdfunding. Crowdsourcing is the process by which an agent uses networks, usually on the web, to tap into the productive energies of a wider group of people. The concept of crowdsourcing was originally introduced by *Wired* magazine writer Jeff Howe, who used it to describe a disparate range of practices, including Netflix's contest to invite users to improve their recommendation algorithm, Eli Lily's use of the InnoCentive platform to develop new pharmaceuticals, and the Doritos advertising contest, in which amateur film-makers competed to have their ad shown during the Super Bowl. The term combines the idea of outsourcing—usually negatively associated with sending US manufacturing jobs overseas—with the concept of the crowd, building upon the assumption that large groups of people are able to find more effective solutions than a small number of geniuses working independently.

Crowdsourcing was further popularized by media critic Clay Shirky, who celebrated the power of online tools to enable disaggregated groups to organize quickly in order to complete a task, support a political cause, or share information quickly and easily, often with millions of readers across the globe. In particular, Shirky cites the example of *Wikipedia*, the online encyclopedia written and maintained by millions of voluntary authors and editors across the globe, alongside other events such as a woman who sparked a national protest when she complained on her blog about her experience as an airline passenger. For Shirky, these online tools have contributed to "a remarkable increase in our ability to share, to cooperate with one another, and to take collective action" (20–21). As a result, he suggests that culture is undergoing a "tectonic shift" that promises new opportunities for individual citizens. Instead of relying on existing networks, creators using web tools can organize quickly and easily, often within a matter of hours or minutes.

Crowdfunding, by comparison, refers to the practice of using such networks to raise funds in order to support the production of a creative product. Within the creative industries, two major web services, Kickstarter and IndieGoGo, have emerged as tools for automating the crowdfunding process. Both services invite creative workers to solicit donations towards a fundraising goal. In most cases involving fundraising for the production of a movie, the director and, in some cases, the stars of the film will appear in a short pitch video explaining the project— often framed in terms of the director's vision—and how the funds will be used. In addition, the film's producers can offer perks or gifts for donating. Typical gifts for smaller donations include movie posters and DVD copies of the completed film, but larger donations can result in being invited to visit the film's set or to appear in the film. In the case of *The Canyons* (2013), director Paul Schrader offered a cherished collectible: the belt buckle given to him by Robert De Niro as a gift for his work on the movie *Taxi Driver*. More recently, the producers behind the cult TV series *Veronica Mars* engaged in a similar—and even more dramatic— crowdfunding campaign. Using the Kickstarter platform, the film-makers reached their $2 million fundraising goal in just ten hours, on their way to collecting a total of $5.7 million from 90,000 individual donors (Tassi). Other established independent film-makers, including Zach Braff and James Franco, eventually sought donations for their projects, leading to complaints that fans were being pressured into supporting projects that were also being funded by massive corporations and were therefore not truly independent. However, such complaints assume that donations to crowdsourced projects entail a zero-sum game. In fact, most of the supporters for *Veronica Mars* were first-time donors who likely would not have discovered Kickstarter otherwise. Fans supported the project not only because of their intense love of the show and their wish to revisit the characters associated with it, but also because the show had been dumped from network television without offering audiences any resolution. In this sense, crowdfunding became a way for fans to express what kind of programming they would like to see. Crowd-coordinated efforts to revive cult TV shows, including sf efforts such as *Star Trek*, *Firefly*, and *Jericho*, have a long history; however, crowdfunding alters this relationship, as fans directly invest in the production of a TV series or movie, explicitly funding a project, usually in advance of the actual production. Of course, in the past, production companies have sought to have potential backers or "angels" buy stock in an unreleased, and often incomplete, film. However, in such instances the fundraising typically served as a potential investment, even if investors knew in advance the long odds of making a profit on the film. In some cases, these projects sought to leverage online resources, as was the case with Civilian Pictures, a Hollywood–Wall Street collaboration partially

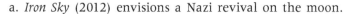

a. *Iron Sky* (2012) envisions a Nazi revival on the moon.

b. The first female American president (Stephanie Paul) warns of the
Nazi menace in *Iron Sky* (2012).

funded by actress Diane Keaton, in which the public would be invited
to buy shares of individual film titles with the hope of getting a cut
of the film's profits and with the added enticement that their name
would appear in the film's closing credits, providing them with a tiny
slice of "celebrity" (Tunick). By comparison, supporters of contemporary
crowdfunding practices provide funds without any expectation of a
financial return on their investment, but instead seek to "buy in" to
the idea of supporting a project they want to succeed, often with the
added bonus of gifts and other perks that might provide them with a
unique connection to the film.

In this sense, crowdsourcing in particular seems to challenge
traditional discourses of authorship and professionalism. However, even
if a film's director cedes some control of the production process to
the crowd, it should just remind us that most movies are collabo-
rative productions that involve the labor of many other people. Thus,
while crowdfunding and crowdsourcing are frequently aligned with
the discourses of fandom, these practices often entail a much more
complex set of motivations and desires. While many participants will
support projects with their time or money primarily for altruistic
reasons or simply to be entertained, others are motivated by professional
factors. In his research on the crowdsourced services iStockPhoto and
Threadless.com, Daren Brabham found that many people who work
on crowdsourced projects do so to make money, to develop professional credentials, or to expand their professional networks (68). Other
critics of crowdsourcing have complained that it has the potential to
dilute the vision and skill of qualified creative industry workers. This
complaint is also driven by professional motivations. If people who are

perceived as amateurs are able to produce logos or advertisements that match the quality of a professional, then it potentially undermines the professional group. Writing for the American Institute of Graphic Artists, Richard Grefe complained that crowdsourcing "compromises the value designers can provide their clients." In this sense, crowdsourcing challenges traditional production discourses, even while it foregrounds the degree to which audiences have long been involved in producing a text's cult status.

Because of these new modes of circulation and promotion, cult films have increasingly become linked to the mainstream. In some cases, cult status can become "ripe for industry exploitation," as Barbara Klinger notes in her discussion of the fan cultures that emerged around the Coen Brothers' *The Big Lebowski* (2). In fact, studios have sought to exploit participatory cultures by producing what might be called a "prefabricated cult" around films that have some of the common aesthetic traits of cult cinema—camp, genre parody, quotability—and in some cases by encouraging fans to join in the film's production through crowdsourcing techniques. However, these prefab cult practices have often backfired when their use comes across as nothing more than a cynical marketing technique, as when New Line sought to rebrand the Samuel L. Jackson action film *Snakes on a Plane* (2006) as a campy cult movie, even to the point of reshooting several scenes to include lines of dialogue suggested by fans that parodied Jackson's screen persona ("Enough is enough! I have had it with these motherfucking snakes on this motherfucking plane!"), as well as glimpses of nudity that would have aligned the movie with the tradition of exploitation films. As one critic of the movie complained, New Line was "cynically manufacturing its own cult mythos" rather than allowing that audience to emerge organically (Bromley). While these techniques likely contributed to a slight bump in the opening weekend box office, the fan audience that New Line sought to capture never embraced the film. In fact, as the *Snakes on a Plane* example illustrates, fan attachment remains a crucial test for whether a film or media property achieves cult status. Instead of becoming a film that fans embraced intensely, it was a brief source of amusement for an online culture that moved quickly and seamlessly from one distraction or internet meme to the next. The *Snakes on a Plane* phenomenon illustrates that cult status typically cannot be manufactured deliberately, even if many of the aesthetic properties associated with cult cinema are present in the film. These same debates about crowdsourcing and crowdfunding helped to shape the reception of *Iron Sky*, both in production and upon theatrical release. Instead of simply another B sf movie that might have played a few film festivals before disappearing into DVD remainder bins (or, more likely, deep inside Netflix's extensive streaming catalog), *Iron Sky* became attached to a number of other narratives about its unusual production process.

Narrative, Cult, Parody

Although *Iron Sky*'s energetic fan base played a crucial role in turning the film into an sf cult property, the film's narrative was also consistent with a cult film aesthetic. The plot, after all, can help establish participatory elements as a crucial aspect of a film's significance as a textual artifact. *Iron Sky* uses tropes from B-movies, speculative fiction, and a broad range of sf films to satirize militarism and American politics, drawing from an sf tradition that includes Robert Wise's *The Day the Earth Stood Still* (1951) and Stanley Kubrick's *Dr. Strangelove or: How I Learned to Stop Worrying and Love the Bomb* (1963). *Iron Sky* is set in the year 2018, when the first female American president (Stephanie Paul), a power-hungry, manipulative hunter and fitness fanatic modeled on former Alaska governor Sarah Palin, works with her assistant Vivian Wagner (Peta Sergeant) to arrange a moon landing that (they hope) will dupe voters into re-electing her by providing a naïve public a camera-ready moment, filled with disingenuous patriotism. Cynically hoping to capture the African-American vote, the President dispatches the aptly named black fashion model James Washington (Christopher Kirby), as one of the astronauts to "Black the Moon," as the President's campaign posters describe it. However, things go awry when the astronauts discover a lunar colony built secretly by Nazis on the dark side of the moon (a location that inevitably invokes a number of Pink Floyd references) in the aftermath of the Second World War. The Nazis kill the other astronaut, capture Washington, and then conduct "scientific" experiments on him that include turning his skin white.

Washington learns that the Nazi colony has been patiently waiting and developing resources to invade the earth. The Nazis are led by a new Führer (Udo Kier); Doktor Richter, a mad scientist loosely modeled on Joseph Mengele; the scientist's daughter, Renate, a somewhat naïve English teacher; and her scheming fiancé, Klaus Adler, who hopes someday to take over as Führer. Eventually, Klaus discovers that Washington's iPhone will provide them with the computing power necessary to conduct an invasion, leading to several jokes about the vast expansion of computing power and the ubiquity of these communication devices. Recognizing that they need more iPhones and computers, Klaus asks Washington to take him back to earth so they can get them, with Renate stowing away on the saucer that initially returns them to earth. Upon landing, Klaus insists that Washington bring them to the President, which he is able to do through his connection with Vivian, the President's campaign manager. The two women are initially pleased to welcome the visitors to their campaign team, and Vivian even appropriates Renate's goodwill speech—which directly quotes Nazi propaganda minister Joseph Goebbels—as a campaign speech for the President, drawing a not-so-subtle connection between political ideologies.[1]

Vivian gradually begins to deduce the true purpose of this visit: an imminent invasion meant to install the "Fourth Reich," and once again, she and the President are thrilled because wartime presidents, they reason, always get re-elected. To announce a response to the Nazi invasion, the President goes before the United Nations and describes plans for sending out a new ship, the *USS George W. Bush*, which is joined by a range of allies from Australia, England, and Canada, much to the chagrin of the President, who wishes to take sole credit for defeating the Nazis. Because of her campaign success, Vivian, who is also bitterly angry with Klaus for rejecting her sexual advances, takes over as leader of the *USS George W. Bush*, leading a nuclear assault on the moon Nazis, even though she is told that the bombs will kill women and children, again offering an unsubtle critique of the use of overwhelming military force during the wars in Iraq and Afghanistan. Eventually, the Nazis are defeated, Washington has a second operation that restores his skin pigmentation, and Renate sees Washington's natural beauty. Meanwhile, the invading force discovers that the Nazis have been mining and storing vast quantities of Helium 3, a resource that will provide energy independence. The President immediately claims ownership rights, provoking a brawl in the United Nations building and, perhaps, setting up a possible plot for a sequel.

Much of the film's humor and its political critique derive from references to older films. Renate, for example, shows a heavily edited version of Charlie Chaplin's *The Great Dictator* to her students to depict the goodness of Nazism (all scenes depicting the cruelty of Dictator Hynkel are omitted), only to discover Chaplin's real intentions with the film when she returns to Earth. The film also overtly borrows from and parodies *Dr. Strangelove* during a scene in which Washington, briefly transformed into an Aryan by Doktor Richter, gets up from a wheelchair and tries to stop himself from giving a Nazi salute. Perhaps the most notable allusion, however, is to the power and creativity of social media itself. A scene depicts Vivian exploding with rage at her subordinates and demanding that everyone who is not "a department head" leave the room. The sequence is a virtual shot-for-shot re-enactment of a similar scene in Oliver Hirschbiegel's film *Downfall* (2004) in which Hitler berates his subordinates.

By the time of *Iron Sky*'s release, the scene from *Downfall* had been reworked thousands of times by web parodists who rewrote the film's subtitles (usually in English) to make it appear that Hitler was complaining about everything from the Barack Obama campaign to the limitations of Microsoft's customer service.[2] In this case, the film directly quotes the kind of work being done by those who joined in making *Iron Sky* (and *Downfall*, for that matter) a cult phenomenon. By citing this bit of fan activity, *Iron Sky* congratulates its viewers on their cinematic knowledge, allowing them to be in on the joke. Here and elsewhere, *Iron Sky* self-consciously engages with the tropes of cult cinema, borrowing from the traditions of exploitation film and low-budget sf, gently mocking the conventions of both categories in a way that includes its audience. Through its extensive citations, it reinforces an sf canon, placing Stanley Kubrick front-and-center, even while, in its own sort of "double feature," subverting that canon by celebrating the cinematic parodies produced by various online fan cultures.

Crowdsourcing and *Iron Sky*

While *Iron Sky*'s narrative makes use of what might appear to be a prefabricated cult approach, the film-makers also positioned the project as a cult artifact at the level of production and distribution. *Iron Sky* was conceived and promoted as a crowdsourced and crowdfunded project from its very inception. The film's director, Timo Vuorensola, had already achieved a certain level of celebrity in the fan community for his *Star Trek* fan films, most notably *Star Wreck: In the Pirkinning* (2005), which had reportedly been viewed several million times by the time *Iron Sky* began production. In this sense, Vuorensola, like many other independent artists, depended heavily upon his existing reputation and celebrity within the fan film community, a reputation that took several years to develop.

During the film's production phase, the film-makers actively solicited financial contributions online through an unusually creative crowdfunding initiative that tied into the film's Second World War elements. Fans of the film could buy "war bonds" for 50 euros, which would entitle them to a DVD of the teaser trailer, a booklet about the film, and a certificate of participation in the fight against the Nazis—a creative reference to the role that propaganda played during the war (Kirsner

70). At the same time, the film-makers invited fans to contribute their talents to the film through their "Wreck a Movie" platform, now available for use by any production using crowdsourcing techniques. "Wreck a Movie" allows users to volunteer their skills to a film production of their choice. Users can search the site by film title, participants, or by requested tasks. Thus, if an aspiring visual effects artist wants to gain experience on a crowdsourced movie, he/she can search the website and arrange to contribute. Conversely, if a director needs an editor for his/ her film, the director can browse the profiles posted on the website to find someone willing to work on that crowdsourced project.

This use of crowd labor was an explicit part of the film's promotion and led to a scenario in which the primary creative team, led by Vuorensola, and the fans were, in a sense, co-creating *Iron Sky*'s cult status. Vuorensola characterizes his decision to use crowdsourcing and crowdfunding techniques in pragmatic terms: "we wanted to find a way to take advantage of the Internet communities in the film industry, and bring resources otherwise unavailable to the hands of independent filmmakers" (quoted in Albrecht). In some cases, these contributions included a request for fans to suggest taglines that could be used to promote the movie, while in other cases fans became involved in set design by creating fake movie posters for a scene set in a theater. These invitations to contribute served as "paratexts" that helped to establish the film's significance several years before it was completed. Thus, through these fan contests, Vuorensola was able to inform participants not only about the content of the film (an sf parody featuring space Nazis) but also about the "content" of the film's production and distribution plans. By getting others to participate, Vuorensola used social media tools to build a cult audience, even before *Iron Sky*'s international premiere.

The motivations for participating in a crowdsourced project vary widely. Although Vuorensola solicited contributions from the fan community associated with the *Star Wreck* and *Iron Sky* franchises, this approach should not imply that the fans had no professional training in film-making. In fact, many of the "Wreck a Movie" contributors work professionally in the media industries and choose to support the work of friends or to gain experience that could be used to obtain other professional jobs in the future. As Brabham notes, many of the participants behind *Star Wreck* and *Iron Sky* contributed their time because it was "fun" and because "they liked sharing knowledge and skills with others, among other altruistic reasons" (67). This process of sharing suggests a collective experience, one built around not just the movie itself, but also the extra-textual features that it involves.

Finally, *Iron Sky*'s unique distribution model helped position it as a cult object. In fact, *Iron Sky* depended heavily on what Roman Lobato describes as "informal media economies" as a means of circulating outside of the international film industry (39–47). Although the film received traditional theatrical distribution in some countries, the film-makers also encouraged fans to demand that *Iron Sky* play in a theater in their community, using a Google Maps mashup that would allow users to pin their location on an online map. If enough people in a city or town demanded to see *Iron Sky*, the producers could then negotiate with a local theater to have the film play there. At the same time, Vuorensola took a more relaxed view of digital piracy, choosing to allow *Iron Sky* to remain on Bit Torrent and other file sharing sites because, he reasoned, these types of informal sharing could also promote the film. Users who downloaded it might like it enough to eventually buy the DVD, or they might support it by purchasing some of the merchandise—t-shirts, fake dog tags—associated with *Iron Sky* as a means of expressing their allegiance. As a result, even the distribution models associated with *Iron Sky* helped to convey the film's different, indeed cult status.

Iron Sky illustrates many of the intersections between a cult cinema and contemporary film-making practices, such as the models of crowdsourcing and crowdfunding. Textually, *Iron Sky* deliberately engages with techniques associated with other sf cult films through its use of genre parody. The film also generally circulated outside of traditional modes of distribution and exhibition. Although it had a small theatrical run in the United States and a slightly larger one in Europe, it circulated largely on VOD and streaming video. More crucially, *Iron Sky* built upon an enthusiastic fan base that helped to finance, produce, and in some cases distribute or exhibit the film through venues traditionally ignored by major studios. Thus, *Iron Sky* reminds that a film's cult status depends on both textual properties and on audience activity. Of course, suggesting that cult status requires both a set of distinct textual features and an engaged audience is nothing new. However, what makes *Iron Sky* unusual is its ability to cultivate this status months—or even years—before the film was officially released. Through a wide range of extra-textual features, ranging from the promotional videos that established the film's tone to the crowdsourcing initiatives that helped to build a vibrant, energetic audience, *Iron Sky* illustrates the potential for participatory cultures to become involved in what might seem like a kind of sf activity: the contemporary process of co-creating cult cinema.

Notes

[1] Vuorensola discusses his intentions to draw connections between Nazism and contemporary political discourse in Jones.

[2] For a discussion of the Downfall meme, see Chuck Tryon, *Reinventing Cinema*. See also Virginia Heffernan's thoughtful analysis of how the Downfall meme "can be made to speak for almost anyone in the midst of a crisis."

Works Cited

Albrecht, Chris. "*Iron Sky* Opens up the Filmmaking Process." *GigaOM*, May 12, 2008. Web. Accessed 30 August 2013.

Benson-Allott, Caetlin. *Killer Tapes and Shattered Screens: Video Spectatorship from VHS to File Sharing*. Berkeley: U of California P, 2013.

Brabham, Daren C. *Crowdsourcing*. Cambridge: MIT Press, 2013.

Bromley, Patrick. "Take Two: *Snakes on a Plane*." *F this Movie*, June 27, 2013. Web. Accessed 30 August 2013.

Clark, Brian. "Berlin 2012 Review: IRON SKY." *Twitch Film*, February 11, 2012. Web. Accessed 30 August 2013.

Corrigan, Timothy. *A Cinema without Walls: Movies and Culture after Vietnam*. New Brunswick: Rutgers UP, 1991.

Duong, Senh. "'Iron Sky' Reviews from the Berlin Film Festival." *Movies with Butter*, February 12, 2012. Web. Accessed 30 August 2013.

Gray, Jonathan. *Show Sold Separately: Promos, Spoilers, and Other Media Paratexts*. New York: New York UP, 2010.

Grefe, Richard. "What's the Harm in Crowdsourcing?" *AIGA Insight*, June 24, 2011. Web. Accessed 30 August 2013.

Heffernan, Virginia. "The Hitler Meme." *The New York Times*, October 24, 2008. Web. Accessed 30 August 2013.

Hills, Matt. *Fan Cultures*. New York and London: Routledge, 2002.

Howe, Jeff. "The Rise of Crowdsourcing." *Wired* 14.06 (June 2006). Web. Accessed 30 August 2013.

Jancovich, Mark. "Cult Fictions: Cult Movies, Subcultural Capital, and the Production of Cultural Distinctions." *The Cult Film Reader*. Ed. Ernest Mathijs and Xavier Mendik. New York: McGraw-Hill, 2008. 149–62.

Jenkins, Henry. *Convergence Culture: Where Old and New Media Collide*. New York: New York UP, 2006.

Jones, Emma. "What's the Fuss over *Iron Sky*?" BBC.com, May 27, 2012. Web. Accessed 30 August 2013.

Kirsner, Scott. *Fans, Friends, and Followers*. New York: CinemaTech Books, 2009.

Klinger, Barbara. "Becoming Cult: *The Big Lebowski*, Replay Culture, and Male Fans." *Screen* 51.1 (2010): 1–20.

—. *Beyond the Multiplex: Cinema, New Technologies, and the Home*. Berkeley: U of California P, 2006.

Lobato, Ramon. *Shadow Economies of Cinema: Mapping Informal Film Distribution.* London: Palgrave MacMillan, 2012.

Rooney, David. "Iron Sky: Berlin Film Review." *The Hollywood Reporter,* February 12, 2012. Web. Accessed 30 August 2013.

Roxborough, Scott. "'Iron Sky' Sequel Gets $150,000 in Crowd-Funding." *The Hollywood Reporter,* July 8, 2013. Web. Accessed 30 August 2013.

Sconce, Jeffrey. "'Trashing' the Academy: Taste, Excess and an Emerging Politics of Cinematic Style." *The Cult Film Reader.* Ed. Ernest Mathijs and Xavier Mendik. New York: McGraw-Hill, 2008. 100–18.

Shirky, Clay. *Here Comes Everybody: The Power of Organizing without Organizations.* New York: Penguin, 2008.

Tassi, Paul. "When Kickstarter Works: The First Footage from the Veronica Mars Movie." *Forbes,* July 21, 2013. Web. Accessed 30 August 2013.

Telotte, J. P. "*The Blair Witch Project*: Film and the Internet." *The Cult Film Reader.* Ed. Ernest Mathijs and Xavier Mendik. New York: McGraw-Hill, 2008. 263–74.

Tryon, Chuck. *Reinventing Cinema: Movies in the Age of Media Convergence.* New Brunswick: Rutgers UP, 2009.

Tunick, Britt. "Tinseltown and the Street Team Up to Offer Movie IPOs." *Investment Dealers Digest,* May 14, 2001. Lexis Nexis. Web. Accessed 30 August 2013.

8. Transnational Interactions: *District 9*, or Apaches in Johannesburg

Takayuki Tatsumi

In 2009, several friends recommended that I see *District 9*, a new film produced by Peter Jackson and directed by the hitherto unknown Neill Blomkamp. They knew that since I was something of a missionary for cyberpunk and avant-pop texts, I would appreciate this film, an unlikely export from South Africa that had quickly attracted a cult following. They were right. Blomkamp's ideas and shocking images immediately reminded me of Shinya Tsukamoto's cyberpunk Tetsuo films (*Tetsuo: The Iron Man*, 1988, and *Tetsuo II: Body Hammer*, 1992) which had inspired me to write my first book, *Full Metal Apache* (2006). However, after seeing *District 9* again, I realized that my first reading was a bit one-dimensional, and I became convinced that this cult film offered significant insight not only into the history of sf film, but also the cultural history—and contributions—of sf itself. At first glance, and like many other films with a cult reputation, *District 9* seems very cheaply done, a seemingly slight, even offhand work. However, that simple low-budget appearance masks an incredible narrative complexity and challenging cultural commentary. This essay explores how that combination of simplicity and complexity has helped to make *District 9* a contemporary cult classic.

District 9 Revisited

The central concept of *District 9* is relatively familiar. Certainly, it recalls the traditional "invaders from space" narrative, as one day the inhabitants of Johannesburg, South Africa, find hovering overhead a huge UFO, inhabited by crustacean-like aliens that the South Africans nickname "prawns." Fans of sf might well suppose that they are either superior invaders, as in Roland Emmerich's *Independence Day* (1996), or god-like supervisors of human affairs, much like the Overlords Arthur

C. Clarke describes in his novel *Childhood's End* (1953), advanced beings who will help us evolve from humans into a higher form and solve our problems. However, Blomkamp twists Clarke's canonical formula for such "Imperialist" sf narratives, a formula that redefines humans as a kind of cattle who have been domesticated and overseen by superior aliens since the dawn of human time. He creates a situation in which it is not the human beings on Earth but the aliens from outer space who need help. Their spaceship is disabled, so they will have to stay here while they find a way to repair their ship. However, the aliens are required to begin living in a zone of Johannesburg called "District 9"—an area that quickly comes to resemble a variety of human ghettoes, thereby establishing a link to familiar contemporary racial conflicts.

In our own history, the 1980s coincided with the period of the director's childhood, when resistance to the racial segregation of apartheid was accelerating. Then 1990 saw South African President Frederik Willem de Klerk's negotiations to end apartheid, culminating in multi-racial democratic elections that, in turn, led to the victory of the African National Congress under Nelson Mandela. But, as Blomkamp has pointed out, *District 9* should not be read simply as an sf caricature of South Africa's history of apartheid, but as a commentary on what is going on even now in Johannesburg, where racist attacks against Nigerian and Zimbabwean immigrants are taking place, where other sorts of apartheid thinking, among both black and white South Africans, still linger. For example, in one of the opening scenes, various protests against the aliens break out, leading several black South Africans to shout comments like:

"I think they must fix that ship and they must go."

"A virus, a selective virus. Release it near the aliens."

"They must just go. I don't know where, but they must just go!"

"If they were from another country, we might understand ... but they are not even from this planet." (italics added)

This last statement is particularly intriguing, since it ironically parodies segregationist discourses of the 1980s. However, in this alternate history set in another 1980s, even black South Africans, those who had suffered through a long history of discrimination, urge segregation for the aliens, who are "not even" foreigners, but unknown visitors from another planet. At this point, Blomkamp penetrates a universal truth about the racist unconscious of Earth's inhabitants: its universality and, despite the lessons of history, its continuity.

This complex situation is the reason why the ghetto-like zone of *District 9* is inhabited not only by aliens from outer space but also by a more familiar sort of alien, in this case Nigerian arms dealers and black marketeers. Their belief in native magic (represented by African traditional medicine or "muti") is here compared with the special knowledge of the aliens, as we see when they purchase a number of alien weapons that they believe will work as another kind of muti, at least, as they later learn, if they are managed by someone with alien DNA. However, we should note that while Blomkamp develops the prawns as parallels to the Nigerians and Zimbabweans, he misrepresents muti here, as one of the characters, Dr. Sarah Livingstone, a sociologist of Kempton Park University, suggests in the introductory sequence of the film:

> "Muti" is a South African word. Today, it's synonymous with witch-doctory and magic ... The Nigerians were consuming alien body parts. They believed that by doing so, they were ingesting their power ... to use alien weaponry.

Here the director replaces muti as traditional magic with muti as a literal form of cannibalism through which the Nigerian gangs believe human beings might become capable of controlling alien weapons, thereby gaining hegemony over their world, and thus a sense of power that has seemingly been denied them in their current situation.

The film's protagonist is Wikus van de Merwe (Sharlto Copley), who works for Multi National United (MNU), a developer of advanced technology and weaponry. He is apparently a good husband to his wife Tania (Vanessa Haywood) and an average bureaucrat, proud of having recently been appointed Field Officer in charge of moving the aliens from District 9 to a new, expanded settlement, District 10. When he is introduced in the film's prologue, we note the documentary tone of the work, suggesting that the whole film has been completed after Wikus has already gone through the unspeakable events that the rest of the film details. This prologue is telling, particularly with its ambiguous references to Wikus's fate, for it makes the audience curious about what happened to him after he began working as the Field Officer in command of this obviously controversial operation. The initially arrogant Wikus and his men require the aliens to sign contracts of eviction, conduct random tests on their strange possessions, and at one point confiscate a cylinder containing an apparently precious black fluid—something that, we later learn, might enable the aliens to fix and energize their disabled craft. After the fluid is accidentally sprayed in his face, Wikus takes the rest of it with him to the laboratory at MNU. While the alien Christopher Johnson (Jason Cope) has struggled to collect the liquid with the aim of going back home, Wikus is just trying to carry out his bureaucratic duties. This simple accident is the genesis of what is revealed to be a genetic infection and ultimately a fundamental transformation in Wikus's character as he is forced to live the life of an alien.

When he subsequently becomes badly ill, Wikus goes to the hospital, where the doctor is amazed at his arm, which is mutating because of a genetic fusion of human and alien DNA. He is promptly taken to MNU bio labs, where scientists are revealed to be conducting live alien experiments, reminiscent of notorious Nazi medical experiments. At these labs, Wikus reluctantly succeeds in doing something no one else has been able to accomplish—firing the alien weapons—a development that turns him from a simple bureaucratic worker to a highly valuable commodity, a kind of human-alien hybrid technology worth billions. However, Wikus only wants to recover from the infection and escapes, returning to the only place he might be safe, the alien District 9.

In the meantime, his father-in-law Piet (Louis Minnaar) suggests to Wikus's wife Tania that the fatal infection may have been caused by a sexual relationship with an alien, and that she should just forget him. In the District, Wikus hides out in the alien Christopher's shack, and the two plan to storm NMU headquarters and take back the fluid, which will allow Christopher's hidden ship to take off. Wikus dons a powered suit, one that recalls various Japanese giant robots, such as those of the *Gundam* or *Evangelion* series, and he survives a battle with the Nigerian arms dealers, who want to cut off and appropriate his alien arm. Functioning much like a superhero at this point, Wikus helps Christopher and his son to go "home," although Christopher promises to return within three years and transform Wikus back into a human being. The film's last sequence shows Tania cherishing a metal flower found on her doorstep, and Wikus, now fully transformed and living as a prawn, trying to fashion another flower, a symbol of both his enduring love for his wife and the cyborgian fusion of the organic and mechanic within him, and also hinting at the subcultural heritage of Blomkamp himself, as I will clarify later.

Intersections between the Prawn, Apache, and Lo-Tek

The film's central conceit of transforming human beings into bio-weapons has an obvious ancestry in Japanese cyberpunk director Shinya

Tsukamoto's Tetsuo series, especially *Tetsuo II: Body Hammer* (1992), a film that appeared exactly ten years after its cyberpunk precursor, Ridley Scott's *Blade Runner* (1982), based on Philip K. Dick's 1968 novel *Do Androids Dream of Electric Sheep?* and eight years after William Gibson's canonical cyberpunk novel *Neuromancer* (1984). Globally embraced by cult fans, *Tetsuo II* won numerous prizes at international film festivals. Its plot structure leaves nothing ambiguous in its own treatment of transformation, as it deals with metallization, not as symptomatic of a new type of plague, but as the effect of medical experimentation on a living person—much as we see in the MNU laboratories of *District 9*. Thus, *Tetsuo II* starts with the conspiracy of a mad scientist, who is trying to transform a group of skinheads into bio-weapons by instilling a conditioned reflex so that whenever they feel the impulse to murder, they automatically transform into powerful cyborg soldiers with metallic rifles growing out of their bodies. But then the next step in his experimentation becomes how to make the murderous impulse even stronger, so they can be more useful as soldiers. The solution is to kidnap the child of an ordinary petit-bourgeois salaryman so he will nurture within himself a revenge impulse, a more sinister intent to kill. This is how the protagonist Tomoo Taniguchi is selected as an appropriate victim. But

a. The Japanese cult film *Tetsuo: The Iron Man* (1989) depicts the human transformed into technology.

b. Evoking the "city destroyers" of *Independence Day* (1996), the Prawns' starship settles over Johannesburg in *District 9* (2009).

the experiment conducted on him is far more successful than expected. As children, Tomoo and his elder brother had already been trained by their own father, another mad scientist, to become bio-weapons. Tomoo's father began his experiment by fusing a cat with a kettle, and later he applied the same methods to the transformation of his own children.

Tsukamoto's notion of a fusion of flesh and metal superseding the limits of human physicality seems to have had an obvious impact on Blomkamp's blending of human and alien DNA, the same blending that enables the hero to manage the aliens' powerful weapons. And, indeed, most sf fans would naturally consider Tsukamoto's Tetsuo series and Blomkamp's *District 9* to be hardcore cyberpunk narratives. Yet what might go unnoticed is the way both interweave the cultural heritage of another subgroup, the Japanese "Apache," an influence more visible in *Tetsuo II*. As I describe in *Full Metal Apache*, the Apaches of Japanese culture, who made their living as scrap thieves in the postwar Japanese wasteland, trace their origins to the day before the end of the Second World War, August 14, 1945. On that day, the Osaka Army factory, the largest munitions plant in Asia (located in Sugiyama-cho between Osaka Castle and the Nekoma River), was totally destroyed by B-29 bombers. Since the plant comprised three large factories, a munitions plant, and a school for engineers, this air raid meant the complete devastation of the center of the Japanese munitions industry. In the postwar years, the American army removed most of the usable weaponry and dangerous materials that had simply been abandoned in the wreckage, and in 1952 the Japanese government designated the whole ruined complex national property. But even at that point, more than 30,000 machines of various sorts remained there, largely intact and partially buried in the ground.

It was then that some of the people living in the shabby shelters on the other side of the Nekoma River came to notice that these wrecked machines might prove highly marketable. That community, almost a cult itself, consisted of Koreans, Okinawans, and some Japanese, ranging from bank robbers and bicycle thieves to get-rich-quick schemers. The junkyard of the Osaka Army factory stimulated dreams of wealth or deliverance from their poor conditions, and prompted them to dig precious scraps out of the ruins which they would then exchange for considerable sums of money. It was not the scrap thieves themselves who selected the term "Apache" as a kind of tribal name, but contemporary journalists who, in their commentaries on this subculture, set up a strong analogy between the scrap thieves in Osaka and the Apache tribesmen often portrayed in popular westerns of the period. In such postwar westerns as *Fort Apache* (1948), *She Wore a Yellow Ribbon* (1949), and *Rio Grande* (1950), John Ford had dramatically described the war between the Americans and the Apache Indians. By the early 1950s, the Apache chief Geronimo had become a familiar figure of Hollywood films and his people found a new popularity in Japanese culture. By 1958, the journalistic analogy between the Hollywood Apache and the multicultural Japanese scrap thieves had become well established, with contemporary journalists noting how the scrap thieves would carry away scraps right in front of policemen, while speaking in Korean or Okinawan, just the way the Apaches brazenly fought the American soldiers. In the May 28, 1958 issue of the *Osaka Nichi-nichi Shinbun* (*Osaka Daily News*), a headline read: "The Japanese Apache Bust: 53 Members of the Tribe Arrested." Later that same year, Ken Kaiko would publish the first "Japanese Apache" novel, *Nippon Sanmon Opera* (*The Japanese Threepenny Opera*), later followed by Sakyo Komatsu's second "Japanese Apache" novel, *Nippon Apacchi-Zoku* (*The Japanese Apache*, 1964). A subculture had not only been established but had found its own cult popularity.

I outline this cultural heritage of the Japanese Apache, which influenced Tsukamoto's *Tetsuo II*, because I believe that in cutting up, sampling, and remixing a variety of the images and narratives peculiar to Japanese popular culture, Blomkamp has imbibed the spirit of postwar Japanese poor who made a profit on scraps in the junkyard, and has incorporated it into his aliens-as-scavengers in *District 9*. The aliens trading their weapons for cat food in the zone, modeled upon the Nigerians and the Zimbabweans segregated in Johannesburg between the 1960s and the 1980s, conjure up the Japanese Apaches of the 1950s, particularly the Okinawans and Koreans who were discriminated against in Japan. Just as Komatsu's Apaches, in their metaphoric linkage of human and machine, become imaginatively fused with various metals and transform themselves into a new tribe of superhuman beings, and just as the tradition of the Japanese Apache inspired Tsukamoto to create a hardcore cyberpunk film, Blomkamp fashioned his alien scavengers as South African Apaches, outcasts whose esoteric technology transforms the ordinary human being Wikus into a Tetsuo-like bio-weapon.

Of course, here the term "Apache" also serves as a catachresis for subversive Native Americans raiding and re-appropriating dominant culture. In his sf alternate history *Apacheria* (1998), published 40 years after the first "Japanese Apache" novel by Ken Kaiko, Jake Page narrates a history in which the original Apaches, led by their new leader Juh, triumph over the armies of the United States and establish a sovereign Apache nation in 1885. That triumph is predicated upon Juh's new, yet also historical vision of the "Apache Way":

> He had a vision that appealed to the young men who had been brought up hearing stories of Apache heroism and glory, of lightning-like Apache raids, of the evident superiority of the Apache Way over any other, be it Mexican, American, or any other tribal people who now lived like zoo animals on reservations. (*Apacheria* Chapter 25).

With Blomkamp's *District 9* enjoying a wide cult popularity, we might well redefine this notion of the "Apache Way" as referring not only to the western hemisphere but also to the eastern, and denoting the specifically cyberpunk vision of resistance and survival that it denotes and that would ultimately inspire a cult appreciation.

This similarity may be one reason why *District 9* also recalls the "Lo Tek" (outlaw technologist) way of life so vividly described in a William Gibson short story of 1981, later adapted by Robert Longo as the cult film *Johnny Mnemonic* (1995). The following passage illustrates the connection:

> The graffiti followed us up, gradually thinning until a single name was repeated at intervals.
> Lo Tek. In dripping black capitals.
> "Who's Lo Tek?"
> "Not us, boss." She [Molly] climbed a shivering aluminum ladder and vanished through a hole in a sheet of corrugated plastic.
> "Low technique, low technology." The plastic muffled her voice ...
> "Lo Teks, they'd think that shotgun trick of yours was effete." (19)

We should not misunderstand Lo Teks as descendants of the simple-minded Luddites who resisted big industry in eighteenth-century England. Pynchon redefined the Luddites in his famous 1984 essay "Is It O.K. to be a Luddite?", as he noted: "Machines have already become so user-friendly that even the most unreconstructed of Luddites can be charmed into laying down the old sledgehammer and stroking a few keys instead." Furthermore, he offers:

> It may be only a new form of the perennial Luddite ambivalence about machines, or it may be that the deepest Luddite hope of a miracle has now come to reside in the computer's ability to get the right data to those whom the data will do the most good. (Pynchon)

Note that Pynchon's redefinition of Luddites corresponds to the rise of the Gibsonian Lo Tek sensibility that is peculiar to many computer hackers or cyberspace cowboys. Lo Teks make use of whatever is at hand or available on the street in order to outwit giant multinational corporations, just like the Nigerian arms dealers headed by Obesandjo in *District 9*.

Intrigued by this hardcore Lo Tek sensibility, Blomkamp in his second feature film *Elysium* (2013), has expanded the possibilities for this sort of resistance into outer space, skillfully blending the outlaw image of District 9 in Johannesburg with that of a future Los Angeles, which has become another version of Mexican border cities like Juares, the seat of a huge drug cartel, as described in Gregory Nava's film *Bordertown* (2006) and Ridley Scott's *The Counselor* (2013). When seen in this context, *District 9* becomes a multiply resonant cyberpunk intersection where the prawn-shaped aliens identify with multinational Apaches and Gibsonian Lo Teks, reviving the spirit of canonical outlaw cities like Chiba City in Japan, described in the opening of Gibson's *Neuromancer*.

Towards a Poetics of South African SF

What renders *District 9*'s particular version of this cyberpunk intersection especially noteworthy is that—as its opening narration reminds us—the aliens' gigantic UFO did not "come to a stop over Manhattan or Washington or Chicago, but instead coasted to a halt directly over the city of Johannesburg." The screenwriters seem to have been keenly aware of such films as *Independence Day*, in which huge starships, the so-called "City Destroyers," storm New York, Los Angeles, Washington D.C., and other high-profile international centers.

That effort at differentiation from mainstream sf also surfaces in the aesthetic difference between the gorgeously streamlined and gleaming UFOs designed by Steven Spielberg, Roland Emmerich, and others—spaceships based upon an aesthetics peculiar to the Modernist age of the early twentieth century, that is, what Gibson called "The Gernsback Continuum"—and the dirty, almost steampunk look of the South African UFO conceived by Blomkamp, quite possibly inspired by Japanese anime and clearly reminiscent of imagery crafted by anime master Hayao Miyazaki. These revisions alone might well have garnered *District 9* and Blomkamp special note and a cult following, particularly among those in the cyberpunk community.

Yet what may be most revealing is the film's more fundamental cultural revision. For while traditional sf has consistently represented aliens from outer space as superior beings, Blomkamp has recast them here in a fashion much more significant for the Third World experience: not as Overlords but as slave-like poor, as worker types needing leadership, and all too easily brutalized and victimized by both white and black bureaucrats. Indeed, despite their apparently high intelligence and technological accomplishments, the prawns' cosmological status seems lower than that of humans.

In this context we might once more recall the works of Arthur C. Clarke—especially his novels from *Childhood's End* (1953) through *2061: A Space Odyssey* (1987), which often depicted highly imperialistic alien races that treat human beings as lower life forms, almost resembling cattle. However, the most essentially cattle-like figures in Clarke's works are not humans but rather beings like the Monolith, which are variants of the Overlords. Such figures serve as mediums or midwives to the future super-evolution of human beings. They possess great intellectual powers, but while human beings are endowed with limitless creative potential, these beings are already trapped in some "evolutionary cul-de-sac" (206). In short—and this is the key point—while they possess superior intelligence, their status is inferior and their fate circumscribed, as seems to be the case for the prawns. Of course, within the limits of the film narrative, Blomkamp's aliens do not serve as such midwives for the future *physical* evolution of mankind. Subverting the traditional hierarchy between human beings and aliens, the director instead focuses on the friendship between Wikus and Christopher, slightly reminiscent of the Spielbergian friendship between the children and E. T. in *E. T., the Extra-Terrestrial* (1982). Shocked by what MNU did to the aliens at the bio lab, Christopher and Wikus exchange promises:

Christopher: I will not let my people be medical experiments!

Wikus: I'm a fucking medical experiment. You hear me? I'm a fucking medical experiment, man.

Christopher: I must go home and get help. I must use all the fluid to travel quickly.

Wikus: I'll just stay here, Christopher. I'll just stay here in this shack. And I'll see you in three years' time?

Christopher: I will come back. I promise.

Behind that bond is the radical transformation Wikus has undergone, for as that genetic transformation proceeds, their friendship becomes deeper. If the aliens are modeled after Africans who are still subject to discrimination, Afrikaners like Wikus, the film implies, can only fully come to understand their predicament by literally going native. So while Blomkamp's prawn-like aliens do not help humans to undergo a super-evolution, they unwittingly make Afrikaners like Wikus literally *live* as aliens themselves. Through this hybrid experience, it is implied, humans (aka whites) and aliens (aka non-whites) might finally evolve a productive coalition, one based on mutual understanding.

This perspective on *District 9* might also allow us to reread a tutor-text like Clarke's *Childhood's End* with its by now hackneyed formula of giant alien spaceships invading the Earth. Although Clarke has often been considered a typical British imperialist, his deep interest in marine biology led him to migrate to Sri Lanka in 1956, three years after the publication of *Childhood's End*, one of whose major characters is himself a hybrid figure, Jan Rodricks. He is "an engineering student from the University of Cape Town" (155) whose blond but expatriate father spent all his life in Haiti, but whose black mother lectured in advanced probability theory at Edinburgh University. Historically speaking, Cape Town was the most important junction between Europe and Asia until the discovery of gold in Johannesburg, which helped ignite the Boer War. After the Union of South Africa was established in 1910 as a Commonwealth realm, Cape Town housed its legislature until 1961, when the Union was reorganized as the Republic of South Africa, independent of Britain. What matters here is that Johannesburg's gold rush and the Boer War caused the gradual decline of Cape Town's significance and central place in South African culture.

Although Johannesburg is the richest city in South Africa today, in *Childhood's End* Clarke's Commonwealth unconscious led him to regard Cape Town as still superior and a place that might, appropriately, produce an important hybrid figure. Although the novel's insights into the future remain illuminating, what still captures our imagination is Clarke's narrative of the African Jan Rodricks stowing away on the Overlords' starship. Clarke's Overlords are not only a medium of super-evolution, but also almost Satanic figures, with their "leathery wings, the little horns, the barbed tail," standing "in ebon majesty" (73–74). This image is imprinted on humans' mythical unconscious as a memory of the future, that is, the memory of "those closing years when your race knew that everything was finished" (243). Jan is a typical African boy whose skin color "would have been a tremendous, perhaps overwhelming, handicap" a century before (102). In this passage Clarke is not trying to characterize Jan in a conservative or negative way, for he explains the status of blacks as follows: "The inevitable reaction that had given early twenty-first-century Negroes a slight sense of superiority had already passed away" (102). As Clarke was writing, the African-American civil rights movement was growing stronger and stronger, and he even seems to predict the global romanticization of black power in the era of Obama. Despite the novel's rigid hierarchy, Clarke is able to imagine a possible intimacy between such a typical South African boy and the Satan-like Overlords as he conjures a vision of potential hybrid development.

While this imagery might suggest a conventional analogy between the Miltonic Satan of *Paradise Lost*, the black man, and the serpent in Eden, we might simply consider what becomes of the hybrid Jan when the Overlord Karellen discovers that he has stowed away, and another Overload, Rashaverak, wants Jan to stay on Earth and report what will happen to the planet at the moment of total apocalypse, assigning him a role like that of Ishmael in Melville's *Moby-Dick* (1851): "The picture that reaches your eyes will be duplicated by our cameras. But the message that enters your brain may be very different, and it could tell us a great deal" (251). What Blomkamp does in *District 9*, if unwittingly, is to transfigure this Socratic master-disciple relationship between the Overlords and Jan into a Huck-and-Jim buddy relationship between the prawn-like alien poor and the posthuman hybrid Wikus, who also might witness what will transpire in this changing world and, as a result, "tell us a great deal."

In extending this parallel, we might note that Wikus describes his wife as an angel in his self-introduction part of the documentary, which, ironically, appears as part of the film's final sequence. Holding up a picture from their wedding, he says:

> You guys haven't seen my wife. Let me show you my wife. She's my special angel. She Even looks like an angel with a halo. You want to see? With the white veil over her head, she even looks like an angel.

But given that image, how are we supposed to interpret the subsequent narrative commentary: "Everyone says his wife's an angel, but this is a real angel that you're seeing." At this point Wikus's wife Tania enters, a virtual widow given his "disappearance." She then displays the metal flower she has discovered and offers a closing commentary: "I found this at my front door, as though somebody had just left it there. My friends say I should throw it away because it's just a piece of rubbish. And it couldn't possibly come from him. I know it's true." But while Tania cannot believe this flower is a secret gift from her husband, she obviously seems to cherish it. And the final scene featuring Wikus, now completely transformed into a prawn, should convince us that *District 9* is not only a black comedy mocking the Clarkean super-evolution narrative, but also a dangerously planetary love story that goes far beyond any earthly coalition. Is Wikus himself a real angel or a fallen angel? This question will remain unresolved; the ambiguities here, as in most works with a cult following, remain seductively alive. All we can know is that it is this form of love that helps support *District 9*'s status as an sf cult film, a work for a new, global-minded audience, and one that could not have been produced within the Cold War discursive frameworks that had so inspired an earlier generation of alien invasion narratives.

Works Cited

Clarke, Arthur C. *Childhood's End.* 1954. New York: TOR, 1990.

—. *2001: A Space Odyssey.* New York: Signet, 1968.

—. *Profiles of the Future: Millennium Edition.* London: Indigo, 2000.

District 9. Dir. Neill Blomkamp. Sony. 2009.

Gibson, William. "Johnny Mnemonic." *Burning Chrome.* New York: Avon, 1986.

—. *Neuromancer.* New York: Ace, 1984.

Mes, Tom. *Iron Man: The Cinema of Shinya Tsukamoto.* Godalming: FAB, 2005.

Page, Jake. *Apacheria.* New York: Del Rey, 1998.

Pynchon, Thomas. "Is It O.K. to be a Luddite?" *The New York Times Book Review,* October 28, 1984: 40–41. Web. Accessed 16 June 2014.

Tatsumi, Takayuki. *Full Metal Apache: Transactions between Cyberpunk Japan and Avant-Pop America.* Durham: Duke UP, 2006.

Tetsuo. Dir. Shinya Tsukamoto. Kaiju-Theater, 1989.

Tetsuo II: Body Hammer. Dir. Shinya Tsukamoto. Kaiju-Theater, 1992.

9. A Donut for Tom Paris:
Identity and Belonging at European
SF/Fantasy Conventions

Nicolle Lamerichs

Decades ago, fans were usually adults who had the economic and social liberty of going to conventions or clubs. Recently, the discourse on fandom has become entwined with that on new media audiences, who are not only portrayed as younger, but also seen as especially exemplary of fandom in terms of their online activity. As a result of the increase in online participatory culture, criticism has followed suit, often focusing more on the "online" than the "offline" dimensions of fandom. However, concerts, conventions, movie theaters, and fan clubs remain relevant sites where media fandom is performed today, and these venues are especially revealing for the study of both cult and sf, one of the media genres in which cult texts have most flourished. In fact, only offline, amongst those who embody the enthusiasm of cult activity, can the scholar witness the key role that intimacy plays in enabling and characterizing the typical cult audience and cult relationship.

Academic commentary has often defined cult texts in relation to their media fandom and the intense and critical commitment of their audiences (Mathijs and Sexton 17–18). These definitions of cult reception echo the social and affective patterns that are often mentioned as characteristics of fandom (see Grossberg; Fiske, *Understanding*; Jenkins, *Textual Poachers*). Of course, differentiating between the fan and the cultist is problematic, since both are adoring, active audiences, but two differences are especially noteworthy here. First, while fandom of movies and television series is historically grounded and organized, for instance through early fan magazines and clubs, cult largely emerged in the 1970s and ties viewers to a critical discourse and a vintage identity of that era (Mathijs and Sexton 3). Cult fans invest in specialized media texts and knowledge (Abercrombie and Longhurst 138–39), and by defining their tastes as oppositional from the mainstream, they maintain a sense of distinction (Mathijs and Mendik 2). Second, academic studies on fanship have differentiated fans from other audiences through their productivity (see Fiske's "Cultural Economy"). In their creative fan practices, fans rework, extend, and appropriate popular culture through creative writing, costumes, fan art, and other activities (Jenkins, *Textual Poachers*). While cultists are recognizable through their knowledge practices, media fans seek to deepen the text through transformation. However, neither attitude is fixed; in fact, as Matt Hills notes, they often conflate in the identity of the cult fan who celebrates niche media (see his *Fan Cultures* 3–6).

Especially in terms of affect, the identity of the fan and cultist appear to converge. Ironic distance has often been mentioned as one quality of the cult audience, but it also characterizes other fandoms. That is, interpretation in fandom often lingers between an affective intimacy and critical distance (see Kelly's *Fanning the Flames*). This is a complex dynamic that I want to explore in relation to the fan convention, which offers a rich space where such affective structures are constructed and played out. Like the cult text itself, the convention is characterized by an ambiguity or doubling pattern. The event promises an immersive and affective experience that is highly personal and intense, but it is also one that is negotiated through detachment and self-reflexivity. Moreover, these critical stances may be provoked through negative emotions, such as shame for other fans or jealousy of their skills. Thus, the fan convention is an excellent space to see how audiences negotiate the cult experience of film and television texts, and to observe the intimacy that the cultist and fan share.

Broadly defined, the fan convention is an event organized by fans of a particular genre such as sf, often focusing attention on particular films, series, or celebrities. Audiences gather to meet actors, authors, or other figures and to discuss their favorite texts amongst each other or with their creators. While many cons are non-profit endeavors, some have commercial intents. Fan cons may also include "expos," which might be loosely defined as events that focus primarily on the market area rather than on the entertainment represented by such features as workshops, videos, and lectures. While I shall describe these venues in more detail below, I would stress that studying these rich social spaces can help us understand the function of cult, not through the text, as so many others have sought to do, but through its audience.

Until recently, the convention has been underexplored as a site of such research. Scholars sometimes attend one event and frame this experience as an introduction into fan practices (see, for example, the work of Bacon-Smith and Taylor). However, few have examined cons and especially their social dimension in detail. Moreover, such studies typically emphasize large American conventions, which are arranged differently from European ones and from many smaller, local events. My research incorporates the richness and diversity of these other sites, as I consider the convention central to the articulation of popular narratives and their related fan practices. This study will explicitly show how fans contribute to offline communities rather than the online communities that other fan studies explore. By combining this ethnography of offline sites with the methods and theories of the humanities, we can gain a better understanding of both cult and sf audiences. My approach involves analyzing three European sf/fantasy cons as pivotal research sites for the sort of ambiguous textual relationship described above. These sites are broadly representative of continental sf fandom and the attendant construction of fan identity, and they show us how sf fandom can be played out through different performative stances, thus illustrating the diversity of that fandom and indeed of the genre itself. To specify these three local field sites, I shall connect the events to three fan figures that I identify as the *nostalgist*, the *collector*, and the *autograph hunter*.

Fan Conventions

Both cons and cult activity are intimately tied up with the history of sf audiences. The first large fan convention, the World Science Fiction Convention, or "Worldcon," was held on July 4, 1939, and is still held annually. In 1953, the literary society that sponsors the event presented the first Hugo Award, now the most critically acclaimed prize for sf and fantasy authors. Before the establishment of Worldcon, some sf fans had already organized public events related to their fanzines or fan clubs (Coppa 42–43). In recent years, such conventions have become far more popular. Specifically, the emergence of anime fandom in the 1990s gave a new impulse to media cons by emphasizing "cosplay" (a portmanteau of "costume" and "playing"), the dressing up as fictional characters. Even though anime cosplay was inspired by the dressing up of Western sf fans, the Japanese redefined it through their own visual designs and craftsmanship culture. When anime fandom gained ground in Western countries, dress-up became more visible and was redefined through its Japanese appropriation (see my "Stranger than Fiction"). Today, fan conventions are among the most popular festivals all over the world. The San Diego ComicCon in 2012 had over 120,000 visitors, while the Japanese comic fair Comiket drew several hundred thousand.

My interest in such cons lies partly in their relationship to narrativity. The convention is a space where fan practices flourish—a landscape filled with the discourses of fan creativity. It is a rich social event that dynamically transforms an ordinary physical space into a media environment rife with allusions to collective fantasies. Scholars have remarked that fans are more engaged with a text that leads to specific structures of close reading and a more emotional form of reception (see Jenkins's *Fans, Bloggers, and Gamers*; Kaplan). This affective reception also characterizes the joy of what we might term *media places*, spaces that include not only cons, but also movie sites and theme parks. The experience is comparable to a type of media tourism, wherein fans visit a place that is integral to the cult text, either as a fictional setting or site of production, such as the tours of settings from *Battlestar Galactica* (2004–09) that are offered in Vancouver. That tourism helps audiences access, interpret, and actualize the beloved narrative anew (see the commentaries by Couldry and Reijnders). Creating this intimate relationship with fiction is similar to the cultural logic of the typical fan convention.

However, the con is also a deeply social platform, albeit one that does not establish a socially coherent community. The convention is one platform where the heterogeneity of fandom can be observed, and where the similarities and differences between individual fans are broadly played out. Hierarchies of taste may be evoked within this community, based on differences between interests in genres (e.g., sf, fantasy), media (animation, films, novels), or characters. More delicate tropes and figures that interrelate these forms may also be pitted against each other, such as steam punk, space operas, or time travel narratives. Fans rely on visual signs of belonging, such as costumes, that grant them status, but conventional roles also provide social status, as in the case of the volunteer, staff member, or lecturer. Some members may also be identified as new or old-timers, a lineage that also contributes to and constructs their fan identity.

Behind the logic of these social "memberships" lie affective regimes, characterized by a private sense of entitlement to the media text and regulated by feelings and investments. Fans may deploy this sense of ownership to include or exclude other fans—to "other" particular individuals in a celebrated, collective space. It is important to note that during my field work, these communities also occasionally were divided, based on crucial social differences like gender, ethnicity, and age. These identity markers were a clear focus for my observations, as were the ways in which fans performed, re-enacted, and socialized based on their favorite narratives. The fictional space of the con thus functions to maintain a fictionalized relationship with the self, other fans, and the text itself.

Beyond Genre

Sf in particular provides a most appropriate genre platform for viewing critical and creative fan activities, since it features a strong "hyperdiegesis," which Matt Hills deems essential for cult activity ("Transcultural 'Otaku'" 137). That is, the genre helps establish a large narrative space of which viewers see or interact with only a small fraction. The long history and lore of the sf world appeals to audiences who can fill in its blanks and debate mentioned characters or events. At the typical sf con, this potential may be witnessed when fans dress up as their favorite or original characters, debate plot lines in panels, or create their own art inspired by film and television texts.

Informing this analysis is the idea that sf especially represents a "transgeneric phenomenon" composed of recognizable aesthetic and structural elements. This term was coined by R. Barton Palmer (30) to describe how another genre, the film noir, migrated across various media platforms. Like sf, its structural elements do not form a coherent whole, but rather emerge in texts that bridge genres, repertoires, and media. That broad emergence underscores that genres are partly what audiences believe them to be and depend on interpretation (see the commentary by Kwasnik and Crowston), even in the case of relatively consistent tropes, such as time travel, dystopias, or cyborgs. Thus, genres are socially situated and closely related to other genres that, together, help demarcate and identify each other's qualities. I shall trace the implications of the increased hybridity of sf through con fans, emphasizing how they explore and perform their loyalties. At these conventions, sf films and shows are constantly put to the test and mixed with fantasy texts, Japanese animation, and video game genres. My analysis will thus include the cultural practices of fans, such as cosplay, that help account for this transgeneric spreadability. Ultimately, I will show that sf's transgeneric qualities do not mean that fans engage with the genre in all its hybridity, but that they navigate by interest.

Method and Approach

My ethnographic approach situates fandom as a lived culture, and involves the researcher observing and participating through different roles, including dialogue with other con participants. For this study, my participant observation is grounded in 20 fan events, often visited multiple times from 2010 to 2013. The sites include anime conventions in Europe (e.g., Animecon), the US (e.g., Otakon), and Japan (e.g.,

Comiket). As a fan, I have attended conventions since 2005, and these past experiences have shaped my research. This discussion specifically focuses on three European events: the Elf Fantasy Fair (2010–12), F.A.C.T.S. (2010–12), and Fedcon (2011). As a cosplayer myself, I dressed up during most of these events or participated at times in costume and at others in casual attire. This visible insider status allowed me to address photographers and other cosplayers more freely. Also informing these accounts and encounters is my own interest in a variety of sf/fantasy works, such as *Star Trek: Voyager* (1995–2001), *Battlestar Galactica*, and *Buffy the Vampire Slayer* (1997–2003).

The selected field sites mark the heterogeneity of sf fandom, as they provide three possible formations of this audience. I examine these events as fields to explore the changing structures and mediation of sf as a genre. While the genre structures of sf are highlighted, I also emphasize the fluidity and diversity of the genre's audiences and the construction of its fan identity. As noted above, three figures in particular emerge from my data and have helped conceptualize this identity: the nostalgist, the collector, and the autograph hunter. These figures are by no means mutually exclusive and should not reduce the complexity of fan investments. Rather, I believe they can be profitably used as conceptual lenses through which to examine the contemporary sf fan and with which we can understand the site specificity of these three conventions.

Nostalgic Sentiment in Elfia

Often promoted as the biggest fantasy event in Europe, the Elf Fantasy Fair, held over a weekend, involves about 25,000 people each year, most attending the festival only for a day. The fair is held outdoors at Castle De Haar in Haarzuilens near Utrecht. Fantasy fairs are a typical continental event, but amply inspired by American Renaissance fairs. In the US, Renaissance fairs are sometimes combined with elements of mythology or folklore, while the Netherlands has often foregrounded the fantasy dimension. Such a setting may not seem like an obvious site to explore sf fandom, but in recent years the Elf Fantasy Fair has steadily become the epitome of Dutch geek culture, which is heavily informed by sf, and since its first edition in 2001 has included a broad range of genres and media, including literature, anime, and even historical re-enactment.

The Elf Fantasy Fair typically engages in a type of world building around its event. Its lore and myths are built on the idea that the terrain of Haarzuilens is transformed into the mystic land of Elfia. Rituals and parades in honor of Elfia, symbolized by an annual king and queen, foster this fictional immersion, which is also supported by visitors who dress up as characters from different media and in a variety of street styles, including "gothic Lolita" and colorful punk outfits. The fair's geography additionally hints at the fictional bricolage of Elfia, since it often includes a *Star Trek* "holodeck" to celebrate sf and a "manga square" for anime fans. In 2010, these two genres were even combined in a "manga holodeck," signifying the perceived commonalities between the audiences. However, in practice this holodeck—hosted in a large tent—caused conflicts because the sf fan groups brought many different props, including a home-made "Stargate," while the manga fan clubs focused on selling tickets for their conventions and hosting workshops. The division of the holodeck was insecure, resulting in a rather empty tent, reflecting not only organizational constraints but also the absence of dialogue between parties.

This situation captures the overall atmosphere of the fair: a highly diverse bricolage of fictional characters and genres, but also of different, not always compatible, fan communities. But the encounters with such different texts and people create the enjoyment of the fair, as the visitor never quite knows what to expect or whether s/he will run into Jafar from *Aladdin* (1992), Katniss from *The Hunger Games*, or Spock from *Star Trek*. The visitors thus help establish the boundaries of Elfia through their own dress-up and interests. At the same time, this diversity can also cause problems, as some fans openly show disregard for some mainstream texts that are personified by visitors' attire and costumes. In 2010, for instance, I observed participants calling the many *Naruto* cloaks and blue *Avatar* (2009) costumes a sign of bad taste and juvenility. Fan hierarchies are clearly imposed and judgments are made at the fair, based on what people wear, what they do, and what they seem to represent.

For many, the fair is about seeing and being seen, or "nerd spotting," as one of my participants dubbed this behavior. The situation recalls Benjamin's description of the *flâneur*, the citizen who strolls the boulevards of the modern city to grasp its sensations and merge with the crowd. While this figure relates to many modern spaces and is not specific to cons, fans do purposely foster this disposition through dress-up and highly immersive environments, such as those at this fair. Particularly evident through such "spotting" is the emergence at Elfia of "steampunk," a subgenre of sf that restructured fan identity and also aligned it more closely with current street styles. This influence can be observed in the dress of the visitors, the increase in the sale of particular merchandise, narratives, and attire, and lectures about the phenomenon, such as "The Origin of Steampunk" by Helene Smits (2012).

The Steampunk form seems a particularly appropriate development for the fair because, like the event itself, it represents a reorganization of existing tropes and genre elements within a new structure. Steampunk is also an obvious nexus whereby the diverse visitors to the fair find common ground, since it bridges the genres of fantasy, sf, history, and anime. Commonly, this form is defined in terms of its historical interest in mechanical and steam-powered technology, which not only evokes a particular era, but is also reflected in specific attire or styles of music and art. Steampunk is a multimedia phenomenon that can be witnessed in different texts and subcultures. While its settings and objects often reinterpret the Victorian era or the Wild West, they can also be integrated in a fantasy setting. Another strand of steampunk fiction focuses on a possible post-apocalyptic future in which mechanical technology has been re-evaluated and purposed anew. The genre is rife with "technostalgia," a colloquial term that signifies an affective longing for past technologies and material objects, as well as an earlier type of sf.

Steampunk is also characterized by its culture of craftsmanship and related performances. This creativity does not just pertain to dressing up, but also to the customization or "modding" of commodities, such as cars or computers that have been refashioned in a pseudo-Victorian mechanical style. The interest in crafting is reflected in both visitors' attire and in the stands that sell gears and ornaments that can be used to modify objects. This nostalgic disposition, an essential character of steampunk, fits well in the larger setting of Elfia, where fiction is blended with history, a theme already invoked by its setting at an historical castle.

a. Varieties of cosplay at the German science fiction convention FedCon 2014.

b. FedCon 2014 attendees celebrate *Stargate* (1994) and *Aliens* (1986).

The fair cross-fertilizes different genres and their audiences, while also connecting them through historical engagement and nostalgia. And yet these sentiments are constantly compromised by the highly reflexive atmosphere that also marks the fair, where the visitor must constantly adjust to different types of fiction and tropes.

Collecting Toys and Merchandise

The Belgian F.A.C.T.S. (an acronym for Fantasy, Anime, Comics, Toys, Space) con promotes itself as the "largest comics, science fiction and anime festival of the Benelux" (Belgium, the Netherlands, and Luxemburg). Like many other cons, the visitor numbers are large, estimated at 10,000 each year, although since many fans attend for only one day, the convention never hosts quite that many visitors at the same time. F.A.C.T.S. is also more commercial than most cons. In fact, while dubbing itself a convention, it is closer to an "expo" that specializes in trade and commerce.

The event is now held in a large lodge at the outskirts of Ghent, and it resembles a market place, favoring the commodity culture of fandom over events, panels, and workshops. F.A.C.T.S. does, however, include special guests who emphasize the media experience. For instance, in years when I attended, I gathered autographs from such actors as Robert Picardo (*Star Trek: Voyager*) and Richard Hatch (*Battlestar Galactica*). However, the earliest tagline of F.A.C.T.S. was "kopen, verkopen, ruilen" (buying, selling, trading), and this motto remains today, as F.A.C.T.S. specializes in merchandise, which seems to be the object of most fan attention. This increased commercialization of the fan space suggests one way in which cult activity itself may be in transition, as the emphasis of both audience and texts shifts away from critical interpretation to object-oriented fandom.

Still, traditional fan practices can be observed in both the visitors' performances and the artists who represent fandom, such as those who sell prints or self-made comics. While lectures, workshops, and panels are an exception at F.A.C.T.S., since 2012, workshop plazas have been included in the con's large dealer room. There, visitors can engage in cultural activities such as martial arts, drum performances, and flower arranging. However, the most important fan event is a cosplay competition hosted on a small stage. Most participants do not engage in elaborate theatrical skits, but rather perform in a kind of choreographed fashion show. Others dance or quote lines from their favorite shows. Though F.A.C.T.S. prides itself on being international in scope, its language culture is primarily French and Dutch. Thus, the cosplay competition is presented in these two languages so that most attendees can follow the event. However, the dialogue of the skits themselves is usually in English—echoing the vocabulary and language from the main source-texts.

F.A.C.T.S. might also be described as the ultimate treasure hunt through popular culture, catering as it does to many fandoms and interest groups with its diverse merchandise. A visitor can search for comics and DVDs, as well as trading cards, action figures, posters, and statues. The typical products for sale at the 2010 con included merchandise as diverse as *Thunderbirds* dolls, swords from *The Lord of the Rings*, a bathrobe from *Rocky*, Japanese *Pokémon* candy, and special edition Barbie dolls. In fact, it seems that anything can be bought at F.A.C.T.S., and indeed many visitors attend expressly to buy rare objects. This pattern is reflected in the convention's layout, which leaves little room for hanging out or socializing. The café is small with few places to sit. Visitors are simply expected to move around and buy or admire things. Artists here pay slightly less for their tables than commercial dealers selling general merchandise. Some of the artists are special invited guests like Dave Gibbons (in 2010), who drew the critically acclaimed graphic novel *Watchmen*. However, most artists are locals who sell small-press graphic novels or manga, prints, or drawings commissioned by visitors. Moreover, representatives of other fan conventions are present to sell tickets for their events, particularly from Belgium and the Netherlands.

The main focus, then, is commerce, for even though many people note that they come to F.A.C.T.S. to socialize or dress up, they also

admit that the largest part of the con experience is that treasure hunt
for special items. In fact, the organization of the collector's experience
is what makes this convention fundamentally different from others.
The various panels are held in the lodge behind a small curtain, right
next to the crowded vendor area. This organizational choice results in
a situation whereby, despite good audio equipment, most visitors cannot
hear the Q&A unless they are in the front rows. For example, I attended
the panels of sf television stars Charisma Carpenter (2011) and James
Callis (2012), only to find these figures relegated to a small space and
barely audible. While I valued seeing them live and hearing them talk
about their shows, my relationship to them was disrupted by the practical
set-up, the social environment, and even my own awareness of what
the stars were going through.

While not myself a collector, I too was swayed by the items that
F.A.C.T.S. had to offer. In 2010, I bought a *Rose of Versailles* statue of
Lady Oscar, one of my favorite fictional characters. In 2012, I unearthed
a rare *Wizard of Oz* independent comic. Many fans seem to shop until
they drop, as they look for figurines and comics missing from their
collections. They bring bags and ask vendors for rare items, as they
make a hobby out of completing a line of something. For particular
fans, these collections or buys may also be an investment, as they go on
to resell the items for higher prices, as in the case of special animation
cels and autographs related to particular films or shows. While most
fans are simply looking for commodities they like for a good price, some
are clearly trying to collect all the merchandise related to a particular
franchise. The latter want to be all-inclusive, thereby adding a further
dimension to Jenkins's idea of "transmedia storytelling" in which
media narratives are spread over different platforms (*Convergence Culture*
95–134). To fully enjoy these narratives, the fan feels the need to buy
and consume all the related texts.

Moreover, such collecting is intimately tied up with the idea of
gathering memorabilia of a fictional experience that has touched one
deeply—in effect, collecting material tokens of the characters and events
that have moved us. However, authenticity also plays a role. For instance,
in 2010, several of my friends compared their signed photographs of *Star
Trek: Voyager*'s Robert Picardo, debating which was the best. Some had
opted for a pondering pose of him as the holographic doctor on the show;
others for an intelligent close-up of his face. All of these pictures felt
right on their own terms and the autographs were personalized, but they
evoked different sides of Picardo as the doctor. Later, I engaged others
in a conversation about the merchandise being offered in conjunction
with *Toy Story 3* (2010). The movie had only recently played and, having

grown up with the previous two films, I was captivated by its anthropo-
morphized toys. However, several attendees saw most of the merchandise
as flawed. "If you want a Buzz, you want it to be the actual thing, the
correct size," said one, staring intently at a Buzz Lightyear figure that
was not quite right; "Otherwise it's beside the point." She suggested
that the toys of toy-characters needed to be exact replicas and clear
look-a-likes or they could not be satisfying representations. Here, the
desire of fans to actualize the narrative in an intimate or self-satisfying
way is central as a form of reception. That desire reminds us that the
merchandise "texts," often overlooked in the study of cult texts, are
also crucial to understanding the fan's affective relationship to the cult.

Seen from these perspectives, merchandise cannot simply be
considered as memorabilia that symbolizes the initial experience with
fiction. Rather, these objects become material texts in their own right,
interpreted and appraised through the narrative value of their source-
texts. Strikingly, collecting and admiring merchandise also seem to
involve one in the dual mechanism of the typical cult text, as a
constant pull between affective longing—realism, intimacy, a hands-on
experience of the text—and critical distance. The fan collectors at
F.A.C.T.S. repeatedly displayed these values through their inclusive and
exclusive strategies while buying and selling.

Stardom and Autographs

The third con under consideration, Fedcon, has been held since
the mid-nineties and currently convenes in Hotel Maritim next to
Düsseldorf's airport, an accessible location for all European visitors
and special guests. This two-day event especially celebrates sf film and
television, emphasizing such series as *Babylon 5* (1994–98), *Battlestar
Galactica* (2004–09), and *Stargate SG-1* (1997–2007), while major films
like *Star Wars* (1977) are not as well represented, perhaps because of
an old rivalry between the fan communities of *Star Trek* and *Star Wars*.
While F.A.C.T.S., as we noted, focuses on merchandise and includes
several guests, Fedcon specializes in inviting a long line-up of actors and
production staff, so a major reason for attending this con is to see one's
genre heroes in real life. In 2011, for instance, I went to see the actors
who played Tom Paris and Harry Kim in *Star Trek: Voyager*. And indeed,
the main attractions at this convention are not merchandise, events,
or workshops but such stars, already advertised on the Fedcon website
when the visitor purchases a ticket. The program booklet also focuses on
the invitees, providing detailed biographies—often a full page each—of

all the guests. To further promote them, the schedules emphasize the many celebrity autograph and photo sessions. Here, it is difficult to find the floor plan in the booklet, and many events, like lectures, are not even mentioned, as the construction of a highly immersive space seems secondary to the presence of the actors.

The emphasis on celebrity culture at Fedcon is striking and far more advanced than at F.A.C.T.S. Fedcon establishes a rich culture of stardom and encourages fans to engage with actors and get their autograph. A large portion of the first day is reserved for one-day visitors to get signed photographs, while the second day is devoted to what some pejoratively refer to as "autograph hunters." However, I use the term to suggest a positive fan activity. Much like the collector, the autograph hunter engages with the text and its production culture by collecting various tokens of fandom. However, the singularity of the autograph—one addressed directly to the individual fan—has a different meaning than any collected merchandise. The autograph is a sign of intimacy with the celebrity and of an affective encounter in the convention space itself. Its singularity and exclusiveness thus create an item of memorabilia that does not simply reflect a textual love but a feeling for the actor. And the context of getting the autograph adds to its import, as the fan can often interact with the celebrity for a minute and ask a question. This personal dimension gives a sense of intimacy with the celebrity and, by extension, the text itself

My own experiences with the con and autograph signing can help to explain this aspect of the cult sensibility. At Fedcon 2011, I attended many panels featuring guest actors, as well as lectures by fans. I was especially taken by Robert Duncan McNeill or "Tom Paris," one of my favorite characters from *Star Trek: Voyager*. On his panel, he described his production experiences on both *Chuck* and *Star Trek: Voyager*, the intimate details giving me a different perspective on the cast and crew of *Voyager*, while also making for a valuable experience. During the session, he mentioned his love for donuts. I looked forward to the autograph session later, and, mindful of his remark about donuts, decided to buy him one. However, I could not decide whether doing so would be seen as kind or creepy. Finally, I decided that I would play it comically and use the donut as a witty reference to his panel. This approach also gave me an alibi in case he tossed the food in the bin afterwards.

The line to get autographs was a long one leading to the center of a room—the repurposed main theater of the hotel—where all the stars were seated. I went to McNeill immediately and found him to be approachable; he even asked me about my trip—my pilgrimage from the Netherlands to Fedcon. I was hesitant to explain how much I liked his work and how much *Star Trek: Voyager* meant to me when I was younger, so instead I asked him about his own travel. I had also decided to present the autograph to my father, who had introduced me to *Star Trek*, and McNeill said that was a nice gesture and inscribed it to him. At that point, I grasped the moment and gave him the donut, referring to the panel: "We heard you like donuts!" The donut was slightly squished from the long wait in line, but he thanked me and a staff member next to him put the pastry on the side of the table. Afterwards—when I realized that I should not care about the donut, that it was the gesture that counted—I re-evaluated this affective moment. He was a nice guy, I concluded, but he certainly was not "Tom Paris," the character. He was older, wore glasses, and was a different person altogether. The autograph felt flimsier by the minute, as I realized that a good role-player would have probably brought me closer to the character I remembered than the actor. However, it was clear that, for most of the fans, being so close to the actors—and having that brief conversation when they sign the photograph—meant a lot.

In fact, for many fans, autograph hunting is not about the hunt itself, or the trophy, but the brief intimacy that this simple act allows, including the chance to talk or give something to the star. In these autograph sessions, the affective encounter with the actor and his or her oeuvre is represented, while the different autographs together form a personalization of television and the production culture around it. Through these sentiments, the autograph—like so much else in the cult experience, including a possible donut exchange—effectively affirms fan identity.

Conclusion

These fan conventions have proved to be vital sites of research, where an ethnographer can socialize with other fans, while also observing different fan practices. Given the heterogeneity of these large festivals, I would argue that these sites are not only an effective offline way to approach fans, but also important phenomena in their own right as media spaces where fiction, perhaps most prominently sf, is continued in new and unexpected ways. The three fan events described here provide different field sites where I was able to observe fan identity as performed, and sf had a different role in all of these cases, the first celebrating its relation to other genres, the second its relation to franchising, and the third its relation to television stardom.

The three cases also illustrate how fan conventions can be given shape and what the focuses of a single event may be. While scholars and fans often speak of the con as a structural phenomenon that can be reprised all over the world, the national and specific contexts of these conventions are important as well. The particular profile of an event is constructed not only through its organization, but also in how visitors, vendors, and different participants contribute to its unique atmosphere. The various texts being celebrated and the shifting nature of cult fandom also constantly press convention staff to revisit their events and sharpen the identity of their festivals.

In these cases, I have focused on three fan figures or themes—that of the nostalgist, the collector, and the autograph hunter—representative types I teased out of the con encounters where they were most central. The three figures have in common a complex play with both past and present in which fan identity is grounded. They echo past experiences with the sf media text and are rife with nostalgia. Moreover, these figures seem to emerge most clearly in the context of sf or speculative fiction. Generally speaking, the sf text is characterized by its intimate play with both historical and futuristic tropes that can give ground to nostalgia; its large worlds and franchises motivate the collection of keepsakes and memorabilia that mark off parts of those expansive worlds; and the intimate history of sf fandom with production companies and actors has strengthened and formalized a culture of autograph hunting.

The key to these figures is the establishment of a new relationship with the media text through the mixture with other texts, through material texts, or through the affective encounter with an actor, creator, or other participatory figure. Fan involvement with and interpretation of the cult texts can thus be pursued along lines and experiences that perform the affective relationship with the text anew. These figures can help us understand how, and in what practices, contemporary media fandom is grounded, and how it consciously works to re-establish a cult-like connection with the text.

Works Cited

Abercrombie, Nicholas and Brian Longhurst. *Audiences: A Sociological Theory of Performance and Imagination*. London: Sage, 1998.

Bacon-Smith, Camille. *Enterprising Women: Television Fandom and the Creation of Popular Myth*. Philadelphia: U of Pennsylvania P, 1992.

Benjamin, Walter. *The Writer of Modern Life: Essays on Charles Baudelaire*. Ed. Michael William Jennings. Cambridge: Harvard UP, 2006.

Coppa, Francesca. "A Brief History of Media Fandom." *Fan Fiction and Fan Communities in the Age of the Internet*. Ed. Karen Hellekson and Kristina Busse. Jefferson: McFarland, 2006. 41–59.

Couldry, Nick. *Media Rituals: A Critical Approach.* New York: Routledge, 2003.

Fiske, John. "The Cultural Economy of Fandom." *The Adoring Audience: Fan Culture and Popular Media.* Ed. Lisa A. Lewis. London: Routledge, 1992. 30–49.

—. *Understanding Popular Culture.* 2nd ed. London: Routledge, 1990.

Grossberg, Lawrence. "Is There a Fan in the House? The Affective Sensibility of Fandom." *The Adoring Audience: Fan Culture and Popular Media.* Ed. Lisa A. Lewis. London: Routledge, 1992. 50–65.

Hills, Matt. *Fan Cultures.* London: Routledge, 2002.

—. "Transcultural 'Otaku': Japanese Representations of Fandom and Representations of Japan in Anime/Manga Fan Cultures." *Media in Transition* 2 Conference. Cambridge: Massachusetts Institute of Technology. May 10–12, 2002. http://cmsw.mit.edu/mit2/Abstracts/MattHillspaper.pdf. Web.

—. "Virtually out There: Strategies, Tactics and Affective Spaces in on-Line Fandom." *Technospaces: Inside the New Media.* Ed. Sally Munt. London: Continuum, 2001. 147–60.

Jenkins, Henry. *Convergence Culture: Where Old and New Media Collide.* New York: New York UP, 2006.

—. *Fans, Bloggers, and Gamers: Exploring Participatory Culture.* New York: New York UP, 2006.

—. *Textual Poachers: Television Fans and Participatory Culture.* London: Routledge, 1992.

Kaplan, Deborah. "Construction of Fan Fiction Character through Narrative." *Fan Fiction and Fan Communities in the Age of the Internet.* Ed. Karen Hellekson and Kristina Busse. Jefferson: McFarland, 2006. 134–52.

Kelly, William W. *Fanning the Flames: Fans and Consumer Culture in Contemporary Japan.* Albany: State U of New York P, 2004.

Kwasnik, Barbara H. and Kevin Crowston. "Introduction to the Special Issue: Genres of Digital Documents." *Information, Technology & People* 18.2 (2005): 76–88.

Lamerichs, Nicolle. "Stranger than Fiction: Fan Identity in Cosplaying." *Transformative Works and Cultures* 7 (2011). Web.

Mathijs, Ernest, and Xavier Mendik. *The Cult Film Reader.* New York: McGraw-Hill, 2008.

Mathijs, Ernest, and Jamie Sexton. *Cult Cinema.* Oxford: Wiley-Blackwell, 2011.

Palmer, R. Barton. *Hollywood's Dark Cinema: The American Film Noir.* New York: Twayne, 1994.

Reijnders, Stijn. "Watching the Detectives." *European Journal of Communication* 24.2 (2009): 165–81.

Taylor, T. L. *Play between Worlds: Exploring Online Game Culture.* Cambridge: MIT Press, 2006.

10. *Robot Monster* and the "Watchable ... Terrible" Cult/SF Film

J. P. Telotte

As Lincoln Geraghty reminds us, early 1950s sf cinema, typified by films like *The Day the Earth Stood Still* (1951), *The Thing* (1951), *Invaders from Mars* (1953), and *War of the Worlds* (1953), was often marked by a rather serious tone and effect, presenting "America and the world in the grip of emergencies ... that jeopardized the future of the [human] race" (23). Despite their sometimes strange monsters and strained plots, the "emergency" visions in these films urged audiences to contemplate the trajectory of their newly atomic-driven world, to reconsider the tense and potentially destructive relations between nations, or, simply, as *The Thing* prompted viewers, to "watch the skies, keep watching the skies" for possible threats—from aliens of the extraterrestrial *or* earthly sort. Yet other films of the same era, works like *Plan 9 from Outer Space* (1959), *Cat-Women of the Moon* (1953), and *Robot Monster* (1953)—all similarly invoking the specter of monsters, invasion, or what Susan Sontag famously described as the "imagination of disaster" (215)—just as often moved viewers in rather different ways. While tracking many of the same concerns and anxieties of the era, these works and their monstrous visitors prompted, both then and now, a less than serious, at times even a laughing response—albeit, I want to suggest, one that only underscores the sorts of strains and exaggerations that often characterize sf films.

As most will readily recognize, *Plan 9 from Outer Space*, *Cat-Women of the Moon*, and *Robot Monster* are also typically cited as cult films, movies that have a special following and special appeal; in fact, films that often seem to traffic in or derive an element of their popularity from that very tension between the serious and the strained that, for some, is the downfall of many sf films.[1] Some commentators describe these as exploitation films, some as camp texts, and others, like Jeffrey Sconce, simply as "bad" films that have been effectively redeemed for viewers and critics by a "paracinematic sensibility" they project ("Trashing"

102), that is, by their tendency to make us mindful of conventional film aesthetics and, in the process, to subvert those same aesthetics. Yet, thanks to such key verbal indicators as "space," "moon," and "robot," we also readily recognize their science fictional status, as works that draw much of their identity from the way they treat science, technology, and reason, the triad at the heart of the film genre. But, of course, that treatment is often different in these cult/sf films, somewhat monstrous in its exaggerations, cheapness, or general artlessness, such that those strained effects come center stage and tend to dominate our response to the works. However, this intersection with the cult is noteworthy since it affords an insight into how the sf film appeals to its audience, and indeed how both sorts of texts are, at their cores, often driven by what we might term paradox.

Admittedly, many sf films from this and other eras have found a similar cult reputation and following, works like *The Phantom Empire* (1935), *Attack of the 50 Foot Woman* (1958), *Santa Claus Conquers the Martians* (1964), *Zardoz* (1974), *The Rocky Horror Picture Show* (1975), and *The Man Who Fell to Earth* (1976). The frequency with which such sf texts cross into a cult embrace might give us pause, since it hints at a relationship between what we might prefer to think of—distinctly—as serious sf and cult sf. These films find this sort of dual citizenship, I would suggest, not simply because they are bad films or in some way "paracinematic"—although several clearly answer to both charges—but rather because, either intentionally or not, they seem to tap into a double character that, for better or worse, quite often marks the sf film: that ability to seem by turns quite serious, conventional, and compelling, but also more than a bit strained, unserious, even absurd, especially in instances when their special effects become dated and appreciably less appreciated, that is, through a kind of slippage that can make viewers overly conscious of how these works function as films and/or as generic texts, and thus of the special effects' own relationship to these texts.

But that is only one connection and, indeed, even without such "slippage," many sf films often seem to be in negotiation between the serious and the strained, to verge on the cult, and this potential kinship can tell us much about both the science fictional and the cult. Until relatively recently, sf has been something of an outlier in the film world. It has often been seen as an inflection of other, dominant, and longer-lived forms, such as the horror film.[2] It has been identified through a constantly expanding—and changing—pool of icons or events that has suggested a certain generic instability or indeterminacy, as one-time iconic elements of the genre, such as television or hand-held communicators, shift into a different register and become instead signs of the everyday and of a decidedly non-science fictional reality. Additionally, the genre of sf has an audience that often sees itself as different from the mainstream, especially appreciative of the *alternative* vision that is part of sf's stock-in-trade, even its *raison d'être*. Moreover, as Patrick Lucanio reminds us—and as we have already noted—there is a certain "over-the-top" sensibility shared by many sf films, a "ridiculousness" (43) that is hard to ignore. Yet, as he provocatively adds, and as I would endorse, there might also be a "meaning and value that arises [*sic*] from" that character (131).

Of course, cult works have typically drawn similar comments—critics describing them as inflections of other forms, as generically unstable or indeterminate texts, as works that deliberately appeal to a different and self-aware audience, or as, very simply, campy.[3] I want to pursue the implications of this intersection by considering the "meaning and value" of one of those examples of textual coincidence, *Robot Monster*. It is an interesting case in part because it so clearly foregrounds that relationship between the serious and the strained. While not quite, as Bill Warren offers, one of the worst movies of all time, it is, I would agree, "one of the most watchable of all terrible movies" (701). And indeed that paradoxical description suggests the kinship I want to explore, for it not only points to a sort of double vision I have been describing—one that is by turns highly serious and strained, the sort of mix that has often brought criticism of the genre—but also suggests the ease with which many sf films edge over into the cult.

Robot Monster has been commonly perceived as an exercise in quick, cheap, and badly scripted film-making—by no means the hallmarks of an established "quality" cinema, but perhaps just the sort of characteristics that might generate a "paracinematic" appeal. Shot in four days without real sets on exteriors around southern California's Bronson Canyon, the film had a reported budget of approximately $16,000, and the weak production values support that report. Its script was cobbled together in a few days and then rewritten by a relative of producer Al Zimbalist (Warren 703–04). The narrative contains a variety of mismatched shots, continuity lapses (as when the girl Alice is shown tied up in one shot, untied in the next, but fully bound in the immediately following one, as if she had somehow tied herself up), dialogue scenes with no audible dialogue, and other credulity-straining images. The "robot monster" or Ro-Man, is reported to have taken definitive shape when renting a robot costume proved too costly for the production and actor George Barrows offered his own gorilla suit instead, mating it with a television antenna and diving helmet supposedly rented at the Santa Monica pier (Sconce, *Haunted* 118). The combination suggests something completely beyond normal experience, a paradoxical union of primal beast with contemporary icons of advanced technology. As a result, the alien invader has been described in similar "watchable ... terrible" terms—as "one of the least convincing monsters of all time," yet "for just that reason" strangely appealing (Warren 703). So while *Robot Monster* may be, by conventional standards, badly done, even laughable to some,[4] it is also a film that, for a number of the same reasons, has gained a cult following, as if its very badness offered audiences not just the sort of "challenge to aesthete taste" that Sconce observes and appreciates in many other cult texts ("Trashing" 104), but also a *different way* of seeing, a kind of seeing through its clumsily constructed science fictional lens—just as I think it can offer us.

While its production and narrative problems have made *Robot Monster* less discursively coherent than we normally expect from the commercial cinema (91), that very troubled coherence, that is, the ill fit of its parts or structures, results in what Ann Jerslev terms a kind of "meta-textual presence" (95). That is, for most of the film, its *seams* show, and as a consequence its *semes* too show themselves, pointing up how this sort of film typically generates meaning and invites audiences to reposition themselves as knowing players in that revealed game of meaning—a game that is always closer to the surface, nearer self-revelation in sf, and by the same token nearer to the sort of special audience/text "interaction" that marks much cult activity and to efforts to define the cult cinema as, most fundamentally, "a mode of reception,"[5] rather than a set of formulaic/generic structures.

Further compounding that sense of "meta-textual presence" in *Robot Monster* is the fact that it closely resembles so many other alien invasion films of the same period, including a more esteemed and more often-discussed entry from the same year with a remarkably similar plot, *Invaders from Mars*.[6] Both films frame their central narrative as a young boy's dream of alien invasion, a nightmare from which he apparently awakes at the film's end to reveal the illusory nature of those events, thus metaphorizing how film too envelopes audiences in its dream-like experience, offering them its unsettling fantasies and then allowing them to awake to their less troubling—if less clearly visualized or understood—reality. Yet both films also revisit and even trouble that implication of invasion at the end, suggesting that their respective dream narratives might have only been premonitory, and that their messages are indeed important warnings.

But then sf has always been marked by such broadly generic self-consciousness, by a tendency to show its seams and semes, thanks to both its technological emphasis and its recurrent imagery. As

Annette Kuhn points out, one of the cinematic genre's abiding—and most telling—characteristics has been its persistent "mobilization of the visual" (6), that is, its emphasis on various technologies and screens that inevitably generate a reflexive sense, letting us glimpse how the medium produces itself—but also how it *situates* itself as a communication to its audience, inviting a cult-like special audience connection. Underscoring this characteristic is *Robot Monster*'s repeated emphasis on video communications devices, especially those used by the humans to talk to the monstrous Ro-Man and by the monster when he reports to his leader, the "Great Guidance." Little more than fake screens, these devices serve to update the action of the narrative and allow Ro-Man to consult on—and thus forecast—his next move. So not only do those scenes effectively rehearse the plot and tell us what is to come, but they also provide a kind of mirror image of events, allowing us to watch actions unfold by watching characters watching events unfold. And since the Great Guidance is actually nothing more than the image of Ro-Man himself—there was, after all, only one gorilla-diving-helmet-antenna outfit, so George Barrows had to play both roles—there are several scenes in which the monster seems to be watching his own image, or, as we might offer, watching the same movie as the audience, even modeling their interaction with this "watchable ... terrible" text.

And the film's dream-like nature only furthers this reflexive effect, as the frame produces a dream that comments upon the narrative situation and eventually blends with it at the conclusion, blurring the lines between fantasy and reality—or the serious and the ridiculous. As we might recall, young Johnny, while playing in a space costume, encounters two scientists who are studying the remains of an extinct human species in nearby caves. But after napping with his mother and two sisters, he awakes to encounter the new circumstances that form the bulk of the narrative. In this dream reality, the older scientist becomes the father he has lost, the young scientist turns into his older sister Alice's fiancé, and all inhabit a world deeply imperiled by the sort of space invaders we earlier saw him pretending to be fighting, but now embodied in the monstrous Ro-Man. And that creature, as we learn, has already wiped out most of humanity and only needs to finish off Johnny's family, along with the inhabitants of an orbiting space station, to complete his task of conquest—in effect, turning them into the extinct human species that was being studied as the film began. However, that plan goes awry when something very unscientific, non-technological, and pointedly irrational—yet also very science fictional—interferes, as the ape-robot Ro-Man develops an unlikely passion for Alice, hesitates in his mission, and is then destroyed by the Great Guidance, who vows to complete humanity's destruction. But, as in *Invaders from Mars*, the young boy then wakes to find that he has only dreamt this apocalyptic scenario, that those who were killed—his little sister Carla and the young scientist—are still alive and well, that Alice has not been kidnapped and horrendously assaulted by an amorous monster, and that the Earth has not been devastated. However, that relief is itself short-lived, for after the humans walk off, we see the supposed dream-character Ro-Man emerge from a cave, presumably to begin that vision of world conquest and human eradication, thereby linking dream and waking narrative, past and future, and lending to *Robot Monster* a further meta-narrative potential.

And yet it is a bit inaccurate to suggest that the dream vision either ends or restarts at this point. For the film has all along, like so many other sf—and cult—films, repeatedly asserted, through these and other reflexive elements, that it essentially lives and breathes the stuff of dreams, including the sort of contradictions that always seem to mark our dreaming, that it inhabits a fantasy borderland wherein the deadly serious and the ridiculous—*can* co-exist, as if it were just a kind of

a. Young Johnny begins his dream of the Ro-Man invasion of Earth in *Robot Monster* (1953).

b. *Robot Monster* (1953) demonstrates its "condensed cultural logic" in
the amalgam of gorilla and space-helmeted alien.

pastiche of other films and other sf texts. And, indeed, we easily note
that pastiche element in its use of footage from other fantasy films,
including *Flight to Mars* (1951), *Rocketship X-M* (1950), *The Lost Continent*
(1951), and *One Million BC* (1940), some of which, such as a brief shot
of a rocket on a launching pad, support the narrative; and some, like
the fighting lizards-badly-disguised-as-dinosaurs from *One Million BC*,
seem just as ill-fitting here as Ro-Man's costume. The film also cobbles
together a variety of found footage from real natural disasters, presented
as the results of Ro-Man's actions. Moreover, Johnny's bubble-shooting
device seen in the film's opening, as well as Ro-Man's "calcinator death
ray," must have instantly recalled—for a 1950s audience—the dizzying
inventory of such strange devices popularized by television programs like
Captain Video and *Space Patrol*, which weekly paraded before audiences
technology like the Captain's Opticon Scillometer, the Ultraplanetary
Transmitter, the Discatron, and the Mango-Radar. But then, the covers
of the lurid pulp magazines that form the backdrop for the opening
credits should have primed audiences to expect just such a pastiche
dream, the kind of stitched-together text that, Ingeborg Hoesterey has

suggested, is common to sf, typically generating what she terms a "double visuality" (60) due to its "conflation" of different forms, "anachronistic juxtapositions" (65), and even deliberate "paradox" (67)—here all readily figured in the character of the Ro-Man monster itself.

More to the point, those pastiche-like juxtapositions, seemingly fashioned within and from dream, are part of a larger pattern that further links sf and cult films. In these ill-fitting parts and jarring juxtapositions, we glimpse one of the great attractions—and dimensions—of the cult film: what we might describe as its *accidental strategy* for showing us new connections and new understandings, for finding unforeseen and indeed quite serious links between our mundane world and, especially in the case of sf, a world newly inflected by rapid scientific and technological development. For just as the sf film consistently plays a kind of "what if" game, or, in some cases, through the genre's strategy of "cognitive estrangement,"[7] primes us to react either seriously or with incredulity to the new, often utopian developments it depicts or forecasts, the cult work too poses the question of the different ways we might read and understand a text, even discover in it unexpected meanings or implications, as if it were drawing its special character from something other than what it was supposed to be.

Here especially, *Robot Monster*'s monster offers us the most obvious clue. Working through what Sconce, in describing another set of alien creations, terms "a highly condensed cultural logic" (*Haunted* 121)—in this instance, of a furry creature, antennae denoting electronic communication, and the fishbowl-like helmet required for an alien environment—Ro-Man suggests a number of profound cultural anxieties or contradictions, both embedded in the film's era and linked to the sf genre. One is the very monstrous physical threat posed by the new, highly technologized postwar world, a threat further emphasized here, perhaps ironically, by the film's cheap production values, which result in the *absence* of most of the common markers of culture—the buildings, cars, and personal appurtenances glimpsed in some of the found footage employed, but nowhere in sight in the rocky Bronson Canyon and caves where most of the action takes place. As we noted at the outset, in this period the sf film was often driven by just such anxieties, so it might be argued that here an element of the film's "terrible" character effectively, and again paradoxically, produces part of its serious and quite "watchable" aspect.

Another anxiety is that bound up in the sort of absent presence which the monster figures for us. For as the single and manifestly powerful representative of the *planet* Ro-Man, he attests to all that, we were coming to suspect in this era, is "out there," still unseen, still unknown, and apparently quite formidable. Communicating with the Great Guidance, who has already determined that all of Earth must be wiped out because, thanks to its rapid development, it now poses a threat to other planets and their civilizations, he fully legitimizes *The Thing*'s chilling warning to "keep watching the skies," as well as the period's repeated political warnings against a Red Menace. He becomes, in effect, the monstrous "other" that, in so many other sf films of the period, would take many different shapes—or in the case of the Blob of that 1955 film, *non-shape*—so that his ridiculously cobbled-together form becomes not only a logical and even accurate figuration or representation, but also the sort of multiply allusive form that commonly populates our cult texts, as they, almost in spite of themselves, signal other concerns, other anxieties that seem almost accidentally to assert their presence.

But a more important anxiety binds together both the film's generic thrust and its cult attraction. It is one bound up not in the characters and the seemingly blasted landscape of Earth so effectively suggested by that very real canyon locale, but in Ro-Man's existential dilemma, which surfaces in the course of the narrative and recalls an abiding concern of our sf films. Ordered to destroy the last remaining humans, including Alice, for whom he has suddenly developed his strange—cross-species—passion, he asks his leader in a strained and pointedly blurred logic if he might "save" one human "for reference in case of unforeseen circumstances." When the Great Guidance questions this logic, admonishes him to remember "the law" of their species, which is to "produce, correlate, eliminate error," and eventually recognizes that something is amiss, that Ro-Man is no longer properly and rationally detached, but has been emotionally infected by these humans, a surprisingly human complaint emerges. When commanded to "kill them all" or himself be destroyed, Ro-Man wavers, noting aloud, "I cannot—yet I must. How do you calculate that? At what point on the graph do 'must' and 'cannot' meet? Yet I must—but I cannot." The monster, it seems, has become divided in purpose and stunned into immobility by this paradox, at least momentarily—and in another paradox, into an inability to go on being the absurd monster he so manifestly appears.

Of course, that monologue seems a bit ludicrous coming from this strange amalgam of gorilla and space-helmeted alien, particularly since we never see his face, and thus cannot register the apparent strain of these new, human-like emotions on this apparently very inhuman creature—one who is, as he says, "built to have no emotions." But that speech rather directly voices the sort of double edge that marks both the typical cult film and much of our sf cinema—their curiously intersecting concerns and strategies, here foregrounded in this angst-laden yet ridiculous dialogue. For just as the cult film often seems to work against itself or its narrative intentions, seems driven by paradox or the play of accident, and typically champions the "truth" of raw, accidentally exposed emotion, so too does this film and its eponymous monster, in the process voicing a theme common to many other sf texts, from *Metropolis* (1927) to *Invasion of the Body Snatchers* (1956). It is also one echoed by the father—or older scientist, depending on whether we read the narrative from within its dream or without—as he reminds his family of the importance of their emotions, of their feelings for each other, noting that they are "the very thing that makes us different from Ro-Man" and his race, and that which sustains their resistance to him.

But more importantly, that shift in the monster simply plays out another intersection between the cult and the sf text. For in the larger world of sf cinema, science, technology, and reason repeatedly find their sway challenged in precisely this way, by human emotion or feeling. In the traditional sf narrative, it is a challenge that often serves a kind of saving or liberating function, as if accidentally surfacing at the last moment to draw us back from the brink of the thoroughly technologized future to which we seem drawn, the overly rationalized line of action, or some scientific apocalypse, by reminding us—while also affirming in the face of an increasingly rationalized world, one advancing so quickly that it might seem to threaten both our own and other worlds—just how deeply rooted our humanity is in that realm of emotion or feelings, how important this part is, as the father/scientist suggests, to all that we ultimately are.

Perhaps this is why *Robot Monster*'s strange, dream-like ending—as well as the apparent finish of Ro-Man—evokes some consternation, as if the final and surest sign of the film's "watchable ... terrible" character. For that conclusion, in which the dream dissolves only to reappear just as suddenly, prompts what Sconce terms a shift in "reading protocol" ("Trashing" 101) that is crucial for the cult text. This shift functions not simply like some monstrous eruption of importance, that is, a portent of serious things to come, such as a real invasion, nor as an additional sign of badness, a repetition that, ridiculously, functions to add another minute or trick ending to an otherwise short, unsatisfying, and narrative-bedeviling conclusion. Rather, this double possibility invites the viewer to interrogate this text precisely in terms of its slippage between such possibilities, with Ro-Man becoming a recurrent return of the repressed, an image of the monstrous haunting itself, of the sort that characterized sf in this era—as well as all of American culture. He becomes a sign of both the attraction and the at times appalling presence that marks the sf genre as it, seemingly by turns, announces its importance and admits its exaggerations, as it plays out the central paradox that was driving the entire genre, namely, its struggle with the inevitable attractions of science, technology, and reason, that had to be consistently balanced against our anxieties about those elements and their potential to undermine—or even destroy—our *real* humanity. The result is the equally inevitable affirmation of our need for feeling, emotion, even the sort of mad passion that renders, if only momentarily and in the strangest of all paradoxes, the monstrous Ro-Man not really robotic after all, but strangely sympathetic, much like the gill-man of the following year's far more successful *Creature from the Black Lagoon* (1954).

If, through their eventual cult status, films like *Robot Monster, Plan 9 from Outer Space*, as well as *Devil Girl from Mars* (1954), *The Giant Claw* (1958), and other similarly "watchable ... terrible" texts from this period seem to encourage audiences to stand at some distance from their worlds, to enjoy an almost reflexive mindfulness of their—badly—constructed narratives, pointedly artificial sets, and clumsy dialogue, even to ridicule their unseemly monsters and monstrous effects, their giant buzzards, intellectual carrots, and diving-helmeted gorilla robots, they also, almost accidentally, make capital out of that very distance or detachment by further helping us to discern some of the problems associated with that informing sf triad. And here we might just note Paul Virilio's recent linkage between accidents and the work of science and technology. For he suggests that in the unplanned and unplanned-for event, which is, as I have argued elsewhere, one of the cult's prime characteristics,[8] we can make out "a revelation of science and technology's original sin": "Science and technology are flawed," he says, "in the same way that we are" (Zurbrugg 154). Thus he suggests that great accidents, like the meltdown of the Japanese nuclear reactor at Fukushima, are not just unavoidable elements of our scientific and technological endeavors, but an important trace of their—and our—"original sin." They signal our own "flawed" nature, while providing us with a "flawed" mirror that we can hold up to ourselves—as we do in the sf film, with the hope that we might respond to and correct those same flaws.

In so far as the cult film resembles our sf cinema, and often seems to intersect with it, then, it may be precisely because of the manner in which it *accidentally* evokes that sort of mirroring or revelation to which Virilio refers and which so often seems to be the genre's own great goal—its own paradoxical interrogation of its nature. Whether it is through its particular textual components, such as the meta-narrative elements on which both Jerslev and Annette Kuhn focus, through its dream-like or pastiche arrangement noted by Hoesterey, or through the shift in audience relationship or "reading protocol" suggested by

Sconce, the cultish sf text like *Robot Monster* practically forces us to *see* differently, even to see sf itself in a more revealing light. For these flawed narratives surprisingly confront us with our own flawed selves, show us our own mismatched parts, and remind us of the genre's own, unacknowledged but informing, paradox: of how we always hope to correct those flaws—of science, technology, even the self—through the same forces of science and technology that have themselves repeatedly proved to be both compelling and problematic, so very "watchable" yet also at times so "terrible."

Notes

1   As an example of this attitude, we might note scientist Sidney Perkowitz's *Hollywood Science*, a work that, while generally appreciative of the efforts of our sf films, also tends to gauge their value—and for the most part *devalue* them—in terms of their efforts at a rigorous scientific accuracy.
2   As a gloss on this difficult differentiation, we might note how Carlos Clarens's seminal 1967 study *An Illustrated History of the Horror Film* was, 30 years later and after his death, reissued under a new title, *An Illustrated History of Horror and Science-Fiction Films*.
3   Taken together, these characteristics also recall two key modes of thinking about the cult text: as a form that cobbles together different structures of meaning and as one marked by certain patterns of behavior, or, as Anne Jerslev offers, by "a certain interaction between a text and an audience" (92).
4   This laughable potential is certainly one of the key reasons why *Robot Monster* would have been featured in the January 2, 1990 episode of *Mystery Science Theater 3000*, a television program in which a trapped astronaut and his robot companions are forced to watch bad sf films. To maintain sanity, the group mocks the films they are shown or, as Jeffrey Sconce describes such activity, shifts the "reading protocol" ("Trashing" 101).
5   See the overview on cult definition "The Concepts of Cult" offered by Ernest Mathijs and Xavier Mendik in *The Cult Film Reader* (15).
6   There is certainly some possibility, given the quickness with which *Robot Monster* was made and released, that it was actually modeled on the better-known *Invaders from Mars*. *Invaders* was released on April 22, 1953, and *Robot Monster* on June 10, 1953.
7   This note of "cognitive estrangement" is, of course, a reference to Darko Suvin's well-known and influential definition of the sf genre as a "literature of cognitive estrangement" (4). See his *Metamorphoses of Science Fiction*.
8   See my discussion of another sf cult text, the "failed" television series *Firefly*, in "The Accident of *Firefly*" in David Lavery's *The Essential Cult Television Reader*. It is a point also implicit in Bruce Kawin's suggestion that a cult film should not simply be seen as a movie with a *following*, but

as a movie that, as if by chance, *finds* its audience in a kind of "walking after midnight" encounter (19), as the moviegoer, frustrated with the sort of film that "eats and breathes and oils itself with compromise" or sameness goes out hoping for a chance encounter or, as he puts it, "searching for the films that are searching for me" (24–25).

Works Cited

Clarens, Carlos. *An Illustrated History of the Horror Film.* New York: Capricorn, 1967.

Geraghty, Lincoln. *American Science Fiction Film and Television.* Oxford: Berg, 2009.

Hoesterey, Ingeborg. *Pastiche: Cultural Memory in Art, Film, and Literature.* Bloomington: Indiana UP, 2001.

Jerslev, Anne. "Semiotics by Instinct: 'Cult Film' as a Signifying Practice between Film and Audience." *The Cult Film Reader.* Ed. Ernest Mathijs and Xavier Mendik. New York: McGraw-Hill, 2008. 88–99.

Kawin, Bruce. "After Midnight." *The Cult Film Experience: Beyond All Reason.* Ed. J. P. Telotte. Austin: U of Texas P, 1991. 18–25.

Kuhn, Annette. "Introduction." *Alien Zone: Cultural Theory and Contemporary Science Fiction Cinema.* London: Verso, 1990. 1–12.

Lucanio, Patrick. *Them or Us: Archetypal Interpretations of Fifties Alien Invasion Films.* Bloomington: Indiana UP, 1987.

Mathijs, Ernest, and Xavier Mendik. "The Concepts of Cult." *The Cult Film Reader.* New York: McGraw-Hill, 2008. 15–24.

Perkowitz, Sidney. *Hollywood Science: Movies, Science, and the End of the World.* New York: Columbia UP, 2010.

Sconce, Jeffrey. *Haunted Media: Electronic Presence from Telegraphy to Television.* Durham: Duke UP, 2000.

—. "'Trashing' the Academy: Taste, Excess and an Emerging Politics of Cinematic Style." *The Cult Film Reader.* Ed. Ernest Mathijs and Xavier Mendik. New York: McGraw-Hill, 2008. 100–18.

Sontag, Susan. "The Imagination of Disaster." *Against Interpretation.* New York: Dell, 1966. 212–28.

Suvin, Darko. *Metamorphoses of Science Fiction: On the Poetics and Discourse of a Literary Genre.* New Haven: Yale UP, 1979.

Telotte, J. P. "The Accident of *Firefly.*" *The Essential Cult Television Reader.* Ed. David Lavery. Lexington: UP of Kentucky, 2010. 111–19.

Warren, Bill. *Keep Watching the Skies!: American Science Fiction Movies of the Fifties.* The 21st Century Edition. Jefferson: McFarland, 2010.

Zurbrugg, Nicholas. "Not Words But Visions!" *Virilio Live: Selected Interviews.* Ed. John Armitage. London: Sage, 2001. 154–63.

11. Science Fiction and the Cult of Ed Wood: *Glen or Glenda?, Bride of the Monster,* and *Plan 9 from Outer Space*

Rodney F. Hill

> One is always considered mad when one perfects something that others cannot grasp.
>
> —Dr. Vornoff, *Bride of the Monster*

As a body of work, the films of Edward D. Wood, Jr., virtually defy classification. Wood's career output included exploitation films, short subjects, industrial films, commercials, pornography, and unproduced screenplays, as well as various forays into sf. Yet even at an individual level, several of Wood's best-known films elude our grasp in terms of genre: *Bride of the Monster* (aka, *Bride of the Atom,* 1955) freely traverses the borders between sf and horror; and recent criticism has noted the avant-garde qualities evident in Wood's sf opus *Plan 9 from Outer Space* (1956, released 1959), as well as the exploitation film *Glen or Glenda?* (1953). As this volume's topic suggests, such blurring of borders is central to sf and "cult" films alike, resulting in the frequent overlapping of the two categories, as Wood's *Plan 9 from Outer Space* and *Bride of the Monster* well illustrate. While known primarily for their cult status, these films abound in sf iconography and thematics—with their flying saucers and intergalactic intelligences, mad scientists and mutant creatures, and ruminations on the use of advanced technology. Even *Glen or Glenda?*, while not quite sf, features a subplot devoted to the then-revolutionary medical procedures involved in sex-change operations, combined with the psychological aspects of its characters' transgendered experiences.

In addition to blurring generic boundaries, as Ernest Mathijs and Xavier Mendik point out, cult films often challenge the distinctions between innovation and "badness," between high and low culture, between acceptable and forbidden subject matter (2–3). As a result, our experience of the cult is frequently marked by confusion: a confusion not only of categories, but also of response (De Seife 2). Are we to be repelled by these films, elated by them, or both? In Wood's case, are we to regard him as a misunderstood auteur (even, perhaps, an accidental artist of the avant-garde), or do we merely dismiss him as one of the "worst" directors of all time?

The "badness" attributed to Wood's films may be seen as a hallmark of cult cinema, yet their almost gleeful silliness stands in marked contrast to Wood's apparently serious aims. Most notably, the quasi-autobiographical *Glen or Glenda?*, with its cross-dressing protagonist (portrayed by Wood, himself a "transvestite"), clearly has an agenda of raising public awareness about transgendered persons. *Bride of the Monster* and *Plan 9 from Outer Space* also proffer misunderstood outsiders as central characters; and if we think of Wood as cult auteur, then it is tempting to see these figures as addressing the same set of concerns that *Glen or Glenda?* takes on more directly: the need for healthy societies to carve out spaces of acceptance for unconventional ideas and ways of life—even film-making. Furthermore, if *Bride* and *Plan 9* warn us of the potential catastrophic effects of misused technology, then *Glen or Glenda?* reminds us of the power of medical science and psychology to transform our lives for the better. Given such an agenda, it seems fitting that Wood would turn repeatedly to the sf genre, where the overlapping (or transgression) of borders often points up humanity's relationship to technology as a potential source of salvation (or, conversely, of destruction)—while also offering up the opposing forces of science versus religious or mythological tropes as possible keys to that salvation. In fact, Rob Craig identifies a "fixation on religion which haunts all of Wood's films," as he notes: "Wood's films are filled to the brim with sacred rituals, the dead coming to life, spiritual battle in the very heavens, and always at root, puny man's horrible freedom of will ... In the end, Wood shows his audience how to achieve personal salvation through unconditional love" (6).

Curiously, some of Wood's most devoted followers have found something akin to religious epiphany, even salvation, in these films, well beyond the level of active celebration, commitment, communion, and community that most cult movies elicit from their audiences. Certainly, *Plan 9* has garnered quite an active fan base, with an "Ed Wood Appreciation Society"—extant at least into the 1980s—which published a short monograph on Wood's films (Hoberman and Rosenbaum 265); and others who are "in the know" with regard to Wood at times take on the attitude of a "congregation" of "converts." One fan/critic, reviewing Tim Burton's *Ed Wood* (1994) for a trade magazine, wrote: "I have the distinct feeling it was made for about 14 people, and I know every damn one of them! ... For dedicated Ed-heads, it's probably the movie of the 1990s; the uninitiated may be less impressed" (Weaver). Still more fanatical devotees have taken the notions of commitment, communion, and community to greater heights, in the formation of the Church of Ed Wood. Founded in 1996, "Woodism" is a registered, pop-culture-based religion which, according to its internet site, "currently boasts over 5,000 legally baptized followers worldwide" ("Ed Wood's Holy Haven"). Wood may thus be the only "cult" film-maker whose work has inspired an actual "cult" and found the kind of "worshipful audience" that J. P. Telotte associates with the "cult film experience" ("Beyond" 5).

The seriousness with which these devoted, even worshipful fans approach Wood's films may mystify mainstream critics and scholars, who find it difficult to get past their apparent "badness." The very idea of Ed Wood as a cult auteur may seem absurd, since auteurism implies a level of authorial intent and technical competency. However, as Jeffrey Sconce points out so well, the longevity and appeal of such "bad" films depend largely upon the countercultural readings of them by an audience actively opposed to the mainstream, a mode of viewing and reception that he terms "paracinema" (380). Sconce elaborates: "In cultivating a counter-cinema from the dregs of exploitation films, paracinematic fans ... explicitly situate themselves in opposition to Hollywood cinema and the mainstream US culture it represents" (381). And Wood's films invite such countercultural readings against Hollywood norms, as they so often deal with outsider protagonists, challenging dominant ideologies and world-views.

Sconce also notes that fan-oriented magazines such as *Film Threat* look to "transgressive aesthetics/genres of the past as avant-garde inspiration for contemporary independent filmmaking" (375, 392). It is within this framework that, Sconce suggests, "Wood is now seen, like Godard, as a unique talent improvising outside the constrictive environment of traditional Hollywood production and representation" (388). However, I would argue further that the avant-garde qualities evident in some of Wood's films are not entirely the product of later readings by an oppositional audience. Rather, elements of the avant-garde, which Sconce sees as a "retrospective reconstruction" by paracinematic viewers (392), are unmistakably present in Wood's texts themselves—most prominently in *Glen or Glenda?*, but also in his other sf films.

Although *Glen or Glenda?* might appear to fall outside this volume's scope, it lies not far afield from Theodore Sturgeon's conception of good sf: "a story with a human problem, and a human solution, which would not have happened at all without its science content" (qtd. in Sobchack 19). We may thus regard *Glen or Glenda?* as at least a kind of "cousin" to the sf film, in its concerns with cutting-edge medical science surrounding sex changes, along with its psychologist-as-narrator who attempts to explain various transgendered characters, viewed as "Other" by the mainstream. Additionally, a consideration of the film's pointed departures from classical Hollywood structures can help us to contextualize and better understand the same tendencies found in Wood's other sf films. We might even say that these films' departures from dominant cinematic practices are essential to their overall aims of challenging mainstream thought. That is, Wood frames the kinds of subject matter and characters that Hollywood marginalizes; and in rebelling against (or ignoring) the narrative conventions of Hollywood cinema (a fundamentally conservative institution), his films imply that a different approach to filmic narration is needed in order to articulate their progressive themes. As Rob Craig notes, Wood "used his meager films as a soapbox upon which to preach his message of love, peace and tolerance ... for unconditional acceptance of the outsider, the eccentric and the rebel in a society which seems bent on ostracizing and/or destroying same" (7).

Like its eponymous, transgendered protagonist, *Glen or Glenda?* occupies a fractured filmic identity, inhabiting multiple generic categories. Although the film is well situated within the exploitation genre (echoing the contemporaneous sex-change case of Christine Jorgensen), J. Hoberman and Jonathan Rosenbaum rate it as "[i]n a class by itself ... [e]ons ahead of its time" (265). *Glen or Glenda?* also takes the form of an essay film, offering—even if unintentionally—an early instance of the *caméra-stylo* (camera-pen) approach to film-making, which later became a hallmark of auteurism and the French New Wave. In any case, its narrative structure blatantly departs from classical Hollywood norms, with nearly one-quarter of the film—14 minutes out of 68—consisting of a remarkable, pointedly experimental sequence, which directly calls to mind the psychodramas of the American avant-garde movement of the late 1940s and early 1950s, epitomized in the "trance films" of Kenneth Anger and Maya Deren, among others.

Although produced in Hollywood in 1953, *Glen or Glenda?*—like *Plan 9*—departs significantly from the narrative conventions that David Bordwell links to the classical Hollywood cinema:

> [I]n the classical cinema, narrative form motivates cinematic representation. Specifically, cause-effect logic and narrative parallelism generate a narrative which projects its action through psychologically defined, goal oriented characters. Narrative time and space are constructed to represent the cause-effect chain ... The viewer makes sense of the classical film through criteria of verisimilitude (is *x* plausible?), of generic appropriateness (is *x* characteristic of this sort of film?) and of compositional unity (does *x* advance the story?). (560)

While the characters of Glen and his "double," Glenda, are somewhat well defined psychologically, others in the film are not. In fact, the film begins with a baffling character, portrayed by Bela Lugosi, whose identity and relationship to the film go unexplained. In the credits, he is identified as "Scientist," but he also seems to be a puppetmaster of sorts, "pulling the strings" that set in motion the sometimes cruel fates of the film's other characters, causing them to "Dance the dance which one is created for." Lugosi's character is a throwback to the magical mysticism of the fantastic, an alchemist, more Dr. Faustus than Dr. Frankenstein; and as a god-like figure, he conflates science and religion. He also serves as a commentator on the film's action, often addressing the audience directly; and his lair, suggestive of a musty library/study, as well as an alchemist's laboratory, bears no discernible spatial or temporal relationship to the film's main events.

Those events are divided roughly into two separate "stories," which never converge—another violation (or disregard) of classical Hollywood norms of unity. These stories concern the cross-dressing Glen/Glenda (Wood) and his fiancée, Barbara (Dolores Fuller), on the one hand, and the transsexual Alan/Anne, who eventually undergoes a male-to-female sex-change operation, on the other. These separate case studies are both related by the character of Dr. Alton (Timothy Farrell), a psychologist who serves as another narrator/commentator, attempting to explain transvestism and sex changes to a police inspector (Lyle Talbot) as well as to the audience. In this regard, *Glen or Glenda?* approaches what Judith Merril identifies as one subgenre of sf: the "Teaching Story, whose function seems to be the popularization of science and technology" (qtd. in Sobchack 18)—or in this case, the popularization of a phenomenon made possible by science. Narrative time and space are disjointed, with no clear cause-effect chain moving the story along. In fact, we might say that the film is not primarily interested in telling a story at all, although it *uses* stories in pursuit of a larger agenda: Wood seems to be *making an argument*, in favor of accepting transgendered people so that they need not lead lives of secrecy, shame, and rejection. The film thus takes on a rather rhetorical form, roughly divided into two sections, presenting the two "case studies" of Glen/Glenda and Alan/Anne.

In between these two "stories," however, the film veers off into the realm of what we might identify—not unreasonably—as *experimental film*, with a prolonged dream/trance sequence that bears unmistakable ties to the "psychodrama" subgenre of the avant-garde. This astonishing sequence begins at roughly the film's halfway point, as Glen is trying to decide whether or not to tell Barbara about his cross-dressing alter-ego, Glenda. Glenda enters her living room and faints, presumably from mental turmoil, and the ensuing 14 minutes symbolically enact that turmoil, fairly dripping with psychological and religious imagery. As Glenda collapses, Lugosi's "scientist" character launches into one of his most obtuse bits of dialogue, warning against the "green dragon" that "eats little boys," admonishing (us, the viewers? or Glen/Glenda?) to "Beware ... take care ... beware!" Next we see Glen and Barbara fully lit against a totally black backdrop, suggesting a remove from the diegetic world of the film (or a retreat into Glen's interior world), followed by a shot in Glen's living room of Barbara trapped under a fallen tree, with Glenda standing helplessly by. Glen replaces Glenda and rescues Barbara from under the tree/log, an act whose Freudian dimensions seem self-evident. A wedding scene follows, again with Glen and Barbara staged against a totally black setting, a Devil character appearing as the ring-bearer. In place of diegetic sound, the entire sequence features overbearing music of varying genres, further demarcating it from the rest of the film and aligning it with experimental cinema. The dream/trance proceeds with close-ups of Glen in obvious mental anguish, underlit with smoke swirling around his face—one of the film's most iconic and haunting images—as well as a series of scantily clad women being whipped, bound, and raped by male characters, the action staged on a sofa against a black background. (Although there is some doubt whether or not these specific shots originated with Wood, they do "fit" aesthetically with the rest of the sequence; and certainly Wood was known for freely using stock footage in his films [Craig 50; Grey 54].) These images are intercut with shots of Lugosi's god-figure looking on, sometimes leeringly, sometimes disapprovingly, as well as shots of Glen's horrified reactions. Next we return to Glen's apartment, now in total disarray (with even the fireplace askew on the set), where he is surrounded by many of the characters we have seen in the dream/trance. Here, Wood blatantly plays with discontinuity editing, as Barbara's costume changes in jump cuts from one shot to the next, from a white angora sweater to a black one, emphasizing the dual, oppositional structures already established by the God/Devil, male/female, and Glen/Glenda figures. Then, as all of the dream characters descend upon Glen, he transforms into Glenda and fights them off. The dream/trance sequence ends with Glenda looking at herself in the mirror, a troubled expression on her face. We then return to the film's main storyline, such as it is, as Dr. Alton explains that "Glen has made the decision to tell Barbara."

P. Adams Sitney characterizes the avant-garde subgenre of the "psychodrama" as marked by "the quest for sexual identity ... a highly personal psychological drama ... [and] a strong autobiographical element" (qtd. in Small 44). Further, Sitney observes that psychodramas often are "self-acted films ... [involving] the film-maker's use of herself or himself as a protagonist," with the result that "film becomes a process of self-realization" (14). In *Glen or Glenda?* Wood-as-actor dramatizes his own process of self-discovery as a transvestite, hetero-sexual male, arguing (as writer-director) for broad societal acceptance of his and others' sexual/gender identities. Edward S. Small observes that the American avant-garde cinema typically involves such "oneiric, fragmented narratives" as the scene described above, and that these films "reflexively revise the already well-established conventions of Hollywood's classical continuity" (43, 44). While citing films such as *Fragment* (Curtis Harrington, 1946), *Fireworks* (Kenneth Anger, 1947), and *Meshes of the Afternoon* (Maya Deren, 1947) as iconic examples of the psychodrama (44–45), Small and Sitney could just as well be describing the above-referenced dream/trance sequence from *Glen or Glenda?*.

My point here is not to cast Wood as an avant-garde film-maker, but rather to suggest his *awareness* of the avant-garde and of an "underground" tradition from which *Glen or Glenda?* clearly borrows—proof of which is in the viewing. The sequence described above demands to be read as a psychodrama if it is to be understood at all. In keeping with this reading, J. Hoberman refers to "the ineffable *Glen or Glenda*"

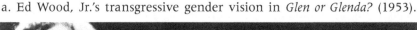

a. Ed Wood, Jr.'s transgressive gender vision in *Glen or Glenda?* (1953).

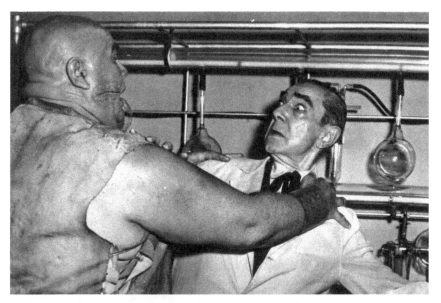

b. *Bride of the Monster* (1955) shows the mad scientist (Bela Lugosi) menaced by his monstrous creation (Tor Johnson).

as "a transvestite psychodrama more surreal than *Blood of a Poet*" ("Normalsleaze" 74), while Rob Craig likens the film to the experimental works of Buñuel and Deren (23). Even a brief commentary in the popular magazine *Premiere* asserts that "Wood's better films have an endearing absurdity approaching Dada" ("Edward D. Wood, Jr." 140).

If we accept Wood's awareness of experimental film, as evidenced in *Glen or Glenda?*, then we might also begin to see his other films as deliberately tapping into the avant-garde's agenda of challenging Hollywood norms, even as they rely upon the established genre traditions of sf and horror. While Wood's intentions are lost to us now, the fact remains that his films *are* significant departures from the mainstream, whether we see those qualities as arising entirely from "oppositional" readings (à la Sconce) or as conscious constructs intrinsic to the films themselves. In *Ed Wood: Mad Genius*, Rob Craig makes a reasonably convincing case for the latter position, casting Wood as "a daring and utterly unique outsider film artist, a wildly creative producer of bizarre personal art, and a filmmaker of sublime stature," whose films are "neither bad nor good—they are art; astounding, bizarre film-poems with many, many flaws, and many more hypnotic charms" (1).

Considered side-by-side, *Bride of the Monster* and *Plan 9 from Outer Space* cast these opposite possibilities in relief. Despite its lack of resources (quite apparent in its bare-bones sets, inept special effects, and bargain-basement exploitation of Lugosi as "star"), *Bride of the Monster* otherwise falls rather comfortably within the realm of classical cinematic norms, with its straightforward, linear plot, clearly defined protagonists and villain, and fairly consistent observance of the rules of continuity—thereby offering an interesting counterpoint to the other two films considered here. In contrast, *Plan 9 from Outer Space* offers something more akin to the avant-garde, or at the very least the art cinema, with its scattershot plot, aimless characters, multiple points of view, overt commentary on the human condition, and unconventional approach to continuity. (Some might suggest that *Plan 9* merely takes a slipshod or careless approach to classical continuity; but as *Bride of the Monster* fairly well follows the basic "rules" of continuity editing, Wood seems to have been aware of those conventions.) Taken in tandem, these films bespeak Wood's dual position *vis-à-vis* classical Hollywood: as presumptive insider and *de facto* outsider—that is, as a writer-director who aspired in some cases to make "classic" Hollywood films, while never being accepted by the Hollywood mainstream, as well as one who also questioned the very nature of Hollywood-style cinematic expression and its suitability for addressing the sort of subjects he chose to tackle.

Bride of the Monster opens with a convincing enough model of an "old dark house," dimly lit, cloaked in rain and lightning—already a long-standing trope of gothic literature by the time of James Whale's 1932 film, *The Old Dark House*. The next scene similarly has roots in dozens of classic horror stories: two wandering men, caught in the thunderstorm, seek refuge in the house, which is inhabited by Dr. Vornoff (Bela Lugosi) and his Igor-like servant, Lobo (Tor Johnson). Clearly, Wood is attempting to draw from established traditions of horror in a fairly conventional manner, and indeed to recreate the kind of motion picture that might have starred Lugosi 20 years earlier. The film's very title suggests a throwback to the iconic *Bride of Frankenstein* (1935) from the golden age of Universal's horror/monster films, while also recalling the series of B horror/sf hybrids that Lugosi made for various Poverty Row studios in the 1930s and 1940s.

To this formulaic opening, Wood then adds various sf elements, as we learn of Vornoff's atomic experiments, which echo numerous earlier examples of such genre mixing, notably *Frankenstein* (1931), *The Invisible Ray* (1936), *The Devil Doll* (1936), and *The Devil Bat* (1940). In fact, Wood's original title, *Bride of the Atom*, underscores this generic duality, a duality then played out in a narrative that has Lugosi portraying Dr. Vornoff, a mad scientist who has created the eponymous "monster" (or, more properly, "creature")—a gigantic octopus that dwells in nearby Lake Marsh. As we later learn, Vornoff had been ridiculed by the scientific community in his home country for his outrageous theories, and he seems to have been driven insane by his desire to prove the establishment wrong. Now in exile, he conducts deadly experiments intended to produce a race of giant super-beings.

The narrative then introduces dual protagonists: one representing patriarchal authority and order, police Lieutenant Dick Craig (Tony McCoy), the other signaling an impulse towards intellectual curiosity and a desire to uncover the truth, Craig's girlfriend, investigative reporter Janet Lawton (Loretta King). While the police insist that "there is no such thing as monsters," Lawton is determined to investigate the supposedly abandoned house near Lake Marsh, and she eventually brings Vornoff's twisted experiments to light: perversions of his earlier work which might have benefited humanity, now tainted by his mad desire to rule the world. In the end, the police rescue Janet as Vornoff is killed by his own creation, the octopus-monster, with a policeman somberly intoning in the film's last line: "He tampered in God's domain."

As a horror/sf film, *Bride of the Monster* bears few remarkable qualities, aside from the star presence of Bela Lugosi. It simply offers up the standard oppositions of reason vs madness, and science's potential for good or ill use—tropes already well established by the beginning of the 1950s, as Vivian Sobchack notes, with the "pro-science" *Destination Moon* (1950), and the "anti-science" *The Thing from Another World* (1951) (21–22). However, *Bride* has become remarkable—and attained cult status—largely because of its director's reputation, earned primarily through *Glen or Glenda?* and *Plan 9 from Outer Space*. As such, *Bride of the Monster* offers a curious illustration of Wood's very stature as cult auteur. If this were a stand-alone B- or C-grade film, one made by some other, unknown director, it would scarcely have attained the level of critical attention or the cult status it has. Its reputation rests almost entirely on its status as "an Ed Wood film." But *Bride of the Monster* does fit comfortably within the critical boundaries ascribed to "cult films" as a category, in addition to its clear generic heritage in horror and sf. In their introduction to *The Cult Film Reader*, Ernest Mathijs and Xavier Mendik suggest that definitions of the "cult" traverse four major areas of concern: 1) the film itself; 2) consumption; 3) political economy, including exhibition; and 4) cultural status, or the film's relation to the larger culture (1). While the last three areas of concern resonate more with *Plan 9 from Outer Space*, *Bride of the Monster* meets several of their criteria for "the film itself": aesthetic "badness," a blurring of genres, intertextuality, narrative loose ends, and nostalgic appeal (2–3).

Mathijs and Mendik find particularly interesting "those films being valued for their 'ineptness' or poor cinematic achievement, often placing them in some kind of opposition to the 'norm' or mainstream in that they attain a status of 'otherness'" (2). They specifically cite *Plan 9* as an example, but their description easily extends to *Bride of the Monster*. The "monster" that "attacks" various characters in the film is an obvious fake, a rubber octopus that was supposed to move hydraulically (as dramatized in Tim Burton's 1994 biopic, *Ed Wood*) but which lies almost comically inert, as the actors attempt to animate it with their own flailing arms. Wood intercuts these shenanigans with stock footage of a living octopus, perhaps in an attempt to push the Kuleshov experiment to its limits, or perhaps out of sheer economic necessity. Add to this shortcoming the wooden acting that pervades the film, and one can see why some audiences might value *Bride of the Monster* especially for its "bad" aesthetics. Indeed, one of Wood's fiercest champions, Rob Craig, interprets the film as a Brechtian exercise in "epic theater," reading the rubber octopus and minimalist sets as intentionally fake, allowing us to see through the constructed illusionism of conventional narratives and spot the artist's hand at work (88–89).

We might further note in *Bride of the Monster* a degree of self-awareness or intertextuality, that is, direct or implicit references to the genres of sf and horror, to specific films, and to other cultural texts and trends. Craig notes parallels between *Bride* and the 1944 Poverty Row production *Return of the Ape Man* (1944, dir. Phil Rosen), wherein Lugosi portrays a mad scientist who subjects his victims to a "freezing chamber" similar to Vornoff's "atom ray" (84). Such intertextual references invite, as Mathijs and Mendik put it,

> comparisons, connections and linkages with other films and other parts of culture ... This involves not only the inclusion of references to other film texts in the form of quotes or cameos but also the calling into reflection of cultural myths, historical backgrounds and archetypes. (3)

Additionally, the plot element of atomic research links the film not only to the real-life cultural dilemmas of the post-Hiroshima, Cold War era, but also to other sf and horror texts of the period that deal symbolically with the same concerns, perhaps most notably *Gojira* (1954) and *Them!* (1954).

Against such troubling aspects of contemporary culture, cult films often offer a sense of nostalgia, a "yearning for an idealized past" (Mathijs and Mendik, 3). One might argue that *Bride of the Monster* provides a nostalgic "trip down memory lane" for fans of classic horror movies; but, significantly, the film also incorporates a similar sense of nostalgic yearning into its own storyline. Talking to his former colleague, Strowski, who offers the possibility of returning home, Vornoff ruefully replies, in one of the film's most touching moments: "Home? I have no home. Hunted, despised, living like an animal! The jungle is my home!" These lines receive special emphasis in Tim Burton's film, suggesting a parallel between the forgotten, washed-up character of Vornoff and Lugosi's own sense of being abandoned by Hollywood, his glory days forgotten. Indeed, according to some of Wood's collaborators, one of the director's greatest hopes was to help revive Lugosi's career, with a planned series of films together. Although Wood may have been driven by more practical concerns (i.e., the ability to get a name star for very little money), perhaps part of his motivation came from his own cult-like, nostalgic desire to see Lugosi, his idol and friend, back on the big screen once again (see *Flying Saucers over Hollywood*).

However, Wood and Lugosi would work together just once more before the actor's death in 1956. On various locations and with no particular story in mind, Wood filmed Lugosi in a series of vignettes— some featuring his *Dracula* cape costume—that would eventually form the basis of the director's most widely discussed film, *Plan 9 from Outer Space*. In contrast to *Bride of the Monster*, *Plan 9* does not simply rehash horror and sf tropes, but rather uses those genres as a point of departure for its less conventional, at times arguably experimental approach to cinematic narrative, making it a far more compelling and revealing entry in the cult film lexicon. Not only does the film depart from classical narrative strategies; it openly defies basic rules of continuity and directly confronts the audience with its anti-violence "message." (If *Glen or Glenda?* is a variation on the kind of sf text that Merril terms the "Teaching Story," then *Plan 9* offers an example of the "Preaching Story, which essentially warns and prophesies," in this case against the violent use of technology [qtd. in Sobchack 18]).

The plot structure, or lack thereof, in *Plan 9* is one of the chief elements separating it from the norms of classical cinema and thus casting the film as "Other." According to actress Maila Nurmi (aka "Vampira"), Wood "didn't start with a master design ... He worked like decoupage" (*Flying Saucers over Hollywood*). In light of the film's origins, in those random scenes shot earlier with Lugosi, perhaps a traditional approach to narrative structure was out of the question. Gregory Walcott, who plays the airline pilot Jeff Trent, recalled that he could not "make heads or tails" of the script (*Flying Saucers over Hollywood*). Indeed, the plot defies easy summary and involves no fewer than ten separate but intersecting groups of characters and arenas of action. A quick overview here will illustrate the film's hodgepodge plot construction, while also pointing out its key sf elements and themes.

In brief, aliens have come to conquer the Earth by reanimating human corpses into an army of zombies; this stratagem, which they term "Plan 9," affects the lives of all of the main characters in various ways. Trent, a commercial airline pilot and one of the first to see the flying saucers, later encounters some of the reanimated ghouls near a cemetery that serves as the aliens' terrestrial base of operations. Two of the zombies, played by Lugosi (as well as an unconvincing stand-in) and Vampira, in their normal lives had been husband and wife, offering curious doubles of Mr. and Mrs. Trent; and a third zombie (Tor Johnson) had been a police inspector named Clay. Numerous scenes take place in the graveyard, with policemen bumbling about and zombies stalking. Other subplots revolve around the military response to the UFOs (including such ludicrous voice-over narration as "Meanwhile, at the Pentagon ..."), as well as the aliens' strategizing aboard their flying saucers and space station.

The narrative shifts freely (sometimes randomly, it seems) from one group of characters to another, with neither a clear protagonist nor villain to root us in the narrative. While a more conventional horror or sf film might rely on the zombies as monstrous villains, *Plan 9* undercuts that strategy, letting us get to know two of the characters before their deaths and resurrections. Even the non-zombie characters lack the clear goals that normally drive a classical narrative forward, giving *Plan 9* a rather meandering story structure. Furthermore, *Plan 9* delays much of its expository material until the end, when we finally discover the aliens' motives for wanting to attack the Earth: humanity is advancing too rapidly in its destructive capabilities and must be stopped, much as in *The Day the Earth Stood Still* (1951).

As a result, not even the aliens emerge as clear-cut villains and, indeed, Wood uses one of them, Eros (Dudley Manlove), as a mouthpiece for the film's pontifications against violence and military machismo. We might expect such overt commentary in the international art cinema or in Brechtian theater, but not in a B genre film. Nor do we expect the sort of direct address to the camera that we find in the opening, pre-credit sequence of *Plan 9*, in which the "psychic" Criswell, of period newspaper and radio fame, ruminates upon our desire to know the future. Curiously, though, amid his ramblings about the *future*, "where you and I will spend the rest of our lives," Criswell introduces the "future events such as these" of our story, while simultaneously alluding to *past* events, that is, to "what happened on that fateful day." Thus the film begins with a confusing yet pointed reference to the duality of past and future; whatever "lesson" or "moral" the film finally offers has something to do with learning from the lessons of the past in order to shape a better future. Given Wood's own background as a US Marine during the Second World War (involving the traumatic killing of a Japanese soldier, according to Rob Craig), we may take the film's admonitions against our violent nature as being offered with the utmost sincerity and seriousness, suggesting, perhaps, in this past-future confusion the time-worn adage that those who do not learn from history are doomed to repeat it.

Criswell's initial hint of a past-future duality should also cue us into the dual nature of the film as a whole. It is at once an sf film and an exploitation film—a close relative of the cult film, as Roger Corman has noted (xvii). Furthermore, *Plan 9* is both Hollywood film, proudly brandishing the credit "Made in Hollywood, USA," and something that begs to be read counter to Hollywood conventions. As Sconce and others have noted, *Plan 9* approaches the avant-garde in its extreme disregard for continuity editing. In J. Hoberman's view, Wood

> puts the principles of [classical] montage to one of their most severe tests. Not only does he employ a cape-shrouded stand-in a full head taller than his erstwhile star [Lugosi], but he employs nonexistent points of view, consistently mismatches day and night shots, and reuses the same stock footage with impunity ("Plan 9" 2).

If Wood demonstrates some minimal competence with regard to continuity in his more traditional *Bride of the Monster*, such concerns no longer appear relevant here; and it is tempting simply to regard the flagrant lack of continuity in *Plan 9* as a deliberate, even aesthetic choice.

It might be no surprise, then, that noted experimental film-maker George Kuchar finds much to admire in Ed Wood's work—the familiar adage "it takes one to know one" comes to mind—and he articulates his admiration in poetic terms. Kuchar observes:

> His work had that memorable, stark, and easy to read look that reminded me of ... the "Farmer Grey" cartoons ... Ed Wood's pictures seemed a natural next step in the live action evolution of these characters, as these two-dimensional constructions moved into a more adult, urban setting, which was just as flat as a sheet of animation paper. It also seemed that the storyboard backgrounds were all jumbled out of order in this new two-dimensional experience, but since the characters moved very slowly or not at all, it sort of glued the whole thing together ... These movies were

fun and approachable, with a better reflective surface to mirror the
dreams and despair of those who labored on them. (11)

Similarly, as with his analysis of *Bride of the Monster*, Rob Craig likens *Plan
9* specifically to Brechtian and absurdist theatrical traditions, whether
such tendencies are intentional or not in Wood's work (141).

Of course, such innovative and experimental moves are primary
aesthetic qualities of cult films; Mathijs and Mendik describe such effects
as "shocks to the system" (2) for viewers. In fact, they specifically cite
Plan 9 from Outer Space as an outstanding example of another major
characteristic of cult films, their aesthetic "badness." We might pause
here, however, to note that the reputation of *Plan 9* as the "worst movie
ever made" (and, by extension, Wood as the "worst director") is dubious
at best. The "worst ever" designation seems to have originated in Michael
and Harry Medved's 1980 book, *The Golden Turkey Awards*. Yet in the 1991
documentary *Flying Saucers over Hollywood: The Plan 9 Companion*, Harry
Medved refers to Wood as an "artist" and to his films as "classics." He
notes, "They try so hard ... to make some kind of statement that's going to
move you." Other commentators point out that there are certainly worse
films than *Plan 9*. Writing in the trade magazine *Video*, one critic asserts:
"There are movies much worse—that is, duller—but this cornucopia of
cardboard sets, preposterous plotting, arch dialog, atrocious acting, and
missing-in-action special effects is endlessly watchable in a way that few
'good' movies are" (M. F. 64). Thus it could be that the Medveds were
engaging in a sort of "alternative canonization" (which, according to
Mathijs and Mendik, is also typical of cult film consumption) in creating
their list of "worst movies"; and indeed Rob Craig credits them with
introducing Wood to a far larger audience than the director ever would
have dreamt possible (138). No doubt, many a neophyte has been drawn
to Wood's films simply out of a curiosity to see how "bad" they can be,
only to discover in them a surprising element of the sublime.

Writing in 1964, Susan Sontag famously linked such "bad art" closely
to the concept of "camp," which she ties in turn to a "cult usage" (42–44);
and we might note that much of the appeal of Wood's films, especially
Plan 9 from Outer Space, comes from the viewing pleasure associated with
such "camp" qualities. Indeed, many of Sontag's observations on camp,
which she characterizes as "the sensibility of failed seriousness, of the
theatricalization of experience" (49), seem tailor-made to describe *Plan 9*:

> the essence of Camp is its love—of the unnatural: of artifice and
> exaggeration ... In naïve, or pure, Camp, the essential element is
> seriousness, a seriousness that fails. Of course, not all seriousness

that fails can be redeemed as Camp. Only that which has the proper mixture of the exaggerated, the fantastic, the passionate, and the naïve ... The pure examples of Camp are unintentional; they are dead serious. (42, 46, 47)

Again, the artifice in *Plan 9* may be deliberate or not, but it seems clear that the film's campiest moments, such as the over-the-top speeches of Eros (who derides all humans as "stupid, stupid ... idiots!") are presented in total seriousness. That is to say, *Plan 9* offers an example of what Sontag would term "pure camp" in that Wood is not attempting to be campy; rather, the camp qualities of his films emerge in spite of (or thanks to) the impassioned seriousness of the ludicrous dialogue and performances. In a similar vein of seriousness, beyond the curious case of the religion known as "Woodism," the films of Ed Wood do offer fabulistic, archetypal, and ideological dimensions, which Mathijs and Mendik view as central to cult cinema's relation to the culture writ large. We have already noted the anti-war sentiments offered in *Plan 9 from Outer Space*, as well as the references to nuclear paranoia in *Bride of the Monster*. But these two films share an added meaning perhaps more evident in *Glen or Glenda?*, a film that Harry Medved sees as "a plea for the world to understand" not only transgendered individuals, but anyone who falls outside the mainstream into the category of "Other" (*Flying Saucers over Hollywood*). This appeal for acceptance of the "Other" is probably the strongest link between these three films, and while it finds its clearest and most forceful articulation in *Glen or Glenda?*, it runs powerfully through *Bride* and *Plan 9* as well.

In *Bride of the Monster*, Vornoff sees himself as an outcast, literally in exile, shunned by his colleagues, ridiculed for what he considers to be his greatest work, simply because it lies too far outside the mainstream—a problem faced by Wood himself. Certainly at this stage in his career, Wood could not have known that he would eventually be regarded by some as the "worst filmmaker of all time." Yet, as both Rob Craig (277–78) and Rudolph Grey (10) point out, Wood's films failed dismally upon their initial theatrical runs, ridiculed by critics and audiences alike; and Wood associate Mildred Worth recalls that he was visibly upset by the guffawing audience at a preview screening of one of his films (Grey 70). Thus it is tempting to read the character of Vornoff as an incarnation of Wood's own resentment at occupying a similar "outsider" status, and the same could be said of the misfit protagonists of *Glen or Glenda?*.

Similarly, in *Plan 9 from Outer Space* Wood offers up his alien characters as fabulistic, psychologically symbolic figures, going so far as to name one of them "Eros," after the Greek god of love. This pointed reference to mythology encourages an interpretive reading and is reinforced by other oblique references to archetypal figures. For instance, the aliens refer to the Lugosi character as the "old man" and "the old one," and several other characters, including the zombies and police, function as character *types*. (In interviews for *The Plan 9 Companion*, Vampira repeatedly refers to her character as the "anima.") Thus the naming of Eros underscores what might be read as a plea for love and understanding (not war), which the human characters seem unable to comprehend. Furthermore, the aliens' physical appearance similarly invites an interpretive reading: anatomically, they seem no different from humans; they are coded as "Other" only by their manner of dress and behavior, much like the transgendered characters of *Glen or Glenda?*; and, furthering that connection, we might note that Eros and his commander are both portrayed with effete affectations.

In situating some of the thematic concerns from *Glen or Glenda?* within a more clearly sf context in *Plan 9*, Wood actually lends them a more mythological, universal aspect. No longer is he simply calling for an acceptance of his own way of life as a heterosexual cross-dresser; rather, he seems to be advocating for a much broader acceptance of diversity, years before the mainstream culture was ready to take on such matters. In this regard, Eros's frustration that the people of Earth refuse to acknowledge the existence of aliens also assumes a deeper significance, in such lines as: "We came to ask your aid; your government refused to accept our existence, even though you've seen us!" Combined with the aliens' stated plan of having an army of zombies march on Washington as "proof of our existence," such dialogue takes on added symbolic and ideological weight, especially at a time in American history when minority groups of all stripes were denied fundamental rights and recognition, and were already staging their own marches.

This demand for acknowledgment speaks directly to the cult audience's need to transcend the status of "Other"—paradoxically by embracing the very "other"-ness of both cult and sf films and thus connecting with a community of like-minded fans. The ability to find value in overlooked or discarded cinematic works (which often take the margins as their very subject matter) and in marginalized figures such as Ed Wood, Vampira, and Bela Lugosi, distinguishes a cult/sf audience from the mainstream. In fact, herein may lie the very essence of the cult sensibility that surfaces in Wood's films and elsewhere: the affinity that these films find with an audience of "outsiders" and the power of this "other" cinema to transform its audience into knowing "insiders." In parallel, we might see the appeal that Wood found in sf as lodged in the power of science as a means of transformation, of promising to remake oneself or the world. As *Bride of the Monster* and *Plan 9* warn, science often attempts to remake the world through violent means, but *Glen or Glenda?* offers the more progressive possibility—of remaking the self through science and claiming one's place in the world. Ultimately, Wood seems to be calling into question the arbitrary nature of conventional life, pleading for a wider acceptance of alternative ways of living—and doing so by means of a highly unconventional, alternative mode of film-making. Given the potentially transformative powers of the realms of sf and cult film within which he worked, it seems little wonder, then, that today some 5,000 baptized followers worldwide regard Edward D. Wood, Jr. as a savior.

Works Cited

Bordwell, David. "The Art Cinema as a Mode of Film Practice." *Critical Visions in Film Theory*. Ed. Timothy Corrigan, Patricia White, and Meta Mazaj. New York: Bedford/St. Martins, 2010. 558–73.

Bride of the Monster. Dir. Edward D. Wood, Jr. Banner Productions, 1955.

Craig, Rob. *Ed Wood, Mad Genius: A Critical Study of the Films*. Jefferson: McFarland, 2009.

De Seife, Ethan. *This Is Spinal Tap*. London: Wallflower, 2007.

Ed Wood. Dir. Tim Burton. Touchstone Pictures, 1994.

"Ed Wood's Holy Haven." Yahoo groups. Web. Accessed 14 July 2013.

"Edward D. Wood, Jr.," *Premiere*, October 1994: 140.

Flying Saucers over Hollywood: The Plan 9 *Companion*. Dir. Mark Patrick Carducci. Atomic Pictures, 1992.

Glen or Glenda? Dir. Edward D. Wood, Jr. Screen Classics, 1953.

Hoberman, J. "Normalsleaze." *Village Voice*, February 1, 1983: 74.

—. "*Plan 9 from Outer Space*." Rev. *Village Voice*, January 13, 1982: 2.

—, and Jonathan Rosenbaum. *Midnight Movies*. New York: Harper & Row, 1983.

Kuchar, George. "Ed Wood." *Wide Angle* 14.3 (1992): 11.

M. F. "The Ed Wood Collection." Rev. *Video*, March 1995: 64.

Mathijs, Ernest, and Xavier Mendik, eds. *The Cult Film Reader*. New York: McGraw-Hill, 2008.

Plan 9 from Outer Space. Dir. Edward D. Wood, Jr. Reynolds Pictures, 1959.

Sconce, Jeffrey. "'Trashing' the Academy: Taste, Excess, and an Emerging Politics of Cinematic Style." *Screen* 36.4 (1995): 371–93.

Sobchack. Vivian. *Screening Space: The American Science Fiction Film*. 2nd ed. New Brunswick: Rutgers UP, 1997.

Sontag, Susan. "Notes on Camp." *The Cult Film Reader*. Ed. Ernest Mathijs and Xavier Mendik. New York: McGraw-Hill, 2008. 42–52.

Telotte, J. P. "Beyond All Reason." *The Cult Film Experience: Beyond All Reason*. Austin: U of Texas P, 1991. 5–17.

—. *Science Fiction Film*. Cambridge: Cambridge UP, 2001.

Weaver, Tom. "Ed Wood: The Man, the Myth, the Movie." Rev. of *Ed Wood*. *Video Scope* 15 (1995): 20.

12. Visual Pleasure, the Cult, and Paracinema

Sherryl Vint

Cult and sf are both categories that suggest a skewed perspective on reality. Jeffrey Sconce uses the term "paracinema" to denote this different perspective, as he describes cult and other kinds of "bad" cinema that are often appreciated, ironically, for their deviation from—perhaps resistance to—dominant aesthetic codes. Sconce maintains that the resulting celebration of such "trash" is a rejection of the hegemony of academic film criticism, championing the trashy as "a final textual frontier that exists beyond the colonizing powers of the academy, and thus serves as a staging ground for strategic raids on legitimate culture and its institutions by those (temporarily) lower in educational, cultural and/or economic capital" (382). Through much of its history, sf has been similarly regarded. In *Metamorphoses of Science Fiction*, Darko Suvin calls it a "paraliterature" (vii) but celebrates its promise to interrogate dominant ideological codes that pass, unquestioned, as natural and apolitical in realist modes of representation. While Sconce's and Suvin's analyses of such different perspectives emphasize their foregrounding of class issues, this essay will focus on gender in the intersection of cult and sf. Both cult and sf have often been regarded as masculine forms, and the pleasures of excess that cult films celebrate often include the visual pleasures of scantily clad female bodies, images frequently associated with pulp sf's lurid magazine covers of the 1920s and 1930s. Yet sf also has a rich history of interrogating gender attitudes, using images such as aliens to express and examine patriarchal fears.

This essay explores cult's claims to transgression in this context of gender difference, focusing on a number of low-budget sf films of the 1950s and 1960s that have attained cult status, including *Cat-Women of the Moon* (1953), *Devil Girl from Mars* (1954), *The Astounding She-Monster* (1957), *Attack of the 50 Foot Woman* (1958), *The Wasp Woman* (1959), *Monstrosity* (aka *The Atomic Brain*, 1963), *Attack of the Puppet People* (1957), and *The Brain that Wouldn't Die* (1962). I argue that these films demonstrate a dialectic of indulgence and critique that characterizes cult sf's treatment of gender difference, revealing how such difference—as well as differences in educational, cultural, or economic capital—informs the "raid" on legitimate culture that such films stage. Their laughably bad plots, dialogue, characterization, and special effects position them as seemingly trivial entertainment when compared to "serious" contemporary sf films such as *The Thing from Another World* (1951) or *The Day the Earth Stood Still* (1951), both concerned with nuclear armament and the Cold War. Yet the 1950s saw significant shifts in gender roles, such as the struggle over women's employment outside the home, which undermined traditional, working-class masculine identity. Domestic culture was changing as significantly and rapidly as civic culture during this period, and the "othering" of gender that resulted is a significant part of sf's history.

Cult sf films both question the naturalness of gender roles and demonstrate anxiety about this shifting culture of gender in their sexualized representation of female bodies (also characteristic of other Hollywood films, of course) and their narratives about the dangers of female power. This dual fascination with and fear of the feminine might also be understood as foundational to the cult film, as Joanne Hollows observes when she points out that "cult is naturalized as masculine and the mainstream as feminine," thereby mitigating cult's claims to transgression because "if the mainstream is persistently gendered as feminine, cult would seem to reproduce existing power structures rather than simply challenge them" (37). Similarly, Steve Chibnall points out that the academic culture which paracinema resists is one informed by feminist cultural critique, since paracinema "has provided opportunities for (predominantly) young straight white male academics to reclaim marginalized areas of cinema's history and to resist the dominant paradigms of film theory which have tended to problematize and pathologize male heterosexual pleasure in the text" (87–88). Cult sf films of the 1950s and 1960s exemplify these tensions between cult's transgressive potential and its often conservative gender views. While the pleasures viewers continue to find in these texts emerge from an ironic, almost dismissive stance—it is so bad, it is good—I want to tease out a thread of what we might call *sincere* anxiety: about female agency, changing gender relations, and especially female desire.

Barry Grant argues that the metaphor of "othering" commonly links cult and sf cultures, suggesting that "in the cult film the Other becomes a caricature that makes what it represents less threatening to the viewer," so that just as with the genre fan, "the viewer ultimately gains the double satisfaction of both rejecting the dominant cultural values and remaining safely inscribed within them" (124). This dynamic explains the appeal of films that obsessively return to gender. Female power is domesticated by the silliness of low-production values, enabling the articulation of anxiety but disavowing it as a serious problem. Further, for the paracinematic audience that embraces such films as sites of ironic pleasure, viewers can simultaneously experience the "othering" of women while denying its appeal through an ironic viewing stance. Yet these films are not simply veiled depictions of misogyny; they do provide significant pleasures for female viewers. Their often monstrous women, although punished for their transgressions, have moments of great cinematic power before their demise. In this power we can see how these cult sf films offer complex and contradictory viewing pleasures to male and female viewers alike in their struggles with gender ideology.

Women's Sexual Power

Cat-Women of the Moon is among the earliest of these films. It begins in the vastness of space as a voice-over notes the mysteries of the cosmos hidden behind a barrier that "will be pierced" some day, reminding us of Victor Frankenstein's project to pursue nature to her hiding-places and the Baconian vision of science as penetrating enquiry enacted on a feminized nature. The secrets of the cosmos are thus linked to the secrets of the titular Cat-Women and, through them, to the secrets of femininity itself because of the Cat-Women's telepathic power to control the sole female crewmember of a moon mission, Helen (Marie Windsor). The mission is led by the staid Laird (Sonny Tufts), whose timidity and investment in rules are constantly challenged by the dashing second-in-command Kip (Victor Jory). Romantic and naïve Doug (William Phipps) and entrepreneurial Walt (Douglas Fowley) round out the crew, which thus offers a range of contemporary masculine identities: the company man in Laird, the frontier hero in Kip, the gullible innocent in Doug, and the self-starter of commercial culture in Walt.

On the journey out, one of the ship's engines fails, requiring Kip to demonstrate manly heroics and establishing him as better suited than Laird for leadership—and for Helen's affections. On the moon, they discover the beautiful Cat-Women, all of whom wear identical body suits and jewelry, and welcome the crew, offering them food served by equally seductive women who seek to learn how Earth technology operates. Through these various enticements, the film expresses anxieties about the treacherous power of female beauty and the limitations of certain kinds of masculinity: Laird, a helpless bumbler, is easily taken in, and his later death suggests that his mode of masculinity cannot secure the future; Walt pursues gold deposits, abandoning any commitment to the mission in favor of personal gain, and he too dies; Doug falls in love with a Cat-Woman, Lambda (Susan Morrow), and jeopardizes the mission, until she also falls in love with him and betrays her own people. Only Kip displays the right combination of manly action and self-reliance, scornfully refusing to partake of the Cat-Women's banquet and later breaking their telepathic control over Helen.

The developing relationship between Kip and Helen is key to the film's "othering" of (some kinds of) women. Kip discovers her complicity with the Cat-Women when confronting Helen about a sexual tension between them, twisting her arm when she tries to leave and silencing her protest with "come on now; I'm not hurting you that much." A little bit of pain proves precisely what Helen needs to shock her out of Cat-Woman control, and she confesses to Kip that she really loves him and was with Laird only because the Cat-Women forced her. By physically imposing his will on Helen—albeit in the name of love—Kip saves her and the mission from the Cat-Women's plans to steal their ship. In contrast to the pliant Helen, the queenly Alpha (Carol Brewster) has no use for love or men (whose minds the Cat-Women cannot penetrate). She proclaims, we "will get their women under our power and soon we will rule the whole world," thereby expressing the film's central anxiety: that if women are not dependent on men they will disdain and reject them. Showing love as more important than power, the film emphasizes that women who desire power are dangerous and must be destroyed—as are all the Cat-Women, even Lambda, who sacrifices herself to help the humans. The cult pleasures of *Cat-Women of the Moon* lie partly in the spectacle of the beautiful Cat-Women, but perhaps more powerfully in the spectacle of them tamed.

Devil Girl from Mars similarly defines its titular character, Nyah (Patricia Laffan), through her costume, a short mini-dress with high boots and a long leather cape. While such provocative and shiny costuming is typical of many screen sf females of the period, when combined with Laffan's performance of command over and contempt for men, Nyah reveals the hint of BDSM that informs such costuming choices. While the Cat-Women are named for the animal's connotations of sexuality and witchcraft, Nyah is defined as a Devil Girl because she comes from a matriarchy. Like a dominatrix, Nyah is authoritative and cold, telling those who resist her invasion that she "can control power beyond your wildest dreams," and that it amuses her "to watch your puny efforts." She is deeply desirable but also deeply threatening. As in *Cat-Women of the Moon*, the film offers the double pleasure of the spectacle of the sexy Nyah striding about and issuing orders, while safely containing this female power in the human women who serve as her foils. Once Nyah arrives, the shrewish Mrs. Jamieson (Sophie Stewart) stops badgering her henpecked husband and looks to men to save the day. The aloof and beautiful fashion model Ellen (Hazel Court) comes to regret her affair with a powerful but married man and wishes she had settled down and done something "proper" with her life, such as raise children with the ordinary but steadfast reporter Carter (Hugh McDermott). Also echoing *Cat-Women of the Moon*, a less perfect masculine model, the escaped prisoner Robert/Albert (Peter Reynolds), must sacrifice himself to save the future, sabotaging Nyah's spacecraft so that she will never arrive in London. Indeed, even the Martian matriarchy is proven to *need* men, as Nyah has come to Earth in search of male breeding stock.

Devil Girl from Mars shows a monstrous vision of a woman who has power, but it also moderates this threat by showing men triumphing. The normative patriarchal assumptions that structure the film are evident in the way the human women quickly cease any challenge to male authority when confronted with the frightening spectacle of female power, while Nyah's provocative sexual costume is a well-established technique of patriarchal representation that manages the threat of powerful women by making them sites of male visual pleasure. These pervasive links among fears of women's sexual power, provocative costuming, and damsels in need of male rescue are so successfully established as tropes of the B sf genre that *The Astounding She-Monster* (1957) is simply a mélange of these elements with little narrative or character development of its own. The woman who learns to appreciate proper manly aggression is socialite Margaret (Marilyn Harvey), who falls for geologist Dick (Robert Clarke) when he rescues her not only from kidnappers but also from the titular She-Monster from space.

The Astounding She-Monster has not been embraced as widely by fans of the paracinematic, but its aesthetic failures—for example, an awkward scene in a car that includes no dialogue or other diegetic sound, or the impossibly slow "chase" scenes as the She-Monster stands gawkily in shot waiting for the other actors to flee—are precisely the sort of effects usually celebrated in such films. However, the She-Monster lacks sex appeal; although she is supposedly "nude," she is filmed through a blurry haze to suggest her radioactivity, but also to hide any titillating features. She has the sculpted, highly slanted eyebrows of the sexy Cat-Women, but her expression is harsh and dangerous, rather than sensual and alluring. Even her name bluntly reveals that what is really frightening is simply her femininity, and only in the film's final moments do we learn that she came to Earth not to take over or to steal its men, but to deliver a message of peace from a pan-planetary entity. Margaret and Dick, the only survivors of her attack, find this message in an amulet after the She-Monster has been burned with acid, and realize she used violence only defensively. *The Astounding She-Monster*, then, ends asking us to interrogate the pleasures we have taken in her destruction and our own projections in seeing her as a threat.

Evil Beauty Queens

Vivian Sochack has written compellingly about the combined hatred and fear of sexual desire in aging women that we find expressed in a number of cult sf films. Discussing the vengeful protagonists of films such as *Attack of the 50 Foot Woman* and *The Wasp Woman*, she writes:

> Subjectively felt, she is an *excess woman*—desperately afraid of invisibility, uselessness, lovelessness, sexual and social isolation and abandonment, but also deeply furious at both the double standard of aging in a patriarchal culture and her acquiescence to male heterosexist values and the self-contempt they engender. Objectively viewed, she is sloppy, self-pitying, and abjectly needy or she is angry, vengeful, powerful, and scary. Indeed, she is an *excessive woman*, a woman in masquerade, in whiteface. (81)

The enmity directed towards such women, she contends, is a projection by male viewers who deny their own aging bodies, a viewing position possible equally for original viewers and those who embrace it as a cult experience. Sobchack argues that such films offer female viewers the gratification of seeing these women transform from being scared into *scary* woman. While I agree, I am also troubled by the way the discourse of "othering" so successfully makes these women seem monstrous such that audience sympathy for them disappears when they are transformed from victimized to vengeful. The cost of power for women, it seems, is to no longer be regarded as human.

The heiress Nancy is multiply victimized in *Attack of the 50 Foot Woman*, first in her encounter with the giant from outer space, which hints at sexual assault—the camera cutting from a huge arm reaching for her to an extreme close-up of her screaming face—and then by her philandering husband, Harry (William Hudson). Ultimately, both are interested only in her wealth: the alien wants her diamond to power his craft, while Harry schemes to have her committed, allowing him to spend her wealth with his suggestively named girlfriend, Honey (Yvette

Vickers). Indeed, Harry's excessive womanizing and drinking seem to function as compensation for the fact that Nancy holds the wealth, and that he is in the feminized position of trophy husband, hence his nickname of Handsome Harry. "The community property routine only works for women," he grumbles, "man doesn't have a chance," echoing Miles's (Kevin McCarthy) complaint in *Invasion of the Body Snatchers* (1956) that, as fellow divorcees, he and Becky (Dana Wynter) are members of the same club, but he pays "dues" while she collects them. In both films, women's emerging financial and legal power is one aspect of male fear, while their sexual choices are another. (We might recall Miles's comment, "I never knew the meaning of fear until ... until I kissed Becky": he knows she is inhuman when she looks back at him not with admiration but "with indifference.)".

Some aspects of *Attack of the 50 Foot Woman* encourage us to condemn Harry and side with Nancy: the opening scenes intercut her ordeal with the alien and Harry's drunken flirting; the couple's butler clearly holds Harry in contempt for his disregard of his wife's mental and physical health; and when he too finally sees the alien craft, Harry abandons

a. The sexual tensions of *Cat-Women of the Moon* (1953) are visualized as Kip (Victor Jory) twists Helen's (Marie Windsor) arm.

b. The powerful—and dangerous—woman (Allison Hayes) in *Attack of the 50 Foot Woman* (1958).

Nancy and flees for his life. Nancy's cloying attempts to placate Harry, begging him not to leave and to love her are painful to watch, and thus it is something of a relief when her alien encounter transforms her into a giant, and she begins to blame Harry rather than herself for their failed marriage. However, the film encourages us to sympathize with Nancy only when she is pathetic and weak, as in *Cat-Woman of the Moon*, where powerful women are monstrous and women in love are sympathetic. Although both Harry and Nancy are killed in the electrical explosion that finally ends her rampage, Dr. Cushing's (Ray Gordon) closing comment—"she finally got Harry all to herself"—lays the blame more firmly on Nancy's desire for fidelity than on Harry's selfish behavior.

The Wasp Woman similarly begins with a sympathetic protagonist, Janice Starlin (Susan Cabot), who runs a successful cosmetics company, but whose market share is threatened by her aging body. The opening scene shows her power over a group of male executives as she complains about falling sales, but they quickly turn the tables and suggest that her once-beautiful face—now aged—is to blame for lost profits, that "not even Janice Starlin can remain a glamour girl forever." Compared to this loss of sexual appeal, her 18 years of experience with the company mean nothing, and Janice becomes obsessed by a scientist's work on royal jelly that promises to reverse the aging process. The link to bees and wasps, animals whose social organization seems to privilege the queen and reduce the males to subservient roles, is central to the film's anxieties about female power—anxieties supported by the notion that wasp queens kill their mates. The threat that Janice as CEO poses is contained by her failure as a woman, and this failure as woman reduces her to a monster when overdoses of royal jelly transform her into a wasp-human hybrid that indeed kills. The film's final moments depict a struggle between Janice and a younger female rival, the secretary Mary (Barboura Morris), which ends with heroic male Bill (Anthony Eisley) killing Janice, stepping into a more powerful role in the company, and firmly establishing his romance with Mary. The visual pleasures this film offers are less the spectacle of Janice's beauty, and more those of the destruction of the inhuman wasp-woman hybrid. However, like *Attack of the 50 Foot Woman*, this film also shows patriarchy's unfair treatment of women by reducing Janice's value to the company to her looks alone. Janice may be a monster, but it is clear that she is made one by patriarchy, so there are simultaneous pleasures to be had in watching her period of power.

The horror attached to an older woman desiring a young woman's sexual power is also explored in *Monstrosity*. In this case the old woman, Mrs. March (Marjorie Eaton), has both the power of wealth (like Nancy) and the power of corporate control (like Janice); she funds research into brain transplants with the hope of transferring her brain to the body of a young woman. This film lacks the catharsis of a scared woman being transformed into a scary woman, since Mrs. March is domineering and cruel throughout. She badgers her partner Victor (Frank Fowler), knowing that his financial dependence compels him to acquiesce, and she taunts him for his interest in the bodies of the young candidates, implying that once her brain has been transplanted, she will seek a better sexual partner. The transplant scientist Dr. Otto (Frank Gerstle) blames Mrs. March alone for the immorality of the project, implying that indulging her unnatural desire for youth is his only way to fund the worthwhile medical work he wants to accomplish. In the end, both Otto and Victor side with the young candidate Nina (Erika Peters)—although each extorts financial promises from her. Mrs. March is transplanted into a cat she mistreated, a result presented as a kind of poetic justice, and these three control her estate. *Monstrosity* lacks ironic or ambivalent pleasures, offering only the *schadenfreude* of Mrs. March's downfall, while a properly submissive version of femininity is celebrated in Nina. It thereby reinforces the dominant culture's misogyny, instead of offering an ironic distance from this fear of women.

Male Stalkers

Another group of gender-focused cult sf films expresses these same anxieties by showing women as victims, not monsters. The villainous male figures in these films are presented with considerable sympathy, and their crimes are shown to be motivated by a desire, even a *need* for female attention which they fear might be withdrawn. However, the capriciousness of female desire and the power that desirability gives women over men links these films to the ones discussed above.

One example is *Attack of the Puppet People*, in which both men and women are victimized by Mr. Franz (John Hoyt) and his technology that reduces people to doll size. His motivation stems from his wife abandoning him for another man. Obsessed with ensuring that he will never again be vulnerable to rejection, he transforms his secretaries into doll-size entities he can control, preventing them from leaving for better jobs or for marriage instead of a career. Franz tries to be kind to his doll people—he brings them out to have parties and sing for him—but he clearly cannot interact with others, especially women, as equals. He must have total control, as is seen by his threats to put them to sleep again unless they feign enjoyment of the activities he selects. His investment in keeping women in traditional female roles is further suggested by the dolls for sale in his workshop, which he describes as coming from a "full range" of walks of life: bride, housewife, and nurse. The men in his entourage are investigators who get too close, not chosen companions like the women. In the end, when the dolls—mainly through the men's efforts—escape and restore themselves to full size, he pleads, "don't leave me, please don't leave me, I'll be alone," as the camera gradually pulls away, leaving him isolated in the upper right corner of the screen, seeming more pitiable than sinister.

Scientist Bill Cortner (Jason Evers) is a more threatening figure in *The Brain that Wouldn't Die*, and his victim, Jan Compton (Virginia Leith), becomes monstrous, though, unlike characters such as Janice Starlin, whose desire produces her monstrosity, Jan is deformed entirely through Bill's actions. A brilliant transplant surgeon who has discovered a medium that will allow him to keep organs alive outside of bodies for an extended period, he tries to save his girlfriend when her head is severed in a car crash (caused by his reckless driving). The film opens with a black screen and a women's voice begging, "let me die, let me die," before we cut to an operating theatre in which Bill demonstrates his skills and saves a patient. Called away to his country house to deal with an emergency—which proves to be caused by a horrible creature he made by grafting together numerous cadavers—he crashes his car, runs off with Jan's head, and hooks it to a fluid that will preserve the brain while he seeks another body for it. As soon as Jan regains consciousness in her new situation, she insists that it is monstrous, that she has become the "ultimate" horror, and that he should have let her die.

In the subsequent scenes, as Bill searches for a new body, he essentially becomes a killer, stalking attractive women, suggesting how his desire to defeat death has made him as monstrous as Jan's unnatural existence as an animated head. The venues Bill investigates—a strip club, suburban neighborhoods in which he leers at attractive women, a "Miss Body Beautiful" pageant—make clear that his interest in his partner's *body* is paramount; he spends no time talking to Jan, explaining the situation, or comforting her. Bill is thus monstrous in the way of Mrs. March but is not portrayed with the same degree of hostility. His interest in *having* an attractive female body available to him seems more understandable than her "unnatural" desire to *be* an attractive female body after she has aged. Nonetheless, the film shows Bill's pursuit as sinister, revealing the lust that informs his quest. Many shots cut between the image of a body he is considering and a close-up of his face, as he bites his lower lip in a lecherous way. Thus, while Jan *looks* monstrous, the film vilifies male lechery rather than female power.

Bill eventually selects a young woman he knows, Doris (Adele Lamont), whose body is so perfect that she makes her living as a figure model. A former boyfriend scarred her, however, and in her modeling shots her face has to be obscured to hide these scars. Her image—both within the diegesis as she is photographed and in the film itself—epitomizes the fragmentation of women's bodies that Mulvey has observed in classical Hollywood narrative, and Bill's plan to literally cut off her head and replace it with Jan's makes this fragmentation concrete. Yet, Doris's dialogue suggests that *The Brain That Wouldn't Die* works against the grain of monstrous female films. She tells Bill, "I don't date men. Because I pose like I do, your mind works overtime. You get ideas. You're all alike," and his manipulation of her (promising to fix her face) reinforces the idea that she is right: men want only her body, Bill just more literally than others. In the end, though, Jan destroys Bill, as the transplant elixir gives her a telepathic connection with the monstrous creature, whom she orders to kill Bill, and her head is destroyed in the resulting fire. Her dialogue in the last third of the film (mainly addressed to the creature) is entirely about vengeance—a vengeance we might at least partially understand as an expression of her resentment of men's attitudes towards women. The film makes literal the problem explored in many of these cult sf films: masculine anxiety, due to the fact that women's bodies are desirable but their heads might resist men's plans or even ridicule men, as Jan does repeatedly.

Ironic Returns

As many critics of cult film have noted, a large part of its appeal emerges from an ironic sense of distance from the text. Cult audiences appreciate films such as *Cat-Women of the Moon* or *Attack of the 50 Foot Women* in spite of their pedestrian special effects and bad plots, and perhaps in spite of their overt sexism. Yet, as a critique via paracinematic viewing might suggest, such ironic pleasures are partially pleasures of disavowal. Allison Graham, in her examination of cults forming around films of the 1950s, argues that cult viewership always involves a dialectic of irony and its absence: "For while the hip knowingness of the cult audience, reveling in its suspension of belief, may appear ironic and seem to stand outside the 'naïve' spectacle of postwar popular culture, it is deeply rooted in the very culture it mocks" (110). Similarly, the pleasure that comes from mocking films that denigrate female agency as monstrous is always at least partly an expression of the anxiety produced by gender difference itself. I do not mean to reduce these films to "sexist" texts and dismiss their cult appeal as misogyny, but to underscore the doubled pleasures they entail, the way their cult appeal is simultaneously a resistance *and* capitulation to their themes.

Perhaps the most famous—or notorious—film that would resurrect these stereotypes and their gender anxiety is Roger Vadim's *Barbarella* (1968), defined by the many costume changes of Jane Fonda's eponymous, sexy heroine. The opening sequence seems a primer in the fragmentation of women's bodies on screen, as Barbarella strips off her spacesuit piece by piece in zero gravity, revealing sensual bare flesh as she rotates in acrobatic pose, her face only the blank screen of her helmet until she finally removes it, throws back her head, and shakes her hair like Rita Hayworth in *Gilda* (1946). Indeed, Barbarella's sexual performance is so exaggerated that one cannot help but laugh: she goes to sleep on a see-through bed as the camera looks from beneath as her visible nipples squash into the surface; she wears a number of short skirt and tall boot ensembles that have see-through nylon mesh cutouts over her nipples and navel; she is attacked by carnivorous dolls whose waist-high biting leaves her stockings in tatters and her thighs bloodied as if she were a rape victim; and so on. These outfits and scenarios are so ridiculous and overplayed that the film invites a distanced, cult viewing. Yet at the same time, of course, Jane Fonda's toned body remains on display for un-ironic viewing pleasure.

The plot similarly vacillates between scenes of the hyper-sexualized Barbarella seemingly designed to gratify heterosexual male viewers and other scenes that are so openly exaggerated as to accomplish the reverse. For example, when Barbarella agrees to have sex with the Catcher (Ugo Tognazzi) in the "old fashioned" way—via an exchange of bodily fluids—instead of through the modern technology of "the pill," his masculine prowess is praised to such a degree that it tips over into sarcasm. In a later sexual encounter with Pygar (John Phillip Law), this old-fashioned technique is enough to restore flight to the angel, who has been struggling with confidence issues. Finally, when Durand Durand (Milo O'Shea) tortures Barbarella with his "sex organ," her capacity for pleasure is such that rather than being killed by overwhelming sensations at the moment of crescendo/orgasm, she breaks the device, leaving him to shriek, "The energy cables are shrinking ... you've exhausted its power ... it couldn't keep up with you. What kind of girl are you?" And, indeed, this question structures the cult appeal of the film: Barbarella is powerful and too much for an effeminate man such as Durand Durand, but can be sated by a "real" man such as the Catcher, and even prefers such "real" sex to the liberation of "the pill." At the same time, her performance of sexual satisfaction is so extreme that it draws attention to itself *as performance*. Thus, while some aspects of the film quaff male anxieties about women's sexual liberation, others exaggerate them.

Invasion of the Bee Girls (1973) similarly captures this dynamic of indulgence and irony. It focuses on men who are dying of sexual overstimulation, a topic treated more seriously here than in *Barbarella*. The investigating officer Neil Agar (William Smith) traces the problem to Dr. Susan Harris (Anitra Ford), the lone woman working at a biomilitary research facility. Recalling the plot of *The Wasp Woman*, she is using the bee genome to transform women into hybrids who can kill men with an excess of sexual pleasure. Susan is sexually attractive and intelligent, but her accomplishments are linked to the threat she represents to male authority in the workplace and beyond. Her co-workers talk about her sexual frigidity, taking her reserve as a challenge to their manliness and suggesting that great sexual pleasure lies beneath her cool exterior. A scene of the transformation emphasizes how the women form a communal group, even have a capacity for sexual self-sufficiency, as seen in the shots of them sensually spreading wax across the inductee's breasts. But, as in the other films we have discussed, female agency and sexual independence are safely contained. Biology proves to limit women: the bee girls are made sterile and then driven by their sterility to mate with men (and here we might recall that menopause was offered as a reason to explain Nancy's instability in *Attack of the 50 Foot Woman*).

Yet the men come across as womanizers, insensitive to their aging wives and generally giving them good reasons for rebellion. Eventually the women are destroyed by Agar, with the help of his love interest and lab assistant Julie (Victoria Vetri), a woman who keeps to her proper place. In the final moments, Agar ends Julie's long and tedious discussion of the case, and her preparedness for physical self-defense, by walking into the bedroom, throwing her on the bed, and silencing her with a kiss. Yet, even as the proper sexual order is restored, the film's final cut to a bee on a flower, as we hear the opening bars of "Thus Spoke Zarathustra," might lead us to believe that a sexual evolution remains at hand.

Ernest Mathijs and Jamie Sexton have argued that an "affection" for low-budget sf films, such as those addressed here, may be "related to nostalgia: for a period when imagining the future was more quaint and innocent, or before science fiction had fully entered the mainstream and turned sophisticated and serious" (208). Certainly, these cult sf films about sexual difference suggest a certain amount of nostalgia for a time of "quaint and innocent" gender roles, when masculinity seemed more culturally secure. However, the cult pleasure we continue to take in them speaks also to complexly entwined and contradictory desires to which we are all prey: for simpler gender roles, for the experience of ironically looking back on ideals we no longer share, and even for the dialectic of desire and disavowal between these positions.

Works Cited

Chibnall, Steve. "Double Exposures: Observations on *The Flesh and Blood Show.*" *Trash Aesthetics: Popular Culture and its Audiences.* Ed. Deborah Cartmell, I.Q. Hunter, Heidi Kaye, and Imelda Whelehan. London: Pluto Press, 1999. 84–102.

Graham, Allison. "Journey to the Center of the Fifties: The Cult of Banality." *The Cult Film Experience: Beyond All Reason.* Ed. J. P. Telotte. Austin: U of Texas P, 1991. 107–21.

Grant, Barry Keith. "Science Fiction Double Feature: Ideology in the Cult Film." *The Cult Film Experience: Beyond All Reason.* Ed. J. P. Telotte. Austin: U of Texas P, 1991. 122–37.

Hollows, Joanna. "The Masculinity of Cult." *Defining Cult Movies: The Cultural Politics of Oppositional Taste.* Ed. Mark Jancovich, Antonio Lázaro Reboll, Julian Stringer and Andy Willis. Manchester: Manchester UP, 2003. 35–53.

Mathijs, Ernest, and Jamie Sexton. *Cult Cinema.* London: Wiley-Blackwell, 2011.

Mulvey, Laura. "Visual Pleasure and Narrative Cinema." *The Routledge Critical and Cultural Theory Reader.* Ed. Neil Badmington and Julia Thomas. New York: Routledge, 2008. 202–12.

Sconce, Jeffrey. "'Trashing' the Academy: Taste, Excess, and an Emerging Politics of Cinematic Style." *Screen* 36.4 (1995): 371–93.

Sobchack, Vivian. "Revenge of *The Leech Woman*." *Uncontrollable Bodies: Testimonies of Identity and Culture*. Ed. Rodney Sappington and Tyler Stallings. Seattle: Bay Press, 1994. 79–91.

Suvin, Darko. *Metamorphoses of Science Fiction: On the Poetics and History of a Literary Genre*. New Haven: Yale UP, 1979.

13. "Lack of Respect, Wrong Attitude, Failure to Obey Authority": *Dark Star, A Boy and His Dog*, and New Wave Cult SF

Rob Latham

Stanley Kubrick's 1968 film *2001: A Space Odyssey* was a *cause célèbre* within the sf genre, dividing Old Guard fans, who deplored the film-maker's purported contempt for reason and scientific inquiry, from younger fans aligned with contemporary counterculture, who embraced its trippy imagery, its fusion of science and mysticism, and its tone of apocalyptic transcendence. At the time of its release, *2001* became a kind of litmus test of fan sentiment towards the New Wave movement, a rising sf avant-garde that sought to remake a genre traditionally inclined towards technocratic scientism and conservative narrative style into a more experimental, counterculturally savvy mode of writing whose perspectives on technological modernity had a subversive critical edge. As Golden Age author Lester del Rey fulminated in his review of *2001* for *Galaxy* magazine, "It's the first of the New Wave-Thing movies, with the usual empty symbolism. The New Thing advocates were exulting over it as a mind-blowing experience. It takes little to blow some minds. But for the rest of us, it's a disaster" (194). On the other side of the generational divide, sf fan Alex Eisenstein proclaimed the film "a prodigious work of art" and "a grand and eloquent message of the spirit" (qtd. in Pohl and Pohl 167, 169), while Earl Evers found the Star Gate sequence a revelation, "one of the most beautiful things I've ever seen" (45).[1] By becoming fodder for this intra-generic debate, the film marked a significant moment of crossover between sf and youth counterculture, a connection long championed by the New Wave's partisans.

In this essay, I want to examine the imbrication of the New Wave with contemporaneous sf cinema, highlighted by *2001*, but with a special focus on two low-budget films of the 1970s that have developed a cult reputation and had clear links, textually or tonally, with the movement: *Dark Star* (1974) and *A Boy and His Dog* (1975). These two works share not only ideological terrain but also a certain mode of cult reception with New Wave fiction, coming to constitute—along with Kubrick's sf films of the period, *2001* and *A Clockwork Orange* (1971)—a kind of New Wave cinematic canon.[2] In the years before *Star Wars* (1977) changed the genre landscape irrevocably, these movies—and others such as *Silent Running* (1972), *Westworld* (1973), *Zardoz* (1973), *Phase IV* (1974), *Death Race 2000* (1975), *The Man Who Fell to Earth* (1976), and *Damnation Alley* (1977)—began to absorb some of the attitudes and ambiences that New Wave fiction shared with youth counterculture: an abiding suspicion of technoscientific modes of knowledge, a casual contempt for social authority, and a downbeat assessment of the human prospect in a nuclear age. Indeed, this thematic repertoire—combined with antiheroic characters, disorienting (if not overtly psychedelic) imagery and editing, and an atmosphere of cynical alienation—would constitute the recipe for constructing a cult sf movie during the period.

That the New Wave literary movement itself represented a sort of cult was a common claim of its detractors. Attacks on the New Wave as a partisan clique were endemic in the era's fanzines, with enemies of the movement especially attacking its aggressive avant-gardism, which dismissed all earlier sf as aesthetically impoverished and ideologically reactionary, while promoting itself as innovative and radical. In a 1968 speech to the Science Fiction Writers of America, Frederik Pohl opined that the New Wave "is trying to change the rules. That's not an evil, in itself ... But I would suggest that any body of rules is wrong when it includes, as rule one, the idea that only the new thing is any good and everything else is slop"; he further suggested that the genre would survive the New Wave's vanguardist posturing as it had survived "Dianetics, Dowsing, the Dean Drive ... and any number of other transitory cults" (30). A more sweeping critique was articulated by the crusading anti-New Wave fan John J. Pierce: the New Wave cult, he claimed, amounted to a "Religion of Negation" (11), undermining and threatening to destroy the genre as a bastion of disciplined rational imagination.[3]

For their part, supporters of the New Wave often presented themselves as sf connoisseurs whose tastes were more refined than the average fan's. In a 1964 letter to the fanzine *Zenith Speculation*, British author Michael Moorcock—then editor of *New Worlds*, the New Wave's flagship magazine—contemptuously dismissed Old Guard fans, who had avidly consumed a "30-year diet" of pulp sf, as "unable to appreciate caviar, even when it's presented to [them] in a porridge plate" (15). Likewise, Moorcock's associate editor, Charles Platt, responding to a fan who had complained that much New Wave fiction was offensive or unintelligible, condescendingly declared that "[h]ere is the small-minded cry of the illiterate masses, yearning for simple entertainment, scared of anything that remotely tries to stretch the mental abilities of the audience. One can only view such protests with contempt" (46). In a somewhat less truculent but equally damning assessment, sf author Harlan Ellison spoke on behalf of "an entirely new crop of writers"—"Artists with the cap-A, if you will"—who insisted that sf should "hew to the same standards of excellence to be found in legitimate mainstream fiction," but who were resisted at every turn by "tunnel-visioned editors and critics (mostly fans) who loathed any movement off the dead-center of commercial sf" ("A Few" 40). New Wave fans shared the cult-like sensibility that they were part of a transformative movement destined to bring higher standards and more socially relevant perspectives to the field.[4]

Similarly, many scholars who have written on cult film stress the sense of superior judgment displayed by cult fans—those who, according to Greg Taylor, place "a high value on connoisseurship ... glorify[ing] the critic-spectator's heightened ability to select appropriately, and tastefully" (15). While the objects of their devotion might seem quirky or marginal—just as many New Wave works of fiction did to the vast majority of mainstream fans during the 1960s—the fans' exalted appreciation functions to validate both the cult texts and themselves for having the foresight to identify and champion them. J. P. Telotte has spoken of this mode of reception as a kind of veneration, "nearly worshipful" in its "excessive attachment or identification" (5), and Matt Hills has similarly used the term "neoreligiosity" to describe the practices of cult fans, who "create cultural identities out of the *significance* which certain texts assume for them" (134). This "unfolding project of the self" is, according to Hills, what distinguishes the typical cult fan from the average fan—and, indeed, we can perceive precisely this sort of process of cult identity-formation in the aggressive distinction from the general run of sf readers that New Wave fans adopted through their aesthetic preferences.

In a similar vein, Mark Jancovich cites Sarah Thornton's concept of "subcultural capital" (derived from Pierre Bourdieu's influential analysis of taste formation) as the boon accruing to cult fans whose superior aesthetic judgment allows them to distinguish—to use Moorcock's terms—caviar from porridge in their sf reading. Yet Jancovich goes on to argue that defenses of cult fandom which simply accept its claims to transgressive avant-gardism ignore the institutional matrix within which these claims are articulated: the encompassing networks of distribution and consumption, and the differential positioning of audiences, that make such distinctions possible in the first place. In his words, "cult movie audiences are less an internally coherent 'taste culture' than a series of frequently opposed and contradictory reading strategies that are defined through a sense of their difference to an equally coherently imagined 'normality'" (157).

Ellison's broad contrast between mainstream fans who preferred "commercial" sf and New Wave fans who cherished Art with a capital "A" thus obscures both the essentially commercial nature of *all* sf (indeed, the New Wave would not have been possible without the diverse marketplace spawned by the paperback revolution of the 1960s) and the complex situation of writers, editors, and fans who, for all the stark partisanship of the era, did not always sort neatly into dichotomous categories.[5] Yet, as Ernest Mathijs and Jamie Sexton point out, while cult consumption is not *necessarily* opposed to commercial exchange, it does usually articulate itself in opposition to "particular *types* of commercialism (corporate and conservative as opposed to independent and 'renegade')" (62; emphasis in original)—and many New Wave outlets during the 1960s, especially Moorcock's *New Worlds* and some of the more counterculturally oriented anthologies such as the *Quark* series edited by Samuel R. Delany and Marilyn Hacker, were definitely perceived as falling into the latter category.

Critics who argue that cult fandom involves a mode of exceptional connoisseurship or an amassing of subcultural capital take pains to distinguish this mode of consumption from "camp" reception strategies, which valorize the sensibility of the consumer rather than any putative value inhering in the object consumed. As Greg Taylor puts it, "camp criticism is more process-oriented than cultism; instead of celebrating happy exceptions, it demonstrates that potentially *any* mass culture object can be re-created aesthetically" (16). Janet Staiger agrees that cult connoisseurship involves an "elitism" that venerates the text's marginality as the index to a superior form of taste, even while it might on occasion—as with camp—affectionately mock its "stylistic excess" (127). Many New Wave fans, for example, generated homages to favorite authors that playfully echoed their characteristic styles, J. G. Ballard's mordant, sententious voice being a particularly frequent target of mimicry.[6] However, such fond pastiches merely reaffirmed the fans' esteem by displaying their capacity to analyze and reproduce a cherished singularity. These forms of imitation were very different from New Wave texts that mischievously simulated Old Guard styles for purposes of aesthetic or political critique—such as Harry Harrison's travesty of space opera, *Star Smashers of the Galaxy Rangers* (1973), or Norman Spinrad's *The Iron Dream* (1972), in which Hitler is reimagined as a pulp sf writer.

I thus see the avid readership of New Wave fiction as a kind of cult fandom in the terms outlined by many cult film critics. Yet it is a harder move to establish links between this readership and the viewers of such films as *Dark Star* and *A Boy and His Dog*, which I have argued were aligned with New Wave fiction as a kind of cult sf during the 1970s. Part of the challenge is establishing a common audience for sf fiction and sf film. While it is true, as Henry Jenkins has claimed, that sf cons or conventions—traditionally venues where fans gather to celebrate favorite writers and types of fiction—also "provide a market for commercially produced goods associated with media stories" (443), the main such connection, prior to the *Star Wars*-led explosion of crossover fandoms, was the TV series *Star Trek*, novelizations of which were produced by sf author James Blish starting in 1967. The relative poverty of the sf media landscape during this period—at least as descried by many sf fans— can be gleaned from the Hugo Awards for Best Dramatic Presentation, established in 1958, which for the first 15 years were dominated by *The Twilight Zone* (three awards), *Star Trek* (two awards), and Stanley Kubrick (three awards); in five other years, no award was given. Only 28 theatrical films—many of them fantasy or horror rather than actual sf—were even nominated during this period, compared to 74 in the 15 years following the release of *Star Wars*.

Yet, sandwiched between these two eras, in the period when the traditional studio system had largely expired but the blockbuster machinery of contemporary Hollywood had not yet emerged, was a five-year window during which all manner of quirky fare made its way onto the ballot, including a soft-porn pastiche (*Flesh Gordon*, 1974), a rock opera (*Phantom of the Paradise*, 1974), and several cult sf films: *Silent Running, Zardoz, Dark Star, The Man Who Fell to Earth*, and *A Boy and His Dog*, the last of which won the prize in 1976. It is also fair to say that the coverage of media in sf fanzines picked up in the wake of *2001*, yet it still remained spotty until *Star Wars* changed the game entirely, inaugurating an historic shift in the relationship between print and media sf.[7] At least prior to *2001*, and certainly prior to *Star Trek*, many sf authors and fans looked on sf film and television as a poor relation, unable to capture the ideational complexity of the best print sf. Frederik Pohl uses the oft-despised term "sci-fi" to describe most of the film genre, although he acknowledges that much pulp writing also deserves that label: "What science fiction in print sometimes does, sci-fi does not bother to. No sci-fi film (or novel) has ever troubled its reader's intellect" (Pohl and Pohl 13). An occasional genius like Kubrick might be able to produce movies that rise above the dross, as some critics admitted, but these were rare exceptions.

Aside from the countercultural appeal of *2001*, the most significant factor in driving the growing visibility and reputation of media sf among fans during this period was the multifarious work of Harlan Ellison.

An author of screenplays and award-winning teleplays for such series as *Star Trek* and *The Outer Limits*, Ellison was also a prolific media critic, reviewing film and TV for multiple venues, including the short-lived '60s journal *Cinema* and *The Los Angeles Free Press*. His irreverent column for the latter, "The Glass Teat," gave him a strong countercultural presence to complement his rising reputation as a sf author. While he was hardly the first sf writer to make a living in Hollywood, he was certainly the most voluble about it, persistently mocking the dismissive attitude towards the mass media adopted by his genre peers. In 1977, in protest over the Science Fiction Writers of America eliminating their Nebula Award for best dramatic presentation, he ostentatiously resigned his membership, delivering a furious speech at the organization's annual gathering in which he railed against the "provincial, insular, hidebound, cocoon kind of thinking" that prevented most sf writers from pursuing the creative challenges—and lucrative possibilities—involved in producing media sf ("How" 89). Arguably, one of the main reasons *A Boy and His Dog* won its Hugo was the fact that it was based on a story by Ellison, who by that point had secured a big following among New Wave fans.

It is highly likely that, were it not for sf and/or counterculture fans, very few people would have seen this film—or *Dark Star* for that matter—upon initial release. Both were savaged by the rare mainstream reviewers who bothered to notice them, with *Variety* calling *A Boy and His Dog* "a turkey" and *Dark Star* a "limp parody" of *2001* with little appeal

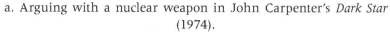

a. Arguing with a nuclear weapon in John Carpenter's *Dark Star* (1974).

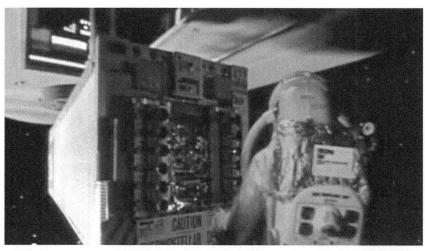

b. *A Boy and His Dog*'s (1975) post-apocalyptic vision.

beyond "the university circuit" (Willis 298, 291). Their budgets were miniscule—*Dark Star* began as a student film of director John Carpenter before being acquired by an independent producer, while *A Boy and His Dog* was mounted by a pair of minor character actors, Alvy Moore and L. Q. Jones (who wrote the script and directed)—and their stays in the few theaters that booked them were short-lived. *Variety* was prescient, however, in forecasting a prospective subcultural reception: both films made the drive-in and midnight-movie circuits later in the decade, but it was not until the advent of the VCR revolution in the 1980s that either reached a wide audience or began to acquire a significant cult viewership.[8] Yet a cult reputation for both movies was already building within sf fandom, as evidenced not only by their nominations for Hugo Awards but also by the accolades they received from prominent figures in the field: Richard E. Geis, for example, praised *Dark Star* warmly, while in an interview Ellison lauded the makers of *A Boy and His Dog* for staying true to his creative vision (Shay).[9] Likewise, sf author John Brosnan's 1978 book on sf film, *Future Tense*, extolled *A Boy and His Dog* as "a superior piece of science fiction cinema" (234) and *Dark Star* as "the best sf film of 1974" (229)—views that were certainly not shared by most mainstream critics at the time.

While *Dark Star* was not based on a specific work of New Wave sf (its main precursor text, as several critics have noted, is *2001*), it shares with the movement an eagerness to traduce accepted formulas, mocking space opera's pretensions to scientific rigor and militarist discipline with an impish relish. The eponymous "scout ship" is on an ill-defined mission to destroy "unstable" planets, its dazed, hippified crew spouting nonsensical jargon in bored monotones: "I show a quantum reading of

35. Three-fiver." Degenerating into apathetic anarchy following the death of Commander Powell, who is electrocuted by a faulty seat panel, they can barely be stirred to trouble themselves over the accumulating crises besetting their disintegrating ship: a renegade alien that looks like a dayglo beachball, an asteroid storm that disables their communication and fail-safe systems, and an intelligent A-bomb that—like *2001*'s HAL 9000—refuses to obey orders and eventually detonates onboard. Instead, they affectlessly pursue their own aimless pleasures: the stolid Boiler practices his laser marksmanship, the dreamy Talby communes with the universe, and the whiny Sgt. Pinback keeps a video diary recording his petty grievances. "Don't worry about it," their nominal leader, Lt. Doolittle, says when the computer warns of an impending problem. "We'll find out what it is when it goes bad."

These whacked-out spacemen are avatars of what Colin Greenland has called the "Mad Astronaut," a "new fictional stock type" pioneered by New Wave writers as a calculated thumb-in-the-eye to the frontier heroics of pulp-era space fiction (49). Instead of the traditional sf pose of technological mastery and transcendent adventure, *Dark Star* gives us "the banality of spaceflight," the vacuous repetition of meaningless routines, and "the tedium of planet-hopping" (47).[10]

New Wave novels and stories such as Barry N. Malzberg's *The Falling Astronauts* (1971) and John Sladek's "The Poets of Milgrove, Iowa" (1966) had already mined similar terrain, anticipating—and preparing New Wave fans to appreciate—*Dark Star*'s genre spoofs and demystifications. Moreover, the formal play characteristic of many New Wave texts is echoed in the film's intertextual references, especially to *2001* but also—as Robert Cumbow has pointed out (14)—to such '50s-era B movies as *It! The Terror from Beyond Space* (1958). One can even perceive metafictional overtones in the film's thematics of failed communication: its buzzy intercoms, unheard warnings, and comical misreckonings. Like a series of genre signals gone awry, the movie persistently sabotages and subverts the conventional mechanisms of sf meaning-making, replacing action with ennui, sense with absurdity. The opening sequence illustrates the strategy: the computer's portentous announcement of an "INCOMING COMMUNICATION" reveals merely a smooth-faced, smarmy NASA official emitting rah-rah bromides ("swell job," "we're all behind you guys"), while pouring cold water on any hope of relief or rescue, a situation the crew accepts with bored indifference. This breakdown in communication and control affects the story itself, which digresses and wanders until the snowballing malfunctions and disabled genre conventions literally blow the contraption—spaceship and narrative—to pieces.[11]

The erosion of narrative authority mirrors the film's depiction of decaying social structures and military hierarchies, conveying a vision of terminal *ataxia* that both reflects a countercultural world view and subtly reproves it. These wasted cosmonauts are, in Cumbow's words, "the long-haired, sweaty fallout of the hippie generation" (13), and their hapless stumble towards collective disaster functions as a "metaphoric swan song of the psychedelic era" (17). The decidedly low-tech special effects are at times quite trippy, culminating in the weirdly glowing Phoenix asteroids that take starchild Talby towards a cryptic apotheosis. A sense of foreclosed options and discontinued futures haunts the proceedings, as it does many works of New Wave fiction. J. G. Ballard in particular was a master at weaving tales of technocratic dead ends and abortive gestures of transcendence, often featuring burned-out or schizoid astronauts as key figures. That the New Wave amounted to little more than a dystopia of ennui was a common charge of the movement's opponents: Old Guard fan and editor Donald A. Wollheim, for instance, inveighed against the relentless pessimism of this "sick fiction" written by "embittered distortionists" who had forfeited traditional sf's "innate belief in the rightness and goodness of mankind" (4). *Dark Star* cheerfully traduces these Golden Age verities, lining up squarely with the New Wave camp.

Whatever one may think of Wollheim's charges, I believe that the downbeat nature of much countercultural sf—literary and filmic—contributed immensely to its accrual of a cult following during the era. As J. P. Telotte has observed, an element of transgression lies at the core of the cult film phenomenon, whose appeal "gains in potency by suggesting a lack of real meaning, significance, or relevance in the everyday world" and thus promises an escape from "the routine, repetitive, and impersonal nature of modern technological societies such as ours" (12–13)—even if this escape takes the nihilistic form of surfing space flotsam to a blazing death, as Lt. Doolittle does at the end of *Dark Star*. Historically speaking, the parlous state of countercultural politics in the early to mid-1970s—in the wake of the Kent State Massacre, the FBI's campaign of covert monitoring and subversion of dissident groups, and Richard Nixon's triumphal re-election on a law and order platform—contributed to an atmosphere of resignation and frustrated longing upon which films such as *Dark Star* powerfully capitalized. The film's depiction of its quasi-hippie crew as ineffectual and jinxed, yet still in touch with mysterious forces they only dimly comprehend, captured the ambivalence of the era in much the same way as did the contemporaneous fictions of New Wave authors such as Norman Spinrad, Robert Silverberg, and Harlan Ellison, with their similar mix of fatalism, satirical swagger, and restless aspiration.

Ellison's 1969 novella "A Boy and His Dog" similarly captures this ethos and, as Ellison himself acknowledged, the film adaptation effectively conveys its basic narrative and world view. The story is set in a post-apocalyptic wasteland—a desert hellscape of murderous nomads and radioactive mutants, where our protagonist Vic and his intelligent, telepathic mutt, Blood, survive on scavenged food and their feral wits. Blood longs to go "Over the Hill," to some vaguely pastoral site of abundance that Vic sneers at as a dippy "pipedream"; for his part, Vic only wants to get laid, and he deploys Blood's considerable reconnaissance skills to find prospective targets. One of these, Quilla June, turns out to be "bait" dangled in his path by a sub-surface city that needs periodic infusions of fresh genetic material to keep its inbred community vital. Much of the second half of the film is set in this false utopia "down under"—known quaintly as "Topeka"—whose grimly cheerful denizens live out a dead fantasy of 1950s normalcy. Their cheeks rouged to hide their subterranean pallor, they desultorily attend proceedings of the three-person "Committee," a kind of totalitarian city council that issues death sentences to dissident citizens with the same blasé good humor as they do blue ribbons in the annual canning festival. The charges are invariably the same: "lack of respect, wrong attitude, failure to obey authority."

Clearly, the film is staging a fairly predictable contrast between "straight" society and counterculture rebels, one that might be encountered in any number of other movies from the era. Yet, as in *Dark Star*, any unproblematic identification a youthful audience might make with the countercultural "hero" is systematically undermined. Vic, a cynical lout whose arrogance is habitually punctured by Blood's caustic barbs, comes across as a preening study in selfishness and moral cowardice, first abandoning his wounded dog to follow Quilla June down under, then—after escaping from Topeka—casually murdering the girl and feeding her to Blood to revive his flagging strength. This grisly ending, combined with the offhand expression of Vic's misogyny, led feminist sf author Joanna Russ to denounce the film as a vicious scapegoating of women, and it cannot be denied that the story trades on the stereotype of the faithless female who tempts men to their doom. Yet the film makes clear how predictably *scripted* the entire world of Topeka is, including this socially handy role of temptress: Quilla June is expressly a patriarchal lure, one of many dangled by the head of the Committee, Mr. Craddock, to manipulate and control other men. Even as she and Vic are making their escape, the Committee is already drawing up plans to lasso its next victim. As Russ observes, "The Nice Girl is socially powerless, useful at best for the minor policing of teenage boys, useful as a reward or a 'responsibility' but hardly a citizen in her own right—after all, the major policing in a sexist society is done by others, overwhelmingly by adult males." Yet while Russ means this as a critique of the film's perspective, it seems that her analysis actually *describes* the situation the film rather unflinchingly depicts and criticizes.

Part of the problem with a reading such as Russ's is that it takes Vic much too straightforwardly as the locus of (male) audience identification, as if we were meant to share his churlish sexism, when in fact he too is being satirized (much more so than the character in Ellison's original story). Vic's seemingly sentimentalized friendship with Blood can, after all, hardly escape the strictures directed at Topeka, given how valorized boy-and-his-dog relationships were in the '50s-era sitcoms out of which this nightmarish subterranean suburb has so clearly been forged. Yet Russ reads the film's depiction of this relationship with a straight face: "Above all, Vic and Blood are lovable and good, and Quilla June is manipulative and bad, so Vic's final choice is a foregone conclusion." It's a foregone conclusion because even the counterculture "hero" of the story is enmeshed in the coercive scripts of a dying world he nominally professes to despise.

The multivalent, corrosive irony of this set-up is one of the main reasons for the movie's cult appeal. Just as *Dark Star* gave its counterculture viewers an ambiguous portrait of themselves as a motley crew of shirkers and slackers implicated in the technocratic world they so evidently scorn and whose inanity and self-absorption contribute directly to their fiery demise, so *A Boy and His Dog* presents them with a posturing antihero whose animal sidekick is smarter than he is, whose default option is a selfish hedonism, and who has no prospects at the end of the narrative save for a sketchy Shangri-la "over the hill."

Barry Keith Grant has alleged that the cult film is essentially recuperative, trading on transgressive images of otherness only to shore up conventional ideologies; as he puts it, "the viewer ultimately gains the double satisfaction of both rejecting dominant cultural values and remaining safely inscribed within them" ("Science Fiction" 124). Yet I would argue that the transgressive charge of cult films like *Dark Star* and *A Boy and His Dog* lies precisely in the lack of any secure grounding for spectatorial identification that would allow for such a neat resolution. Like much New Wave fiction, these texts do not simply flatter the pretensions of their counterculture audience but rather adopt a pose of bemused irony that satirically deflates those countercultural ideologies, even as the stories themselves work to feed them.

In short, I believe that most New Wave cult films gain their charge from a relentless deconstruction of heroism, of the traditional or countercultural variety, as well as from an uncompromising pessimism. Like much New Wave fiction, these films feature either nihilistic antiheroes (Alex in *A Clockwork Orange*, Vic in *A Boy and His Dog*, Mr. Frankenstein in *Death Race 2000*) or ambiguous—sometimes savage, sometimes reluctant—messiahs whose transformative promise is either inscrutable or quixotic (Freeman Lowell in *Silent Running*, Zed in *Zardoz*, Thomas Jerome Newton in *The Man Who Fell to Earth*). In fact, most of these films end on downbeat notes, with at best a vague gesture at transcendence (such as Talby's joyride on the Phoenix asteroids), or else they depict the ironic triumph of a murderous violence. Texts that deviate from this pattern come across as specious or forced: *Damnation Alley*, for instance, sentimentally redeems its amoral antihero (who is much more scabrous in Roger Zelazny's original novel) and culminates in the maudlin embrace of a Norman Rockwell-esque small-town utopia. In their foreclosure of pulp-era heroics and felicitous futures, these movies forged a model that low-budget sf films would often follow in the subsequent decade. *Liquid Sky* (1982) and *Repo Man* (1984), for example, responded to the dreamy effusions of *Star Wars* with a derisive nihilism (while also giving a piquant punk twist to '60s-era psychedelia). In many ways, then, the New Wave proved as transformative for the filmic as it did for the literary history of the genre.

Notes

1   Evers acknowledged that he was high on LSD when he viewed the film, a mode of "head" spectatorship then making significant inroads into sf fandom—as evidenced by del Rey's "mind-blowing" put-down. For an analysis of *2001* in terms of divergent generational readings, see Palmer; for an anatomy of head spectatorship, focusing especially on its gender dynamics, see Gallagher. For a fuller discussion of the reception of *2001* within the sf community, see my "Journey beyond the Stars."

2   As applied to 1960s sf, the term was originally borrowed from filmic discourse—specifically, the debates over the French Nouvelle Vague and its influence on other European cinemas in the late 1950s and early 1960s. (For an overview of the emergence and consolidation of the term within the genre, see my "*New Worlds* and the New Wave in Fandom.") Like these modes of art film, sf's New Wave was formally and ideologically iconoclastic, breaking with conventional modes of narration and forcefully confronting charged sociopolitical realities. Interestingly, many of the major French New Wave directors produced their own sf films: Jean Luc-Godard with *Alphaville* (1965), François Truffaut with *Fahrenheit 451* (1966), and Alain Resnais with *Je T'aime, Je T'aime* (1968). For a discussion of low-budget sf films such as *A Boy and His Dog* as "the true heirs of New Wave sf cinema," see Csicsery-Ronay (504).

[3] My essay "Inside the New Wave Wars" canvasses Pierce's self-styled *jihad* against the movement.

[4] See, for example, Angus Taylor's response to Pierce's anti-New Wave crusade, "Don't Make Waves," where he defends the new fiction as aesthetically serious and ideologically forward-looking. Some fanzines during the late 1960s and early 1970s—e.g., *BeABohema, Energumen, Prehensile, Psychotic, Starling*—essentially became platforms for New Wave debates, with the factions squaring off against one another in issue after issue.

[5] Ellison himself occasionally acknowledged as much, as when he asserted that his version of the "new thing" in sf "is neither Judith Merril's 'new thing' nor Michael Moorcock's 'new thing.' Ask for us by our brand names" ("Introduction" xxv). For a fuller discussion of the New Wave's avant-gardism in the context of evolving markets and audiences, see my essay "A Rare State of Ferment."

[6] See the hilarious parody by Angus Taylor, "J. G. Ballard Viewed as a Cross-Country Chandelier Race between a Spider and a Fly."

[7] Acknowledging the change, Richard E. Geis's well-regarded fanzine *Science Fiction Review* established a regular column on film by Bill Warren starting with its May 1978 issue. Not all fans at the time were pleased with the media invasion, however; see Mansell's "The Selling of *Star Wars*."

[8] For background on *Dark Star*, see O'Bannon (who co-wrote the screenplay with Carpenter), and on *A Boy and His Dog*, see Triplett. For a discussion of the role of "aftermarket" reception in fostering film cults, see Klinger.

[9] An exception to this chorus of acclaim was sf author Joanna Russ's denunciation of *A Boy and His Dog* as vilely misogynistic.

[10] See also Butler for a more extensive discussion of this New Wave subgenre (38–50). If Sgt. Pinback is to be believed, he owes his spot on the *Dark Star* mission to a literally deranged astronaut who committed suicide by jumping naked into a liquid fuel tank.

[11] Grant's essay "Disorder in the Universe" offers an excellent analysis of themes of chaos and breakdown in Carpenter's films, specifically as they relate to patterns of generic expectation.

Works Cited

Brosnan, John. *Future Tense: The Cinema of Science Fiction*. New York: St. Martin's, 1978.

Butler, Andrew M. *Solar Flares: Science Fiction in the 1970s*. Liverpool: Liverpool UP, 2012.

Csicsery-Ronay, Jr., Istvan. "Sound is the New Light." *Science Fiction Studies* 38.3 (2011): 501–07.

Cumbow, Robert C. *Order in the Universe: The Films of John Carpenter*. Lanham: Scarecrow, 2000.

del Rey, Lester. Review of *2001: A Space Odyssey*. *Galaxy* 26.6 (July 1968): 193–94.

Ellison, Harlan. "A Few (Hopefully Final) Words on 'The New Wave'." *Science Fiction: The Academic Awakening.* Ed. Willis McNelly. Shreveport: College English Association, 1974. 40–43.

—. "How You Stupidly Blew $15 Million a Week, Avoided Having an Adenoid-Shaped Swimming Pool in Your Back Yard, Missed the Opportunity to Have a Mutually Destructive Love Affair with Clint Eastwood and/ or Raquel Welch, and Otherwise Pissed Me Off." *Sleepless Nights in the Procrustean Bed.* San Bernardino: Borgo, 1984. 87–98.

—. "Introduction: Thirty-Two Soothsayers." *Dangerous Visions.* Ed. Harlan Ellison. Garden City: Doubleday, 1967. xix–xxix.

Evers, Earl. "2001 Light Years from Home." *Shangri L'Affaires* 74 (1 September 1968): 43–45.

Gallagher, Mark. "Tripped Out: The Psychedelic Film and Masculinity." *Quarterly Review of Film and Video* 21.3 (2004): 161–71.

Geis, Richard E. "Out of Phase for a *Dark Star*." *Science Fiction Review* 13 (May 1975): 54.

Grant, Barry Keith. "Disorder in the Universe: John Carpenter and the Question of Genre." *The Cinema of John Carpenter: The Technique of Terror.* Ed. Ian Conrich and David Woods. London: Wallflower, 2004. 10–20.

—. "Science Fiction Double Feature: Ideology in the Cult Film." *The Cult Film Experience: Beyond All Reason.* Ed. J. P. Telotte. Austin: U of Texas P, 1991. 122–37.

Greenland, Colin. *The Entropy Exhibition: Michael Moorcock and the British "New Wave" in Science Fiction.* London: Routledge & Kegan Paul, 1983.

Hills, Matt. "Media Fandom, Neoreligiosity and Cultural Studies." *The Cult Film Reader.* Ed. Ernest Mathijs and Xavier Mendik. New York: McGraw-Hill, 2009. 133–48.

Jancovich, Marc. "Cult Fictions: Cult Movies, Subcultural Capital and the Production of Cultural Distinctions." *The Cult Film Reader.* Ed. Ernest Mathijs and Xavier Mendik. New York: McGraw-Hill, 2009. 149–62.

Jenkins, Henry. "'Get a Life!': Fans, Poachers, Nomads." *The Cult Film Reader.* Ed. Ernest Mathijs and Xavier Mendik. New York: McGraw-Hill, 2009. 429–44.

Klinger, Barbara. "Becoming Cult: *The Big Lebowski*, Replay Culture and Male Fans." *Screen* 51.1 (2010): 1–20.

Latham, Rob. "Inside the New Wave Wars." *The Eaton Journal of Archival Research in Science Fiction* 1.1 (Spring 2013). Web. Accessed 29 March 2013.

—. "'A Journey beyond the Stars': *2001: A Space Odyssey* and the Psychedelic Revolution in Science Fiction." *Science Fiction and the Prediction of the Future: Essays on Foresight and Fallacy.* Ed. Gary Westfahl, Wong Kin Yuen, and Amy Kit-sze Chan. Jefferson: McFarland, 2011. 128–34.

—. "*New Worlds* and the New Wave in Fandom: Fan Culture and the Reshaping of Science Fiction in the Sixties." *Extrapolation* 47.2 (2006): 296–314.

—. "'A Rare State of Ferment': SF Controversies from the New Wave to Cyberpunk." *Beyond the Reality Studio: Cyberpunk and the New Millennium.* Ed. Graham J. Murphy and Sherryl Vint. New York: Routledge, 2010. 29–45.

Mansell, Mark. "The Selling of *Star Wars.*" *Science Fiction Review* 24 (February 1978): 17.

Mathijs, Ernest, and Jamie Sexton. *Cult Cinema.* Oxford: Wiley-Blackwell, 2011.

Moorcock, Michael. Letter to the Editor. *Zenith Speculation* 7 (December 1964): 12–15.

O'Bannon, Dan. "The Remaking of *Dark Star.*" *Omni's Screen Flights/Screen Fantasies:* Ed. Danny Peary. Garden City: Doubleday, 1984. 147–51.

Palmer, R. Barton. "*2001*: The Critical Reception and the Generation Gap." *Stanley Kubrick's* 2001: A Space Odyssey: *New Essays.* Ed. Robert Kolker. New York: Oxford UP, 2006. 13–28.

Pierce, John J. "The Devaluation of Values." *Algol* 16 (December 1970): 4–11.

Platt, Charles. Letter to the Editor. *Habbakuk* 2.3 (February 1967): 45–46.

Pohl, Frederik. "Speech to the Science Fiction Writers of America." *Algol* 14 (Fall 1968): 27–30.

—, and Frederik Pohl IV. *Science Fiction Studies in Film.* New York: Ace, 1981.

Russ, Joanna. "*A Boy and His Dog*: The Final Solution." *Jump Cut* 12–13 (1976): 14–17. Web. Accessed 29 March 2013.

Shay, Don. "Tripping through Ellison Wonderland." *Cinefantastique* 5.1 (Spring 1976): 14-23.

Staiger, Janet. *Media Reception Studies.* New York: New York UP, 2005.

Taylor, Angus. "Don't Make Waves." *Energumen* 3 (August 1970): 10–11.

—. "J. G. Ballard Viewed as a Cross-Country Chandelier Race between a Spider and a Fly." *Energumen* 2 (May 1970): 6–7.

Taylor, Greg. *Artists in the Audience: Cults, Camp, and American Film Criticism.* Princeton: Princeton UP, 1999.

Telotte, J. P. "Beyond All Reason: The Nature of the Cult." *The Cult Film Experience: Beyond All Reason.* Ed. J. P. Telotte. Austin: U of Texas P, 1991. 5–17.

Triplett, Gene. "Producer is Unique; His Cult Film is Too." *The Oklahoman,* October 30, 1983. NewsOK. Web. Accessed 29 March 2013.

Willis, Donald, ed. *Variety's Complete Science Fiction Reviews.* New York: Garland, 1985.

Wollheim, Donald A. "Donald Wollheim's Guest of Honor Speech, LunaCon 1968." *Niekas* 20 (Fall 1968): 1–6.

14. Capitalism, Camp, and Cult SF: *Space Truckers* as Satire

M. Keith Booker

Set in worlds that are different from our own and often featuring civilizations and customs (or even species) that are different from our own, sf is *the* genre of difference. And sf fans, with a long history of fandom that dates back to the letters columns in the pulps of the 1930s, tend to be regarded as a sort of subculture, different from the mainstream, though alike in their difference and in their common interest in sf. In like fashion, cult films and other cult objects achieve their cult status both because they are different from the perceived norm in some way and because they have the ability to create a community of intensely devoted followers. Cult and sf films would thus seem to be a natural match, especially since both seem to embody the contradictions of capitalism (which seeks to create a smoothly functioning, well-organized collective, based on an ethos of each against all), perhaps more directly than other cultural forms, even as they typically announce their contempt for values often associated with capitalism—but in a seemingly apolitical way that congratulates their fans on being different from it all.

Stuart Gordon's *Space Truckers* (1996) exemplifies this vision of the cult film, while introducing (through its satirical engagement with capitalism) interesting questions about the relationship between the cult film and sf in general. The film begins as a reasonably conventional sf narrative, as officials of a sinister "Company" (of the kind common in many previous sf films) test a new high-tech robot warrior on Triton, largest moon of Neptune. These officials look coldly on as the battle-bot decimates a contingent of human soldiers, proving its efficacy in combat. The story then takes a turn as Company CEO A. J. Saggs (Shane Rimmer) takes control of the bot and orders it to destroy its developer, Company research chief Dr. Nabel (Charles Dance), just to make sure the bots stay a well-kept secret so that he can use them to take control of the Earth, whose global government seems in a state of near collapse. While this early portion of the narrative sounds a little over-the-top, it offers a relatively conventional collection of sf iconography. But then the narrative cuts, rather jarringly (but not surprisingly, given the film's title), to the title sequence, accompanied by countrified trucker music that heralds a sudden generic clash: a sequence in which veteran "space trucker" John Canyon (Dennis Hopper) eases his big rig, loaded with genetically modified "square pigs" from Mars, into a hokey-looking outer space trucking depot.

The film quickly moves into a sequence that, except for its outer space setting, seems largely drawn from the trucker films that were popular in the 1970s; it becomes clear that Canyon is an individualistic, independent trucker, often at odds with the corporate forces for which he is forced to work in order to make his living. Here, he delivers his load to the Inter Pork corporation, which may or may not (the film never makes clear) be affiliated in some way with the unnamed Company of the film's opening. When Inter Pork cheats him on his load of pigs by refusing to pay more than one-fourth of the agreed compensation, Canyon refuses the offer, leading to an altercation with the company's local manager, Keller (George Wendt), and his thugs. The action then shifts to another locale on the station, where Canyon visits a diner that caters to truckers—and makes a deal with his old flame Cindy (Debi Mazar), who agrees to marry him if he can get her to Earth, where her mother is having an operation. While space travel is routine in this future, travel to Earth remains expensive—far more expensive than Cindy can afford on what she makes in the diner. Another altercation with Keller and his thugs results in the rotund Keller being sucked (with some difficulty) through a porthole into open space. By this time, though, Inter Pork has stolen Canyon's cargo of square pigs altogether, so he decides that it is best to get out of Dodge. He then arranges with his underground connections to get a black market load of sex dolls to take to Earth, and heads out, towing the load behind his old Pachyderm 2000 space truck, accompanied by Cindy and neophyte trucker Mike Pucci (Stephen Dorff). In other words, the characters declare their independence of the corporate bosses of the space trucking world, even as the film declares its independence from the usual conventions of big-budget (corporate-produced) sf film, where even "outlaw" space jockeys such as Han Solo would not likely be found hauling a cargo of sex dolls.

But by this point in the narrative, it is clear in all sorts of ways that *Space Truckers* is no ordinary outer space adventure. Of course, fans of director Stuart Gordon or, for that matter, Dennis Hopper, would never have expected anything ordinary from either of them. Gordon's principal previous sf film was the offbeat 1989 post-apocalyptic *Space Jox*, which features deadly mechanical fighting machines that are the clear forerunners of the battle bots of *Space Truckers* (eventually described in the film as "genetically engineered biomechanical super warriors"). However, while it has a minor cult following, *Space Jox* is a weak effort that takes its premise seriously while executing it sophomorically. One might say that *Space Jox* achieved what cult status it has accidentally, while *Space Truckers* seems to have been designed to attract a cult following all along, somewhat in the spirit of Gordon's better-known cult horror films, such as *Re-Animator* (1985) and *From Beyond* (1986), both rooted in the horror fiction of H. P. Lovecraft, though both include sf elements as well. Both begin with visuals and plots that would be very much at home in the fictional worlds of Lovecraft, but then they push to ridiculous, over-the-top extremes, turning motifs from high horror into high (if rather dark) comedy.

Space Truckers does much the same with its basic sf premises, except that it also adds a much stronger and more overt element of social and political satire than can be found in the two horror films. However, Lovecraftian horror still exerts a strong influence on *Space Truckers*, especially in the visual design of the "super warriors," which include lots of hoses and tentacle-like extrusions, even though such features would not necessarily be efficient in mechanized combat. In fact, the warriors seem a lot like robotized versions of the eponymous alien from the *Alien* film franchise, itself designed by H. R. Giger under the strong influence of Lovecraft. And, of course, the fact that the Company of *Space Truckers* has developed these devices specifically as weapons echoes the hope of the similarly evil Company (eventually identified as the Weyland-Yutani Corporation) in *Alien* to weaponize the deadly aliens of those films. Indeed, many aspects of *Space Truckers* recall the *Alien* films, including the fact that the crew members of the ship *Nostromo* in *Alien* actually *are* space truckers. Moreover, *Space Truckers* offers an entire sequence in which the virtually indestructible warriors threaten the film's heroes on board their spaceship, while the heroes (Cindy and Pucci, anyway) spend much of the film in their underwear, echoing (and perhaps spoofing) the eventual state of dishabille of *Alien*'s Ripley. Indeed, given the fact that *Alien* was originally conceived as a low-budget film to be made for Roger Corman, it is tempting to view *Space Truckers* as a more comical version of what a Roger Corman version of *Alien* might have looked like.

The link to *Alien*, of course, can be taken as a knowing nod to sf fans, and thus might be part of the cult appeal of *Space Truckers*. *Alien* is perhaps the best-known example of a sf/horror hybrid in all of American film, and such generic hybridity is often a key feature of cult films, since lack of respect for generic boundaries is a relatively common mark of such texts. However, *Alien* is deadly serious, whereas *Space Truckers* mixes these genres a bit more playfully, while enhancing the playfulness of this mixture by foregrounding the trucker film as a third element of this generic mix. Additionally, while the *Alien* films, especially in representing the Company as a rapacious manifestation of corporate capitalism, already have a strong potential as critiques of capitalism, *Space Truckers* is much more overtly satirical—possibly to the point of undermining its own satire, which is always in danger of becoming a parody of satire because of its very comic tone.[1]

Much of this more overt satire derives directly from the later film's greater engagement with the trucker film, which has quite often been built upon an opposition between virtuous, hard-working, blue-collar, individualist truckers and the corrupt corporate bosses for whom— and *against* whom—they work. While *Alien* does almost nothing with this generic connection, *Space Truckers*—through plot elements, visual representation, and even background music—constantly calls attention to this connection, which places it in direct dialog with such films as *Smokey and the Bandit* (1977), its sequels, and other trucker films, such as Jonathan Kaplan's *White Line Fever* (1975), John Leone's *The Great Smokey Roadblock* (1976), Don Hulette's *Breaker! Breaker!* (1977), Sam Peckinpah's *Convoy* (1978), and Norman Jewison's *F.I.S.T.* (1978). As Andy Johnson has argued, these films establish the trucker as an iconic working-class hero, devoted to following his own individualist code, but also able, when necessary, to work in union with other working-class individuals to make common cause against the corporate (and, in some cases, government) forces that oppose them. As a result, the clear identification of John Canyon as such an outlaw trucker brings with it an assemblage of anti-establishment messages even as the incongruity of the displacement of his free-spirited hijinks from the open highway to open space creates a level of ironic humor.

Of course, the trucker film is itself a hybrid form that is connected to other genres, most obviously the western. Indeed, as Jane Stern has pointed out, the trucker is in many ways a modern version of the Old West cowboy. Meanwhile, as films like Clint Eastwood's *Space Cowboys* (2000) have made explicit, the astronaut might be seen as an even more modern version of the cowboy, venturing forth into the realm that both John F. Kennedy and *Star Trek* identified as our "new" or "final frontier." Meanwhile, the connection to the western is made explicit early on in *Space Truckers*, as the altercation in the diner, though not unlike the fight scenes that sometimes punctuate trucker films, is quite clearly choreographed after the manner of the classic western saloon fight, complete with appropriate, high-spirited background music.

Beyond such localized images, *Space Truckers* is linked to the western on a more fundamental level through its evocation of the "waning of the West" story, one of the classic versions of the western narrative, especially from the 1960s forward. This narrative has often been figured as a case of greedy capitalists routinizing the once-wild frontier to maximize profits, thus leaving outlaw individualists (such as, for example, Butch Cassidy and the Sundance Kid), who were once at home in the West, with no place to go. In like manner, the Company of *Space Truckers* has effectively converted the last frontier of outer space into still another profit zone, and much of the point of this film has to do with the way in which the wide open spaces of the solar system have been both colonized and capitalized, leaving little room for free spirits like Canyon (whose very name evokes the western) to operate.

When Canyon and his crew set out for Earth with their black market load of what they believe to be sex dolls, they quickly reinforce their outlaw status by having to evade the space police, during which sequence they take an asteroid hit that knocks out their cooling system. This event leads to what might have been a relatively conventional bit of sf space adventure. However, the narrative again veers away from the conventional, as Canyon goes outside the "truck" to effect repairs, while Cindy and Pucci remain inside, stripping to their underwear because of the growing heat inside the cabin. They then predictably start to generate heat of their own as sparks fly between them, although Cindy eventually rebuffs his advances because of her "engagement" to Canyon, even though she clearly does not really wish to wed the aging trucker. Meanwhile, they all try to keep cool by downing beers that Canyon has stashed in a Styrofoam cooler, since his vehicle lacks a refrigerator. Refrigerators, we learn, are extras, and Canyon, refusing to play the conformist/consumerist game, does not buy extras.

The problem of the rising temperature in the cabin, however, quickly moves to the background when space pirates arrive, taking them all prisoner and hijacking their load, while seemingly hijacking the film by taking the narrative in still another generic direction. Pirates, of course, are an additional staple of American popular culture, often carrying many of the same anti-establishment resonances as truckers and cowboys. And yet, pirates are also a bit more complex than these other individualist figures, partly because, however unconventional they might be, they do, by the very nature of their enterprise, work in large groups rather than as a few rugged individuals. In addition, pirates are fundamentally concerned with making a profit, no matter what it takes to do so, making them predatory figures of capitalism as much as opponents of it. However, *Space Truckers* makes it clear that the more "reputable" capitalist enterprises that appear in the film, such as the Company, are also pirates of sorts, who differ from the narrative's literal pirates in the same way that bankers differ from bank robbers: they steal bigger and are usually aided by the law, rather than hindered by it. While the space pirates operate in opposition to official capitalism, they follow an inexorable capitalist logic, and fittingly so, as they are a literal "spin-off" of the Company, captained by a rebuilt Dr. Nabel, who has survived the earlier attempted assassination by rebuilding himself with electromechanical parts, re-emerging as the cyborg Macanudo, now devoted to revenge against Saggs and the Company. Turnabout, in this case, is fair play, as the pirate Nabel/Macanudo attempts to strike blows against a piratical company.

Nabel/Macanudo's piracy clearly serves as a sort of economic guerrilla campaign against the interests of the Company. But this is a film in which economic transactions go beyond those that are strictly business. Macanudo takes a liking to the scantily-clad Cindy, who (still desperate to get to Earth for her mother's surgery) quickly offers to have sex with him if he will take her to Earth—although she also clearly hopes thereby to secure the safety of Canyon and Pucci. He immediately agrees, then takes her back to his quarters, where he prepares to impress her with his fancy electromechanical penis, complete with pull-cord starter. This scene, of course, could be interpreted as a sort of rape, which might undercut its potential for humor. However, Cindy is hardly an innocent and helpless victim, and this is not a tragic scene, but a comic one, and one that seems to have been included in the film almost entirely as a sort of gag. It is, in fact, the single moment of the film that most closely approaches the sensibility known as "camp," especially as famously described by Susan Sontag in her 1964 essay "Notes on 'Camp.'"

For Sontag, the "ultimate camp statement" is the aesthetic judgment that "it's good *because* it's awful" (295), something that might well seem to apply to the entirety of *Space Truckers*. Moreover, Sontag notes that "the essence of Camp is its love of the unnatural: of artifice and exaggeration" (275), a description that easily applies to this film's over-the-top situations that occur in completely manufactured environments. However, she sees camp as essentially a mode of reception rather than production, and "pure" camp can only be achieved accidentally—by works that aspire to seriousness but fail to achieve that aspiration, so a film such as *Space Truckers*, which is intentionally ridiculous, would not seem to qualify. In addition, because of its unremitting critique of capitalism, *Space Truckers* violates Sontag's insistence that camp is fundamentally apolitical and disengaged from such critique, although we might argue that the "political engagement" of *Space Truckers* is itself a campy spoof of political engagement. For example, even the "sex" scene between Macanudo and Cindy is part of the film's critique of capitalism, since the exchange involved is so clearly an economic one, the action involved more prostitution than rape, as Cindy offers her "virtue" to Macanudo in exchange for transportation to Earth, just as she had offered it to Canyon. Then again, in this future realm of capitalist triumph throughout the solar system, everyone seems reduced to prostitution of one sort or another, and all of the film's characters are constantly involved in deals that see them offer up whatever assets they might have in exchange for whatever advantages they can get in return.

In this case, the deal is never quite consummated, presumably because that would spoil the comic effect, even if a completed rape scene might have made a more powerful satirical point about the rapaciousness of not only Macanudo, but the company whose strategy he emulates, even as he opposes it. Appropriately, Macanudo is again hoist on his own petard, or at least done in by his own technology: he has trouble starting his mechanism, and even after he finally gets it up and running, his system overloads and explodes, obliterating him (again). Thus, Macanudo, who is a sort of counterpart to Canyon as a rebellious figure who bucks the company, fails because he opposes the Company by trying to be *like* it. Lacking both the Company's resources and Canyon's basic code of honor, he almost *must* fail.

The resourceful and opportunistic Cindy, meanwhile, dons his jacket and hat so she can try to impersonate him and take charge of the ship. The impersonation, not surprisingly, is not very effective, but it is also

a. *Space Truckers* (1996): The Big Rig in outer space.

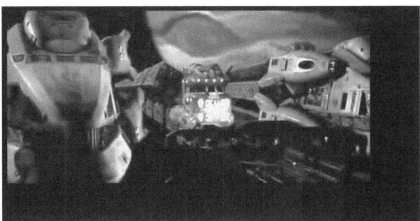

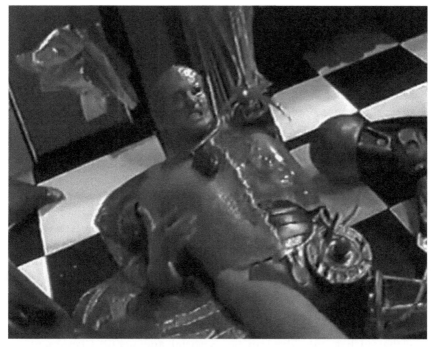

b. Technological sex aids in *Space Truckers* (1996).

beside the point, because the pirates themselves are soon overwhelmed by Canyon's cargo, which, in another of the film's sudden plot twists, turns out not to be sex dolls after all. In a substitution that vaguely echoes the intermingling of sexuality and economics that circulates throughout the film, the shipment of "sex dolls" turns out to be a shipment of the electromechanical warriors featured in the film's opening scene. The pirates' subsequent defeat by the warriors allows Canyon and his crew to escape the pirates, although they still undergo considerable trials in battling the warriors, some of whom manage to cling to the exterior of Canyon's ship/truck and are finally defeated only when it reaches the Earth's atmosphere, burning up the remaining bots on re-entry.

The arrival on Earth marks the beginning of the film's fourth segment, in which, among other things, we learn that the surgical procedure undergone by Cindy's mother Carol provided a cure that was unavailable when she first developed a terminal condition 20 years earlier. Carol, we learn, has been in suspended animation, waiting for a cure to be developed. As a result, now awakened and cured, she is still young and beautiful—and in fact looks exactly like scream queen Barbara Crampton, who had played the female lead in Gordon's *Re-Animator* and *From Beyond*. The casting of Crampton here, of course, provides a bonus recognition for fans of Gordon's horror films, essentially inviting them, as insiders, to become cult fans of this film as well. And this development is particularly fortunate, because Canyon has already ceded Cindy to Pucci, allowing for the trucker to pair up with Carol and resulting in a double romance ending.

The only remaining obstacle to this connubial bliss is that Saggs and the Company have already seized political control of the planet by privatizing Earth's government and installing Saggs as president. However, Saggs realizes that the newly-arrived travelers, who know about his robotic warrior plan, represent a dangerous loose end and, again demonstrating the murderous extent to which the Company will go to further its ends, schemes to kill them all. Since *Space Truckers* is a comedy, the scheme is turned against Saggs, and the bomb with which he plans to assassinate the travelers blows him up instead, events of the film leaving little room for audiences to regard this as anything other than a happy event.

Space Truckers makes it abundantly clear that, in its future world, capitalism is unquestionably an evil. The question, of course, is just how effective such a cult film can be as social and political commentary, given that the portrayal of the Company as a malignant entity is so overt and heavy-handed as to make it a sort of cartoon villain. In addition, while all of the corporate forces in the film are evil, that evil is personified in the figures of Saggs and Keller, suggesting that the problem might not be corporate capitalism itself, but simply a few unscrupulous individuals who have unfortunately risen to positions of power. This problem, of course, resides in almost all American films that purport to critique capitalism and the corporate system, the plot structures and film language of American cinema as a form having evolved to focus on the operations of specific individuals, who are easy to portray on screen, as opposed to large, amorphous organizations that cannot be represented visually. But this convention evolved largely because it is consistent with (and provides support for) the dominant ideological structure of American capitalism, which consistently seeks to deflect attention from fundamental flaws in the system, attributing its obvious evils to the work of specific villains who can be identified and defeated without any challenge to the system itself. Additionally, the political thrust of *Space Truckers* further suffers because Saggs and Keller are so *comically* evil, while the film itself combines its cartoonish representation of the Company with an overall tone that is so lighthearted and silly that, as we have noted, its commentary almost becomes a parody of political critique. And since an individual like Canyon, with a little help from his friends, can defeat the combined sinister forces of an interplanetary corporate empire, we have to ask how scary can that empire be, really?

Part of the problem is that we live in an age when even the most serious-minded political critique is not taken seriously. In a kind of weird postmodern doublethink, we have reached the point where the vast majority of Americans (except for intellectuals in the academy, who are thereby themselves rendered suspect in the majority view) accepts capitalism as the best possible system, even while feeling (at some level) that capitalism is corrupt, exploitative, and downright evil. Critiques of capitalism by this measure appear inherently silly and pointless, because they are simply restating the obvious. At the same time, as this same majority also thinks that all alternatives to capitalism would necessarily be even worse, criticisms of capitalism that include the suggestion of possible better alternatives (especially if that alternative happens to be socialism) appear even worse than purely negative critiques. The Cold War demonization of socialism is, of course, crucial here as the phenomenon that created the conditions in which this attitude thrives, although it certainly does not help that Soviet communism seemed to validate this demonization, the vast distance between "actually existing socialism" and anything remotely resembling socialism not being something that anyone wants to hear about. To a public conditioned for decades to believe that any genuine challenge to received traditions of capitalism is by definition wrong-headed—and thus seems either shrill or totally ludicrous—is likely to seem silly, although critiques that are knowingly silly might actually seem more sophisticated than critiques that take themselves seriously. In on the joke, such silly critiques attract audiences who think they know better than serious critics of capitalism, and thus may have a better chance of communicating with those knowing audiences in a way to which they are receptive.

Here again, *Space Truckers*, in the comic extravagance of its critique, draws on the strategy of camp, which Sontag sees partly as a reaction to the fact that traditional means of irony and satire often seem "inadequate to the culturally oversaturated medium in which the contemporary sensibility is schooled" (288). But of course the media environment in which *Space Truckers* was released, more than 30 years after Sontag's essay (not to mention our contemporary environment, nearly 20 years after *Space Truckers*), was even more saturated with a variety of different works, including cult films, to the point that is hard to see the film as being about capitalism so much as being about other films, as perhaps more a pastiche of *Alien* and other well-known sf films than a satire of capitalism. What is worse, it is in danger of appearing more like a *lampoon* of critiques of capitalism than a critique proper.

The increasing saturation and commodification of culture and media that have occurred between Sontag's essay in 1964 and *Space Truckers* in 1996 are, of course, merely a continuation of a long-term process that was only beginning to enter its final, or at least latest, phase in 1964. By 1996, that phase, which in the cultural realm we have come to know as postmodernism, was nearing full status as a cultural dominant, at least in the West, marked by a collapse of the crucial distinction between the economic base and the cultural superstructure that had been a central element of capitalism's social structure in its earlier manifestations. This process, as influentially characterized by Fredric Jameson, deprives cultural products of any critical distance from which to launch politically powerful assaults against the capitalist system, of which they are always already a part and in which they are inherently implicated. However, following the lead of Darko Suvin,[2] Jameson has consistently privileged sf as a holdout genre that might retain some vestiges of critical power, even in these later stages of capitalism, both because its "science" draws upon an older, modern (rather than postmodern) worldview and because its "fiction" produces a cognitive estrangement that is crucial to the project of cognitive mapping that Jameson sees as central to any attempt to resist the obfuscating power of late capitalism.[3] *Space Truckers*, though, is not built on any sort of scientific logic and seems designed to produce amusement more than thoughtfulness.

Indeed, if one accepts Suvin's definition of sf as the literature of cognitive estrangement, then *Space Truckers* (like most other sf comedies) probably should not be read as sf at all, but as a sort of postmodern simulation of sf that deploys clichéd versions of the genre's tropes (not only iconic hardware, as in the battle-bots and the spaceships, but also plot elements, as in the evil corporation and a technology that turns on its maker) to the effect of making the potential expansion of capitalism throughout the solar system in the coming centuries seem more annoying and hilarious than threatening and horrifying. Yet it still matters, I would argue, that these tropes *are* from sf: *Space Truckers* may be a comedy, but it would not be funny without the ironic incongruity of telling its trucker story (and its pirate story and its western story) within the context of sf, all of these forms mixing in a way that calls attention to itself in good postmodern fashion, somewhat like the war movie and spaghetti western hybrid of Tarantino's *Inglourious Basterds* (2009).

For Suvin and Jameson, the cognitive estrangement produced by sf is a key to the genre's special utopian potential, unsettling received notions so that readers become more receptive to the consideration of alternatives to the status quo, asking why things are the way they are and wondering if they might not be different. *Space Truckers*, as a comedy, is more comforting than unsettling, which might diminish this effect. But the same might be said for cult films in general, as they become cult texts largely because they offer a sort of comfort zone to which their niche audiences can return with pleasure again and again—something that is encompassed, for example, in Umberto Eco's well-known declaration that even something as mainstream as *Casablanca* can be considered a cult film because it provides:

> a completely furnished world so that its fans can quote characters and episodes as if they were aspects of the fan's private sectarian world, a world about which one can make up quizzes and play trivia games so that the adepts of the sect recognize through each other a shared expertise. (198)

There would seem to be a fundamental conflict between cult films (whose major utopian energies arise from the comforting collective experience of being "in" on what makes a particular film special) and sf films (whose major utopian energies arise from the uncomfortable experience of realizing that one's assumptions about the world might be flawed). However, the very dissonance between the jokey, cultish texture of *Space Truckers* and its sf iconography creates a mild cognitive dissonance of its own. This dissonance may be played mostly for laughs, but if *Space Truckers* does not prompt viewers to ask why and how its world is different from their own, it just might, somewhere, deep down, prompt them to ask why this future world is so familiar, so very much *like* our own. In this sense, the film, however loudly silly its surface, faintly whispers a commentary on the difficulty, amid the pressures of late capitalism, of imagining any real alternatives to the current system. Attending to these whispers, the viewer might not, like Macanudo, declare that "I rebuilt my mind!", but might at least start to wonder whether his or her mind might *need* to be rebuilt.

Notes

1 Perhaps the most overtly satirical treatment of capitalism in the *Alien* films occurs in a scene in *Alien: Resurrection* (1997) in which we learn that the Weyland-Yutani Corporation no longer exists, having been absorbed in a hostile takeover by an even larger, more predatory company.

2 Suvin's well-known vision of science fiction as the "literature of cognitive estrangement" has been put forth in a variety of places. See *Metamorphoses*

(3–15). See also Parrinder for an extended discussion of Suvin's ideas on this topic.

[3] Jameson has acknowledged his debt to Suvin on multiple occasions, including in the introduction to *Archaeologies of the Future*, his most extended meditation on science fiction (iv).

Works Cited

Eco, Umberto. "*Casablanca*: Cult Movies and Intertextual Collage." *Travels in Hyperreality*. Trans. William Weaver. New York: Harcourt, Brace, 1986. 197–211.

Jameson, Fredric. *Archaeologies of the Future: The Desire Called Utopia and Other Science Fictions.* London: Verso: 2005.

—. *Postmodernism, Or, The Cultural Logic of Late Capitalism*. Durham: Duke UP, 1991.

Johnson, Andy. "Road Work: *Smokey and the Bandit* and the Trucker Film." *Blue-Collar Pop Culture*. Ed. M. Keith Booker. Santa Barbara: Praeger, 2012. 103–15.

Parrinder, Patrick. "Revisiting Suvin's Poetics of Science Fiction." *Learning from Other Worlds: Estrangement, Cognition, and the Politics of Science Fiction and Utopia*. Ed. Patrick Parrinder. Durham: Duke UP, 2001. 36–50.

Sontag, Susan. "Notes on 'Camp.'" *Against Interpretation and Other Essays*. New York: Dell, 1966. 275–92.

Stern, Jane. *Trucker: A Portrait of the Last American Cowboy*. New York: McGraw-Hill, 1975.

Suvin, Darko. *Metamorphoses of Science Fiction: On the Poetics and History of a Literary Genre*. New Haven: Yale UP, 1979.

15. *Bubba Ho-tep* and the Seriously Silly Cult Film

Jeffrey Andrew Weinstock

By looking at the example of Don Coscarelli's unapologetically silly 2002 film, *Bubba Ho-tep*, I want to propose that we consider sf, fantasy, and indeed cult films of all stripes as both literal and figurative "strange attractors." Excluding perhaps what J. P. Telotte refers to as "classical" cult films in *The Cult Film Experience*—mainstream Hollywood films such as *Casablanca* (Michael Curtiz, 1942) that have inspired fiercely loyal fan followings—cult films typically are works that foreground their thematic, structural, and/or aesthetic deviation from loosely defined Hollywood norms. They *literally* attract due to their strangeness. Borrowing from chaos theory, however, we can find another sense in which cult films might be considered as strange attractors. Chaos theory studies the behavior of non-linear systems (such as weather) that are extremely sensitive to initial conditions. Small variations in those initial conditions can yield widely varying outcomes, making long-term prediction impossible. Within chaos theory, a "strange attractor" is the focus of a pattern of seemingly chaotic behavior—it is, according to James Gleick in his famous study *Chaos*, "the trajectory toward which all other trajectories converge" (150). Moreover, the strange attractor—much like a cult film—is posited retroactively; the pattern signals the presence of a focus that cannot otherwise be identified.

In his *Looking Awry*, an explication of Lacanian psychoanalysis, Slavoj Žižek appropriates this idea of the strange attractor as a way to explain the working of a concept intimately related to human desire, the Lacanian *objet petit a* (opa). For Lacan, human subjects are fundamentally marked by lack. The *objet a*, the unattainable "object cause" of desire, is that which the subject fantasizes would complete him or her, what one loves but cannot fully grasp or possess. In Seminar 11, Lacan—sounding as though he is discussing the sf cult fans of *Rocky Horror* and *Mystery Science Theater 3000*—expresses this relationship as, "*I love you, but, because inexplicably I love in you something more than you—the* objet petit a—*I mutilate*

233

you" (268). Žižek, after a brief synopsis of chaos theory, then asks, "Is not the very form of the 'strange attractor' a kind of physical metaphor for the Lacanian *objet petit a*?" (38). Arising out of (and indeed consti-tuting) the subject's lack, the *objet a* is that indefinable something—the strange attractor—that sets in motion and regulates the dynamic system of human desire.

It is in this sense that the cult film, whether it be a straightforward sf work like *Blade Runner* (Ridley Scott, 1982), a campy, comic sf text such as *Barbarella* (Roger Vadim, 1968), or a fantasy hybrid like *Bubba Ho-tep*, figuratively can be construed as a strange attractor. For not only is the cult film retroactively constituted as such on the basis of fan response, but more particularly because it produces and regulates the turbulence, eddies, and whirlpools of a kind of chaotic desire that marks the cult—a desire that, in going "beyond all reason," as Telotte offers (7), manifests itself both on the level of conscious intellectualization and on the level of affect, that is, the experience of feeling or emotion. What one loves in the cult film is something more than the film—it is the idea of the film as well as the affect produced by the film, the "visceral forces beneath, alongside, or generally *other than* conscious knowing, vital forces insisting beyond emotion" (Seigworth and Gregg 1).[1]

The Attractions of Silliness

As Mathijs and Sexton describe in their *Cult Cinema*, the strangeness of the cult film can take many forms, as film-makers "design films to include transgressive, exotic, offensive, nostalgic or highly intertextual narratives and styles" (8). However, the majority of cult film criticism arguably has tended to emphasize the aggressive strangeness of the cult film. Mathijs and Sexton observe that discussions of cult films and their modes of reception cluster around "transgression" and "freakery" as "instruments" through which cult films may "break boundaries of morality and challenge prohibitions in culture, ... dispute commonsense conceptions of what is normal and acceptable," and "confront taboos" (97). They add that, "In particular, cult cinema receptions negotiate *negative* forms of affect such as disgust, revulsion, and aversion" (97). Mathijs and Sexton here echo various other analyses of cult cinema, such as Barry K. Grant's "Science Fiction Double Feature: Ideology in the Cult Film," in which he proposes that cult films, to the extent that they have been discussed at all, are typically addressed in terms of a transgressive quality that forms the basis of their appeal and which manifests itself in terms of subject matter, attitude, or style (123). Telotte proposes that "What the film cultist embraces is a form that, in its very difference, transgresses, violates our sense of the reasonable. It crosses the boundaries of time, custom, form, and—many might add—good taste" (6).

To this catalog of "comfortable differences" (Telotte 5)—or strange attractors—that are typically embraced by cult film fans, I would like to add a sensibility or disposition qualitatively different from disgust, revulsion, and aversion, but of perhaps equal importance: *silliness*, which I conceive of as a sensibility or disposition that is related to, but not quite the same as carnival, camp, satire, and absurdity. To be silly is to be *innocently* playful—silliness is in earnest and lacks guile. We expect silliness from children; adults who are or act silly are goofy, foolish, or, using an older definition, daft or idiotic. In any case, the moment of silliness is one of absorption, as one is caught up in the movement of laughter—not the laugh of the Medusa, which is one of scorn, but rather the child's laugh of surprise and delight. It is laughter as affirmation rather than negation or denigration. Silliness thus serves as a rebuke to Heideggerian angst and Lacanian lack, as it is an act or moment of fullness, of plenitude, and of effervescent good humor. True silliness is also its own end—one is silly for no other reason than to be silly, and laughter is the manifestation of its excessiveness. The *pleasure* of silliness inheres in being silly, and silliness is both inwardly and outwardly directed—as an internal disposition that manifests itself through laughter, through the body, it is inward; however, silliness, as fullness to overflowing, also bubbles over into the world.[2]

In contrast to carnival, camp, and absurdity, silliness, finally, is gentler and takes on smaller targets. It plays acceptingly with the given world in ways we hadn't realized or remembered were possible. Rather than functioning as cogent or caustic social critique, it presents itself as ostensibly lacking a political dimension. For these reasons, it generally is dismissed as childish or deficient in social import. To say that a film is silly is to say that it finally lacks depth and sophistication—that it is all surface, lacks profundity, and is not worth the serious viewer's time. Post-Bakhtin and post-Sontag, the carnivalesque, the campy, and the absurd can all be justified or recuperated as canny social commentary or as avant-garde transgression that marks the viewer's tastes as rebellious or elite. But what does one do with something that, as we have construed it here, simply seems silly?

Part of the cult attraction of the silly movie—its comfortable difference, I would argue—inheres precisely in its *appearance* of unrecuperability. Whereas many if not most cult films incorporate a metatextual element through an implicit or explicit critique of the conventions of

Hollywood film-making and consumption, the silly film often presents itself as being a film about nothing more than itself. Silly cult films—and in this category we might think of such works as *Monty Python and the Holy Grail* (Terry Gilliam and Terry Jones, 1975), which foregrounds its own silliness by explicitly referring to Camelot as "a silly place," as well as a host of sf films like *The Adventures of Buckaroo Banzai Across the 8th Dimension* (W. D. Richter, 1984), *Weird Science* (John Hughes, 1985), *Earth Girls are Easy* (Julien Temple, 1988), *Spaceballs* (Mel Brooks, 1987), *Bill & Ted's Excellent Adventure* (Stephen Herek, 1989), or the focus of this essay, Coscarelli's *Bubba Ho-tep*—are all what might seem like "childish" films aimed at adults, and they are therefore often dismissed by those who associate silliness not with a subversive effect, but with immaturity and a failure to assume expected adult social roles and responsibilities, and who thus view the silly film as a *waste of time*. For them, the fundamental transgression of the silly film is *in* its being silly, which is to say refusing to be mature, serious, deep, and so forth.

It is this ostensible unrecuperability of the silly film, however, that is often embraced by the cult film fan who loves the film *precisely because* it presents itself in this way: as childish, as lacking depth, as socially disengaged (and therefore, from the serious critic's perspective, irresponsible), and, significantly, as a waste of time. The silliness of the silly cult film functions as the strange attractor inaugurating and, as we shall see, regulating a chaotic system of desire. For the silliness is what one loves in the silly film more than the film. It is what stuffs the film to the point of overflowing and invites the viewer to participate in an imaginary economy beyond lack and scarcity.[3]

The Hero's Hallway: *Bubba Ho-tep*

My conceptualization of silliness here is grounded in Don Coscarelli's *Bubba Ho-tep*, his adaptation of author Joe. R. Lansdale's short story of the same name, which originally appeared in a collection of fantastic, if not silly tales, *The King is Dead: Tales of Elvis Postmortem* (1994). *Bubba Ho-tep*, it must be acknowledged, is on every level an example of the intentional cult film—a film seemingly ready-made for cult consumption. Indeed, to establish the film's cultic pedigree, one need look no further than Coscarelli, a director most famous for his *Phantasm* films, and its star Bruce Campbell, beloved by cult fans everywhere for his roles in a variety of quirky films—most especially Sam Raimi's *Evil Dead/Army of Darkness* series.[4] Beyond this pedigree, this limited-release, low-budget film has many hallmarks of the cult cinema, including a ridiculous plot, campy special effects, and a playful mixing of genres (horror, comedy, sf, fantasy).

My argument, however, is that *Bubba Ho-tep*'s true cult appeal inheres in what I have come to consider its fractal silliness—its aura or ethos of silliness that manifests on all scales, from the macroscopic levels of plot and character to the more microscopic levels of scene, image, and line. Consider, for example, the unabashed silliness of the plot itself: protagonist Sebastian Haff (Bruce Campbell) is an elderly inhabitant of the Mud Creek, Texas, Shady Rest Convalescent Home who claims that he is in fact Elvis. Having grown tired of the pressures of his career, he explains, he exchanged places with an Elvis impersonator named Haff who indeed died in 1977, and he has since lived happily pretending to be himself (that is, performing as an Elvis impersonator) until a hip injury sustained during a performance led to an infection and subsequent coma. Haff, now mostly bedridden, spends his time contemplating his age, choices, and physical deterioration. Haff's only friend is a black man named Jack (Ossie Davis), who also insists he has another identity, that of John F. Kennedy. He claims that, following the assassination attempt in Dallas, he was dyed black by Lyndon Johnson and abandoned in the nursing home.

Haff and Jack are propelled into action when they trace a sequence of deaths in their nursing home to the machinations of a reanimated and bizarrely cowboy-garbed ancient Egyptian mummy who sustains himself on the souls of the living and has targeted the nursing home because the deaths of the elderly are unlikely to raise suspicions. Haff and Jack devise a plan to destroy the mummy, dubbed "Bubba Ho-tep" by Haff, and equipped with a makeshift flamethrower, a motorized wheelchair (Jack), and a walker (Haff), they confront the plodding, undead menace. Jack is thrown from his chair, but is saved from having his soul sucked by the mummy when Haff interrupts the act. When Jack then dies (with soul intact), Haff must contend with the supernatural predator on his own. As a last, desperate act, Haff commandeers Jack's motorized wheelchair and, crashing into the mummy, propels both of them over a riverside embankment and down a steep hill. Although Haff sustains a mortal wound in his side as a consequence, he summons his remaining strength to douse the mummy in gasoline and set it aflame. Then, as music softly swells on the soundtrack and the stars overhead organize themselves into hieroglyphics which a subtitle translates as "All is well," Haff winks out of existence with a "Thank you, thank you very much," and the film, too, fades to black.

The sheer silliness of this plot structures a playfulness of character and dialogue accentuated by framing, soundtrack, and effects, which ripples throughout the film. Most obvious—and oft-remarked in reviews—in this respect is the *joie de vivre* with which Campbell embraces his role as an enfeebled sexagenarian rest home-bound Elvis/Elvis impersonator with graying muttonchops and gold sunglasses who delivers outlandish lines with a swagger, a straight face, and a thick Elvis accent.[5] For example, after having searched his soul and concluded that there is a moral imperative for him to come to the aid of his nursing home by confronting the supernatural threat, he exchanges the following bit of dialogue with his friend Jack:

> Haff (calling Jack): Ask not what your rest home can do for you. Ask what you can do for your rest home.
> Jack: Hey, you're copying my best lines!
> Haff: Then let me paraphrase one of my own. Let's take care of business.
> Jack: Just what are you getting at, Elvis?
> Haff: I think you know what I'm gettin' at Mr. President. We're gonna kill us a mummy.

a. Serious silliness in *Bubba Ho-tep* (2002), as Elvis (Bruce Campbell) reads an alien message inscribed in a bathroom stall.

b. Elvis (Bruce Campbell) and JFK (Ossie Davis) head down the
"Hero's Hallway" in *Bubba Ho-tep* (2002).

This resolution on the part of the film's two heroes then precipitates
what might be considered the film's single best moment—the scene
corresponding to the piece of music on Brian Tyler's soundtrack titled
"The Hero's Hallway." Having gone over their checklist of mummy-killing
supplies, the pair agree to reunite at a predetermined time and the screen
fades to black. The next scene opens on a dim rest home hallway. As
the twangy Ennio Morricone-inspired spaghetti western soundtrack—
complete with choral voices—swells, Jack's motorized wheelchair rolls
into view from the left at the far end of the hall and swivels to confront
the camera. He is then joined by Campbell's Haff, who is dressed in
a white Elvis rhinestone suit and cape and supports himself using a
walker. As the two stone-faced and determinedly start down the hall,
there is a cut to a semi-close-up and the camera then pulls back slowly
as they advance.

This scene is arguably the ridiculous heart of the film, its moment of
silliest resolve. First, it is a structural repetition that inverts an earlier

scene and completes the trajectory of Haff's character arc. Having been questioned near the start of the film by the patronizing daughter of a recently deceased rest home roommate as to why he—Elvis—would desire to leave behind his fortune and fame, Haff recalls the road trip to Nacogdoches, Texas, during which he exchanged identities with Elvis impersonator Sebastian Haff. In the flashback, young Elvis—here all dressed in black—and his posse exit the car from the right and determinately advance directly upon the camera as the same piece of spaghetti western-inspired music plays. The flashback concisely documents the moment that Elvis stopped being Elvis—turned his back on his fans and stopped "taking care of business." Its juxtaposition with the "Hero's Hallway" scene reveals the latter moment as the crucial point when Haff—now old, enfeebled, and dressed all in white, by virtue of resolving to face his fears, to do right by his rest home, and once more "take care of business"—reassumes the mantle of being the King. However, even in becoming Elvis again, Haff is not in fact reassuming his actual identity (assuming for the sake of argument that Haff's story is indeed true and that he is the actual Elvis). Rather, as he himself explains in a voice-over, he is becoming the celebrity persona created by the media: "In the movies, I always played the heroic types. But when the stage lights went out, it was time for drugs, and stupidity, and the coveting of women. Now it's time. Time to be a little of what I had always fantasized of bein'—a hero." This meditation on fame suggests that the "real" Elvis was always just as made up and impossible as the mummy Haff is about to confront.

The sheer silliness of the "Hero's Hallway" scene derives from the ironic contrast between the hyperbolic seriousness of the situation and its place within a larger fantasy plot structure that is an extended and good-natured wink at the viewer. On the one hand, the spaghetti western music, the framing of the two determined heroes at the end of the long hall, and their advance on the camera as they go to confront a cowboy hat-and-boot-wearing antagonist and possibly their own demise, establish this scene as the prelude to a gun-fight and, indeed—particularly because of the very compelling soundtrack—the moment is a thrilling one. But the drama of the scene is then twisted by the ridiculousness of both image and plot: in place of the strong and virile cowboy, in place of John Wayne, Gary Cooper, or Clint Eastwood, *Bubba Ho-tep* substitutes an elderly Elvis/Elvis impersonator in a white suit with a walker and a spare tire around the middle and a black man in a wheelchair who thinks he is JFK, both of whom are setting off to confront a poorly made-up mummy who—as I shall discuss below—sucks souls out of people's assholes.

What is endearing to the cult sensibility, I would assert, is precisely this ironic contrast—one that, in fact, structures the entire film: the disjunction between the affect communicated by acting, music, and framing that together convey a sense of epic heroism on the one hand, and the incongruous image of an elderly Elvis in an outlandish costume and a black JFK in a wheelchair setting off to confront a mummy on the other. Importantly, the scene is primarily silly rather than parodic or campy, because Haff and Jack are not being mocked and, within the context of the film, the threat is real.[6] Further, I would argue that it is not a matter of the seriousness of the scene being undercut by the silliness of the plot. Rather, the scene's effectiveness—and, more broadly, the viewer's enjoyment of the film as a whole—depends upon the viewer's willingness to "play along" and appreciate the seriousness of the situation while *simultaneously* welcoming its silliness. Whether or not Haff and Jack are who they insist they are, the viewer is asked to consider them as one would children in costume playing a serious game—and to join in the fun, aware that it is a game but also aware of how much it matters to the participants. This is serious silliness indeed.

What one loves in the seriously silly cult film then—what is in the film more than the film itself—is at least in part the childishness at its core. It is this comfortable difference, a characteristic usually disparaged by serious critics and spectators, that is embraced by the cultist and serves as the strange attractor regulating the spectator's cinematic desire. The unreasonable love for a silly film like *Bubba Ho-tep* is therefore to a certain extent structured by the rebellious refusal to "act one's age" and the impossible desire to recapture the fantasized plenitude of childish play and the fullness of laughter.

Asshole! Asshole! Asshole!

As noted above, the silly film presents itself as ostensibly lacking a serious, much less a political dimension; but this lack is part of its appeal to the viewer who embraces its invitation to come laugh with it: "it's all in good fun!" the film promises. And yet films, even silly ones, are never innocent. They invariably come saturated with political messages, and the silliness of the silly film therefore functions as an alibi, masking various ideological implications and perspectives. Indeed, because the silly film so assiduously disavows political engagement on the surface, it may function particularly effectively as Barthesian myth, naturalizing historically sedimented political significations. In keeping with Grant's meditations in "Science Fiction Double Feature," the transgressiveness of a film like *Bubba Ho-tep*'s silliness masks a recuperative tendency, and this "structural doublethink" is achieved through the "inflection of the figure of the Other," who "becomes a caricature" (78)—rather like an Elvis impersonator.

Bubba Ho-tep's at times poignant meditation on aging and celebrity seems to insist on a postmodern conception of identity as performance. The essence of Elvis and JFK, the film suggests, is in their acting like Elvis and JFK, for Elvis indeed only becomes himself by virtue of imitating the media representations of himself. And yet, beneath the apparent slipperiness of such subjectivity, within the film lies the bedrock of gender, and one way the political subtext underlying the silliness becomes evident in *Bubba Ho-tep* is through an insistent affirmation of conventional masculinity, bolstered by the narrative's staging of what some would describe as homosexual panic.

The narrative proper of *Bubba Ho-tep* opens with the bedridden Sebastian Haff reflecting on his current impotence:

> I was dreamin'. Dreamin' my dick was out and I was checkin' to see if that infected bump on the head of it had filled with pus again. If it had, I was gonna name it after my ex-wife 'Cilla and bust it by jackin' off. Or I'd like to think that's what I'd do. Dreams let you think like that. Truth was ... I hadn't had a hard-on in years.

Haff's masculinity here is doubly impugned—first, by physical abnormality (the suspicious growth on his penis), but more particularly by his inability to achieve an erection, and his frustration gets channeled towards Elvis's ex-wife, Priscilla. This undermining of Haff's manhood is then accentuated by the women who subsequently visit Haff's room: the daughter (Heidi Marnhout) of his deceased roommate, who disregards Haff's attention entirely, and the nurse (Ella Joyce), who routinely applies ointment to his flaccid penis without arousing him. The first, when going through her father's personal effects, bends over, prompting Haff to reflect:

> The revealing of her panties was neither intentional or non-intentional, she just didn't give a damn. She was so sentimental on me that she didn't mind that I got a bird's eye view of her love nest. I felt my pecker flutter once, like a pigeon havin' a heart attack, then lay back down and remain limp and still. Of course, these days even a flutter was kinda reassurin'.

Of the second, Haff muses bitterly, "A doll like this, handling me without warmth or emotion. Twenty years ago, just twenty man, I could have made with the curly lipped smile and had her eating out of my asshole."

Assholes are very much to the point here because the threat that invades the Shady Hill Convalescent Home isn't limited to the souls of its residents, but to their bodily integrity as well. After Jack's initial encounter with the mummy, he reports to Haff:

> Jack: He had me on the floor and had his mouth over my asshole!
> Haff: A shit eater?
> Jack: I don't think so. He was after my soul. Now you can get that out of any major orifice of a person's body. I read about it.

What this conversation establishes is that Bubba Ho-tep is not simply an undead invader from the East, but in keeping with well-established Orientalist stereotypes, a sodomite as well; his unnaturalness neatly conjoins his ontological status and sexual proclivities, resulting in a sexualized monster who simultaneously sucks souls and drains masculinity. Of the two threats, Haff seems more unnerved by the latter, commenting to Jack that he is going to get himself a couple cups of coffee to keep himself awake and avoid the threat: "he comes in here tonight, I don't want him slapping his lips on my asshole."

As overtly silly as it may seem, this concern about assholes—what goes into them, what touches them, what comes out of them, and the implications of this for those involved—runs throughout the length of the film. Clues are first given to the nature of the threat confronting Jack and Haff by bathroom-wall graffiti. Jack points out to Haff hieroglyphics that have been carved into the wall of the visitor's bathroom stall, which he has roughly translated as "Pharaoh gobbles donkey goobers" and "Cleopatra does the nasty." This discovery leads to a conversation about why an "Egyptian soul sucker" would invade a rest home and why he would visit the guest's bathroom. Jack first explains that the rest home provides perfect cover for a creature that feeds off the souls of the living: "if that thing comes back two or three times in a row and wraps its lips around some elder's asshole, that elder is going to die pretty soon. And who would be the wiser?" And why would a mummy use the toilet? Because if he subsists on souls then he craps "soul residue." The implications of this sort of predatory activity, as Jack explains, are that "if you die from his mouth, you don't go to the other side where the souls go. He digests souls until they don't exist anymore"—to which Haff adds, "And you're just so much toilet water decoration." The conclusion could not be more *straight-forward*: allowing an unnatural creature to put his lips to your asshole transforms your soul into filth.

As if to punctuate this underlying homophobic panic, one of the minor characters, an elderly resident of the rest home suffering from dementia and referred to—in a nod to another doubled identity here—as Kemosabe (Larry Pennell), due to his black Lone Ranger mask and the toy six shooters he wields, pursues Bubba Ho-tep down the hallway, clicking his pistols and shouting "Asshole! Asshole! Asshole! Asshole! … Asshole!" before collapsing. An asshole, of course, is what he sees Bubba Ho-tep as, but it is also what he threatens. Following Kemosabe's death, Haff observes, "Kemosabe was dead of a ruptured heart before he hit the floor. Gone down and out with both guns blazing. Soul intact." But in order to protect his own asshole and soul, Haff is forced to "man up" in his own way, which is precisely what happens as his own "six shooter" unexpectedly comes back to life. Reflecting on his successful termination of a notably campy scarab that has invaded his room—a "big bitch cockroach" that he skewers with a fork and fries against a space heater element—Haff finds himself becoming aroused for the first time in years, as his nurse does "that little thing" by applying ointment to his penis. Surprised, Haff considers, "There had been two Presidential elections since I had a boner like that one. What gave here?" and concludes, "I had been given a dose of life again." When his surprised nurse suggests he needs a cold shower, he replies, "You get in there with me, I'll take that shower" and then invites her to continue handling his member. The emasculated Elvis has managed to get his groove back precisely because he has acted "like a man"—that is, by being assertive and vigorous in subduing that "big bitch." Haff is, as a result, half a man no longer, and ready to take on that larger threat posed by the ass-sucking mummy.

The final showdown between Haff and Bubba Ho-tep is precipitated by the newly energized Haff's resolution that, "I'll be damned if I let some foreign, graffiti-writin', soul-suckin', son of a bitch in an oversized cowboy hat and boots take my friends' souls and shit 'em down the visitors toilet!" and Haff's (decorously heterosexual) bond with Jack is then sealed by one last masculinity-affirming question, appropriately about Marilyn Monroe: "What was she like in the sack?", to which Jack responds that such information is classified, but—between friends— "wow!" The culminating battle is thus framed as one between the King—a white, male, heterosexual American who is possibly Elvis and fantasizes about Marilyn Monroe in the sack and, as Haff taunts, an "undead sack of shit," the Oriental ass-sucking soul-devouring mummy—Grant's caricatured Other writ large. Although the mummy curses Haff with the command to "Eat the dog dick of Anubis, you ass wipe" in hieroglyphics that spill from his mouth and then are translated for the viewer's benefit, Haff remains resolute and neither sucks dick nor allows lips to be applied to his asshole. Instead, like his namesake Saint Sebastian, or indeed like another king, Haff is penetrated in his side and his Christ-like sacrifice is affirmed by the cosmos. In the end, it does not matter whether he is or ever was the "real" Elvis: he has acted the hero—that is, he has been a man—and saved the world from an unnatural ass-sucking Oriental.

Silly Politics

Read in light of its gender politics, *Bubba Ho-tep* offers a clear demonstration of the way in which many cult films allow the spectator to gain "the double satisfaction of both rejecting dominant cultural values and remaining safely inscribed within them" (Grant 124). In this instance, however, the recuperation is a bit trickier than in some other cult films, because the transgression and the recuperation operate on such different levels: the transgression is filtered through the film's insistent pattern of silliness, while the recuperation resides in the film's conservative construction of gender and its additional inflection by way of sexuality and race. The silliness, which the cult audience clearly loves, ostensibly drains the malice out of the film's denigration of the caricatured Other. It is just a silly film, audience's readily admit, and to take it seriously is to make too much of it.

In this way, the silliness of the film functions finally as *Bubba Ho-tep*'s strange attractor—the "trajectory toward which all other trajectories converge." It is that which, echoing on all levels of the film's narrative, organizes and regulates the chaotic desire it produces in responsive viewers. It is what one loves in the film to the point of mutilating it— of breaking it into pieces and, as a consequence, not seeing all that is there. The fantasized fullness of childish laughter that it evokes thus acts to minimize, deflect, and obscure the serious politics simultaneously *at* play and *of* play. Drawing on *Bubba Ho-tep*'s cult example, then, let me underscore my argument. First, we need to add silliness to the catalog of qualities that provoke an affective response in many viewers, leading to the establishment of a new category for thinking about how the cinematic cult operates—that of silliness as a strange attractor. Second, we must recognize that silliness inevitably obscures or even defuses political messages, that it becomes a kind of alibi for the doubleness that lurks in these texts. With this perspective in mind, we might consider, for example, how silliness functions in a range of sf cult films: how it deflects attention from the pronounced Orientalism that marks Mike Hodges's *Flash Gordon* (1980) and John Carpenter's *Big Trouble in Little China* (1986), how it excuses the overt and exploitative sexualization of women in *Barbarella* and *Weird Science*, or how it neutralizes the militaristic apologetic that is central to *Buckaroo Banzai*. Of course, even to suggest such readings might represent a strike against their cult status, for they can be enough to arouse the ire of fans who will protest that we are reading too much into the films and their strategies; after all, they are *just silly films*. But this is precisely the power of the silly cult film as we have described it: like a magician, it shows us a hat that appears to be empty. Inside, however, there is always a rabbit—often with big fangs.

Notes

1 The mutilation of the love object proposed by Lacan dovetails in interesting ways with Umberto Eco's assertion in *"Casablanca*: Cult Movies and Intertextual Collage" that, "In order to transform a work of art into a cult object, one must be able to break, dislocate, unhinge it so that one can remember only parts of it, irrespective of their original relationship to the whole" (68). Eco suggest that to be a cult film, a film must be breakable. Lacan suggests that that which we love, we break.

2 We might think of carnival and camp, in contrast, as silliness with teeth. While sharing with silliness the element of play, both are more strategic and even threatening, as they use social outsiders (court jesters, drag queens) or transgressive practices to comment on—or mock—the inside. As Eric Rabkin has suggested to me, carnival is arch—deliberately or affectedly playful and teasing—and I would suggest that camp is as well, as it provocatively elevates bad taste to the level of art (see Sontag, 50 and *passim*). Absurdity, I would suggest, bears an asymptotic relationship to silliness as it deploys something that seems fundamentally impossible. This is not to criticize (although it may feel arch) so much as to destabilize. Like carnival and camp, absurdity depends upon an implicit contrast with conventional generic and social norms.

3 I would here differentiate between silly films and films with moments of silliness. I see silly films as characterized throughout by a sort of fractal silly sensibility—that is, they are governed on both the macroscopic and microscopic level by an orientation towards silliness. Silly moments within the films are structured by that larger silly sensibility.

4 Indeed, *Bubba Ho-tep* arguably alludes to Raimi's 1993 *Army of Darkness* by casting Campbell as Elvis/an Elvis impersonator. Late in *Army of Darkness*, after his character Ash returns to the present, he considers, "Sure, I could have stayed in the past. I could have even been king. But in my own way, I *am* king." Grabbing a nearby woman and dipping her for a

kiss, he then pronounces with an Elvis-like swagger, "Hail to the king, baby."

⁵ Reviews of the film, whether favorable or negative (as of March 7, 2013, the film has a 79% "fresh" rating on *Rotten Tomatoes*), almost universally applaud Campbell's performance. For example, Peter Travers of *Rolling Stone* gave the film three out of four stars, saying, "This absurdly clever caper is elevated by Bruce Campbell's pensive Elvis into a moving meditation on the diminutions of age and the vagaries of fame," and Michael O'Sullivan wrote in *The Washington Post* that, "the film stars Bruce Campbell of the 'Evil Dead' series as Elvis in a touching, funny and at times grotesque performance that is actually the best thing about the movie." Matthew Turner's review for *View London* concludes, "*Bubba Ho-Tep* may not be to everyone's taste, but it's an extremely enjoyable, genuinely original film that's worth seeing for Campbell's performance alone."

⁶ Roger Ebert, in his review of the film, appreciates this as well, writing, "'Bubba Ho-Tep' has a lot of affection for Elvis, takes him seriously, and—this is crucial—isn't a camp horror movie, but treats this loony situation as if it's really happening."

Works Cited

Ebert, Roger. Rev. of *Bubba Ho-tep*. *Sun Times*, October 17, 2003. Web. Accessed 7 March 2013.

Eco, Umberto. "*Casablanca*: Cult Movies and Intertextual Collage." *The Cult Film Reader*. Ed. Ernest Mathijs and Xavier Mendik. New York: McGraw-Hill, 2008. 67–75.

Gleick, James. *Chaos: Making a New Science*. New York: Viking, 1987.

Grant, Barry K. "Science Fiction Double Feature: Ideology in the Cult Film." *The Cult Film Experience: Beyond All Reason*. Ed. J. P. Telotte. Austin: U of Texas P, 1991. 122–37.

Lacan, Jacques. *The Four Fundamental Concepts of Psycho-Analysis*. Ed. Jacques-Alain Miller. Trans. Alan Sheridan. New York: W. W. Norton, 1977.

Mathijs, Ernest, and Jamie Sexton. *Cult Cinema: An Introduction*. Oxford: Wiley-Blackwell, 2011.

O'Sullivan, Michael. "'Ho-Tep': Elvis Hasn't Left the Building." *The Washington Post*, January 8, 2004. Web. Accessed 7 March 2013.

Rabkin, Eric. Email to the author. February 4, 2013.

Seigworth, Gregory J., and Melissa Gregg. "An Inventory of Shimmers." *The Affect Theory Reader*. Ed. Melissa Gregg and Gregory J. Seigworth. Durham: Duke UP, 2010. 1–28.

Sontag, Susan. "Notes on 'Camp.'" *The Cult Film Reader*. Ed. Ernest Mathijs and Xavier Mendik. New York: McGraw-Hill, 2008. 41–52.

Telotte, J. P. "Beyond All Reason: The Nature of the Cult." *The Cult Film Experience: Beyond All Reason*. Ed. J. P. Telotte. Austin: U of Texas P, 1991. 5–17.

Turner, Matthew. Rev. of *Bubba Ho-tep*. *View London*, October 19, 2004. Web. Accessed 7 March 2013.
Travers, Peters. Rev. of *Bubba Ho-tep*. *Rolling Stone*, August 14, 2007. Web. Accessed 7 March 2013.
Žižek, Slavoj. *Looking Awry: An Introduction to Jacques Lacan through Popular Culture*. Cambridge: MIT Press, 1991.

A Select Cult/SF Bibliography

Abbott, Stacey. *The Cult TV Book: From* Star Trek *to* Dexter, *New Approaches to TV Outside the Box*. New York: Soft Skull Press, 2010.

Austin, Bruce A. "Portrait of a Cult Film Audience: *The Rocky Horror Picture Show.*" *Journal of Communications* 31 (1981): 450–65.

Bacon-Smith, Camille. *Enterprising Women: Television Fandom and the Creation of Popular Myth*. Philadelphia: U of Pennsylvania P, 1992.

Benson-Allott, Caetlin. *Killer Tapes and Shattered Screens: Video Spectatorship from VHS to File Sharing*. Berkeley: U of California P, 2013.

Bernardi, Daniel Leonard. *Star Trek and History: Race-ing Towards a White Future*. New Brunswick: Rutgers UP, 1998.

Bignell, Jonathan and Stephen Lacey, eds. *Popular Television Drama: Critical Perspectives*. Manchester: Manchester UP, 2005.

Booker, M. Keith. *Postmodern Hollywood: What's New in Film and Why It Makes Us Feel So Strange*. Westport: Praeger, 2007.

—. *Science Fiction Television*. Westport: Praeger, 2004.

Bould, Mark. *Science Fiction*. London: Routledge, 2012.

Boyer, Paul. *By the Bomb's Early Light: American Thought and Culture at the Dawn of the Atomic Age*. Chapel Hill: U of North Carolina P, 1994.

Brosnan, John. *Future Tense: The Cinema of Science Fiction*. New York: St. Martin's, 1978.

Cartmell, Deborah, I. Q. Hunter, Heidi Kaye, and Imelda Whelehan, eds. *Trash Aesthetics: Popular Culture and its Audiences*. London: Pluto Press, 1999.

Chase, Donald. "The Cult Movie Comes of Age: An Interview with George A. Romero and Richard P. Rubinstein." *Millimeter* 7.10 (1979): 200–11.

Cheng, John. *Astounding Wonder: Imagining Science and Science Fiction in Interwar America*. Philadelphia: U of Pennsylvania P, 2012.

Chute, David. "Outlaw Cinema: Its Rise and Fall." *Film Comment* 19.5 (1983): 9–11, 13, 15.

Cornea, Christine. *Science Fiction Cinema: Between Fantasy and Reality*. Edinburgh: Edinburgh UP, 2007.

Craig, Rob. *Ed Wood, Mad Genius: A Critical Study of the Films*. Jefferson: McFarland, 2009.

Dery, Mark. *Escape Velocity: Cyberculture at the End of the Century*. New York: Grove, 1996.

Eco, Umberto. *Travels in Hyperreality*. Trans. William Weaver. New York: Harcourt Brace, 1986.

Egan, Kate, and Sarah Thomas, eds. *Cult Film Stardom*. London: Palgrave Macmillan, 2012.

Ellis, John. *Seeing Things: Television in the Age of Uncertainty*. London: Tauris, 2000.

Foucault, Michel. *Language, Counter-Memory, Practice: Selected Essays and Interviews*. Ed. Donald F. Bouchard. Ithaca: Cornell UP, 1977.

Geraghty, Lincoln. *American Science Fiction Film and Television*. Oxford: Berg, 2009.

Gray, Jonathan. *Show Sold Separately: Promos, Spoilers, and Other Media Paratexts*. New York: New York UP, 2010.

—, Cornel Sadvoss, and C. Lee Harrington, eds. *Fandom: Identities and Communities in a Mediated World*. New York: NYU Press, 2007.

Hills, Matt. "Academic Textual Poachers: *Blade Runner* as Cult Canonical Movie." *The Blade Runner Experience*. Ed. Will Brooker. London: Wallflower, 2005. 124–41.

—. "Cult Movies with and without Cult Stars: Differentiating Discourses of Stardom." *Cult Film Stardom*. Ed. Kate Egan and Sarah Thomas. New York: Palgrave-Macmillan, 2013. 21–36.

—. *Fan Cultures*. London: Routledge, 2002.

—. "*Star Wars* in Fandom, Film Theory and the Museum: The Cultural Status of the Cult Blockbuster." *Movie Blockbusters*. Ed. Julian Stringer. London: Routledge, 2003. 178–89.

—. "Virtually out There: Strategies, Tactics and Affective Spaces in on-Line Fandom." *Technospaces: Inside the New Media*. Ed. Sally Munt. London: Continuum, 2001. 147–60.

Hoberman, J., and Jonathan Rosenbaum. *Midnight Movies*. New York: Harper, 1983.

Hoesterey, Ingeborg. *Pastiche: Cultural Memory in Art, Film, and Literature*. Bloomington: Indiana UP, 2001.

James, Edward. *Science Fiction in the Twentieth Century*. New York: Oxford UP, 1994.

—, and Farah Mendlesohn. *The Cambridge Companion to Science Fiction*. Cambridge: Cambridge UP, 2003.

Jameson, Fredric. *Archaeologies of the Future: The Desire Called Utopia and Other Science Fictions*. London: Verso: 2005.

Jancovich, Mark, Antonio Lázaro Reboll, Julian Stringer, and Andy Willis, eds. *Defining Cult Movies: The Cultural Politics of Oppositional Taste*. Manchester: Manchester UP, 2003.

Jenkins, Henry. *Convergence Culture: Where Old and New Media Collide*. New York: New York UP, 2006.

—. *Textual Poachers: Television Fans and Participatory Culture*. London: Routledge, 1992.

Johnson, Catherine. *Telefantasy*. London: BFI, 2005.

Johnston, Keith M. *Science Fiction Film: A Critical Introduction*. Oxford: Berg, 2011.

Johnson, William, ed. *Focus on the Science Fiction Film*. Englewood Cliffs: Prentice-Hall, 1972.

Johnson-Smith, Jan. *American Science Fiction TV:* Star Trek, Stargate *and* Beyond. Middletown: Wesleyan UP, 2005.

Kennedy, X. J. "Who Killed King Kong?" *Focus on the Horror Film*. Ed. Roy Huss and T. J. Ross. Englewood Cliffs: Prentice Hall, 1972. 106–09.

King, Mike. *The American Cinema of Excess*. Jefferson: McFarland, 2008.

Klinger, Barbara. "Becoming Cult: *The Big Lebowski*, Replay Culture and Male Fans." *Screen* 51.1 (2010): 1–20.

Latham, Rob. *Consuming Youth: Vampires, Cyborgs, and the Culture of Consumption*. Chicago: U of Chicago P, 2002.

—. "*New Worlds* and the New Wave in Fandom: Fan Culture and the Reshaping of Science Fiction in the Sixties." *Extrapolation* 47.2 (2006): 296–314.

—. "'A Rare State of Ferment': SF Controversies from the New Wave to Cyberpunk." *Beyond the Reality Studio: Cyberpunk and the New Millennium*. Ed. Graham J. Murphy and Sherryl Vint. New York: Routledge, 2010. 29–45.

Lavery, David, ed. *The Essential Cult TV Reader*. Lexington: UP of Kentucky, 2010.

Lavery, David, Angela Hague, and Marla Cartwright, eds. *Deny All Knowledge: Reading The X-Files*. Syracuse: Syracuse UP, 1996.

—, and Cynthia Burkhead, eds. *Joss Whedon: Conversations*. Jackson: UP of Mississippi, 2011.

Lewis, Lisa A., ed. *The Adoring Audience: Fan Culture and Popular Media*. London: Routledge, 1992.

Mathijs, Ernest, and Jamie Sexton. *Cult Cinema*. Oxford: Wiley-Blackwell, 2011.

—, and Xavier Mendik, eds. *The Cult Film Reader*. New York: McGraw-Hill, 2008.

McCarty, John. *Splatter Movies: Breaking the Last Taboo of the Screen*. New York: St. Martin's, 1984.

Milner, Andrew. *Locating Science Fiction*. Liverpool: Liverpool UP, 2012.

Newman, Kim. "Moon Kampf." *Sight and Sound* 22.5 (2012): 44–45.

Orvell, Miles. *After the Machine: Visual Arts and the Erasing of Cultural Boundaries*. Jackson: UP of Mississippi, 1995.

Redmond, Sean, ed. *Liquid Metal: The Science Fiction Film Reader*. London: Wallflower Press, 2004.

Samuels, Stuart. *Midnight Movies*. Macmillan, 1983.

Sconce, Jeffrey. *Haunted Media: Electronic Presence from Telegraphy to Television*. Durham: Duke UP, 2000.

—. *Sleaze Artists: Cinema at the Margins of Taste, Style, and Politics*. Durham: Duke UP, 2007.

—. "'Trashing' the Academy: Taste, Excess, and an Emerging Politics of Cinematic Style." *Screen* 36.4 (1995): 371–93.

Siegel, Mark. "*The Rocky Horror Picture Show*: More Than a Lip Service." *Science Fiction Studies* 7 (1980): 305–18.

Shaviro, Steven. *Post-Cinematic Affect*. Winchester: Zero Books, 2010.

Short, Sue. *Cult Telefantasy Series: A Critical Analysis of* The Prisoner, Twin Peaks, The X-Files, Buffy the Vampire Slayer, Lost, Heroes, Doctor Who *and* Star Trek. Jefferson: McFarland, 2011.

Sobchack, Vivian. *Screening Space: The American Science Fiction Film*. 2nd ed. New Brunswick: Rutgers UP, 1997.

Sontag, Susan. "The Imagination of Disaster." *Against Interpretation and Other Essays*. New York: Dell, 1966. 212–28.

—. "Notes on 'Camp.'" *The Cult Film Reader*. Ed. Ernest Mathijs and Xavier Mendik. New York: McGraw-Hill, 2008. 41–52.

Staiger, Janet. *Media Reception Studies*. New York: New York UP, 2005.

Stewart, Garrett. "The 'Videology' of Science Fiction." *Shadows of the Magic Lamp*. Ed. George E. Slusser and Eric S. Rabkin. Carbondale: Southern Illinois UP, 1985. 159–207.

Suvin, Darko. *Metamorphoses of Science Fiction: On the Poetics and History of a Literary Genre*. New Haven: Yale UP, 1979.

Taylor, Greg. *Artists in the Audience: Cults, Camp, and American Film Criticism*. Princeton: Princeton UP, 1999.

Telotte, J. P., ed. *The Cult Film Experience: Against All Reason*. Austin: U of Texas P, 1991.

—, ed. *The Essential Science Fiction Television Reader*. Lexington: UP of Kentucky, 2008.

—. *Replications: A Robotic History of the Science Fiction Film*. Champaign: U of Illinois P, 1995.

—. *The Science Fiction Film*. Cambridge: Cambridge UP, 2001.

—, and Gerald Duchovnay. *Science Fiction Film, Television, and Adaptation: Across the Screens*. New York: Routledge, 2012.

"*TV Guide* Names the Top Cult Shows Ever." *TV Guide*, June 29, 2007. Web. Accessed 23 May 2008.

Virilio, Paul. *The Art of the Motor*. Trans. Julie Rose. Minneapolis: U of Minnesota P, 1995.

—, and Sylvere Lotringer. *The Accident of Art*. Trans. Michael Taormina. New York: Semiotext(e), 2005.

Waldman, Diane. "From Midnight Shows to Marriage Vows: Women, Exploitation, and Exhibition." *Wide Angle* 6.2 (1984): 40–48.

Whitt, David, and John Perlich, eds. *Siths, Slayers, Stargates & Cyborgs: Modern Mythology in the New Millennium*. New York: Peter Lang, 2008.

Wilcox, Rhonda V., and Tanya R. Cochran, eds. *Investigating* Firefly *and* Serenity: Science Fiction on the Frontier. London: I. B. Tauris, 2008.

Wood, Robert E. "Don't Dream It: Performance and *The Rocky Horror Picture Show*." *The Cult Film Experience: Beyond All Reason*. Ed. J. P. Telotte. Austin: U of Texas P, 1991. 156–66.

A Select Cult SF Filmography

2001: A Space Odyssey (1968). Dir.: Stanley Kubrick. Prod.: Stanley Kubrick. Script: Kubrick, Arthur C. Clarke. Photog.: Geoffrey Unsworth. Cast: Keir Dullea, Gary Lockwood, William Sylvester, Douglas Rain.

The Adventures of Buckaroo Banzai across the 8th Dimension (1984). Dir.: W. D. Richter. Prod.: Richter, Neil Canton. Script: Earl Mac Rauch. Photog.: Fred J. Koenekamp, Jordan Cronenweth. Cast: Peter Weller, Ellen Barkin, John Lithgow, Jeff Goldblum.

The Astounding She-Monster (1957). Dir.: Ronald V. Ashcroft. Prod.: Ronald V. Ashcroft. Script: Frank Hall. Cast: Robert Clarke, Kenne Duncan, Marilyn Harvey, Shirley Kilpatrick.

Attack of the 50 Foot Woman (1958). Dir.: Nathan H. Juran. Prod.: Bernard Woolner. Script: Mark Hanna. Photog.: Jacques R. Marquette. Cast: Allison Hayes, William Hudson, Yvette Vickers.

Attack of the Puppet People (1958). Dir.: Bert I. Gordon. Prod.: Bert I. Gordon, Samuel Z. Arkoff. Script: Bert I. Gordon, George Worthing Yates. Cast: John Agar, John Hoyt, June Kenney, Jack Kosslyn.

Barbarella (1968). Dir.: Roger Vadim. Prod.: Dino De Laurentiis. Script: Terry Southern, Roger Vadim. Photog.: Claude Renoir. Cast: Jane Fonda, John Phillip Law, Anita Pallenberg, Milo O'Shea.

Battle beneath the Earth (1967). Dir.: Montgomery Tully. Prod.: Charles Reynolds, Charles F. Vetter. Script: Charles F. Vetter. Photog.: Kenneth Talbot. Cast: Kerwin Mathews, Viviane Ventura, Robert Ayres, Peter Arne, Martin Benson.

Big Trouble in Little China. (1986). Dir.: John Carpenter. Prod.: Larry J. Franco. Script: Gary Goldman, David Z. Weinstein. Photog.: Dean Cundey. Cast: Kurt Russell, Kim Cattrall, Dennis Dun, James Hong.

Bill & Ted's Excellent Adventure. (1989). Dir.: Stephen Herek. Prod.: Scott Kroopf, Michael S. Murphey, Joel Soisson. Script: Chris Matteson, Ed Solomon. Photog.: Tim Suhrstedt. Cast: Keanu Reeves, Alex Winter, George Carlin.

Blade Runner (1982). Dir.: Ridley Scott. Prod.: Michael Deeley. Script: Hampton Fancher, David Peoples. Photog.: Jordan Cronenweth. Cast: Harrison Ford, Rutger Hauer, Sean Young, Daryl Hannah.

The Blob (1958). Dir. Irvin Yeaworth. Prod.: Jack H. Harris. Script: Kay Linaker, Theodore Simonson. Photog.: Thomas E. Spalding. Cast: Steve McQueen, Aneta Corsaut, Earl Rowe.

A Boy and His Dog (1975). Dir.: L. Q. Jones. Prod.: L. Q. Jones, Alvy Moore. Script: Jones, Alvy Moore, Wayne Cruseturner, based on a Harlan Ellison story. Photog.: John Arthur Morrill. Cast: Don Johnson, Susanne Benton, Charles McGraw, Jason Robards.

The Brain That Wouldn't Die (1962). Dir.: Joseph Green. Prod.: Rex Carlton, Mort Landberg. Script: Rex Carlton, Joseph Green. Cast: Jason Evers, Virginia Leith, Adele Lamont.

Bride of the Monster (1955). Dir.: Ed Wood, Jr. Prod.: Ed Wood, Jr., Donald McCoy. Script: Alex Gordon, Ed Wood, Jr. Photog.: Ted Allan, William C. Thompson. Cast: Tony McCoy, Bela Lugosi, Tor Johnson, Loretta King.

Bubba-Ho-tep (2002). Dir. Don Coscarelli. Prod.: Don Coscarelli, Jason R. Savage. Script: Don Coscarelli. Photog.: Adam Janeiro. Cast: Bruce Campbell, Ossie Davis, Ella Joyce, Bob Ivy.

Cat-Women of the Moon (1953). Dir.: Arthur Hilton. Prod.: Jack Rabin, Al Zimbalist. Script: Roy Hamilton. Cast: Sonny Tufts, Victor Jory, Marie Windsor, Caro Brewster.

Cowboy Bebop: The Movie (2001). Dir.: Shinichirô Watanabe. Prod.: Takayuki Yoshii. Script: Keiko Nobumoto. Cast (Voices): Steve Blum, Beau Billingslea, Wendee Lee, Melissa Fahn.

Dark Star (1974). Dir.: John Carpenter. Prod.: John Carpenter. Script: Carpenter, Dan O'Bannon. Photog.: Douglas Knapp. Cast: Dan O'Bannon, Brian Narelle, Cal Kuniholm, Dre Pahich.

The Day of the Triffids (1963). Dir.: Steve Sekely. Prod.: George Pitcher, Philip Yordan. Script: Yordan, Bernard Gordon. Photog.: Ted Moore. Cast: Howard Keel, Kieron Moore, Janette Scott, Nicole Maurey.

Death Race 2000 (1975). Dir.: Paul Bartel. Prod.: Roger Corman, Jim Weatherill. Script: Robert Thom, Charles Griffith. Photog.: Tak Fujimoto. Cast: David Carradine, Simone Griffeth, Sylvester Stallone, Louisa Moritz.

Devil Girl from Mars (1954). Dir.: David McDonald. Prod.: Edward J. and Harry Lee Danziger. Script: James Eastwood, John C. Maher. Cast: Patricia Laffan, Hugh McDermott, Adrienne Corri, Peter Reynolds.

District 9 (2009). Dir.: Neill Blomkamp. Prod.: Peter Jackson, Carolynne Cunningham. Script: Neill Blomkamp, Terri Tatchell. Photog.: Trent Opaloch. Cast: Sharlto Copley, Jason Cope, David James.

The Fifth Element (1997). Dir.: Luc Besson. Prod.: Patrice Ledoux. Script: Luc Besson, Robert Mark Kamen. Photog.: Thierry Arbogast. Cast: Bruce Willis, Milla Jovovich, Gary Oldman, Chris Tucker, Ian Holm.

Ghost in the Shell (1995). Dir.: Mamoru Oshii. Prod.: Yoshimasa Mizuo, Ken Matsumoto, Ken Iyadomi, Mitsuhisa Ishikawa. Script: Kazunori Ito. Cast (Voices): Atsuko Tanaka, Akio Ôtsuka, Iemasa Kayumi.

Invasion of the Bee Girls (1973). Dir.: Denis Sanders. Prod.: Fred Weintraub. Script: Nicholas Meyer, Sylvia Schneble. Cast: William Smith, Victoria Vetri, Anitra Ford, Cliff Osmond.

Just Imagine (1930). Dir.: David Butler. Prod.: Buddy DeSylva. Script: David Butler. Photog.: Ernest Palmer. Cast: El Brendel, Maureen O'Sullivan, John Garrick, Marjorie White.

Liquid Sky (1982). Dir.: Slava Tsukerman. Prod.: Tsukerman, Nina V. Kerova, Robert E. Field. Script: Tsukerman, Anne Carlisle, Nina V. Kerova. Photog.: Yuri Neyman. Cast: Anne Carlisle, Paula E. Sheppard, Susan Doukas, Jack Adalist.

The Man Who Fell to Earth (1976). Dir.: Nicolas Roeg. Prod.: Michael Deeley, Barry Spikings. Script: Paul Mayersberg. Photog.: Anthony B. Richmond. Cast: David Bowie, Candy Clark, Rip Torn.

The Man Who Wasn't There (2001). Dir.: Joel Coen. Prod.: Ethan Coen. Script: Joel and Ethan Coen. Photog.: Roger Deakins. Cast: Billy Bob Thornton, Frances McDormand, Scarlett Johansson, Michael Badalucco, Jon Polito.

Monstrosity (1963). Dir.: Joseph V. Mascelli. Prod.: Dean Dillman, Jr., Jack Pollexfen. Script: Dean Dillman, Jr., Sue Dwiggins, Jack Pollesfen, Vy Russell. Cast: Marjorie Eaton, Frank Gerstle, Frank Fowler, Erika Peters.

Phantom Empire (1935). Dir.: Otto Brower, B. Reeves Eason. Prod.: Nat Levine. Script: Wallace MacDonald, Gerald Geraghty, Hy Freedman, Maurice Geraghty. Photog: Ernest Miller, William Nobles. Cast: Gene Autry, Wheeler Oakman, Frankie Darro, Betsy King Ross, Dorothy Christy. A serial in 12 chapters.

Plan 9 from Outer Space (1959). Dir.: Edward D. Wood, Jr. Prod.: J. Edward Reynolds, Ed Wood. Script: Ed Wood. Photog.: William C. Thompson. Cast: Gregory Walcott, Bela Lugosi, Tor Johnson, Tom Keene, Vampira.

Re-Animator (1985). Dir.: Stuart Gordon. Prod.: Brian Yuzna. Script: Stuart Gordon, William J. Norris, Dennis Paoli. Photog.: Mac Ahlberg. Cast: Jeffrey Combs, Bruce Abbott, Barbara Crampton, David Gale.

Repo Man (1984). Dir.: Alex Cox. Prod.: Peter McCarthy and Jonathan Wacks. Script: Alex Cox. Photog.: Robby Muller. Cast: Harry Dean Stanton, Emilio Estevez, Tracey Walter, Olivia Barash.

Robot Monster (1953). Dir.: Phil Tucker. Prod.: Al Zimbalist. Script: Wyott Ordung. Photog.: Jack Greenhalgh. Cast: George Nader, Claudia Barrett, George Barrows, John Mylong.

The Rocky Horror Picture Show (1975). Dir.: Jim Sharman. Prod.: Michael White. Script: Jim Sharman, Richard O'Brien. Photog.: Peter Suschitzky. Cast: Tim Curry, Richard O'Brien, Barry Bostwick, Susan Sarandon.

Santa Claus Conquers the Martians (1964). Dir.: Nicholas Webster. Prod.: Paul L. Jacobson, Joseph E. Levine, Arnold Leeds. Script: Paul L. Jacobson, Glenville Mareth. Photog.: David L. Quaid. Cast: John Call, Bill McCutcheon, Pia Zadora, Leonard Hicks.

Serenity (2005). Dir.: Joss Whedon. Prod.: Christopher Buchanan, David V. Lester, Barry Mendel, Alisa Tager. Script: Joss Whedon. Photog.: Jack N. Green. Cast: Nathan Fillion, Gina Torres, Alan Tudyk, Morena Baccarin, Adam Baldwin, Summer Glau, Ron Glass, Jewel Staite, Sean Maher.

Solaris (1972). Dir.: Andrei Tarkovsky. Prod.: Viacheslav Tarasov. Script: Fridrikh Gorenshtein, Andrei Tarkovsky. Photog.: Vadim Yusov. Cast: Natalya Bondarchuk, Donatas Banionis, Juri Jarvet, Nikolai Grinko.

Southland Tales (2006). Dir.: Richard Kelly. Prod.: Sean McKittrick, Bo Hyde, Kendall Morgan. Script: Richard Kelly. Photog.: Steven Poster. Cast: Sarah Michelle Gellar, Dwayne Johnson, Seann William Scott, Mandy Moore, Justin Timberlake.

Space Truckers (1996). Dir.: Stuart Gordon. Prod.: Gordon, Mary Breen-Farrelly, Greg Johnson. Script: Stuart Gordon, Ted Mann. Photog.: Mac Ahlberg. Cast: Debi Mazar, Dennis Hopper, Stephen Dorff, Charles Dance, George Wendt.

Star Trek—The Motion Picture (1979). Dir.: Robert Wise. Prod.: Gene Roddenberry. Script: Harold Livingston. Photog.: Richard H. Kline. Cast: William Shatner, Leonard Nimoy, DeForest Kelley, James Doohan, Walter Koenig, Nichelle Nichols, George Takei, Persis Khambatta.

Tetsuo: The Iron Man (1989). Dir.: Shinya Tsukamoto. Prod.: Shinya Tsukamoto. Script: Shinya Tsukamoto. Photog.: Kei Fujiwara. Cast: Tomorowo Taguchi, Kei Fujiwara, Shinya Tsukamoto, Renji Ishibashi.

They Live (1988). Dir.: John Carpenter. Prod.: Larry Franco. Script: John Carpenter. Photog.: Gary B. Kibbe. Cast: Roddy Piper, Raymond St. Jacques, Meg Foster, Keith David.

Tron (1982). Dir.: Steven Lisberger. Prod.: Donald Kushner. Script: Steven Lisberger. Photog.: Bruce Logan. Cast: Jeff Bridges, Bruce Boxleitner, David Warner, Cindy Morgan, Barnard Hughes.

The Wasp Woman (1959). Dir.: Roger Corman, Jack Hill. Prod.: Roger Corman. Script: Leo Gordon. Photog.: Harry Neumann. Cast: Susan Cabot, Anthony Eisley, Michael Mark, Barboura Morris.

Zardoz (1974). Dir.: John Boorman. Prod.: John Boorman. Script: John Boorman. Photog.: Geoffrey Unsworth. Cast: Sean Connery, Charlotte Rampling, Sara Kestelman, John Alderton.

Index

Please note: all **bolded** numbers refer to illustrations.